A Perfect Revenge

Also by Annabel Dilke

Secret Relations

The Inheritance

A Perfect Revenge

ANNABEL DILKE

ST. MARTIN'S PRESS ✍ NEW YORK

A PERFECT REVENGE. Copyright © 2007 by Annabel Dilke. All rights reserved. Printed in the United States of America. No part of this book may be used or reproduced in any manner whatsoever without written permission except in the case of brief quotations embodied in critical articles or reviews. For information, address St. Martin's Press, 175 Fifth Avenue, New York, N.Y. 10010.

www.stmartins.com

Library of Congress Cataloging-in-Publication Data

Dilke, Annabel, 1942–
    A perfect revenge / Annabel Dilke.—1st U.S. ed.
        p. cm.
    ISBN-13: 978-0-312-37626-0
    ISBN-10: 0-312-37626-X
    1. Revenge—Fiction. 2. Family secrets—Fiction. 3. West Country (England)—
Fiction. I. Title.

PR6054.I388 P47 2008
823'.914—dc22
                                                            2008001805

First published in Great Britain by Simon & Schuster UK Ltd

First U.S. Edition: April 2008

10 9 8 7 6 5 4 3 2 1

Acknowledgements

Thanks to my dear mother, Alice Mary, for invaluable memories of living through the Second World War as a young wife; my friends Neville Abraham, Peter Watkins, John Wilkins and Caroline Weeks for help on such diverse matters as property millionaires, the army, Cistercian abbots and gardens; my uncle, Henry Best, and my sister, Lucy Pinney, for occasional advice on West Country dialect; my agent, Bill Hamilton, for unfailing support and encouragement, Sara Fisher and everyone at A.M. Heath; Suzanne Baboneau and Libby Vernon at Simon and Schuster; Melissa Weatherill; Charlie Spicer at St Martin's in New York; and readers and friends like Jerry Smithson in Phoenix, Arizona, who make me feel it's all worthwhile.

For Sash, with all my love

Chapter One

It isn't normal to loathe your neighbours so intensely that it makes you ill or mad, Laura Delancey reminded herself with newly acquired maturity; and neither is it funny or admirable to spend all your time thinking up ways to torment them.

'And now you're going home,' observed the strange middle-aged woman sitting opposite, who was still hoping for a conversation.

Laura's reaction was to stare down at the floor of the railway carriage, which was extraordinarily clean. The air smelt fresh and tobacco-free and the landscape streaming past the windows seemed unreasonably verdant. Yes, after six months away, she was returning to her family, but as for thinking of it as going home . . .

They would instantly have comprehended the reason for her bleak, shut-off expression.

'You'll have been missed,' the woman added confidently as the train started to lose speed. Obviously, she had summed up the stuffed rucksack in the luggage rack above and the dirty brown feet in sandals. But the girl had a strange expression, she noticed – half dreamy, half apprehensive – like that of a first-time visitor.

There was no arguing with the stranger's statement and Laura nodded, while avoiding eye contact. She'd believed that somewhere on her long journey she'd left the misery behind. But – with each familiar landmark – it was as if her old self were running alongside, threatening to board the train. '*It's different now,*' she thought steadfastly, as she noted the three pines on a cone-like hill, which meant they'd be drawing into the station in approximately two minutes; and recalled some of the numerous existences glimpsed during her long journey. There'd still be women hanging out washing at the back of their huts close by the train tracks on the way to Cochin or picking tea leaves in the cool hills of Munnar. People would still be cooking in the streets, little boys toiling after foreign visitors begging them to buy cans of coke. Regardless of her absence, the sun would continue rising and setting in blazing scarlet and purple splendour all over India. The night before, she'd created a dead-centre parting in her hair, like carrying home a silent plea for justice and tolerance.

'Aching to see you, my precious darling,' her mother had written in the last letter in her typically demonstrative way. There'd been a sticky mark on the fragile airmail paper and Laura had licked it and tasted a sharp sweetness, instantly seeing her mother seated at a disembodied kitchen table, surrounded by freshly filled jars of delicious preserves made from fruit gathered from fields and hedgerows – blackberry jam and rosehip jelly and quince cheese.

Being removed from one's environment made it possible to become someone else, as Laura had discovered along with innumerable other young travellers freed for the first time from punctuality or hygiene or any other sort of personal accounting. So she'd painted herself as a girl with a normal home life. There'd been just one moment of honesty, on a bus. It was because of the noisy pungent camaraderie, like being in a moving slow oven full of friends, and the man, of course – beautiful Chas, who'd just remarked on how crazy his own family was.

'Nuts,' he'd said, as he constructed a roll-up with tobacco and an extra something from a screw of newspaper, bought off a man in Jaipur.

'So are mine.' To her amazement, it emerged as naturally as a cough.

'Yeah?' His amused tone indicated she'd been pigeon-holed. Posh but trying to make out she wasn't. He'd met loads of those on his travels. As for crazy . . . People like her couldn't comprehend the meaning of the word. A little smile played over Chas's wonderfully shaped lips.

'They've got this feud going,' said Laura, eager to engage him now she'd started.

Frowning, he repeated the word, pronouncing it like 'food'.

'A quarrel with another family.' She almost added, 'They used to be our gardeners' before realizing what a colossal mistake this would be.

'Yeah?' Chas flicked his plastic lighter and the mixture caught. He inhaled deeply. He knew about feuds, after all. 'Like, my dad cut a piece off the neighbours' Russian vine and they threatened to neuter our cat?'

'This is different. I mean, everyone's been sort of hating each other for forty years. But we got used to that.'

'Yeah?' He looked confident that nothing she said could ever surprise him. He passed across the reefer and waited for tranquil amusement to steal through her, too.

'It was a joke, really.'

'A joke?' he repeated, smiling beatifically.

'But now . . .'

'Mmm?'

'They've stolen our house.'

Waiting for the train to arrive, her father, Sam Delancey, was still trembling with rage. It was passing the Rolls in the drive that had done it – edging his battered, bird dropping-encrusted old Volvo past Mark Trafford's obscenely clean monster and crushing the grass verge, which for once had been a pleasure.

'Mind my grass!' Trafford had shouted.

'How else can I pass you?' Sam had responded mildly, horrified to find himself actually smiling in an agreeable sort of way. That was the trouble with having been given a decent upbringing – you were programmed to behave well, however murderous your real feelings. It was the word 'my' which had really infuriated him, just as the other man had known it would. Worst of all, the brief exchange had spoilt the anticipation of seeing his beloved daughter again.

'And keep your bloody dogs under control!' was Trafford's parting shot, and then the Rolls was gone, sliding up to the magnificent low-lying Abbey like a silver bullet in Sam's heart.

The station bell had just been trilled. A handful of other people were standing on the narrow station platform waiting for the seven o'clock train. Old Brocklebank was leaning on his shooting stick with his hands clasped on his knees, scanning the blue horizon beyond the empty fields as if praying for a ragged V of honking mallards in flight. The self-styled Lady Bountiful who took it upon herself to organize the church fête was rifling through the basket covered with a white napkin she habitually carried over one arm. Such was life in the environs of a small town in the West Country. Sam nodded courteously at them both and tried to imagine himself with similarly insipid preoccupations. It was impossible.

He made an effort to pull himself together. Laura had been sufficiently distressed by the bad feeling before. It was, after all, why the dear child had been sent away. As the train drew in, he made a resolution. For her sake, he'd keep off the subject of the Traffords.

Scanning the carriages hurriedly, he saw a hunchback squeeze its way out of a door and drop heavily down onto the platform. Then he looked more closely.

'Laura?'

Six months ago, when she'd left them, she'd been pasty-skinned and overweight. Now she was very slender and the colour of tea, with hair that was longer and fairer than ever. Extraordinary what a difference a few months could make, thought Sam. Laura looked tired and in need of a good wash, but suddenly she'd become a beauty. He wondered if there was a man involved; she was nineteen, after all.

He hugged her, noting the new sharpness of bones in her shoulders. 'You look *different!*'

Laura wriggled and blinked, trying to keep the new detachment and hide the shock. In the first instant of recognition while the train was slowing and her father was unaware of being observed, he'd seemed so old and sad, with a lost expression as if he still couldn't believe what had happened to them all. But now that she'd had a good look at him, she assured herself, he was exactly the same really. Same graceful way of moving, as if there was some crazy, shameful, but not quite abandoned ambition to be a dancer lurking in his burly body. Same favoured old clothes with, no doubt, a fresh sprinkling of moth holes. Same undisciplined curl of hair falling over one eye, except that it seemed greyer now. Same intense frowning way of drawing on a cigarette, as if smoking might hold the solution to all his problems. And in between talking to her he was remonstrating with his dogs just like he always had, in affectionate barks, as if speaking their language.

'There's nothing left of you, pet! Yes, she's home at last but you don't need to go berserk about it. No, sir, you do NOT get in the front! SIT, you impertinent bugger! I said SIT!' He went on in the amused, relaxed voice she'd once feared none of them would ever hear again, 'You're a mere shred,' adding a little doubtfully, 'a shrere med?' A spoonerism should be greater than the sum of its parts, he had always insisted. It was hardly one of his best efforts but – she recognized – a form of loving reassurance.

'Well, India . . .' said Laura, climbing into the car, too, and remembering the dysentery that had lasted for weeks.

The interior of the old Volvo hadn't changed either. It was like a travelling office with a non-existent filing system – newspapers and letters strewn everywhere – smelling very strongly of dog. Her father considered it infra dig to bother with keeping a car clean. She wondered if he still stowed his shotgun under the back seat and noticed scribbled notes on an old envelope balanced on the dashboard, which probably meant he'd come up with some fresh scheme to reverse the family fortunes.

'Well, In-dyar!' he repeated mockingly, as he reversed sharply (same impatient way of driving), causing the two Labradors to topple from their obstinate standing positions on the hairy back seat. He'd always come down hard on any suggestion of pretentiousness. ('Why do you think our children are so interesting?' he'd defend himself to his wife.) Then he seemed to repent. 'You must tell us about it,' he said, but not *too* encouragingly because, although he couldn't be more delighted his eldest child was home, nothing was more boring than hearing about other people's holidays. 'Ma's been making a feast,' he went on, sounding very tender. 'All your favourites . . .'

'Oh Pa, the poverty . . .' Laura began, biting her lip and shaking her head and thinking, '*How can I explain to them the difference of what I've seen?*' It had become a mission to carry it all back, her conscience weighing her down like a battered, much-travelled old rucksack.

'There's lasagne,' he went on smoothly, as if he hadn't heard.

'Lasagne?' she echoed blankly, thinking that she hadn't eaten meat since the dysentery or liked lasagne since childhood birthday parties.

'Lasagne,' he confirmed. Laura spoke differently, he noticed. There was a curiously classless twang to her speech now, as if – somewhere on her travels – she'd made a decision to rewrite herself. He decided not to tease her about it for the time being.

'Meringues?' she faltered, because she'd not eaten dairy products for months either.

He nodded briskly, pleased they'd remembered. 'And meringues with strawberries and . . . cripped wheam.' She should have been warned from the way he pronounced the last word, like whistling it, putting the 'h' in front of the 'w'. Her grandfather had used exactly the same mannerism when boiling up into a rage.

Then the look Laura had dreaded, and prayed she'd never see again, came over her father's face – that flushed and glassy-eyed expression that distorted it so – and his voice rose to a frightening shout as he relived the incident with Mark Trafford earlier. All the way back to the Lodge where their family now resided he ranted on, while Laura shifted miserably beside him.

'*Nothing's changed*,' she thought in despair. '*It's as if I'd only slipped out to walk to the village shop.*' She could see that explaining the rest of the world to her family would be just as impossible as trying to explain their crazy feud to outsiders. They were all insane and, now she was once more amongst them, she would be suffocated all over again by their obsession and hatred. '*Back to square one*,' thought Laura, staring down at her wonderfully thin brown legs as if they belonged to someone else.

It was impossible to approach the Lodge, their shrunken new home, without catching sight of the golden shape of the Abbey in the distance, an E with the middle prong missing. Because it was fringed with lavender bushes, it appeared to float over the ground on which it was built, with something about its open form suggesting an embrace. Its mullioned windows glittered with rosy light, like honeycombs illuminated from within, and smoke drifted languidly from the big middle chimney which meant that a fire had been lit in the enormous stone hearth in the Great Hall. Laura let out a ragged gasp.

Her father glanced at her worriedly and muttered through stiff lips, 'Bastards!' as if he really believed that, knowing she was coming home, the Traffords had produced this magical effect out of sheer malice. And then, a moment later, the old Volvo came to a stop outside the red-brick Lodge that seemed so cramped and dark by comparison.

'Our bumble hungalow,' Sam said with a savage smile even

though their new home had two storeys.

Then Laura's mother came running out. She was known as Fred because she'd been christened Frederica. In honour of the occasion, she'd put on lipstick and, as usual, it looked jaunty and strange like a wedding hat.

'You're so thin!' she mourned after the lipstick had left pink kiss marks all over her daughter's cheeks. At that moment, a medley of delicious cooking smells drifted out of the Lodge.

Laura glanced wearily at her father. 'I did have dysentery, Ma.'

'I remember, you wrote. My poor darling!' Then Fred frowned. 'You really should have looked after your skin . . .'

'I know,' Laura agreed meekly. Then she was overcome by emotion once more. Through the open front door she could see a familiar collection of objects and furniture she'd grown up with, but all crammed into a tiny space now. There was her father's favourite chair, its seat bearing a hunting scene embroidered by her grandmother, Hester; and the hand-painted standard lamp that had once lit a corner of the freezing Morning Room. The enormous blue and white bowl which had formerly stood, full of rose petals, on the oak chest in the Great Hall now rested on the floor filled with stray court shoes of different colours. Laura had loved that graceful, lightly chipped bowl all her life but, seeing it now, was reminded only of the sad absence of the oak chest and the row that had erupted around it. The Traffords had tried to hang on to it, arguing that it was too big for the Lodge and no use to her family any more. Though Mark Trafford had offered to pay what he called 'a fair price' – money they, after all, desperately needed – her father had responded, 'Over my dead body!' then affected not to hear the other man's muttered 'I wish!'

Her father had refused to sell anything. He'd given the chest, together with a lot of other nice furniture, to the owners of a neighbouring great house who were good friends, with both sides pretending it was a loan till he reclaimed the Abbey. Of the good stuff, only her parents' four-poster bed, the Refectory table and the family portraits had been left behind.

With reluctance, Laura could understand their decision to leave the long oak table in the Refectory, where it had, after all, stood for centuries. What other house would it fit? Built from a single tree, it measured eighteen feet in length and each scar and stain under its patina of beeswax told a story. The same reasoning could be applied to the enormous four-poster, which was impossible to move from the White Room without being dismantled. But all of them had been astonished by Sam's insistence that the portraits should stay, too.

Laura now believed she understood this, also. Having lost his family its inheritance, her father was desperate to retain some measure of control. Why else had he insisted on keeping the Lodge at the bottom of the drive as a condition of sale? And leaving images of long-dead Delanceys in the Refectory was surely his way of keeping a toehold in the Abbey itself. Perhaps, in his fevered state of mind, he believed their painted humourless stares would caution the Traffords to respect that historic place. He was so proud of his ancestors, and two in particular – Sir Percival Delancey, who would certainly have been Prime Minister, he'd always point out, but for a frame-up by a jealous political rival; and the Admiral, Giles Delancey, whose courage had become one of the legends of the Navy.

With a flourish, he produced the dead, still-warm pheasant from behind his back. It was one of Trafford's, of course – reared for a shoot, he'd informed Laura on the journey home, as 'part of that family's pitiful attempt to ingratiate themselves with the local gentry'. Intercepting it scuttling across the road, trapping it in his headlights just as they were turning into the long drive, had improved his spirits no end. It was fair game and tit for tat for the business with the Rolls. He hadn't even needed his gun. A sharp acceleration had been all that was required.

'Sam!' exclaimed Fred.

He looked momentarily taken aback. Then he said, 'Bloody thing was about to attack us! Sheer self-defence.' He turned to Laura. 'Wasn't it, my love?'

'I'll hang it in the bike shed, shall I?' said Fred, smiling at Laura and beaming the unspoken, reassuring message: 'See what good form Pa's in . . .?'

'No, no! Think I'll string it up here.' Sam was already knotting the pheasant onto the door knocker, where it couldn't be missed by the Traffords the next time they passed, and Laura found herself grinning at the sheer childishness of it.

Her brother and sister hung back a little as they all crowded into the sitting room, where a small table under the window had been laid for supper; and Fred disappeared into the cramped adjoining kitchen to finish cooking on the ancient gas stove that sulked if required to do any more than the minimum. David and Maria would be unchanged, too, thought Laura with a mixture of affection and impatience: eighteen-year-old David the same supercilious, lazy know-all, sixteen-year-old Maria still obsessed with clothes and make-up and boys. She could tell they were delighted to see her yet anxious to retain their new positions in the family. They were probably remembering how her misery had commanded most of their father's attention – even with everything else that had been going on at the time. He'd borrowed money he'd never be able to repay to send her off on her travels. 'Laura's too sensitive for her own good,' he'd told them when they'd questioned the fairness. Laura had heard them all through the flimsy floorboards as she lay weeping in her bed.

She now noticed something that really was new, pinned to a wall where it could not be missed. It was a large plastic board intended for shopping lists, with a felt-tip pen attached by a cord. Scrawled on it in a mixture of her parents' handwriting were five seemingly unconnected statements: 'Today is Friday, 28 June 1985. The Prime Minister is Mrs Thatcher. I will need a bath tonight. I will not need to be driven to Magna Saunter for wool or anything else. I live at the Lodge now, and not the Abbey.' The last sentence had been underlined twice.

Laura glanced at her father enquiringly but, before he could respond, Hester Delancey entered.

For as long as Laura could remember, her grandmother had been elegant, fitting into the Abbey as naturally as the marvellous plaster-moulded ceilings and panelling installed four centuries after it was built. She was as essential a part of its flavour, for her family, as the smell of dried flowers and boiled cabbage, or even the silverfish that skittered across the flagstones. In her pearls and beautifully cut clothes, her style was languid amusement, though it was acknowledged that nobody could have managed the Abbey's staff so efficiently or cared more passionately about its treasures. It was obvious what the house represented to Hester because, even as a child, Laura had observed some dreadful dysfunction in her grandparents' marriage. They lived in beauty and grandeur yet could hardly bring themselves to speak to each other. When she was nine, her grandfather had died very suddenly from a heart attack and her grandmother had handed over control of the house to Fred, as required, though remaining very much an incisive, advising presence.

Now, Laura was horrified to see that she wore a stained twin-set over a pair of old trousers bristling with bits of twig picked up on her mysterious rambles, and thick, carelessly applied make-up: blue eyeshadow that made her look like a parrot, bright-pink lipstick that left greasy smears on every cup and glass. Her hair stood up in a wild white halo, and the once finely plucked brows that had given her face its distinctive quizzical expression crouched over her wandering green eyes like shaggy grey moths. It was as if everything in her had been rendered its opposite by the dementia.

Sam had warned Laura in the car how greatly Hester had deteriorated over the last six months. It was only fragments of the past that she remembered with clarity now – sharp emotions like fear or relief picked out of a cabinet of memories so jumbled that she often made no sense at all. Yesterday, she'd remarked, apropos of nothing, in the maddeningly undisciplined fashion that contrasted so oddly with her refined and careful way of speaking, 'We were lunching at the Caprice. Someone's birthday? I forget . . .' She'd laughed suddenly, as if she'd made a joke. 'And then we heard it right overhead. UH-UH-UH-UH! That's how it sounded! A what do you call it? And everyone dived under the table. It was funny!' She'd stopped short, looking cross and an hour later, when they were all sitting having tea and talking about something entirely different, had suddenly announced very loudly and triumphantly, 'Doodlebug!' Hester had always talked a lot about the war but these days the family never listened. They treated her ramblings like muzak. It was the only way to tolerate them.

Now, she announced very regally: 'How nice!' She was

looking a little curiously at Laura, almost as if waiting to be introduced.

'Gran?' There appeared to be some confusion in her grandmother's eyes, thought Laura, as if two conflicting emotions were jostling for supremacy.

'Supper time,' said Fred coming back into the room and rapping the table as if beating a gong. As usual, she'd taken the same care with presentation as she'd once done at the Abbey. She'd laid out ironed linen napkins and the remainder of the silver cutlery, though the candlesticks had long since been sold. Instead, there were nightlights in pretty, though mismatched saucers; and pink geranium petals were scattered artlessly, like sugared almond treats. 'A welcome home feast for our darling Laura,' she announced, smiling fondly at her elder daughter.

'Oh, have you been away?' Hester asked very graciously, the consummate hostess. And, at that, Laura laughed in exactly the same joyous abandoned way she used to, at the same time giving her grandmother an apologetic and loving kiss. Hester returned the embrace with surprising strength, as if – somewhere beneath the distressing craziness –all the old humour was still there, together with a new warmth. Suddenly, the whole business of coming back became bearable.

Chapter Two

Up at the Abbey, a client of Mark Trafford's was sitting down to supper in the Refectory. He smiled at Janice Trafford as she set a prawn cocktail before him on the enormously long and oddly scarred old table, shook his head regretfully when offered more fine champagne because he needed to keep a clear head.

When his host had taken the seat next to him, he enquired, 'And these are of?' He gestured at the myriad dark and murky portraits lining the huge room. It would have been hard not to remark on them because they looked so odd against the newly done-up walls. The whole place smelt of paint, though there was a faint musty smell underneath as if the old house was grumbling gently.

He was only trying to make conversation until he and Trafford could get down to the real purpose of the evening – two properties in East London he was interested in buying. Trafford was known for his gift of the gab, his brimming confidence, but in his own home he seemed strangely quiet and abstracted, almost as if he were brooding on some private

grievance. He kept frowning and pursing his lips, and once let
out an exasperated sigh. Then he seemed to make an effort. He
bared his teeth in a smile. 'I believe that's Sir Percival Delancey,
a Member of Parliament,' he said, pointing at one of the
pictures, which all looked much the same to the client, 'until he
lost his seat following a scandal.'

'When?'

Mark Trafford ate a mouthful of prawns. 'Late nineteenth
century, early twentieth century? My father knows more about
it than I do.' He shrugged as if he personally couldn't care less.

The client saw him glance at his children, who were absorbed
in conversation with their grandfather further down the table,
then he lowered his voice, at the same time making a
contemptuous face. 'It's rumoured several women at the same
time were involved.' He indicated another picture. 'And that's
Admiral Giles Delancey. He commanded a fleet till he mislaid
it. Leastways he found the sense to go down with his ship! I'm
not aware the others made anything of their lives.'

'You're related to the Delancey family, are you?'

'No,' said Mark, without expression. 'We bought this house
off them.'

'I see . . .' The client felt no more enlightened as he stared at
the portraits overlooking them from every wall of the room. He
waited with an encouraging smile, but it was obvious his host
wasn't about to explain.

The evening was full of surprises. He'd been pleased to be
invited to meet the family, and stay the night, too. He'd have put
good money on them living in the stockbroker belt, cushioned
by mod cons. Instead, he'd been summoned to this remote,
decaying mansion in the West Country. He wondered why on
earth Trafford, who'd made a fortune with his talent for

identifying up-and-coming properties in the inner city, should have decided on this as his principal residence. Especially as it appeared to afford him little pleasure.

The house was very imposing, but chilly even in summer and in the midst of renovation. He'd seen the builders' clobber on the way from the huge hall where they'd had pre-dinner drinks: paint-blobbed old radios, clumsy iron tools, pots of paint with the lids left off, stepladders and stained dust sheets. This room where they sat eating supper had been done up to the nines – apart from the old table and those pictures, of course. Not his style but he had to admit it was cheerful and the brand-new chair he was sitting on was very comfortable. He could see that radiators had been installed under the vast mullioned windows and guessed the whole place would soon have central heating, which would hardly be cheap to run.

On turning into the drive, he'd been taken with its immediate beauty, of course – pale old honey stone embroidered with creeper, a low layout that came at him like a pair of welcoming arms and a long canal in the distance glittering with the last intensity of the sun. The house had long ago been a monastery, Janice Trafford had informed him brightly, and the care that had gone into its construction was impressive. But he'd not missed the sagging – though exquisitely wrought – drainpipes and gutters, and that was just for starters. These old places ate money, as Trafford would be the first to point out. He could certainly afford it though, the client reminded himself. Mark Trafford was a millionaire many times over. Still only in his mid-forties, he was rapidly becoming a legend in the property world.

It was interesting how this famously ruthless businessman deferred so tenderly to his father; it made the client see a whole other side to him. The old man had been introduced as Stanley. He was obviously a permanent part of the household though he didn't seem to fit with the smartly turned-out, carefully spoken couple and their confident children. Stanley had revealed before dinner that he'd originally come from these parts, though Mark had shot him an odd look as if entreating him to shut up. But it explained the funny rural accent. He wielded his knife like a pen. He had blackened teeth with gaps and spoke with his mouth full. It even looked suspiciously as if he hadn't washed his hands.

'Delicious!' the client told Janice Trafford, who'd started clearing away the first course. It wasn't true. The prawns had been soggy and tasteless and the mayonnaise had come out of a jar. But she seemed so anxious to please that it brought out his protectiveness. It occurred to him that she was probably terrified of being replaced, any minute now, by a younger model. He'd seen it so often with these self-made men, desperate to reinvent themselves. Janice's successor was probably even now holed up in a mistress flat somewhere in London. Shame, because she was patently such a nice woman. Good-looking, too, with her carefully done reddish hair and neat figure. He appreciated it when women made an effort. But in Janice's case, he reflected, she probably had little choice.

Mark wasn't going to explain the situation with the Delanceys to his guest because it was none of his business. But for the first time, he believed he noticed echoes of his enemy in many of the portraits. The Admiral had Sam Delancey's polite sneer, the MP his dark and mocking eyes – and both appeared to be observing him sardonically.

'*Damn him!*' Mark thought with frightening passion. The

incident in the drive earlier that evening had ruined his mood and for some reason the rage intensified in this enormous, quiet old room, which should have been so calming.

He regretted his softness about the portraits. Once the Refectory had been redecorated, both he and Janice had wanted to stash them away in the attics. However, to Janice's very great disappointment, Stanley had insisted the pictures be re-hung exactly as before. 'I want to look at 'em,' he'd said with a strange smile, and Mark had given in because if Stanley wanted to gloat over the end of an era, he was entitled. At the heart of the desperate, single-minded striving that had gone into the making of his vast fortune had been the desire to make up to Stanley and his late mother, Effie, for their sufferings at the hands of the Delancey family. 'I'm going to look after you,' he'd promised, even as a young child.

He should never have let Sam stay on at the Lodge, he thought very bitterly, and certainly not for the first time as he set about carving the joint of overdone roast beef Janice had put before him. But what else could he have done? Sam Delancey had made it an absolute condition of sale and, by that time, Mark – with Stanley at his back – was determined to have the Abbey and its estate. He prided himself on his strength of mind, his keen negotiating skills, but he'd got nowhere even when – against all his better judgment – he'd offered to up the price a few thousand. It was his father who'd persuaded him to accept the unusual arrangement. 'Let 'em stay,' he'd decreed with surprising equanimity. 'They won't get in us way.' However, he could hardly have been more wrong.

It was Mark's business to know about property but, oddly, it was Stanley who had noticed when the Abbey came on the market, almost as if he'd been watching and waiting for the moment. He'd seemed extraordinarily excited. It had given Mark an uncomfortable jolt to be shown the photo in the estate agent's details; after all, Melcombe Abbey was associated with the greatest misery his family had ever known. Even so, he thought he could understand why his father seemed so set on it. They were owed, said Stanley implacably. He even used the word 'symmetry', which he must have picked up from one of the children.

Seated further down the long table, masticating his beef with difficulty with the wobbly old teeth Mark was always urging him to replace with dentures, Stanley was talking to his favourite grandchild, Genevieve. Joe, her elder brother, was a dreamer – he wanted to be an actor, for Christ's sake! – and as for Justin, the eighteen-year-old, his smart school had given him a self-assurance that was not entirely pleasing. It was all very well knowing your p's and q's, thought Stanley, but it didn't make you an expert on life. However, Genevieve was a proper Trafford: tough and determined. He and Gen had the same hands, big and square with stubby fingers, though his were stained from handling soil no amount of scrubbing could remove. '*She's not spoilt neither*,' he thought, glancing disapprovingly at the mounds of perfectly edible meat Joe and Justin had left on their plates as usual. Having gone through the war and rationing, he was incapable of wasting food.

'That family pollutes everything,' said Genevieve, glancing at Stanley for approval.

'Who says, miss?' he responded, half teasing, half flirting because, even at his age, it came as naturally as breathing.

'They're like Paraquat,' Genevieve continued, to please her grandfather, the former gardener. 'Only they do nothing.'

*

'Isn't this all perfectly lovely?' said Janice, blotting her mouth carefully, and waited for their guest to compliment her on the first step in her grand transformation plan.

The ancient Refectory bore little resemblance to the icy, whitewashed room lightly traced with cobwebs where monks had once gathered in silence to consume their simple rations. Janice's expensive interior decorator had advised leaving it very much as it was – 'I think it's important to preserve the sense of history' – with, at most, a coating of one of the neutral colours she was so addicted to, like magnolia or buttermilk. She didn't understand Janice's longing for brightness and warmth, her desire to put her own stamp on the house.

Janice was remembering her first sight of the enormous room, when Mark and Stanley had brought her along to view the property. 'Dining area,' Mark had muttered, as if showing around a client, scanning the skirting boards and ceiling for signs of damp – not because anything was going to deter him from the purchase but so he could beat Sam and Fred Delancey down in price. It was the first time she'd met the couple, of course, but, right from the start, she'd felt their antagonism, though Stanley had hung back, trying to make conversation with them, as if determined to savour the extraordinary moment. Even then, knowing she'd have to live in this place, Janice had started to toy with ideas.

After much anxious deliberation, she was very pleased with what she'd achieved. Nobody could say the Refectory wasn't cheerful and welcoming now, and elegant, too. She pictured the Delanceys' poky lounge cum dining room, glimpsed through the Lodge's windows: junk piled everywhere, bolts of material flung over uncomfortable old chairs, a jumble of patterns and colours. It was just like the Abbey had been when she and Mark and Stanley had first viewed it, only on a much, much smaller scale.

'*Serves them right!*' she thought savagely, offloading the hurt at the Delanceys' hostile behaviour and remembering Mark's stories of his harsh childhood. '*See how they like it now!*' It was only a shame, she told herself, that the humble gardener's cottage where Mark had spent his early years no longer existed. To see the Delanceys forced to move there would have been poetic justice indeed. But after Mark and his family were evicted, that little house was, for some strange reason, never again occupied, eventually collapsing through neglect.

It was rather dismaying that the Delanceys' plunge into poverty didn't appear to have affected their social standing. Only last week, walking her dog Scampi, Janice had spotted their new neighbours, the Harcourts, emerging from the Lodge still laughing with Sam and Fred, obviously having enjoyed lunch. She noticed they'd parked their Daimler on the grass verge, squashing it more severely than Sam ever did, but had found herself beaming encouragingly from a distance as if urging, 'Oh do please feel free to wreck our land whenever you like!' However, she might as well have been invisible. 'I'm sure they'd been talking about us,' she'd complained to Mark later.

She was longing to entice the Harcourts to the Abbey. But how did you go about making friends in a place like this? It was so different to the comfortable, affable environment where they'd lived before. It was like moving to a foreign country without a phrase book. People weren't exactly rude, but they failed to respond to overtures. She'd had nice cards printed – gold lettering on pale blue, with 'Mark and Janice Trafford are now the proud owners of Melcombe Abbey' – and dropped them into all the neighbouring houses, but there'd been no feedback whatsoever, certainly no friendly invitations.

'Up their own arses,' Stanley had observed sourly, though he was just as anxious to cultivate relationships with the right folk. Despite years of enforced London-dwelling, he'd never shed his West Country way of speaking, though it was overlaid by vernacular picked up in the city. 'You leave it to me,' he'd promised. Next project was a pheasant shoot. Folk didn't change, he'd chuckled confidently. They'd soon swallow their superiority for the chance of a day's free shooting, 'the greedy buggers'.

'Lily said the elder daughter was coming home today,' Genevieve confided to her grandfather as she helped herself to a second slice of Viennetta.

Half listening from the other end of the table, Janice reflected that there'd been no problem establishing a rapport with their cleaning lady. If it weren't for Lily (who'd worked for the Delanceys till they could no longer afford her but still kept in touch) they'd know nothing of the other family's life. 'They'm off to that big do at the manor tonight, ain't they?' Lily would remark, knowing full well the Traffords hadn't been invited. Or, with a sly glance at Genevieve, 'I tells Maria Delancey, "You should be a fashion model with your figure."' Lily lorded it over the other women who'd been brought in from the village to help service the Abbey.

Janice shook her head slightly at her daughter while maintaining a pleasant smile for the sake of their guest. It was useless. Genevieve was at least a stone overweight.

'Laura,' Genevieve went on, pronouncing the name as if there was something intrinsically ridiculous about it, even though – because her family had only very recently moved in –

she'd never met Laura Delancey or even seen her. 'She's been to India!' she continued, making an incredulous, disgusted face.

'Silly cow!' responded Justin, who was bespectacled, and solid like Genevieve.

Only Joe was slender and good-looking. But actually, thought Janice, if you studied photos of Stanley in his long-ago youth, before the poverty and bitterness were stamped on him, you could find the same dark and sultry looks, the black eyes that, on Joe, shone with gentle dreams. Joe was in a reverie now, not listening of course, a lock of hair falling over his forehead, a little smile on his lips.

In other circumstances, she reflected, it might have been fun for the children to have young people so near in age as next-door neighbours. But Genevieve and Justin loathed the family who'd humiliated their grandfather and now seemed on a mission to provoke their father daily. 'Snobby scumbags,' Justin called them. Why should Laura Delancey be any different?

Only Joe was beginning to question the logic of the feud. 'We've got their house now, haven't we?' he'd remarked the other day, adding gently, 'Anyway, their nan's not all there.'

However, Stanley had responded smartly: 'Two ha'p'orth short of a farthing is Hester these days – a sorry sight. Don't make her any less poison. I know them Delanceys and don't you forget it.'

'Coffee?' Janice enquired of her guest. She was desperate for one herself because she'd slept so badly the night before.

She'd awoken very abruptly at two o'clock, imagining, for an eerie moment, that she caught the sound of sobbing somewhere in the distance. Then, still searching for an explanation, she'd heard their dog, Scampi, who should have been snoring in his basket in a corner of the bedroom, barking frantically down below. In the light of the bedside lamp, Mark looked sweet asleep – years younger, with the tension and irritation wiped away. She'd sighed and caressed his forehead and he'd shifted and murmured as if impatient with her even in his dreams. She wouldn't wake him, she had decided. But the following morning at breakfast she might tell him about braving the depths of this creepy old house.

In case of trouble, she picked up a heavy marble bust they were still using as a doorstop. Its nose looked as if it had been newly knocked off (perhaps with one of the battered unusable croquet mallets, part of an incomplete set, which had also been abandoned when the Delanceys moved out) and it had been given a green paint moustache. '*Very funny!*' thought Janice sourly. One more insult and another piece of Delancey junk. She'd been shocked by the other family's shabby way of life, their careless approach, as if letting moths and decay rampage through a house was something to be superior about.

At least Scampi was a good guard dog, she'd told herself as, snug in her quilted dressing gown, she'd descended the long staircase leading to the ground floor. He was a rescue dog – a patchwork mongrel – because she and Mark had made it a rule only to take in animals that really needed a home. The Delanceys' two pedigree Labradors made a lot of noise, too, and still galloped round the Abbey grounds as if they owned them. Rather disloyally, Scampi had made friends with them. The three dogs were constantly spotted in one another's company.

The snarling and yapping had come from the Refectory. Scampi had sounded quite demented with excitement, as if he'd heard a vixen's ghastly cry outside in the darkness. Then he'd stopped abruptly, with a whimper.

The room was filled with moonlight and, on entering, she'd seen the dog sitting to attention on the new pink carpet, his spaniel's tan and white coat trembling with tension, his big German Shepherd's ears painfully pricked.

'Scampi?' she'd faltered.

But he hadn't even turned his head.

'Scampi!' she'd found herself shrieking, and then the light had been snapped on.

'Janice! What the heck are you doing down here?' Mark had demanded. He was always stressing that he needed his sleep, so of course he was cross.

Then Scampi had bounded up to him, quite his usual undisciplined self, and as they all went back to bed, Janice had decided there was no point in worrying her husband. 'Aren't you happy here?' he'd have demanded because, for all his tough single-mindedness, he needed reassurance. 'It's only what you wanted,' he'd have insisted most unfairly, as if it were he who'd been bullied into giving up their comfortable modern house in Guildford and all their friends, and moving to this enormous, dilapidated, unfriendly place.

She stared unhappily at the portraits as she sipped at her cup. '*Nasty dark old things*,' she thought, transferring the bitterness and rejection onto something inanimate. They spoilt the effect of her pretty new paint. Even Stanley had commented on how dirty they were. He'd gone further. He'd suggested they should be professionally cleaned. They were still the Delanceys' property, of course, but there was no need to ask their permission, he said. 'It's *us* doing *them* the favour!'

They were a team, thought Stanley happily as he slurped at his own coffee and ignored the visitor and drew the strings of family tight. It had always been their strength. And now – thanks to his wonderfully successful son, Mark – here they were living the life of Riley in the house that had haunted him. Hatred was spoken of as a bad thing, wasn't it? But it was hatred, he'd told Mark, which had kept him watching the Abbey for years so that, when the Delanceys suffered their moment of vulnerability, his family could be there in an instant, before anyone else, like a hawk swooping on a rabbit even as it contemplated emerging from its burrow. Hatred, he'd maintain, plus the confidence that sooner or later disaster would befall the Delanceys. 'They've never wanted for nothing, see,' he'd point out. It was unnecessary, of course, because Mark had always understood it was hardship that shaped you. And now, the very best of sons, he'd redefined the family, bearing them from the poverty of the past into a glorious future.

'Here's a turn up for the books!' Stanley would say it often, looking about his grand and spacious surroundings with shining eyes. For, unlike Hester Delancey, his contemporary, he knew precisely who and where he was. Even so, remembering his younger self was like watching a boy standing on a distant hill.

What none of his family – even Mark – knew was quite how familiar he was with every inch of this place, and why. It was like staring at the lines on his battered old hands. Each step in the house and gardens took him further back into the past.

Only yesterday he'd visited the spot where the real part of his story had begun – down by the river, dried to a trickle now. But when he'd shut his eyes, he'd seen the water swollen and twisting with currents and felt the spongy bank beneath his ten-year-old feet. He'd even fancied he heard that terrified though imperious cry.

'*Wish I'd turned away*,' thought seventy-year-old Stanley, but knew in his heart it was not true. '*I'm a champion hater, but I can also love*.' In this beautiful yet sinister place steeped in old passions, he could feel himself humming with new vitality, almost like being young again.

Chapter Three

'Save me!'

As he dawdled along the river bank, looking for otters, Stanley was galvanized by the shriek somewhere in the distance. He guessed it was Edmund Delancey long before he spied him struggling in the tumbling water. He couldn't imagine who else would be in that deserted spot, and – more to the point – only a nob living in a palace full of servants would turn a desperate appeal for help into an order. He wondered briefly and a little sardonically who Edmund expected to come to his aid. The Almighty, perhaps? Was even He expected to jump to it for the all-powerful Delanceys?

Until that summer morning in 1925, Edmund had studiously ignored him, though they were both only children of the same age, living on that magical estate. Once Stanley had come across him accompanied by an equally superior friend, trailing after a shoot while, all around them, dead or dying birds cartwheeled out of the sky. On that occasion his presence had been acknowledged: 'Watch out for the guns!'

Then Stanley had heard Edmund's friend respond in the same highfalutin contemptuous way: 'We don't want to shoot any peasants, do we?'

However, Stanley put this out of his head as he kicked off his heavy boots and peeled away his jacket and dived into the freezing swirling waters of the river. He didn't stop to think about his own safety.

The cold took his breath away. Trying to keep control, swimming desperately against the strong current, he could see Edmund thrashing his arms about, his head disappearing beneath the water, eyes rolling up to show the whites. When he finally managed to grab him by the collar, the other boy behaved as if he wanted to drag him down, too, and, reacting instinctively, Stanley punched him in the face. He tasted the satisfaction even as, terrified for himself now, he struggled to keep both of them from being swept away.

After he'd used all his strength to drag Edmund up on to the bank, he sat there shivering and exhausted, waiting for him to come round. But he was so slack and white, like a piece of uncooked poultry – he seemed lifeless. Stanley rolled the dead weight of Edmund onto his back, took a deep breath and started blowing into his mouth as he'd learnt to with the calves and lambs and piglets on the estate farm when they struggled to survive. Suddenly, there was a cough and a splutter. He moved away just in time and Edmund was violently sick.

Suddenly, everything felt sharp and new to Stanley: the sight of a willow tree trailing its feathery branches in the torrent as if flirting with danger, the fluid trill of a blackbird nearby, even the disgusting sour smell of the vomit. The sun had come out, too, and lovely warmth crept across his puckered skin.

'You punched me!' gasped Edmund when he'd recovered

his breath, sounding more shocked about that than anything else.

Stanley got up abruptly and started forcing his boots over his dripping woollen socks. He'd be off. Ungrateful didn't begin to describe it. He could see that the skin around the other boy's eye was already discolouring from the blow. Edmund would have a field day, getting his revenge. Stanley knew his own father would never believe his version, could already envisage him unbuckling his heavy belt to administer a thrashing.

Then, to his astonishment, Edmund conceded, sounding quite reasonable, in so far as he could, with a permanent plum in his mouth: 'I suppose you felt you'd little alternative . . .' It was so funny the way he said it, as if reciting from a play. He added, sounding slightly aggrieved now (because there was no question he'd been bettered): 'Who taught you to swim, anyway?'

Stanley shrugged, looking very surly as he pulled his jacket over his soaked shirt. *'Taught meself,'* he thought with pride, remembering the frog in a puddle he'd watched for hours.

'You're not just going to leave me here, are you?' Edmund went on plaintively. He had round, pale-blue eyes and straight blond hair cut in a fringe, though it was sadly bedraggled now.

Stanley scowled and might as well have muttered, 'I don't owe you nothing.'

'I suppose we could hold a conversation.' Edmund coughed again and momentarily looked very apprehensive. 'I do dislike being sick,' he said, once it became clear it wasn't going to happen again. 'Don't you?'

At last Stanley spoke. 'I'd sooner cut meself.' Then he bent and picked up a tiny feather gleaming blue-green on the bank. 'I sees Mr Kingfisher been up to his tricks.'

Afterwards, he would remember how Edmund took the feather from him – as if there was no question he and his family possessed every single part of the estate, even down to this casually discarded item – and tucked it into his pocket. He did it with care, as if he intended to make use of it later.

Then he seemed to make a conscious effort to become someone very much nicer, stashing away the arrogance and superiority, too. 'Look,' he said eagerly, 'if we sit here for a bit, our clothes will dry. It's getting quite hot. I had some chocolate in my pocket. It might be all right.'

'There were an apple here,' Stanley admitted grudgingly, feeling around in his own jacket.

'Shall we move a bit?' Edmund suggested, indicating the pool of vomit.

Their unlikely friendship appalled both families, though for very different reasons, and shocked everyone else, too. Edmund never revealed to his parents why the gardener's son had suddenly become his favourite companion. He'd have had to admit to playing in a forbidden place and the stupidity of trying to trap a dragonfly that had nearly cost him his life. However, it did sometimes seem as if he deliberately made the friendship hard for himself.

'Where are you off to now?' his mother would enquire with a familiar, alarmed look in her eye.

'Just – out.'

'Anywhere special?'

'See the swans on the lake, mebbe.'

'*Will* you speak properly, Edmund! And take your hands out of your pockets! Are you going on your own?'

'Thought I'd see if Stanley was about.'

'That's the gardener's son, is it?' she'd say, though she knew perfectly well. 'And don't mumble like that.' Then, as Edmund stood there mutinously, she'd threaten to put an end to the friendship though she didn't specify how. She was in a difficult position. It was true that Edmund was in unwelcome company and picking up all sorts of bad habits. On the other hand, Stanley's father was a consummate gardener, his skills envied by landowners for miles around.

But by then the friendship had become very much more than a debt of gratitude. It was Stanley who was the true custodian of the woods and fields of Melcombe, not choleric old Smithson, the half-blind gamekeeper. Stanley used the old rural terms that made Edmund laugh. He called wasps 'wopses' and ants 'emmets' and moles 'wants'. He seemed to know where every animal and bird lived, too. He showed Edmund the nest of field mice near the hedge in Tinker's Corner where the hay was long and thick; he'd been visiting them since they were born.

Excited by the tiny wriggling creatures, Edmund moved to stamp on them. But Stanley stopped him. 'You should respect living things,' he said – this from Stanley who, at ten, could wring a chicken's neck like an expert. But that was different: it was all right to kill for the table. The exception was hares, he informed Edmund. The servants would cross themselves when the carcasses were brought into the kitchen after coursing. The cook dreaded being instructed to prepare jugged hare: everyone knew the animals were familiars.

'What's a familiar?' Edmund asked.

Stanley told him that a wounded hare had once run into a local cottage fleeing from the hounds and, when the huntsman knocked on the door to warn the old woman who lived there,

there was a long delay before she appeared with a fresh bandage on her left leg, blood seeping through it, exactly where the hare's injury had been. Any coincidence was dismissed.

'I seen her,' Stanley insisted. It was another of his attractions for Edmund that he took witchcraft for granted. It was like glimpsing a whole dangerous other world alongside the one that prevailed at the Abbey.

They didn't discuss their differences. But, then, they didn't talk much. They explored the countryside, whacking at nettles and bracken, jumping streams, trapping adders with a tennis racket purloined from the Abbey so they could observe them at their leisure (though, on Stanley's insistence, later setting them free), occasionally tumbling into fights that were more about bonding than aggression.

Stanley never revealed to Edmund that his own parents were just as opposed to the friendship. However, they could spell out in dreadful detail what would happen to the family if they lost their place on the estate; they could forbid Stanley to go anywhere near the Abbey; they could even beat him. But when Edmund turned up at their cottage asking for his playmate, they were powerless. The only comfort, they assured each other, was there was no way the friendship could last, especially now Edmund was to be sent away to boarding school. This hope was most fervently echoed by the Delanceys.

They were all of them wrong, of course. For a long long while it seemed there was nothing the friendship wouldn't survive.

Only once did the two boys refer to the incident that had brought them so close. Edmund pushed Stanley down a bank. And when he was sprawling in mud and momentarily ridiculous, he told him without expression, as if reading from a book, 'You saved my life, Stanley.'

Stanley stared at Edmund through a mask of dirt before spitting in his direction. 'I'd've done sim'lar for Spot or Molasses,' he muttered. He would just as impetuously and carelessly have risked his life for one of the estate dogs.

'I wouldn't,' said Edmund slowly, as if fascinated by this further difference between them. He continued, still with a strange lack of vitality as if part of him dreaded making the promise: 'Now, whatever you want from me, I have to give it to you. And that means anything, Stanley, and for ever. Don't you forget that.'

Then he kicked more dirt over the gardener's son, as if he despised him (and perhaps himself, too) and Stanley lunged at him and the conversation was over.

Chapter Four

Laura thought, summoning up her new resolve, *'I'm going to put this thing into perspective.'*

It was the morning after her return and, as she leant on her bedroom windowsill where the once-white paint was dirty and broken like part of an old mosaic, she could hear out of sync hammering from the Traffords' builders mingling with sweet English birdsong. She could see the Abbey in the distance, too, but, once over a surge of upsetting emotion, found it strangely comforting. At least that magical place was still in her life. She could appreciate now that it might have been even sadder if they'd moved away and believed she comprehended, for the first time, what had lain behind her father's insistence on keeping the Lodge. After all, she reasoned, wasn't it better to remain within sight of something beloved, even if sadly lost? Melcombe was too deeply embedded in their imaginations and memories: it could have haunted them for ever.

'I'm not going to get sucked back in,' thought Laura.

For the Traffords hadn't stolen the Abbey, she reminded

herself. They might have proved to be disagreeable and hostile but they were hardly wicked thieves. They'd bought the house quite legitimately after her father had been forced to put it on the market. Even her grandmother had accepted there was no other option but to sell. However, that had been before she discovered who was bidding.

The effect had been dramatic. The famously controlled Hester had implored Sam not to allow the sale. When he'd pointed out he didn't like the idea of his family's former servants taking over the Abbey any more than she did, but that needs must because it had become very dilapidated and there were no other buyers in sight, she'd eventually seemed to come round. But then he'd unveiled his secret plan to stay on the premises and keep an eye on things – his condition of sale.

Laura shivered as the past came back to her. It had been the beginning of the end for Hester, but Sam had been strangely obdurate in the face of all that raging and weeping. 'Don't you understand?' Laura had heard him shout at one point. 'We *have* to stay on! Otherwise we lose everything!' Hester went demented and much of his reason deserted him, too. The Traffords were intent on torture, he'd tell anyone who'd listen. They didn't appreciate the Abbey – how could they, as plebs? Their only motive in coming back was to rub it in that it was the former gardener and his family who could now afford to live in splendour in the big house, whereas the true owner was forced to stuff his family into a cramped little cottage. On and on he'd ranted, until Laura had taken to her bed, unable to stop crying.

And yet, for all of her childhood, her father had seemed merely amused by the long feud between the two families. He even turned it into a family joke, borrowing her grandfather's crusty humourless style and pretending to hate the Traffords as unreasonably as he did.

'There's bad blood there,' he'd growl dramatically.

The concept had been quite confusing for Laura and her siblings because they only knew about good blood. Good blood had been spilt in the Abbey centuries ago and their parents had scared them with the ghastly story because it was part of their heritage.

But they were still no better informed about the strange continuing quarrel with a former servant. And how, they wondered, could people continue to hate each other when they never met?

'What do you mean, bad blood?' they'd demand. 'What makes it different?'

'Why don't you ask Grandpa?' their father would reply, knowing perfectly well this was impossible because nobody could talk to bad-tempered old Edmund about anything. He was a disappointment to his grandchildren, in whom he took little pleasure; all he seemed interested in was his own misery. He was plagued by insomnia and nightmares, he'd complain; he never had one second's peace. But, then, he'd been like that for as long as anyone could remember. The Delancey depression was famous. The black dog, the unpredictable mood perched on the shoulder like the gloomy-looking owl on the family crest – '*Sapientia prima stultitia caruisse*'. It was a family blight, like the baldness that had caused Edmund to lose every strand of hair overnight in his early thirties. The children knew it was Sam's secret dread that he, too, would arise from his bed one morning, head like an egg, leaving a pillow of dark hair behind him.

'We're asking *you*.'

Sam mimicked Edmund, exaggerating his petulant, old Etonian drawl. 'Bad blood means people are born rotten to the core.'

'So, it's not the Trafford family's fault, then?'

'Oh, it's their fault orl right!'

'Are they always going to be bad?'

'Till the end of time.'

'But, Pa, how do you know if you've never even met them?'

'I just do.'

'Were they bad before we started hating them?'

'Oh, they were bad orl right.'

'So why didn't we start hating them before?'

'Enough!' Sam would roar, suddenly bored, because it was part of his temperament to tire easily.

Laura smiled as she remembered all this. The fact was, her father didn't even know how the feud had started because he and her grandfather had never got along well enough for him to ask. As she understood it, all Sam knew was that, although his father had sacked Stanley Trafford soon after the war had ended, thus depriving a whole family of its livelihood at a bad time, he'd continued to loathe him. Long after the Traffords had left the Abbey, Edmund went on blaming them for everything. It reached the ridiculous stage where, if the roses suffered mildew or a prized tree blew down in a gale, his reaction was invariably: 'That damned bloody lot again!'

Once, lubricated by claret, he'd muttered that Stanley Trafford had been caught in the act of trying to destroy a valuable vine, and that, on quitting the estate, he'd put a curse on the entire Delancey family for perpetuity. Sam joked about that, too. 'Oi condemns the lot o' you to hell for the rest o' time!' he'd snarl.

The truth was, Sam had long ago discovered that the mysterious feud had its uses. He could deflect his father's legendary rages by invoking the Traffords. If he was feeling particularly unreasonable, he could blame his own troubles on them. So, he casually passed the feud to his children, like handing down a hideous but handy heirloom.

But in those days, the early seventies, Laura and her siblings believed that it was unfair to go on hating the other family, even if their father found it amusing – and besides, they still hadn't found out what bad blood was. So they went in search of their grandmother.

They found Hester, as usual, at her embroidery as she reclined in an ancient stripy deckchair set up on the warm and sunny paving outside the cloisters. From far across the woods and fields, they could hear the hollow punctual sound of a cuckoo and the considered tolling of a bell like the one that had centuries ago summoned monks to prayer before being torn down and melted in the furnace that could so easily have destroyed the Abbey. ('Nothing left but an iron pancake,' their father would say dramatically.) Nearer at hand, there was the noise of fraying canvas straining at dodgy seams as their grandmother shifted in her deckchair, pouring her soul into the creation of yet another miniature depiction of the house she loved so greatly.

'Pa says they've bad blood!' they began indignantly because, being children, they assumed everyone would know what they were talking about.

Hester certainly seemed to. 'Bad blood, darlings?' she said. 'Oh, I know *all* about bad blood.' She didn't enlighten them, though, just nodded with one of her annoyingly enigmatic expressions and continued to spear her tapestry with a fat needle loaded with wool. In and out it went, tracing the blueprint in her mind.

'Tell us, Gran!' they pleaded. '*Why* do we hate them so much?'

But she seemed to slide away from the question, almost as if they'd no business asking. 'This is satin stitch,' she told them. 'See how it brings out the texture of the stone?'

'Bad blood!' they nagged, but her response was so baffling and inadequate that, very soon afterwards, they gave up.

'Oh, it's not blood that's important,' she said, which was quite ridiculous coming from her because she was always going on about family and had been born into a very grand one herself before marrying their grandfather (thus entering Debrett's and Burke's for the second time).

It wasn't until the Traffords bought their Abbey that the Delancey children understood that the long tradition of hatred between their two families had been justified. Taking away their beloved home for revenge, driving their grandmother dotty and upsetting their father to the point of madness made the Traffords into the worst people in the world. It wasn't enough to say they had bad blood – they were demons. All of a sudden, it became entirely logical to tune into the ancient anger and loathing, like picking up a gauntlet.

It was only when Laura had gone away from them that she started to see the sickness in it.

The day was hazy, beautiful and wonderfully fresh and, in the distance, she noted familiar black specks bouncing over the Abbey lawn. 'Traitors,' she murmured with more affection than bitterness. She told herself it might even be a good omen because legend had it that if the Delanceys left the house, then the ravens would disappear too.

Then she stiffened suddenly.

A bent, rather overweight figure in blue overalls had emerged from one of the arches leading to the cloisters. From his attitude, he seemed to be sniffing appreciatively at the air, probably smelling the old yellow roses that twined up the wall there. After several minutes of this, he stooped and fiddled with one of the bushes. He seemed to be pulling off bits, stuffing them into his pockets.

Then a large person in trousers (whether it was a boy or girl was impossible to tell from that distance) cannoned out of the Abbey and hugged the old man, who surely had to be that pantomime villain of Laura's childhood, Stanley Trafford. They stood clasped and swaying for a long moment while he patted the person's back enthusiastically, like slapping a horse.

Laura shivered a little in her nightdress as she watched the Traffords behaving like a functional family. Straining to see more, she observed a tall man in a suit – who had to be Mark Trafford – emerge. There was a dog bounding alongside him and, very faintly – the sound travelling across the still air – she heard him bellow just as her father did, 'Down!' And then the androgynous-looking person shrieked something at the dog, too, and Laura realized it was a girl.

'What are you doing, darling?' asked someone just behind her. It was Fred, who'd quietly entered to see if she was awake – and of course had guessed exactly what she was up to. 'I wouldn't,' she advised with a troubled frown. 'I try to ignore them. It's the only way.'

'I'm fine, honestly,' said Laura, turning from the window and smiling at her mother. For the first time in her life, she felt that it was she who should be protecting her parents rather than the other way round.

*

Fred hadn't wanted to stay at the Lodge, either, but went along with it, as usual, for Sam's sake. Besides, where else could they afford? She was very deeply upset by the loss of the Abbey, the more so because she'd seen it coming for years. For all her love of Sam, she had to concede he was no good at business. But it wasn't his fault, she'd remind herself fiercely, even as she watched him squander the estate's resources (an ambitious venture into pig farming one long dry summer, an ill-thought-out attempt to become a professional cider producer the next). What chance had he ever had, with his upbringing? Granted, there'd been money and privilege, but she'd seen for herself how his father had treated him with a mixture of boredom and contempt, whereas Hester had mollycoddled him in her frosty way, instilling a sense of superiority but no work ethic. Displeased with Sam's lack of acumen – which he'd exacerbated by taking away his confidence – Edmund had prevaricated about making over the estate to him in his lifetime as his accountant had advised . . . only to die at sixty, leaving a bill for death duties that made the eventual sale of the Abbey inevitable.

It was amazing, really, Fred reflected tenderly, that her husband was able to love at all. 'Thank you for saving me,' he'd say, even now – seeming to forget it was he who'd forced their young marriage with a shock pregnancy. He increasingly brought out her protectiveness. There was no way she was going to tell him what she really thought: that it was high time he accepted the Abbey was lost to them for ever and found himself a job.

But being Sam, he'd sworn that the Lodge was only a perch until he won their old home back – impressing on her that this revolution in their fortunes would come about when his next brilliant idea hit the jackpot (because, of course, he'd no intention of working for anyone else). She pretended to go along with the fantasy while quietly taking control of the family finances, trying to eke out the last tranche of money left after the debts had been paid. But, however she scrimped and saved, she knew there was no way it could last the year and her fear grew all the time.

Sam's ego still had to be massaged, though. Only that morning he'd accused her, with a wounded look, 'You don't believe I'll get the Abbey back for us, do you?'

'Of course I do!' Fred had insisted, bolstering him up like always but inwardly dismayed because there was something very frightening about his failure to face reality.

'Don't lie to me. I can see it in your eyes.'

'Darling, I swear!'

'I know how you were looking forward to having the girls' weddings there.' He sounded desolate.

'It doesn't matter!' she assured him immediately.

'What do you mean, it doesn't matter? You *don't* believe it!'

'All I meant was,' said Fred very calmly, 'there's plenty of time, isn't there?'

'There is,' he agreed, slightly mollified.

'Anything could happen.'

'I suppose.'

'They haven't even found themselves husbands yet!'

'I know we've had bad luck,' he conceded.

'We have.'

'But some of it was my fault.'

'None of it was your fault,' Fred told him, trying to sound as if she believed it. She could measure his plunging mood by the fact that he'd spent the whole of the past week painstakingly constructing a model Spitfire aeroplane.

'Listen,' he said, radiating sudden enthusiasm as he turned out bits and pieces of scribbled-on paper from his pockets. 'I've just had an idea for a bestseller. It's about someone trying to murder Margaret Thatcher. He's been hired by a group of self-styled patriots. He's a ruthless assassin, a legend. I thought I'd call him "The Ferret".'

And Fred said, 'Brilliant!' as usual, but couldn't prevent a sigh. As an afterthought, she gave him the sort of kiss that always conveyed a promise.

'Shameless hussy! I'll hold you to that.'

'Just you try,' Fred told him with a fake show of demureness, glad to have restored his spirits. The passion in their marriage had always compensated for the insecurity. But now, for the first time, she was chiefly motivated by pity and felt very sad about it.

When Laura eventually descended from her bedroom washed and dressed, she found her brother and sister still sitting over breakfast. There was a plump cat slumbering on one end of the table next to a dish containing a slab of melting butter which had several tortoiseshell hairs embedded in it, and one of the Labradors, Spectre, was watching David with unblinking attention as he ate a piece of bacon, waiting patiently for a slip of the hand or one tiny lapse of concentration. At least, thought Laura, the pets were behaving true to form.

'Good morning!' said Fred very cheerfully, as she came in from the kitchen with a new pot of coffee and a rack of fresh toast. 'What are you all planning to do with yourselves today?'

David and Maria looked a little affronted.

'I have to read something,' said David pompously, even though everyone knew he was idling away the time until he heard about his A levels and would probably just go back to bed.

'You could tidy your room,' Fred suggested pleasantly, though without much hope.

Coincidentally, Justin Trafford was waiting for the same crucial examination results. David had heard from Lily, their former cleaner, now working for the Traffords, that Justin was expected to get straight A's – 'Top of his class, ain't he? They be right proud.' The same could hardly be said of himself, though he had a good mind – his teachers were always saying so. With their encouragement and his parents' backing, he'd applied to his father's old college at Cambridge. But, of course, Justin Trafford was in with a far better chance, David would point out with a sneer of self-pity. After all, *he* hadn't been obliged to transfer to the local comprehensive when the money ran out.

'I thought I'd talk to Laura about India,' said Maria, smiling encouragingly at her sister though she, too, should probably have been looking for a job. But both girls had been actively encouraged to leave school early, to save money, and were unqualified for anything except perhaps working in a shop, which their parents would never have countenanced. It was Sam's belief that girls didn't need to be educated. He assumed they'd get married early – preferably to someone rich whose parents could pay for the wedding. He and Fred were lucky to have two such attractive daughters, he'd remarked the other day within earshot of the Traffords. It was a dig at Genevieve, of course.

'Anyone know where Gran is?' asked Fred because it had occurred to her that she'd not seen Hester since early in the morning, when she'd taken her a cup of tea. Her bedroom was empty. She'd just checked.

As if in answer to her question, the dogs started up a storm of hysterical barking and raced towards the front door.

Janice Trafford was waiting outside with Hester.

As usual, she'd taken considerable trouble with her appearance. She wore a neat pair of slacks with a smart blouse in a coordinating colour and good shoes free of country muck. Her make-up had been carefully applied and she'd just Carmen-rollered her hair.

By contrast, Hester Delancey was untidier than ever and also dismayingly cheerful, as if – in her demented condition – she genuinely believed she'd spent a useful and productive morning.

'I found her in the Abbey again!' Janice was determined not to appear to have noticed the dead pheasant hanging so conspicuously from the door knocker even though, now the day was warming up, it was beginning to smell.

'I assume you mean my mother-in-law?' Fred responded very coldly.

'Exactly,' Janice agreed a little uncertainly as if the other woman had scored an unexpected point.

'I'm sure Lady Delancey is perfectly capable of making her own way back,' Fred went on with an even icier edge to her voice.

'She was only wrecking one of our new leather chairs, wasn't she?'

'I beg your pardon?'

'Digging holes in it with a stonking great needle!' Janice knew that, by losing her temper, she'd probably surrendered the moral high ground. But Fred Delancey always had that effect on her. It was no good telling herself she was the lady of the Abbey now or remembering Mark's contemptuous nickname for Fred of 'the fridge'. Fred was so effortlessly patronizing. What sort of silly name was that, anyway? Fred and Sam! Stanley, who was famously homophobic, as well as racist and sexist, would splutter, 'Sounds like a couple of perverts to me!'

For a moment, she wished she'd let him bring back the old lady instead. He was always offering, almost as if he *wanted* contact with the other family. But Stanley might have given Fred Delancey the impression it was acceptable for her mother-in-law to barge into the Abbey and destroy valuable property whenever she felt like it. It was becoming a real problem, thought Janice despairingly. You moved to a grand estate, hopefully among people who knew how to behave, only to find you'd inherited a mad old bat who spent her life trying to make yours a misery.

'Ah!' Fred looked amused. She raised her eyebrows. 'Digging holes, you say? I wonder if you're aware of Lady Delancey's reputation?'

Janice smiled, as if Fred had only stated the obvious.

'My mother-in-law's work has been featured in several books on fine needlework. She embroidered most of the chairs in the Abbey.'

'That's as may be. But I'll thank you to keep her hands off ours!'

In the dining room, all three Delancey children were listening to this exchange.

'Don't worry,' Maria whispered to her sister. 'It happens all the time.'

Laura winced. She found it most upsetting. She'd never heard her mother sound this cold and unfriendly. She was watching a wasp imprisoned in an empty honey jar, its angry buzzing growing weaker and weaker.

'It's not poor Gran's fault she still thinks we live there,' said David indignantly.

'I never heard of her trying to embroider a *leather* chair before,' said Laura, frowning. It almost seemed as if her grandmother had been engaged in some private joke.

'Horrible people!' Maria sounded vicious, as frighteningly foreign as Fred had done. 'Horrible horrible horrible!'

Laura could see now that they should never have stayed on at the Lodge. She could feel the bile and bitterness like a noxious cloud, smothering her family's natural humour and niceness. They were probably going to sit here all morning, dissecting the awfulness of the Traffords in minute detail. And meanwhile, the sun was shining and the countryside was beautiful.

'You've not heard the last of this!' Janice warned Fred as a parting shot, and Maria turned with a grim smile to share the joke with her sister.

But Laura had slipped unnoticed from the room and gone for a walk, taking the wasp in the honey jar with her. Once outside the Lodge, she set it free.

Chapter Five

Joe was gently at odds with his father. They were very different in character and it irked Mark to see any son of his lounging about, even on a Saturday. This time, however, his mild irritation was inexplicably boiling up into a fury. What did Joe think he was doing with his precious youth, still sitting in the Refectory when it was nearly eleven, with that dopey expression on his face? The rest of the family had long since breakfasted and gone about their business. Janice was studying a list of suggestions from her very superior interior decorator – none of which she'd accept, thought Mark, the sourness spilling over. Justin was locked away in his bedroom with his books. Even Stanley, who'd earned all the relaxation he desired, was making one of his bonfires with the help of Genevieve. Strange, Stanley's attitude to bonfires . . . He'd attack the task with grim determination but always needed company, almost as if he were afraid. And this was the man who, more than forty years before, had faced down enemy fire to rescue two fallen comrades, earning himself a medal in the process.

'When I was your age, Joe,' said Mark, 'I already had my foot on the ladder.'

'Yes, yes, yes,' Joe muttered under his breath because he knew about the journey from rags to riches – they all did. Then, suddenly compassionate, he gave his ravishing smile, which had the same momentarily soothing effect as patting his father on the shoulder.

Mark complained gently, '*I* couldn't afford to sit around.' As he spoke, he was shuffling papers, scribbling notes in his filofax, glancing at his watch – doing everything he could to make his son feel guilty and idle and yet at the same time admiring his wonderful attractiveness, his sense of ease. '*Handsome is as handsome does,*' he reminded himself sternly. Joe was the family looker but that didn't mean he merited special treatment.

'No,' Joe agreed thoughtfully, oblivious to his father's sudden frown. He could appreciate that he was lucky.

'You've a good brain on you,' Mark said, even though it was not strictly true. Justin was the clever son.

'Yes.'

'Don't let it go to your head. These are crucial years, Joe, and don't you forget it.'

'I won't,' Joe promised his father with another wonderful smile.

Mark couldn't understand Joe's ambition to be an actor. Why should a man wish to spend his working life pretending to be other people? In the last ten years, with the boom in the property market, the family had zoomed so swiftly up the social spectrum that they were still all catching their breath. Of course, Mark had hoped his elder son would take over his empire when the time came. What self-made man wouldn't? Now, that *would* be like stepping onto a stage in front of a huge waiting audience.

You needed talent and faith to succeed at his business and it was always fun, even during hairy moments like the crash of '74.

'They've had it so easy,' he'd grumble to Janice.

'You wouldn't want them to go through what you did.'

'That's true,' he'd agree without hesitation. He'd enjoyed the privilege of spoiling his children – which was why, though an agnostic, he'd always add, 'Thank God!'

But at least he'd been loved as a child; and this certainty that he was cherished had made the worst hardships endurable. 'Two's company,' his father would say. 'Three's perfect.' It was as if he were trying to impress on Mark that the love they all shared would act as magical protection. Three was better than two, even when there was barely sufficient food for one. 'Four lovely black eyes . . .' Stanley would croon, looking into the haggard faces of his wife and child. Family was the only thing in life that truly counted, he'd say over and over again. It was the cornerstone of Mark's upbringing. This closer-than-close bond between the three of them had its negative side, as well: it made them suspicious of anyone outside their tight little unit, for hadn't the very people they'd learnt to trust betrayed them most cruelly?

Life might have been easier with a sibling – especially a brother, Mark had often thought wistfully – but early on, he was made to realize this could not be. He was twelve when he accidentally overheard a tearful conversation between his parents and understood with horror that his mother, Effie, was about to undergo an abortion (which, he simultaneously learnt, was not the first or even the second). That bitter loss – of his innocence too – would become another charge against the wicked Delanceys.

His childhood had been divided into two very different

sections: before and after the banishment. He could remember only odd snippets from before: the rich smell of the cottage; the pain of an invisible sting from a bee; standing on the thatched roof when he was just four, hand in hand with his mother, staring unblinkingly at the Allied planes towing the gliders back after the D-Day landings. He was to remember it for ever, she ordered him tenderly. So he did.

He'd been six when his family was exiled from the Abbey estate one autumn morning in 1947, but he could still remember the acrid taste of desolation as he'd trailed after the others dragging a heavy suitcase, his father carrying his crippled grandfather on his back. It was the first time he'd seen his usually merry and stoical mother cry like that – the tears running from her eyes like a gutter overflow. 'What are we going to do?' she'd kept repeating piteously because there was no job to go to and no home either and the whole country was in post-war meltdown. 'Are we to be gypsies?' she'd whispered. And then Mark had witnessed his father shake his fist and bellow like a crazed bull.

'I curse you, Edmund Delancey, and all your kin for ever!' The terrifying sound had bounced off the surrounding hills, the echo growing fainter and fainter, like someone repeating a promise: the whole estate must have heard him.

Mark had turned round for one final look at the past and there was the Abbey glowing gold in the autumn sun, floating on its base of silvery lavender bushes, beady-eyed ravens bouncing across its emerald lawn in competition with the long shadows. The whole place was utterly tranquil as if it had already forgotten about the family of gardeners who'd striven for generations to make it so exquisite. It had haunted him, of course: the last moment of such beauty for years and years.

He'd been twenty-one and living with his parents in cheap rented accommodation in London, when he bought his first property. His father was delivering for a grocery store then, his mother was working as a cleaner. He'd managed to impress a kindly bank manager with his cocky enthusiasm, and was prepared to risk everything on untested intuition, fired by the iron determination to make something of himself. By then, he was working by day in a post office, sorting letters, and at night in a pub, wiping tables and clearing glasses. The post office could offer a real future, said Stanley, who expressed alarm when taken to view a broken-down, two-bedroomed, ground-floor flat with a bath in the kitchen and a privy in the back yard. Stanley was a countryman. He'd never get used to the city, he'd grumble, with the dirt and the noise, not to mention the different coloured skins.

'Wouldn't stick a pig in there.'

'Soon fix that. Property's the way forward, Dad. I were lucky to find it.'

'Lucky? Your mam and me can't help with them payments, you know.'

'I'll manage.'

'You has to eat, lad! You don't want to saddle yourself with a twenty-year debt. Don't want to fall out with the post office neither.'

'Never said I did.'

'So when does you reckon on finding time for them repairs?'

'Evenings.'

'What about the pub, then?'

'I'm giving that one up.'

'I don't know, son, I don't know . . .'

'Won't take long, the rate I'll be working.'

'If you're not murdered first. You'll stand out like a sore thumb in these parts!'

'The area'll pick up, you'll see.'

'I don't know, son . . . Don't forget now, them lot got the advantage of you in the dark.' He delivered a further warning as they left the crumbling house in the seedy road littered with junk: 'You're setting a trap for yourself.' He gestured at the twitching folds of yellow-grey net in the front window behind them, the hidden suspicious eyes that had witnessed so many changes for the worse. 'You tell me the sense in buying a property that's occupied!'

'Why do you think it's going dirt cheap, Dad? And she ain't going to live for ever.'

Stanley lowered his voice, even if Mark hadn't: 'I'd make damn sure she don't!'

He was joking, of course, but when Mark's 78-year-old tenant died not long afterwards, he couldn't help but be delighted. She'd been a miserable old bat, he gathered, not properly grateful when her young landlord mended all the things that should have been fixed years ago, like the leaking toilet and rotting sills.

Within months of getting sole occupation of the flat, Mark had sold it for almost double what he'd paid and was on his way up. He mastered wiring and plumbing and paperhanging, but his real skill lay in buying. Like a hunter, he'd circle the areas on the tattered edges of the city that lay within his limited budget and then he'd frequent the pubs, getting to know the locals, casually asking questions. It took time he couldn't afford but he learnt who was on their uppers and would welcome a quick sale, with continued tenancy, if need be; who was in poor health and might soon free up a property. He'd an eerie gift for knowing when an old person had died almost before their next of kin had been informed. In a trice, he'd made his offer and was living rough on the property as he blocked up fireplaces, installed radiators, pasted woodchip paper over bumpy walls, hid cracks with lashings of spackle and textured ceiling spray and laid cheap carpet over dull old floorboards.

He left the post office in 1963, when he was twenty-two. Stanley prophesied doom. He was deeply proud of his son's energy and ambition. Even so, he believed it was insanity to give up a job with prospects and, in forty years or so, the security of a pension. Besides, Mark was courting now and it wouldn't be fair to inflict the uncertainty on Janice, he said, let alone any nippers that came along.

'Look what happened to me, son! Thrown out after years of faithful service, without so much as a thank you!'

'I know, Dad,' Mark had agreed extremely soberly. 'That's why I only ever want to work for myself.'

Unlike the rest of his family, Joe relished every moment of living in the Abbey. The others enjoyed the retribution part all right – the triumph of taking the Delanceys' place, rubbing their snooty noses in it – but were uncomfortable with the vaulted, unheated size of the place and the musty odour of old flowers that no amount of Janice's atomizers could dispel, the uneven stone floors that tripped you up, the strange humming silences and occasional tricks of the light.

'It's like I see someone out the corner of my eye,' Genevieve would complain, more cross than frightened.

And once, when they were all in the Great Hall, they heard a faint but persistent drumming as if someone was beating on the oak front door but, when it was opened, there was nobody there. For all his bravado, his grandfather had looked really scared for a moment. But his father had insisted it was just the old wood reacting to the new central heating. He had an explanation for everything.

Joe loved the chaos and the mystery. The Abbey was so different from any of the houses they'd lived in before. He believed he could sense the power of the past clutching at him: a throng of the long dead, pleading with him to tune into their extraordinary stories. He'd tell himself it was a lucky break, since he wanted to be an actor; after all, as an exercise, he often pretended to be other people. So, shivering with importance, he'd crouch in a corner of the Great Hall – which his mother had yet to renovate – and stare at its beautiful moulded ceiling and think of the monks who'd once lived in the Abbey and whisper, 'I'm listening . . .'

It was only logical, he told himself, that, like radio waves, past feelings continued to vibrate in the air – love, of course, but also scary stuff like fear and anger. He'd make his mind quite blank, preparing for the soft shuffle of feet, the faint amorphous rumble of voices. But, though he tried and tried, nothing ever happened. When he finally opened his eyes, he was always alone.

It amazed him, really, that the rest of his family displayed so little interest in the past. His mother was the worst. He knew that for two pins she'd raze this place to the ground and replace it with a larger grander version of the modern house in Guildford she missed so much, though she'd never have dared say so to his father. Instead, she was busy imposing her own exigent standards on the ramshackle Abbey, like someone trying to train a very disobedient dog. The next project was sorting out the plumbing. It was to be a massive undertaking, with en suite bathrooms installed throughout and pumps to service the new showers. Joe thought he'd miss the ancient noisy system and even the brown water that trickled from taps clogged with limescale. It pleased him to imagine all the people who'd lowered themselves, shivering with the icy cold, into claw-footed iron baths whose enamel was so worn and patchy by now it resembled the pattern of leopard skin. Before that, he supposed, they'd have bathed in tubs filled with water heated in kettles on the old kitchen range that his mother was planning to replace with a costly but efficient Aga. Even the monks must have washed sometimes, he reflected, and squeezed his eyes tight shut with concentration as he strove to pick up the stale whiff of their long habits as they filed silently through the Abbey, heavy iron crosses on chains bumping against their bony chests, heads bent in contemplation. '*C'mon, c'mon!*' he urged, mentally snapping his fingers.

'Joe!'

Having very reluctantly left him to his devices, his father was now calling him from somewhere in the distance. No doubt he'd thought up some unnecessary task. In a minute, if there was no response, he was sure to come looking.

Joe rose swiftly from the table, crossed to one of the long windows and opened it. He'd go exploring, he decided.

He was balancing on the Refectory sill on his way out into the full hot brightness of midday – half of him warmed by the sun, half still chilled by the lingering breath of old stone – when he stopped short. Later, he'd swear he'd not imagined it. He'd relive the moment over and over: would even set up the exact same circumstances to entice it to happen again, while cursing his feeble reaction at the time. But for now, on his way out of a room he knew to be quite empty, he was terrified when it felt exactly as if a hand had been laid on his bare left arm. Though there was nothing to see when he looked down, he was certain he could identify its shape and weight as his hairs rose to meet it, and believed he was even conscious of the faint scrape of an invisible nail.

From the window of her make-do study, soon to be adorned with knicker blinds, Janice saw her eldest child race across the sunlit lawns like a dog let loose. He was heading towards the plume of yellow-grey smoke rising in the distance where Stanley and Genevieve were piling rubbish on their bonfire.

'If you're looking for Joe . . .' she called to her husband. Her voice trailed away. He was already in a bad mood. He'd noticed the piles of excrement on the lawn: far too much for one dog to have produced. He hated having the builders around, too, though he paid them extra to work weekends. He was always saying he could do a finer job himself.

A moment ago, she'd heard him open a window and shout, 'Have to do better than that, boys!' which had provoked a storm of vigorous hammering from the roof above, just as he must have anticipated. And now the Delanceys were bound to complain about the noise – again.

'Strongly suggest leaving panelling as it is,' the interior decorator, Lucinda Hartley-Green, had advised on the typed list beside Janice. But *she* didn't have to live with it. Janice picked critically at the ancient uneven wood. It was all so dirty! In her opinion, those knots and grooves should be sandpapered and filled and the whole lot freshly painted. Then the panelling would tone with the built-in cupboards she planned. There was no storage space in the Abbey. It was a major problem. She thought wistfully of the house they'd left. No out-of-reach ceilings. No dusty stone corners. Plenty of wardrobes. Fitted carpeting everywhere. No maddening smell of old rose petals.

She knew better than anyone how ambitious her husband was. Their family life had been regularly interrupted by moves ever further up the property scale, starting with a tiny house occupied by a sitting tenant. She dreaded to think that this might be their final resting place: an enormous white elephant of a property where, once upon a time, his father had been a servant. But she was allowed little say. It was Stanley and Mark – so extraordinarily close – who made all the real decisions.

There was so much to do, suddenly. There were instructions to be given to the huge cleaning staff and meals to put on the table on time (because she was determined to carry on cooking for her family), not to mention thinking about colour schemes. The house and its rooms went on for ever: one chilly yawning problem after another. There were forty-two, Genevieve had announced the day they moved in. What other family occupied a house where they could use only a fraction of the space? It was Justin who'd first discovered the rows and rows of ancient bells on coiled springs outside the kitchen door, each with a faded, ornately inscribed label beneath: Great Hall . . . Refectory . . . Library . . . Cloisters . . . Morning Room . . . White Room . . . Shooting Room . . . Keeping Room . . . The children were always ringing them – tugging curiously at fraying cords or brass contraptions like huge studs, listening in vain for a rusty jangling in the distance.

Janice must have touched a hidden catch because, all of a sudden, a small section of panelling swung open. It seemed there was a space inside. Something gleamed in the darkness from beneath a shroud of cobwebs, and Janice made out a stack of envelopes tied with white satin ribbon. More Delancey junk, she thought wearily, and was about to remove the bundle for Stanley's bonfire when a big spider scuttled out. She shrieked and slammed the section of panelling to. She must see to the flowers now. She'd deal with the old letters later. All the same, she felt a sense of triumph. Quite by chance, she'd discovered a secret place and, with a pencil, she took care to mark its exact location.

After that, she gave the study another dose of air freshener and shrugged on a cardigan because, even in summer, the cold was abysmal in this old house. *'I can't be doing with the past!'* she thought wearily.

Chapter Six

Stanley Trafford and Edmund Delancey were in the village pub, where everyone else was talking about imminent war. They were engaged in a favourite game, acting out the roles of carefree lothario and disapproving maiden aunt.

'I met someone,' announced Stanley, sipping at the beer Edmund had bought him. It was warm and frothy and tasted strongly of hops.

Edmund frowned and raised his eyebrows like someone of fifty-four rather than twenty-four. 'And?'

Stanley was always picking up new girls. Even so, Edmund had noted the unusual excitement in his friend the minute he walked in. Stanley seethed with covert well-being and Edmund knew that if women were permitted in this male enclave of wiped-down mahogany and slow chat, they'd be fidgety and distracted by now, crossing and uncrossing their legs, laughing a little too loudly.

'She'm different,' said Stanley, pushing away the sticky black curl that always tumbled over his forehead.

Edmund assumed a quizzical expression. 'Now, where have I heard that before?'

Stanley fixed him with his liquorice eyes, which were strangely earnest. 'It's the truth, Edmund.'

Edmund waited for more information, while appearing to be far more interested in a measured game of darts being played out in one corner.

However, instead of spilling out the lurid details, as usual, Stanley asked very confidently, 'Will you be seeing her, then?'

It took Edmund by surprise, though, true to form, he murmured very laconically, 'Delighted.' Stanley had never made such a request before. But there'd been no need because his women never lasted long. Stanley liked his freedom. He was always saying so.

To Edmund's absolute astonishment and discomfort – wriggling his shoulders like a man anxious to slough off old bachelor ways – Stanley said, 'I were thinking . . . You, me and Hester . . . Set up a foursome?'

Their friendship had survived the continuing disapproval of both sets of parents, Edmund's long absences at Eton and Cambridge and the influence of new people with whom, on the face of it, he had far more in common. But nothing could alter his affection for the gardener's son. At the heart of it was the astounding memory of Stanley risking his life for him. He couldn't imagine anyone else, even his own parents, behaving like that. Stanley could so easily have walked away, with nobody the wiser. He was so straightforward, too: he said what he thought and in Edmund's world that was unusual. Moreover, Edmund found himself a better person in Stanley's company. On discovering that the other boy could barely read and write, he took it on himself to give lessons, using the

woods and fields for classrooms and the books he'd grown up
with and loved. It was fun teaching Stanley because he was
bright, and Edmund never perceived the sadness of being
clever in a milieu where so little could be achieved with it. He
was the heir to a great estate, but often felt trapped and put-
upon. It didn't occur to him how truly constricted Stanley's life
was.

However, where sex was concerned, Stanley was the tutor.
Nearly all Edmund's knowledge of women came from him.
Once, it occurred to him (in the friendliest kind of way) that
it was a bit like sending a terrier down a hole to flush out a
fox. One could hear the distant yelps and squeals and get a
vivid picture of the mayhem while remaining in control up
above. Encouraged by Stanley, he went to his first prostitute
shortly after his twenty-first birthday. 'Happy?' he was asked
subsequently.

'Ooh arr!' Edmund agreed enthusiastically, imitating his sex-
mad friend.

'Rather splendid, ain't it?' said Stanley, falling happily into the
joke.

Privately, Edmund told himself that sex would be different
with someone he could relate to. But, where girls from his sort
of background were concerned, sex before marriage was out
of bounds – though Stanley the expert would scoff, 'Don't
know what they wants till you gives it 'em.'

Edmund had been able to manage the friendship on his
terms because there'd always been an unexpected delicacy
about Stanley, an acceptance of boundaries without them
needing to be defined. The gardener's son had never been
invited inside the Abbey, of course. Similarly, he'd seemed
happy to accept that this old inn was the only place where they

openly socialized. Their friendship was accepted here: the more so since the country had edged ever closer to war.

'*I should never have told him about Hester,*' thought Edmund, wincing away from the atypical confidence. One thing seemed certain: for Stanley to have made such an unusual request meant this new girl of his was serious.

But then, Edmund reflected, in this last precious summer of 1939, seriousness was like an infection sweeping through an entire generation. Even he, naturally so cautious, was thinking of proposing to Hester, whom he scarcely knew. But very characteristically he kept this to himself. He smiled faintly as his friend gabbled on, interjecting every now and then in his caustic fashion, giving the impression that he was above such foolishness as love at first sight and hoping Stanley would get the message – without the awkwardness of him having to spell it out – that a meeting with Hester was impossible.

'Needed that!' said Stanley, setting down his half-empty tankard and passing his shirtsleeve across his red mouth. 'Effie's her name. She'm a lovely maid, Edmund!'

'So I gather.'

'Soon as I sees her, I knows her.' Rolling his r's, substituting z's for s's, chewing his words like a contented bull, Stanley went on to explain that before Effie had even opened her mouth – ' . . . and it were right beautiful, Edmund' – he'd known her voice would be husky and sweet. He'd guessed she'd be shy, too, and the exact way she'd choose to express herself. He'd known everything, he said, from that first glimpse at a gathering in the village, to which Effie had been brought by a friend. 'I'm daft!' he concluded, shaking his head in astonishment at his own vulnerability, not to mention his strange intuition.

'Ridiculous,' confirmed Edmund affectionately. He was

remembering his own first impressions of Hester. They'd met at a dinner before a dance, at another grand local house. He'd not considered her immediately attractive with her pale colouring and slight build, though she had a style about her that was impressive. She was the same age as him: older than most of the other girls.

'Soon as I sees her,' Stanley repeated. 'And when I gets up close, I thinks to meself: "I knows for a fact you'd smell just like that."'

'Dear oh dear!' said Edmund, tut-tutting away enjoyably.

'She'm a good soul,' said Stanley, confounding him.

'So you've not . . . ?'

'She ain't like that.' But Stanley sounded more proud than disgruntled. It seemed Effie really was different. 'Seventeen, she is. A babby!'

Edmund caught a glimpse of their two reflections, dodging among ranks of bottles in the big murky mirror behind the bar: Stanley brawny and dark and bursting with vigour; himself blond and slender, still with his boyhood fringe.

He could sense the grave tenor of the groups of other drinkers, the alarm coming off them like steam. It was such relief to be talking about something trivial and harmless for a change; so pleasurable being in his friend's company.

'Honey and clotted cream,' Stanley pronounced triumphantly. His expression became soft and doting. It sat oddly with his masculinity. 'Still,' he said as tenderly as if talking about one of the animals or birds he loved, 'she'm only young, ain't she?'

It occurred to Edmund that, beneath a healthy glaze of perspiration, a hint of musk, Stanley gave off the scent of innocence, too. He knew *he* didn't. A discreet sniff at the shoulder of his summer jacket identified a trace of stale lavender mingled with a breath of old cigar smoke – his father's smell exactly. This was unsurprising, since all his suits were passed on. 'Made to last,' his father would boom, but Edmund didn't really object since the suits had been very expensive and, anyway, went with his old-fashioned style. The one he was wearing dated back to the previous century, like all his suits, when his father had been thin. Made of cream linen, it bore very faint but indelible reminders of his father's frailties and passions: ghostly discolorations from late-night hot cocoa on the cuffs, pale greenish marks on the knees from impetuous and quite unnecessary bouts of gardening.

Hester smelt of rose water and talcum powder and, the first time they'd met, of mothballs, too (it was cold and she'd worn a family lynx). After the dinner, he'd been asked to give her a lift to the dance. 'Delighted!' he'd said, though quailing at the thought of more awkward conversation while trying to concentrate on not driving into a ditch after all the champagne and wine. As it turned out, the journey had been unexpectedly enjoyable.

In his father's Daimler, Hester had mocked the distant howling of kenneled spaniels throughout dinner – 'Ever been made to sit through *Parsifal*?' – and the high colour of their hostess – 'Was that make-up? Looked more like toothache to me.' By the time they reached their destination, he was relaxed, and eager to spend the rest of the evening with her.

'That's set, then, Edmund.' Buoyed up by bliss, Stanley sounded surprisingly firm, like a long-standing mistress issuing an ultimatum to a married lover.

'I couldn't very well say no,' Edmund later explained to Hester. 'After all, he did once save my life.'

Hester raised her eyebrows. He understood her seeming lack of enthusiasm, her droll approach. People from their sort of background were taught to play down emotion so that, if misfortune struck, the mechanism for coping gallantly and with dignity was already in place.

'Seriously!' But his amused expression, his mocking drawl seemed to belie his words. 'Wouldn't be here today if he hadn't dived into the river when I was drowning. Didn't give a thought to his own safety.'

'Well done, Stanley,' she said, as if awarding the gardener's son a grateful but dismissive pat on the shoulder.

'Sure you don't mind?'

'I'll survive,' she assured him with a twist of the mouth, not quite a grimace.

'I managed to get out of a dinner,' said Edmund, and a memory came back to him of Stanley attacking a pork pie in the pub as if trying to inscribe a message on it.

'Well, *there's* a mercy.' She sounded very light and casual.

'The White Lion Hotel does an excellent tea.'

'And there's only one way to eat a sandwich,' she reminded him with a smile.

He found it a little sad that she could read him so accurately, but they were very alike. 'Now listen, Hes. After half an hour, maximum, I'm going to scratch the side of my nose like this . . .' He demonstrated. 'And you're to say, "Oh my goodness, I've just remembered – I've an appointment." Got that?'

'It'll be fun,' she said gaily.

'You're a brick and I won't forget it.'

'We must celebrate,' said Edmund, while the dregs of Lapsang Souchong still lay warm in their cups. He clicked his fingers imperiously at a passing waiter: 'Bottle of your finest fizz.'

'You don't have to do that!' protested Stanley with a delighted smile, and he shot a glance at Effie as if to say, '*Told* you!'

'I know I don't!' said Edmund with a slight frown, because gratitude, like compliments, stuck in the craw.

'Beer'd be champion,' said Stanley, who'd have preferred it to champagne. He'd a proper thirst on him after the dish-water tea, he indicated with a cheeky lift of the elbow. He looked handsome and fresh in his dark suit, which – unlike Edmund's – was both new and cheap, and a starched, gleaming white shirt. As always, Stanley seemed confined by clothes, semi-throttled by his tie.

'Oh my goodness!' Hester began. 'I've just remembered . . .' But Edmund shook his head at her in warning. It was remorse that was making him go over the top. The moment dear old Stanley had come in, it had swamped him in a black wave. How *could* he have encouraged Hester to believe this meeting was a reluctant favour, even a chore? What a ghastly snob he'd been. The war was bearing down on them all, for God's sake! There'd be no class differences soon if old Hitler had his way. There'd be not a shred left of the England they knew.

He was reminded of his decision. It had been made last week, after another sombre male conversation over port at the Abbey. When he'd told his father he was going to enlist, he'd said approvingly, 'Good man,' but his mother had wept, remembering the dreadful slaughter of only twenty years before and the loss of two beloved brothers. The dearth of young suitors had led to a marriage with a contemporary of her father, a childless widower desperate for an heir. It was a grand match, certainly, but hardly happy.

Edmund wished Hester had tucked into the cakes and sandwiches as enthusiastically as the others instead of insisting with a dry little smile, 'No, no, it's all for you, truly. Edmund and I have had the most enormous lunch.' (Which meant he felt impelled to hold back, too, though he was ravenous.) He wished, also, that she hadn't chosen to wear her pearls and quite such an obviously expensive dress. He could tell Stanley was impressed by her style and breeding; the casual confidence she exuded. However, he had to admit that, in terms of obvious physical appeal, it was Effie who had the advantage with her dark glossy curls and voluptuous shape and perfect creamy skin. It was sweet how she deferred to Stanley, who was behaving with a rare gentleness. They were like a pair of blackbirds, taking dainty sips of tea, discreetly preening each other. Even so, he could sense the sexual chemistry beneath the show of refinement, like an insistent drumbeat. He glanced at Hester, as if suddenly uneasy, and saw her note the look.

'Stanley tells me you been friends since you was that small.' Effie had the same soft twang to her voice as her boyfriend, his slow and easy way of speaking. But, then, she was native to the area – they all were – only Edmund and Hester were a different kind of local.

Stanley shot a glance at Edmund from under his long lashes. 'Ten, weren't it?'

Edmund nodded brusquely, as if ashamed.

'I think that's lovely!' exclaimed Effie. Her lips were very full and bruised-looking; her dark eyes brimmed with pride.

'He saved Edmund's life,' Hester observed, with a tight smile. 'Didn't he tell you?'

'No.' Effie looked wondering, a little frightened. 'Is that right, my love?'

'More's the pity!' responded Stanley, letting out his great belly laugh like a woman ripping off a corset. It was only what he'd have said to Edmund if they'd been alone together. He was always ribbing him. But it didn't work in this context without an explanation. It caused a hole through which all the carefully constructed goodwill threatened to drain away.

'I seen the Abbey once,' said Effie a little uncertainly, picking up on the sudden tension in Hester without comprehending it.

'Exquisite, isn't it?' Hester responded with languid control, as if to push Effie back in her seat.

Edmund thought, staring down at the knees of his suit (one of which had a very faint, small spherical purple stain on it, as if his father had long ago, by mistake, knelt on a blackcurrant): *'If you say anything to Stanley like, "Your father's done wonders for the garden," then I shan't propose to you even though you're perfect for me, perfect. Today will be the end of it.'*

But he never found out what Hester was going to say next. Even as he waited with a fine mixture of feelings, Stanley dropped the first of his bombshells. He'd joined the Territorials. It had happened earlier that week, he told them all, looking as excited as when he'd first confided in Edmund about Effie. It was news to her as well. In fact, as Stanley later explained to Edmund, the reason he'd been so anxious for company was so she'd feel unable to make a fuss. He was bad at tears. They were getting married in less than a fortnight and she was bound to take it hard.

'Seemed only right,' was all he said by way of explanation for both these impetuous, enormous decisions.

Next day, first thing, Edmund joined up, too. And a week later he proposed to Hester, who reacted as if she'd never doubted his intentions for a minute.

Chapter Seven

The Abbey was a house built for secrets. It had offered a
choice of more than a dozen favourite meeting places, from a
cubbyhole at the top of a winding stone staircase to an ancient
linen cupboard more spacious than any of the Lodge's
bedrooms. But in the Delanceys' compact new home – long ago
occupied by the estate manager – all conversation could be
overheard. Every confidence had to be whispered – and
sometimes even written – when Sam and Fred were around. In
Laura's bedroom, Maria had just scribbled something on a piece
of paper before passing it over with a sickened expression.

'They were having it off again last night!!!' Laura read in
Maria's untidy writing. She raised her eyebrows casually, while
thinking what a child her sister still was, and Maria shook her
head with her eyes shut as if to deny what she'd heard.

'Now!' her mother had cried very urgently. 'Now!' She'd
buried her head under the quilt but later heard her parents
murmuring and chuckling.

'WHY?' Maria added on the piece of paper, underlining the

word twice. Not so long ago she'd confided that she was prepared to forgive her parents just the three acts of sex that had been necessary to produce their family.

Laura shrugged. She was feeling trapped and aimless and as if the past six months had been a dream; and now rain was teeming down outside, overflowing the blocked gutters and clattering onto a piece of corrugated iron nobody had bothered to remove. She was noticing how dusty the house was and thinking without much enthusiasm that she ought perhaps to do something about it. Her mother would polish what little remained of the inherited furniture till the old grain glowed with reflected light and fill vases with flowers poached from the Abbey gardens, but otherwise she neglected housework, especially where the bathroom and kitchen were concerned.

To add to the sense of claustrophobia, the sisters could hear the voice of their former cleaner, Lily, rising through the floorboards. Lily always dropped in for tea on her way back from the Abbey. 'Just a very quick cup, then,' she'd tell their mother reluctantly, as if she needed to be coaxed.

She and Fred were both shouting – Lily because she was partly deaf and Fred because she was becoming so irritated. As they listened, the girls visualized the wig-like frizz of bleached hair, the knees like old cauliflowers below the miniskirt that had never ceded to any other fashion, and the sun-blasted stretch of upper chest that Lily would refer to with a grim chuckle as 'me shammy leather'. She'd worked for the Delanceys for more than twenty years until they could no longer afford her and it was a little shocking how swiftly she'd transferred her allegiance. Mrs Trafford was right house-proud, she'd announce with a disdainful glance at Fred's smeared surfaces and crumby floor, and all the changes 'up there' were lovely. But Fred relied on her, and she knew it. How else could she find out what went on at the Abbey?

'She'm having a ong sweet for the White Room.' After delivering this bombshell, Lily became critical, almost hectoring. 'This here cup wants a good washing.'

'A what?' Fred sounded distracted.

'You try soda crystals. Works a treat. I'll fetch myself another, shall I? Dear oh dear, this one's well buggered, too.'

'She can't do that!'

'Beg pardon?' Lily didn't address Fred as 'Your Ladyship' any more. She didn't call her anything these days. She seemed as confused as everyone else by what had happened to the family.

The sisters had already exchanged a look of alarm. The White Room was the most beautiful of all the Abbey's bedrooms, where the head of the family and his wife had always slept. They'd loved its mix of style and mess: the enormous heirloom four-poster, perpetually in disarray because Fred had never seen the point of bed-making when you only had to do it all over again twenty-four hours later; a dressmaker's dummy sporting a black straw hat and a length of flimsy material flung over one shoulder; clothes spilling out of the inadequate wardrobes and strewn across the floor like a picnic set out for the Abbey's ravenous and uncontrollable horde of moths; the tipping pier glass that threw back a dumpy reflection; elegant heavy silk curtains fraying at the edges. It was like entering an enormous cave full of tatty riches. And now, apparently, a piece was to be sliced out of it in order to create a new bathroom. Bathrooms were in short supply at the Abbey, but this had never bothered their family. Bathing was necessary, of course, but it didn't have to be a profound experience. All you needed was a flannel and a sliver of soap. And they were very used to making do with cold water when the ancient plumbing seized up.

Lily chuckled down below and said in that lazy, drawn-out way of speaking they were so used to: 'Can't be doing with them bee days.'

'Did you say a bidet?' The girls recognized the warning note in their mother's voice, even if Lily couldn't. But then, they'd a lifetime's experience of deciphering the faces their parents presented to the world. The first indication of tension in their mother came when she started twirling a strand of hair round one finger as if winding herself up for confrontation. With their father, it was the smoking. Since the move, he was on forty a day and rising and they were all worried about his health, not to mention the expense.

'She'm a bit quaint,' Lily observed fondly. 'For why don't she wash her feet in the bath like other folk?' There was a pause while she seemed to ruminate on this. 'She'm having one of them round jacoozis with the power sprays, ain't she? The decorator told her white but her heart's set on avocado.' Then she was off on one of her pet rants: 'There be a job I'd like!' She put on a ludicrously exaggerated posh accent, like pulling a mink coat over her old apron. 'Lucinda Hartley-Green in her twin-set and pearls . . . Drives one of them top of the range Golfs but can't come up with a decent idea for to save her life.' She chuckled, then there was a comfortable silence and the girls guessed she was sipping her tea and crunching one of the Jaffa Cakes she enjoyed.

'She can't *do* that!' Fred repeated. There was a grating sound as she pushed back her chair. The sisters visualized her going to the window, hiding the distress. 'More tea?' they heard her enquire, after a moment, sounding tight and clipped, as if she couldn't care less.

'Refectory looks a treat,' Lily went on contentedly. 'Ever so bright and cheerful with her new paints.'

Laura could see Maria's face begin to change as the fury entered her, too. However hard she strove to keep a sense of perspective, it was torture having to stand by powerlessly as their beloved former home was hacked about and vulgarized. It was torment to see their parents more upset by the day. But they had to find a way to deal with it or be driven crazy too. She'd intended to keep Maria in the dark but now she said hurriedly, 'I met someone yesterday.'

The ruse for distraction worked, of course. When did they ever encounter gorgeous strange men in this backwater?

She'd gone to the post office to buy stamps to keep in touch with all the friends she'd made on her travels, when suddenly she was made aware of a nice deep voice behind her.

'They never have anything, do they?' it grumbled, as if the person it belonged to was used to enormous streamlined post offices with stacks of stationery and pens. The village one was operated by 66-year-old Mrs Byers, who augmented her miserable pension by measuring out other people's. With a kettle permanently whistling in the background and the ever-present, delicious smell of fresh baking (currant buns, that day), it resembled a private home, which was unsurprising. The office was Mrs Byers' converted front parlour and, as a sideline, she sold eggs from the clutch of poultry kept in her muddy back garden.

Laura immediately looked around but there were no other customers, so he could only have been talking to her.

'What are you after?' she asked, suddenly shy as she absorbed the stranger's thick dark hair and attractive black eyes. She could hear Mrs Byers' chickens nearby, the monotonous inconclusive clucking rather reminiscent of her grandmother these days.

He said vaguely, 'Oh I don't know,' as if he'd wandered in out of boredom and had simply been making an observation.

'Can I help?' Mrs Byers asked from behind her counter with its grille bearing an exhortation to 'use your local post office'. She was staring in an intimidating sort of a way through her thick spectacles as if she knew all about him; then her gaze fixed on Laura before darting from one to the other in the same inquisitive, malicious way Lily had.

'Just looking.' He gestured at Laura, smiling to show lovely white teeth. 'Why don't you serve her instead?'

'I'll serve who I choose, *thank you*.'

Outside, he said, 'Well, excuse me for breathing!'

They laughed about Mrs Byers all huffed up with offence like one of her hens taking a dust bath, and the controlled chaos of the post office.

'I'm surprised she hasn't moved her bed in there, too,' Laura joked, noting how lithe and fit the young man was in good 501 jeans and a nice dark red shirt that looked as if it had been chosen to compliment his colouring.

As they fell into step together, he asked casually, 'Where are you from?'

But because Laura simply couldn't bear to explain about her family's fall from grace, she found herself being evasive. 'Sort of over there,' she said, gesturing vaguely in the opposite direction from the Lodge. And when he asked her name, she muttered, 'Sandra'.

Maria twinkled encouragingly. 'How did you say goodbye?'

Laura hesitated, as if deciding she'd revealed quite enough, but the shouting was still going on below. 'Actually, he asked me for a drink at the wine bar tomorrow evening.'

'You said yes?'

'What do *you* think?' She frowned. 'You think I want to stick around here?'

'*Really* gorgeous?'

'Yeah!'

'Dark, you said.' Some strange alarm had entered Maria's voice as if, all of a sudden, a dreadful suspicion had occurred to her.

'Dark,' Laura confirmed happily. 'With lovely black eyes. Very tasty.'

'Tall?'

'Tall.'

'Oh, Laura,' Maria began. She bit her lip as if steeling herself to explain why her sister could not possibly go and have a drink with this particular young man, however gorgeous he might be.

But Laura carried on, oblivious. 'He's a carpenter.'

'A carpenter?' Maria echoed, suddenly defused.

'His name's Matt,' Laura went on to explain. 'And he lives in one of the new council houses down by the railway.'

'Ah!' said Maria, sounding profoundly relieved.

'I'm only going for a drink. And if you say anything to the parents I'll kill you.'

Maria was about to explain the confusion – why she'd been so funny a moment ago – when there was uproar downstairs.

'Portraits?' they heard their mother cry, this time with unmistakable anguish and fury. 'What have they *done* to our portraits?'

Chapter Eight

Janice sat in her study reflecting on the situation with the Delanceys, which had suddenly got a lot worse.

The evening before, just as she and her family had started eating, there'd come the sound of a visitor – a melodious rendering of 'D'ye Ken John Peel' from the chiming bell Stanley had just fixed up to replace the old-fashioned iron knocker shaped like an eagle that had probably been there for ever. Of course, there was another motive. 'Flaming heck! You murder one of our pheasants, I'll show you what we think of your flipping eagle.'

Janice had gone to the door to find Fred gasping for breath, seemingly in the grip of some sort of fever, scarlet blotches flowering on her pale unmade-up cheeks. As always, she was baffled by the other woman's strange dress sense and the way she took so little trouble with her appearance – especially as she had to concede that Fred was attractive in a blonde and blowsy sort of way. For this visit, she'd for some reason chosen to wear a multi-coloured waistcoat over a T-shirt which clashed with a long droopy skirt, and a string of big orange beads like unripe tomatoes; and her hair was pinned up in an artless bun with a strange bonnet effect of wild tendrils. As usual, it was only too obvious she wasn't wearing a bra. Janice couldn't imagine feeling happy about displaying her own nipples, and – as she remembered the scene that had ensued – patted her bosom, all trussed up in lacy La Perla lingerie, for reassurance.

There were no niceties. Just an imperious: 'I'd like to look at our portraits.' It had occurred to Janice, for the first time, that the other family's strange decision to leave the pictures in the Abbey might have been a pretext for barging in whenever they wanted.

'Pardon?' Janice had actually been commenting on the rudeness of turning up unannounced, especially when they were eating. Six o'clock was when Stanley liked the evening meal, although everyone else preferred it later. However, Fred merely raised her eyebrows a fraction as if *she* was on the receiving end of the bad manners.

Had she any idea how infuriating it was to be treated so contemptuously? And what did she imagine gave her the right? After all, Janice reminded herself, the Delanceys knew nothing of the grinding hard work and risk and terror involved in building a fortune from scratch. They'd been born sitting on a centuries-old inheritance and, through their own foolishness, had lost the lot. And then they had the cheek to despise what they called 'new' money! They'd been the 'haves' for centuries, lording it over the 'have nots'. '*Well*,' thought Janice grimly, '*we are the "haves" now!*'

'I never asked for those dirty old things to clutter up our dining room,' she'd countered, suddenly furious and out of control, yet knowing full well how the 'our' would wound the other woman. She'd added before she could stop herself: 'Besides, it's not convenient. We're having our tea.'

She could have kicked herself for the slip. But Fred was too angry to have noticed. Janice had actually believed for a second that the other woman would strike her. *'Good!'* she'd thought savagely. *'I've finally got through to her.'*

Then Mark had joined them. He must have heard the gist of the conversation because, to her surprise, he'd said quite agreeably, 'If she wants to see the pictures – let her.'

So the two of them had unnecessarily led the way to the Refectory, where Stanley and the children were seated, about to dig into macaroni cheese set out on one of the new dinner services. They'd all looked up in astonishment and even Stanley, who was seldom fazed, had paused mid-shake of the sauce bottle.

A moment before, when they'd all been sitting peacefully, enjoying family togetherness, Janice had been thinking how lovely and warm and welcoming the Refectory was. It glowed in the last beams of sun shimmying through the multitude of tiny panes Lily made such a fuss about cleaning.

She'd heard Fred catch her breath behind her. Of course, she'd reminded herself, it was her first sight of the room since it had been redecorated. It was bound to be a surprise, because it was such a transformation. But Janice was mortified by what came next.

'This is an abomination!'

Janice had never heard Fred Delancey sound like that before. It was as if some wild force had seized hold of her. Her feet in ridiculous embroidered slippers were planted on the new carpet and she kept looking down at it as if she couldn't believe her eyes. She'd even kicked at the thick pink pile, as if trying to ascertain whether the old flagstones freckled with permanent rusty stains still lay beneath.

'How dare you!' she'd shrieked as the family sat there dumbfounded, although, by this time, as if to make a point, Stanley had picked up his knife and fork and recommenced eating his macaroni cheese.

She was behaving as if they were forbidden to change a single thing about the Abbey; as if she and *her* family had some divine right over it for ever.

Then, suddenly, she'd taken a deep breath, as if striving to recover a measure of control. She'd even assumed a little smile as she stared at the voluminous gold silk curtains that now swooped from beneath a fringe of elaborate pelmeting either side of the huge mullioned windows; and took in the gold paint rag-rolled over a base of deep pink which coated the walls she'd only ever known plain and whitewashed. She'd laid a hand on the ancient table, as yet unrestored, as if challenging anyone to touch it. It was obvious she was about to say something very insulting indeed: all the more lethal for being delivered in her clipped upper-class way.

'I was brought up in a great house,' she'd informed them, with a coldly amused glance in the direction of Stanley, apparently revelling in making as much noise as possible eating his supper. She went on: 'I have been in many great houses in my time' – another pause for them all to be suitably impressed – 'but I have to say that I have never, ever, in my entire life . . .'

And then she'd noticed the portraits.

'*You* don't think I'm vulgar, do you?' Janice asked Mark piteously when Fred had finally returned to the Lodge – shown the door by Stanley, as it happened – and the family had dispersed. What

she meant, of course, was 'Do other people see me as vulgar?'
She was still deeply upset though proud to have given as good
as she'd got. The insults had been all the more shocking coming
from someone usually so controlled.

'Don't you take no notice of that fucking bitch, Janice!' Mark
told her angrily – the coarseness spilling out now the children
were gone.

Usually, she'd have gently remonstrated with him –
'Language, darling!' – but she was far too upset and hardly
inclined to quibble over his description of the other woman.
Besides, to her astonishment, Fred had used four-letter words,
too.

'I can't believe she told us we'd no respect for the past or
beauty!' Janice was truly bewildered. 'The place was falling apart
when we came here! You saw it, same as I did! Look at the
money that's been spent!'

'What've I just told you? Woman's nothing but a stuck-up
frigid bitch with a plum in her gob. Filthy gob, too. She should
be ashamed of herself – woman like that.'

'Those pictures turned out lovely!'

'They cost enough,' he confirmed grimly.

'What sort of person wants dirty things cluttering up their
home?'

'I know, I know,' he said, frowning, because he appreciated
that Janice had never wanted the portraits in the Refectory in the
first place. Neither had he, but that was irrelevant when Stanley
had made his wishes so clear.

'I'm only trying my best!'

'I know that. You hush now. That's enough.'

Janice made an attempt to defend the fine job the picture
restorer had done – the way the colours were so bright now that

you could really make out the expressions on the faces. But Fred's voice, like a whip, still rang in her ears: '*How dare you turn my husband's ancestors into cartoon characters! They look like something out of* The Beano*!*' She wanted the portraits returned to exactly how they'd been, she'd raged, and the Traffords must pay whatever it cost. Her parting shot had been: 'I won't be responsible for what happens when my husband hears about this!'

For all his brisk dismissal of Janice's tears, Mark wrapped his arms around her and kissed the top of her head. For once, they had precious privacy because, after supper was cleared away, Stanley had taken Genevieve to the cinema, Joe had disappeared off somewhere and Justin had retreated to his room with his books.

Janice calmed down a little. Her last withering observation about the other woman was: 'She wouldn't be here today either if Granddad hadn't saved her precious father-in-law!'

'Now, now, you know he doesn't like that sort of talk!' warned Mark, even though it was just the two of them. 'Besides, it's stuff and nonsense!'

It was his mother, Effie, who'd claimed a long-ago rescue from a near-drowning. But it had been at the very end of her life when, doped with morphine, she'd come out with increasingly crazy fantasies. Stanley and Edmund Delancey were once thick as thieves, she'd said! She and Stanley had been guests of honour at an Abbey ball! She'd been unstoppable, despite Stanley's tender, anxious attempts to silence her. 'Hester Delancey were my dear friend,' she'd insisted, chapped lips curved in a happy smile. Poor dying Effie, whose son was even then bearing her into the world of the super rich, had, for some reason, felt the need to invent a Cinderella past for herself. She'd been just fifty-four years old. Mark had never talked to Janice about the pain of it all. His inability to express deep emotion simply intensified. He locked away the suffering in some secret compartment: perhaps as a caution to himself never again to surrender his heart so completely.

A little while later, when the two of them were watching the football on the television set in their bedroom, the new doorbell had rung several times: one jolly cantering tune rippling after the last, giving the impression that the caller was brimming with goodwill.

'You think I'm answering that?' said Mark with a grim smile. He'd relaxed enough to light one of the cigars Janice disliked and the musty scent stained the air.

'You're joking!'

It bonded them even more to picture Sam Delancey safely locked outside, boiling with rage he was quite powerless to express. As the football came to an end, Mark stroked Janice's left breast and nuzzled one of her ears, a familiar prelude. In the unmodernized cold bathroom where they were making do until the builders got round to the en suite, she sprayed perfume over her naked body. Then she slipped on her warm dressing gown to brave the draughty corridor before joining Mark in the four-poster Sam and Fred had left behind. But he was wearing his pyjamas even though a newly installed electric blanket was warming up the bed nicely. 'Leave the light on,' she pleaded, but might not have bothered, since he kept his eyes shut throughout. *'Does he love me, really?'* she thought, as he pounded away on top of her. As usual, it was over very quickly. She found herself identifying with the gold watch he wound up before placing it on the bedside table for the night.

'Nice,' he murmured sleepily, patting her thigh.

'Mmm,' she'd agreed, knowing for sure that by the morning he'd have recovered the usual impatience and distance. She hadn't been ready to relinquish the intimacy just yet.

For all their continuing possessiveness about the Abbey, it looked as if the Delanceys had not known about its hidden cupboard, or the packet of letters stowed within. It gave Janice a sense of triumph, after the dreadful scene of yesterday. She was glad now that she'd not tossed the cobwebby old packet on Stanley's bonfire.

She extracted the top envelope, opened it and started reading, frowning in puzzlement every so often because the language and also the handwriting were so unusual.

'My dearest Pooh, spring has finally arrived and this morning I went for a long walk round the garden and looked at all the evidence of new beginnings that should cheer me: bare twigs unfolding tender leaves, like secrets, and hidden bulbs pushing green spears through the dark soil. Of course I thought of you, for when do I not? But it is forever and forever winter in my soul. I think of you in some unknown place yet under the same moon and stars and my poor heart aches with longing. I know I am considered cold and unfeeling, but that only seems to me to be an advantage now because nobody knows, nobody guesses my secret. But I am so lonely, so desolate. Can you understand the wealth you mean to me?'

Janice thought, '*That has to be "wealth", doesn't it?*' She often used the word herself but found it a little strange to see it employed in the context of love. Reading these old letters was very laborious because the paper was dangerously frail and the writing so faded in places that it had become illegible.

'There! I have dared to speak to you at last, my dearest Pooh, and, to my astonishment, found some measure of relief. Strange, when I am to all intents and purposes, dead. Oh I remember those golden days of ours! I remember everything . . .'

There the letter tailed off, leaving Janice a little shaken. Pooh? What an extraordinary nickname! Was it meant to be insulting? The envelopes bore no address, just as the letters were undated and, quickly opening a couple more without reading them, Janice checked that they too were unsigned, almost as if the writer couldn't bear to say goodbye. Each had been lightly glued down, not – Janice sensed – because the writer had ever intended to send it but, rather, to seal away the emotion once it had been expressed, keep each outpouring separate and contained. She imagined her sighing as she licked each one – because it was a woman, of course. Only a woman would behave like that.

She'd never seen writing like this. In pale grey ink, which might originally have been black, the hand was very precise, with each 'g' inscribed like an almost complete figure of eight, each 'e' like a single-toothed old-fashioned comb; and the whole was a beautiful pattern of words and spaces, as if, along the way, the writer had taken pains to construct a work of art. The precision and inventiveness put into it reminded her of the embroidery of the crazed Delancey grandmother. People had no time for that sort of self-indulgence any more, she thought a little dismissively.

The letter caused her to remember a moment before her

marriage when she'd almost broken off with Mark. She hadn't, of course, and never told him about the wobble. She, too, had written her despair and longing into a pile of unsent letters: 'I need more, Mark . . . I need to feel loved . . . I feel I could be anyone sometimes . . . I know you are capable of tenderness because I have seen it . . .' The difference between herself and this anguished, probably long-dead woman was that she'd destroyed her drift of paper. But the exercise had worked. She'd aired the pain and Mark's seeming inability to express deep emotion became less hurtful.

Janice had an uncomfortable feeling of intrusiveness. The letter was so tormented and yet, at the same time, filled with shame: as if the love had been tamped down like the tobacco in the old pipe Stanley sometimes used, but smouldered on regardless. However, the story it promised was irresistible. She decided to measure out the letters, one at a time, like chocolates. Of course the writer must have been married, too. Why else had she taken such pains to hide her passion away? The whole thing breathed illicitness.

Then Stanley walked in without knocking and she felt quite resentful though she greeted him perfectly pleasantly. 'All right, Granddad?'

'You busy?' He wasn't serious, of course. He was like Mark, who believed only men's work held real significance. They were like two peas in a pod, the way they treated women. Stanley had been much the same with Mark's mother, Effie, though that straightforward, generous woman hadn't seemed bothered. Janice had been very fond of her mother-in-law and devastated, along with everyone else, by her death from ovarian cancer at such an early age. It was *their* fault, said Stanley predictably – for all the stress and worry they'd inflicted.

'Tidying up,' Janice replied. She brushed the letters into a rough pile then covered them with a book on fabrics her interior decorator had left, reasoning that they were unlikely to interest Stanley.

He proceeded to browse her study, picking up photos of the family and putting them down in the wrong place, examining ornaments with a chuckle as if heartily amused by femininity and also his daughter-in-law's strange need for a private place. Even at seventy, he had a way with women. Janice noticed it when he talked to Lily with a cheeky charm that battered through the roughness and the lines, causing the cleaner to don ever shorter skirts and deeper necklines for her trips to the Abbey. For months now he'd smelt sporadically of Old Spice: the cloying sweetness of the aftershave swamping his natural smell of fresh perspiration. (Only his beloved granddaughter, who'd given him a bottle for his birthday, could have cajoled him into a practice he considered despicably effeminate.)

As usual, he was dressed in old blue gardening overalls. He hadn't even removed his dirty boots and Janice noticed that a big gob of mud had smeared her new sheepskin rug. She couldn't understand why, when they employed a whole fleet of gardeners, he continued to want to play at one. But then she thought of the writer of the secret letters walking in the gardens Stanley was so proprietorial about and felt a small glow of satisfaction about keeping something from this self-professed clever clogs.

'Had an idea,' he said, sounding important, as he picked up a treasured possession: a clay hippopotamus Justin had made for her, aged seven.

'Oh yes?' she asked without real interest.

'It's about our lass.'

'Ah!' Now she understood what this surprise visit was about.

After their lovemaking the night before, she'd asked Mark how he thought the children were doing, knowing it was a conversation he could never resist. *'This is what really matters,'* she'd told herself. *'This bond, this link . . .'*

'This acting lark . . .' he'd begun worriedly.

But then she'd pointed out how happy and confident Joe seemed. 'Give him time. He's only young.'

Mark had agreed, of course, because of his own deprived youth. Time was a luxury. How could it not please him to be able to give it to his own children, along with the rest? As always, he was anxious not to spoil them, yet happy to have the chance.

They'd glowed with mutual satisfaction over Justin, whose teachers were delighted with his academic prowess. That left their daughter.

Janice had felt her way in the dark, remembering Lily's words, spilt out with far less tact. She'd seen Genevieve down at the local pub, she'd told Janice that very day, 'snogging that lad what mucks out horses at the Palmer-Smythe stables. Landlord said he'd a mind to throw cold water over the both of them'.

Mark had obviously gone on to repeat her concern about Genevieve to his father. It made Janice a little indignant. She was fond of Stanley, but his influence in the family was too great.

'Come to me in the picture house, when I were sat there with Gen. *There* were a family what understood how to handle themselves – unlike some I could mention!'

'Pardon?' Janice stared at her father-in-law, quite mystified. As usual, he'd seized on any chance to attack the Delanceys, but who was this other family he was talking about?

'The de Winters of Manderley! *There* were a house!' He was silent for a moment. 'Gen's idea, weren't it? Give me *Strangers on a Train* or *The Man Who Knew Too Much*. But *Rebecca*'s a lass's picture, ain't it?'

'Oh,' said Janice, having at last comprehended him. There was a Hitchcock season at the local cinema, where the projector sometimes broke down and customers would be invited to watch films again from the beginning. The whole simple cinema-going experience had been known to take more than six hours. That was nothing, Stanley had claimed (because he always had a better story). When he was young – during the era of silent films – a friend of his had released a lot of moths from a jam jar during a particularly tender scene. Their silhouettes flapping across the screen had reduced the audience to tears of mirth, he'd said, adding with a strange change of mood that he'd disapproved at the time.

'Costume ball,' he pronounced now. 'That's how we circulates our Gen.'

Janice stared at him. It wasn't a bad idea. As a matter of fact, the more she thought about it the better she liked it – though, because it came from Stanley, she'd put up a token show of reluctance. Genevieve was twenty now and needed a push in the direction of suitable young men. Furthermore, like the planned pheasant shoot, a ball would be a good chance for the whole family to expand its social horizons. Stanley's long connection to the Abbey and its traditions was an advantage, as he never stopped reminding them. He'd seen how these things were done.

'The decorators haven't even started on the Great Hall . . .' she began very doubtfully.

'I'll stick a bomb up their arses.'

'Lucinda says cream but I've set my heart on cerise to warm the place up.'

'You have what you wants, girl. Beats me why you wastes your husband's money on that useless lass.'

'People might not come,' she went on, stung by his chauvinism. She was mindful, too, of the absolute lack of response after she'd dropped in her specially printed cards.

'Bollocks!' responded Stanley with vigour. 'Free food – you hire one of them fancy catering firms. Free booze. You tell me who'll turn that down in a hurry! Greedy buggers they are. Mind you,' he went on, his thoughts still on the film he'd seen, 'don't want our Gen upsetting anyone with her gown, do we?' Then, still chuckling at the idea of his beloved granddaughter all done up as glamorously and tactlessly as the second Mrs de Winter at the Manderley ball, he went off to berate the gardeners for allowing a ceanothus to become spindly.

He was surprisingly harsh on them, considering his history. He'd point out with far more indignation than sorrow that it had been different back then. Look at the fortune Mark had to pay out in National Insurance! He couldn't seem to accept that gardeners in the eighties were entitled to paid holidays and sickness benefit; that you couldn't even sack them if they were useless because they'd take you to an industrial tribunal. They even expected pensions, he'd say incredulously, adding that the humblest cottage these days wore a TV aerial like a pair of antlers. '*We* never had nothing like that!' He made it sound as if the grim poverty of the past was something to be proud of.

Left in peace once more, Janice thought of all the jobs she should be doing and, after retying the ribbon, replaced the packet of letters in the secret cupboard. She felt changed by her discovery. Always before, history had seemed to her to be about crumbling old artefacts, dates hammered into the memory like nails. Now, for the first time, she appreciated that it was about people. A woman she could relate to had once lived and very probably died in this house. She felt her humanity like a warm breath: not a cold snob like Fred Delancey but someone who'd suffered and ached for what was out of reach. But who was she? There were no female portraits at the Abbey. It seemed that, in their own way, the Delanceys were as sexist as the Traffords. Janice made a resolution to find out about this mystery woman.

Joe had confided to her recently that he often felt the presence of the folk who'd long ago lived in the house.

'Ghosts?' she'd queried, a little troubled.

He'd seemed to deliberate before saying lightly, 'Just – feelings, Mum.'

'Pardon?'

He'd shrugged, given his wide joyous beam. 'Love and – stuff.'

'Love?'

'Yeah!' And when she continued to frown with puzzlement, he'd gone on to try and explain. 'Like, radio waves.' He'd looked absurdly happy as if he knew what he was talking about.

'*But he's too young to understand about love*,' thought Janice, ruffling the soft hairs at the nape of his neck. To her pleasure, instead of moving away as his father would certainly have done, he rubbed his head against her hand like an affectionate animal.

Thinking about the content of those old letters made her ache with loss. But despite his shortcomings in the romance department, Mark was an excellent husband. She'd never argue with that.

'And you?' she whispered to the shade of the unknown woman. 'Did *you* have a good husband, too?'

Chapter Nine

Effie Trafford grasped Hester Delancey's left hand in her own and placed it on her stomach, snatching at the moment of intimacy like you were forced to seize everything during these ticking wartime days. The two women's wedding bands touched very briefly, like making a silent toast to marriage: the silver ring that had cost Stanley half a crown nine months earlier and the heavy gold affair that had belonged to Edmund's great-grandmother and would pass in the fullness of time (as Effie understood the peculiar ways of the aristocracy) to Hester's daughter-in-law.

She'd noticed that, for all its considerable value, Hester often removed her wedding ring. She'd take it off if she was required to wash her hands or change a dressing for one of the wounded men, and leave it lying around the Abbey as if it were no more important to her than a hat or a scarf, for anyone to pore over the engraved inscription inside: 'Mindful I'll be to cherish thee'. Effie couldn't imagine Edmund coming out with something so poignant and tender unless it was a joke. On the other hand, it occurred to her, men were men – she couldn't even give Stanley a quick hug without him getting ideas – and maybe the long-dead author had written a memorandum to himself on the importance of simple affection untinged by lust. Hester's ring made Effie very thankful that she and Stanley were ordinary folk because there was nothing to stop her from wearing her own wedding band when she was a bundle of bones in a coffin.

'There he be!' she said proudly, patting her abdomen though, predictably, Hester's hand had whisked off straightaway. She didn't like physical contact. Effie had noticed it before.

'You've decided it's a boy, then?' Hester wore the amused but disdainful expression Effie believed she'd the measure of now. Hester was like Edmund. You needed to look beneath the surface, Stanley had advised her authoritatively, sounding for all the world as if the aristocratic Delanceys were like the carrots and onions newly rooted in the Abbey's tennis court. Dig for victory, he'd gone on jokingly, because at that stage Effie had been unsure of Hester's attitude towards her.

'I knows so, Hester.' Effie sounded very serious.

'You'll have to give up your war work eventually, you know.'

Effie bit her lip as if chastised. Hester was right, of course. She couldn't go on working in the munitions factory, unless Stanley's mother looked after the baby. All of a sudden, it seemed deeply unpatriotic to be feeling such happiness.

'What are you, anyway? Four weeks? Five?'

Effie's face cleared suddenly as she thought of the baby growing inside her. 'He'm four week and two day. Remember?'

'How could I not?' Hester responded in her dry fashion, as if really saying the opposite. Then, glancing at her watch, smoothing her starched nurse's apron, said, 'I really must get back.'

Effie had become pregnant on the final night of Stanley's last leave before both he and Edmund left for France for service with the 2nd Battery as part of the British Expeditionary Force. As usual, husband and wife were compelled to part before they could become used to each other again. It played havoc with the emotions, together with the dreadful uncertainty. It made her weepy and angry even as she hated herself for it. That last time, for Stanley's sake, she'd played a secret game of pretend. *'Pretend the war never happened . . . Pretend I ain't sick with fear cos he's going to France.'* It was the only way to manage it.

Their goodbye lovemaking had taken place in a distant field with an old well in its centre. They'd made it theirs on the first night of marriage. It was a lot more private than the gardener's cottage where Stanley's parents lived, which was Effie's home now. The cold didn't matter. You could make as much noise as you liked – and she had, in the absolute silence and darkness and the long sticky grass with its faint old man's whiff of cow parsley.

'You're a right shrieker.'

Effie felt more anxious than complimented. Was she at fault in showing the pleasure so unequivocally? She'd little idea because she'd never been with a man before.

'You'll scare the animals.' But he sounded so proud and fond she knew it was all right.

'You sure that were safe, my love?' she asked after a moment, even though he'd maintain withdrawal was one hundred per cent effective.

'Trust me,' he said with that knowing look on his handsome face that made her feel murderous towards the women who'd preceded her. 'Don't you fret,' he went on comfortably, as if it were none of her business.

'If it ain't, Stanley . . .' she began, but managed to stop herself. For wasn't she determined to behave well?

'What've I just told you, girl?'

'I don't mind. I don't really!' It was too late. She'd said it. It was all the deep emotion that had done it. She was sobbing, even though she knew she mustn't upset Stanley. It terrified her that, after months of playing war on the mainland, he was being sent off to dangerous foreign parts. There'd be casualties, of course – massive ones. Everyone said so. Why else had the Abbey been requisitioned as an officers' convalescent home, with dozens of imported, neatly made beds all ready and waiting? She'd seen them for herself in the Refectory and the Great Hall. Hester had shown her. Hester, whose own husband was now an officer, and who would be helping nurse the wounded men when they most certainly arrived.

'Plenty of time,' Stanley said, kissing the promise into her ear, 'to make us a football team.'

Effie calmed down at that, letting the profound quietness and the velvety darkness soothe her spirit. 'D'you reckon . . . ?' she began slowly, her thoughts now directed towards the east wing of the Abbey, the only part the Delancey family still occupied. Then her voice petered off like a shy night creature. She and Stanley were as one. But it still didn't feel right to be talking this way.

'Them two like us?' It was uncanny how he could tune into her: Stanley, who was in all other respects totally male. It made her fearful, sometimes, of the future and having secrets. 'Hester?' There was a smile in his voice. Then it dropped a note as if he were implying even more doubt. 'Edmund?'

'And why ever not?' she queried a little sharply and he envisaged her pursing her rich mouth in disapproval.

'Maybe.' He said it to humour her. No other couple was like them. The chemistry was extraordinary and it hadn't faded one bit with marriage. The wonder was that, for all her earthiness, she remained such a good girl and shockable too. But, then, women really were closed books, thought Stanley, who'd plenty enough experience to know, and an image came into his mind of the funny old novels Edmund liked to read, a silver paperknife by his side for slicing apart the joined-up pages. *Might even Hester be secretly passionate?* He found himself speculating.

'What's so funny?' Effie asked, huddling against his naked warmth under the blanket they'd brought.

'That's for me to know, ain't it? And you to find out, my pet.'

The war had thrown Hester into Effie's company in a way she'd never have believed possible. Their men had begun military life in the same regiment – the First Searchlight, based some seventy-five miles away, which meant that leave could often be synchronized.

The experience had bound Stanley and Edmund even closer as friends. It was impossible to explain to outsiders; Edmund assured Hester with his usual courtesy, 'I would if I could, my love.' But how to convey the boredom of 'square-bashing' as Stanley called it, the exhausting days of drilling and marching; above all, the strangeness of being flung together with the oddest sorts of people? Men who seemed unable to speak without swearing and talked about women in the most disgusting terms, as if they had only one function . . . Men who couldn't even write their own names. Unsurprisingly, it was Stanley who'd adapted best to the strangeness, who made Edmund laugh at the indignity and occasional pettiness of it all.

And though shared leave would begin with both couples keeping a distance (Edmund and Hester rattling around in their bit of the Abbey, Stanley and Effie crammed into his parents' cottage), this never lasted. Lacking Stanley to jolly him along, Edmund sometimes turned morose. If Hester tried to ask questions about his war, he'd clam up.

In the end, it was she who'd suggest very lightly to Edmund: 'Should we find out what the others are up to this evening?'

'Should we, Hes?' (It gave her a pang to see how suddenly cheered he became.) Then, a little anxiously, as if reminded to think of her feelings, too: 'I'm happy if you are.'

'We could go to that place we discovered last time,' she'd prompt, like throwing him a line.

'We could,' he'd agree with a happy smile, remembering the out-of-the-way inn perched on a low cliff, where delicious crab and cider were served.

Stanley and Edmund. The gardener's son had long ago saved Hester's husband's life, but she now understood it was not the real reason for their closeness. 'He taught me about fun,' Edmund had once confided, sounding gruff and a little fearful as if he'd been brought up to believe enjoying oneself was sinful and even she, his new bride, might turn the knowledge of this weakness against him. After that, she made real efforts with Stanley. The war was on her side, of course, clipping at the barriers that normally precluded people like them from fraternizing. And Stanley *was* fun. He was very lively and occasionally impudent – 'a law to himself', Effie would interject very quickly, lest anyone should take offence. He'd tease the pomposity out of Edmund and make him into an altogether happier and nicer person. He'd pull Hester's leg too, in his sly fashion, and, in the end, the cheeky flirtatiousness won her over.

For Edmund's sake, she'd no wish to be unfriendly to Effie either. But, aside from the huge class difference, she found the younger girl unsophisticated and naive: they really had nothing in common. Then, just before setting off for France, Edmund said very tentatively, 'You will be nice to Effie while we're away, won't you?'

'Aren't I always?' Hester had retaliated lightly.

'The thing is, darling, Stanley says she seems to have got this idea you don't like her.'

'That's ridiculous!' said Hester with a smile.

'I want you to keep an eye on her for him. Will you?'

Stanley put in his own word, too, on the quiet, when they found themselves alone together. 'Effie thinks the world of you, Hester,' he confided with unusual gravity.

This was wartime, after all, so Hester sent a message inviting Effie for tea at the Abbey and found that, once encouraged, there was no stopping her. Effie would seek her out on precious days off from her munitions factory, where the hours were a lot longer and the work harder. She'd be in and out of the Abbey constantly, lending a hand with beds, cheerfully emptying the enamel bedpans, chattering all the while. And Hester warmed to her, along with everyone else. She was so appealing and sweet natured. Even Edmund's normally taciturn old father would ask, 'Where's that lovely child?' Altogether, the war was having a strange effect on him. 'I THINK IT'S WONDERFUL!' he'd boom with a beatific smile, apropros of nothing. He couldn't, surely, be referring to the fighting in France and the terror for his only son and heir, or the bombings and the ever-present danger? Let alone the dreadful mess that had been made of his Abbey . . .

As for Effie, there was no side to her, no restraint. Hester observed the way the men reacted when she was around but Effie never even noticed. Only Stanley mattered to her. He was a wonderful husband, she'd say again and again. 'I'm a lucky girl, Hester, I knows it.' Then she'd smile – her pretty face made beautiful by happiness – because Hester was lucky, too. They were all four of them blessed. And every so often, like shyly producing a gift, she'd ask Hester for advice, as if the older girl were wiser and more sophisticated by far.

Sometimes – in between dashing round the Abbey fetching this, that and the other – Hester would catch sight of the former tennis court in the distance, its net long vanished, its elegant turf peeled away for the planting of vegetables, and reflect that it was a fine metaphor for what had happened to girls like her. It was astonishing to remember just what an idle and carefree life she'd led before the war, her only expectation to attract the right sort of husband. She'd made her good marriage in the nick of time and then joined the genteel stampede to become Wrens or WAAFs or land girls. If she'd volunteered straightaway, along with some of the girls, she could have taken her pick of war work – like her friend Emmeline Carpenter, who was far happier wiring cannon guns in a fighter aircraft factory than she'd ever been hanging around waiting for men to ask her to dance. But Hester had dithered and ended up, like so many girls from her background, joining the Voluntary Aid Detachment and doing nursing. Not real nursing, of course, because she lacked the training, but the menial stuff like scrubbing floors, dealing with bedpans and washing the patients. It was like being a glorified maid, thought Hester. She abhorred the intimacy involved, although at the end of the washing the men were handed a newly soaped flannel and asked to deal with their embarrassing bits themselves. Her mother wasn't pleased about any of it. However, she was a great deal happier than if Hester had joined the forces, and very thankful she could stay on at the Abbey under the protection of her parents-in-law.

And yet, not even remote and beautiful Melcombe was safe. Yesterday there'd been a dogfight just two miles away. So clear was the sky – a beautiful cloudless blue – that they'd seen the whole thing. They'd wheeled some of the badly injured men outside and everyone had cheered when the German bomber plunged from the sky with smoke pouring from its tail. A second later a white parachute had blossomed, drifting after it like a graceful show of surrender.

'It makes a grand hospital,' Effie would say admiringly. But it pained Hester to witness the changes. The Refectory and Great Hall were crammed with beds full of noisy men, and cluttered with the paraphernalia of the wounded: the wheelchairs and stretchers, the trolleys piled with bandages and dressings – and a discreet but unnerving collection of unnaturally pink and shiny prosthetic legs like big fat lengths of sausage meat. There were newly installed locked cabinets, too, full of painkillers. The ancient flagstones were dulled by carbolic soap and – most distressing of all – for bizarre reasons of hygiene, the ancient whitewashed walls in both the Refectory and Great Hall had been painted a dark glossy brown. It gave the house a gloomy feel, in spite of the constant noise. Only the marvellous moulded ceilings remained untouched and aloof. It wasn't that Hester was unpatriotic. Of course it was right to fight this war. But oh, how she longed for elegance and order to return.

It seemed Effie wasn't quite ready to let her go back to her nursing duties and – from her troubled glances and sighs – Hester guessed that a confidence was about to be imparted.

Effie confessed, looking unhappy, that the baby she was so eagerly anticipating had been a mistake. She sounded as if she honestly expected Hester to be surprised. Hester smiled faintly. And then she listened as Effie told her very anxiously that it mustn't happen again. Stanley had told her so.

'Like it were . . .' she began with a helpless shrug. She rootled about in the pocket of her dress and extracted a crumpled envelope. It was like summoning up Stanley himself, with his impetuous virility, his maddening conviction that he was always right: a way of explaining why getting pregnant had been none of her fault. Then she replaced the letter because Hester had already relayed the contents to her. This was because – unlike Stanley, who'd been taught by Edmund – Effie could barely read and write.

Stanley was strangely circumspect in letters home but, then, thought Hester, he must have known she'd read them, along with the official censor. The sentiments were carefully transcribed and frequently misspelt, but Hester would translate them into ones a person such as herself might have written. She'd turned Stanley's 'I is proper thrilled, my own darling' into 'You must know how delighted I am, darling'. And 'I frets hows you'll mange now Mam is porly with her bad leg' into 'I worry about how you'll be able to look after the baby, what with my mother's poor health'. The letter had ended with: 'We'll have us our football team but is there no end to this?' And then, as if he couldn't stop himself, 'I kiss you every bit, my darling wife.' But all Hester had said to Effie was, 'He's worried about the war, though he can't say so, of course – oh yes, and he kisses you.'

'Don't he write beautiful!' Effie had marvelled, when she was through. And Hester had thought how strange it was to be

more intimately connected with a love letter than the person it
was intended for.

'Stanley gets right carried away,' Effie confided now with a
worried frown. Then, as if she'd put a lot of thought into how
to phrase the question, but very shyly and in a rush: 'Oh Hester,
how does you control Edmund?'

She made it sound as if men were like horses, to be curbed
with bits and spurs, thought Hester, more amused than
offended. But typically she raised an eyebrow, gave her mocking
little smile, and saw Effie bite her lip and blush for her own
impertinence. In fact, she hadn't intended to put Effie in her
place. But the incident came to define all future such
conversations with the other girl, who would talk about her own
situation, but never expect more than listening in return.

'She'd be surprised if she knew what I was really thinking,' Hester
reflected.

She was nearly twenty-five and the whole country was at war.
Everywhere she looked, she could see that girls like her had
been given a rare sense of purpose, as if, suddenly, a secret door
had sprung open to beckon them out of the room where they
might otherwise have spent the whole of their lives. Though she
didn't enjoy nursing, there was a part of her that relished the
unexpected freedom, the responsibility, the mixing with such
very different people. And yet at the same time, she felt the
inexorable weight of having become a Delancey bear down on
her. God willing, she and Edmund would have years together,
but he was the only son and there was the ever-present worry
now that he might never come home. She saw the terror in his
parents' eyes at the end of each leave: the unspoken question
for her in the weeks that followed, the slow drift of
disappointment. They loved him, of course, but there was

another consideration. For four hundred years, as she understood it, the Abbey had directly passed from one generation to the next with, usually, the insurance of at least one spare besides the heir. It was early days, of course. But what if she and Edmund became the ones to break the chain? What if the house and all its treasures were lost to some distant relative? It had survived so much. Even now it was battling gallantly with the unfamiliar.

In fact, whenever Hester looked at her heirloom wedding ring, she was reminded what was expected of her.

Chapter Ten

'You look pleased with yourself,' Fred commented as she placed a cup of tea on the table beside Laura's bed.

Laura mumbled something, though she was instantly alerted. Only Hester, who woke with the birds, was accorded tea in bed (though this was mostly to check she was still *in situ*). Her mother must have decided it was the best way to catch her alone.

'Mmm,' Fred went on, though there'd been no satisfactory response.

But Laura kept her eyes tightly closed as if still in a deep sleep. She felt her bed give as her mother sat down on it, and then strands of her long hair were picked up and dropped and her cheek lightly stroked, as if points were being assembled in an argument. Finally she was asked extremely casually: 'Nice evening?'

She blinked up at her mother, rubbed at her eyes, appearing puzzled. 'When?'

'Yesterday, of course! You went out,' Fred reminded her with a smile, remembering Laura rejecting all offers of a lift before setting off up the long drive in a flowing dress and her tattered Indian sandals, carrying smarter shoes in a plastic bag.

She and Sam prided themselves on not interfering in their children's private lives. Luckily, Hester had done the asking for them: '*You* look pretty, darling. Where are you off to?'

But all Laura had replied, looking vague and a little shifty was, 'Just out, Gran.'

'Oh *I* used to go out,' Hester had responded with one of her radiant dotty smiles.

Now Laura said, 'Oh yes!' as if grateful to her mother because she might otherwise have forgotten all about her evening.

'Anywhere special?'

'Um, not really.'

There was a silence while Fred considered and then decided against more direct questioning. Sounding a little disappointed, she said: 'You got back jolly late.'

'Did I?'

'Ten to three.'

'Honestly?'

'I didn't hear a car.' Then Fred added quickly, lest Laura should be under the impression she'd lain awake listening for her, 'One of *them* came roaring up the drive at about two – so inconsiderate! – and then I couldn't get back to sleep.'

'Oh?'

Fred wore a little smile. 'Far be it from Pa or me to be curious about your private life.'

Laura looked amused, too. 'Who said anything about a private life?'

'Nobody. Nobody at all. I'm off to church now.' She'd get

even less out of Maria, who would surely know where Laura had gone. It was maddening to have fenced herself in like this. Nevertheless, she believed she managed to leave Laura with the impression that she and Sam knew a great deal more than they let on.

It had been their first proper date, a week after their encounter in the village post office. Matt had suggested it in the wine bar in Magna Saunter where they'd enjoyed a drink. They had decided to meet up at the same venue and after that they'd climbed into his car, one of those omnipresent Peugeots, and he'd driven them to a good restaurant in High Regis, the next big town. He was obviously doing all right, as a carpenter.

They'd spent at least six hours in each other's company and yet she found it almost impossible to recall any of their conversation. She'd liked him, of course, for his gentleness and courtesy. He must have been funny, too, because her cheeks had ached with smiling. But what she remembered most about the evening was the way his black hair tumbled into his melting dark eyes, his beautiful square hands and red full-lipped mouth. The attraction had seeped out of him in heady waves like perfume. She'd eaten very little of her food, though she'd become quite drunk fairly quickly. They both had. And inevitably they arrived at the moment when they were alone together in his car, parked in a dark wood about half a mile outside the town. He'd switched off the engine and turned to look at her and that moment of gravity made what came next all the more exciting. They'd made love in a grassy clearing, with the moon and stars overhead and an owl hooting softly in a tree nearby, as if cheering on all the abandonment.

She felt very thankful to be young at such a time. Her

mother's generation would have felt it necessary to go on a whole series of dates before having sex. They didn't know about the pleasure of getting to know someone from the inside out. But, then, Laura reflected, the older generation found love and sex inseparable. She thought of Hester, for instance, surrendering to passion with an almost stranger and giggled out loud.

She'd not revealed her true identity to Matt. He was quite incurious and, besides, there seemed no point. When they were at last ready to part, she'd asked him to drop her the other side of the village and then she'd walked home through the pitch dark, sunken lanes teeming with hidden life, guided by her long knowledge of the area. Turning into the gate of the Lodge, she'd seen a light glistening in the Abbey in the distance and idly wondered who was still up at that very late hour.

'Crazy,' she whispered as she climbed out of bed. She decided that she really had liked him and was glad they'd arranged to meet again later that day. She stretched and smiled, luxuriating in the yeasty warm scent of her body, and experienced tender pity for all those not in the same sublime state of fulfilment on that beautiful morning. It seemed to her as if she'd stumbled on the secret of life.

As usual, she leant on her windowsill, staring at the golden E-shape of her old home in the distance. It was becoming a ritual to spy on the family who'd caused hers such misery, although today she felt tolerant to all mankind. It was still early and the Abbey looked very pure and creamy in the weak light, its windows dark and blank, exactly as they must have appeared during all the centuries before the discovery of electricity. She started to play a favourite game. It was also a way of re-establishing superiority over the Traffords, who understood nothing of the house's patient endurance of the ages.

In 1549, ten years after the Abbey's religious community had been dissolved, the King had paid a visit to her ancestor Thomas Delancey, a royal courtier and the then owner of Melcombe. It was he who turned a beautifully built monastery into an elegant home, adding a whole series of apartments above the cloisters and employing the finest craftsmen in the country to create the panelling and ornate ceilings that would help make the house so famous.

Thomas's advancement had been marvellous. Legend was that it had come about because he'd made the King laugh. Laura liked to think it was possible to change one's whole fortune with a joke. If only her father, who used to be very funny before everything went wrong for them, could do the same.

But the royal visit couldn't have been particularly amusing. Thomas had referred to the occasion – '*A fine and gracious honour*' – in a vellum notebook, a treasure passed most carefully through the generations until Sam had been forced to sell it. There was surely another story. As she shivered a little in her nightdress, Laura enjoyed herself imagining the frantic preparations that must have gone on for the weekend visitors from hell. She found herself wishing Thomas's wife had written the diary instead as it would have been nice to know domestic details. They were a lot smaller in those days, as ancient suits of armour testified, but had they eaten more? Or were those innumerable courses one read about mainly to impress? Then, would they have laid straw on the flagstones to catch the tossed-away bones? Or was more refined behaviour expected of royal company? And had conversation possessed a form and rules as precise as the dancing that must have gone on in the Great Hall?

Laura imagined reedy wind music for gliding courtiers and thought of the way her own family cut across each other's speech and picked up jokes and expanded them and shouted and laughed. And what had such company smelt like? Sometimes she'd envisage a sludge of low-lying stink from the rarely washed bodies and clothes and the bad teeth and the disgusting latrines, overlaid by a delicious rich waft of roasting game and crackling log fires and smoky tapers. The farting from the elegant whippets, who'd surely crouched under the long table just like Caesar and Spectre used to, would have passed unnoticed. And had the terrifying King been in a good mood throughout? '*A most pleasaunt visit,*' Thomas had recorded once it was over but must have felt greatly relieved. His advancement had been marvellous but rendered him vulnerable as never before. That which had been given could just as swiftly be taken away. After all, hadn't the King demonstrated over and over again how he could laugh one minute, incarcerate you in the Tower of London the next?

How to explain her sense of history to Matt, who lived in a purpose-built council house? She'd grown up with ghosts and the huge presence of the Abbey as a backcloth, and certain areas like the Refectory where very occasionally and without warning, one could find oneself assaulted by intense anger or sadness. For generations, her family had grown as one with the house and, consequently, parting from it had meant losing all sense of identity and pride. As sweet and sensitive as Matt seemed, how could he possibly understand? He'd probably regard her family as foolish undeserving snobs, just like the Traffords did. As for revealing that they'd been involved in a feud for forty years!

She heard a door close quietly down below and, a moment

later, spotted Hester scuttling out of the house with a large leather handbag looped over one arm. It was her first outing of the day but her style was as unkempt and gaudy as ever: a jumper too thick for summer pulled on inside out, a pair of baggy old trousers with dead leaves clinging to it, a fuzz of unbrushed hair, a smear of make-up. Caesar trotted sociably after her and Hester turned and said in her refined yet languid fashion, '*Will* you go away! *Please!*' The dog looked really put out as it slunk off.

Laura smiled. She wondered if Matt had a crazy grandparent, too. Poor old Gran! She guessed Hester was off to break into the Abbey again and destroy more of the Traffords' belongings. What was she thinking, in so far as she was still capable of it? As Laura watched, Hester took off at impressive speed across the enormous lawn. There was no point in telling the parents, she thought, because they positively encouraged Gran's break-ins these days.

Hester had reached the walls of the Abbey by now and Laura saw her try the handle on the enormous oak front door. It seemed to be locked this time, but – as they both knew – there were innumerable other ways of getting in. At least, Laura thought a little wistfully, Hester had found a way of going back; and maybe, in her addled state, she never even noticed the changes.

'Abominable!' Fred had cried on returning from her confrontation about the portraits. 'I can't bring myself to describe it,' she'd gone on with tears in her eyes. It was just as well because none of them wanted to know. That way, they could keep the Abbey inviolate in their hearts. '*I can still feel it,*' Laura told herself as she conjured up its peculiar mixture of deep peace and uncomfortable old passions.

'Hey!'

Laura heard the faint disembodied shout and watched Hester struggle with the handle more vigorously. Then, all of a sudden, her grandmother turned to face her accuser and, too far away for details, Laura painted in her gracious smile (because nothing could affect Hester's manners).

It was the same bent old man in blue overalls she'd seen before – Stanley Trafford, obviously. He must have been pottering around somewhere in the gardens; might even have monitored Hester's progress across the lawn. Laura shook her head and tut-tutted softly. One of these days, the Traffords were going to report her grandmother to the police.

Then, to her very great surprise, she saw Stanley approach Hester, touching her on the shoulder. Even at that distance, she seemed frozen with disbelief – Gran, whose fine appreciation of her social standing was locked into her bones and who discouraged intimacy even from her own family.

Then another figure emerged from the big oak door – a tall, dark young man, most likely one of the Trafford boys – and immediately Stanley moved sharply away. '*Curiouser and curiouser*,' thought Laura.

It was her first sighting of either of the sons and she reached for her father's binoculars borrowed for just this purpose, while feeling a little cross with herself for being interested. The family was hateful, clearly. So why was she bothering? But with knowledge, came power. And, after all, she was who she was. ('Never forget you're Delanceys,' her father used to tell them all with unusual gravity when they were children.)

The focus in those old leather binoculars was continually slipping. She fiddled around for several minutes before fixing a clear picture then immediately frowned, as if trying to work out a puzzle.

What on earth was *he* – of all people – doing there? Then she smiled. She'd got it! He was, after all, a carpenter so there was no reason whatsoever why he shouldn't be employed at the Abbey, together with all the other workmen. He'd not mentioned this job, so far as she could remember – but, then, why should he have?

'Laura?'

It was Maria, of course, bursting in to find out what had happened on the date. 'You promised to wake me . . .' she began in an aggrieved tone. 'What time did you get in, anyway?'

'The most amazing thing . . .' Laura began, ignoring her sister's question, binoculars still trained on the Abbey in the distance.

'What happened?' Maria asked very impatiently. 'I want to know it all, right from the beginning! Don't you dare leave out a thing!'

The tiny tableau trapped in Laura's view all of a sudden slipped into a different pattern, as if the set of binoculars had magically become a kaleidoscope. Now the old man in overalls was very formally escorting her grandmother off the premises and he . . . Now *he* was in the affectionate embrace of a middle-aged woman who'd just emerged from the front door – Janice Trafford, whom Laura had last glimpsed locked in bitter dispute with her own mother.

'Laura?' said Maria, very concerned.

For her sister was crouching on the floor as if terrified of being spied on in return. And, to Maria's consternation, she was trembling and on the verge of tears.

She saw him first. He was leaning against a pine tree in the deserted and peaceful clearing where they'd arranged to meet. His handsome face was raised to the warm sun and, as she watched, a wonderful smile spread across it. It was like watching a young tomcat lick its whiskers after a particularly rich meal.

'Sandra!' he exclaimed delightedly. He moved to kiss her and looked really puzzled when she took a sharp step back.

'Lying cheating scum!' said Laura, spitting out the words. She wiped her hand across her lips and shuddered violently. 'And to think . . .'

'What?' he exclaimed, even more astounded.

'I know exactly who you are!' she went on, unable to look at him because she was so miserably disgusted with herself. It even felt revolting to be meeting in that beautiful place because, of course, when they'd arranged this rendezvous, the whole intention had been quite different. She hadn't wanted to come at all but, because she could so easily bump into him again, knew she must stamp on this for good.

'Your name's not Matt!' she raged. 'You don't live on a housing estate! You're not even a carpenter!'

He wasn't going to deny it, though he looked a little foolish. In the end, he responded with a helpless shrug: 'So what? It's no big deal!'

'No big deal?' she repeated. 'NO BIG DEAL?'

'Sorry,' he said. 'You've lost me.'

'No,' Laura corrected him. '*You've* lost *me*!' It was time to explain. 'I'm Laura Delancey.'

The effect was gratifying, even a tad over dramatic. Joe Trafford actually blanched and then he shut his eyes and slid down the trunk of the pine tree until he was sitting on a floor of dry needles. After that, he smote one side of his head with a palm as if trying to knock this extraordinary revelation into his disbelieving brain. He kept pausing to stare up at her with wide black eyes. Finally, he pointed out quite reasonably, 'You lied, too.'

'I didn't *lie*,' she corrected him sharply. 'Well, only slightly. I didn't say *anything* much and, anyway, you weren't interested.' She added because she couldn't help herself, 'Why did you do it? Why?'

'I often pretend to be other people,' he admitted with unexpected meekness. 'It's just something I do.'

'Well, I can't say I'm surprised you should want to be someone else,' Laura found herself saying very sharply.

A moment before, he'd been behaving almost as if this huge revelation was beginning to dwindle in importance, might even be smoothed over with the help of a little forgiveness and tolerance – but, then, she'd seen the gentleness and amiability in him the night before. 'Tell me I haven't dreamt all this,' he'd murmured as they exchanged one last long kiss. But now his handsome face darkened, becoming almost brutal. Well, she told herself grimly, he was a Trafford, wasn't he?

'What is it with you lot?' he demanded. 'How come you *still* think you're better than us?'

Once more, Laura reacted as her mother might have. She shrugged and gave a cold smile, as if no answer was needed, knowing perfectly well the offence it would cause.

'See?' he said disgustedly. 'After everything you've done!'

'Everything *we've* done? Oh, I don't believe this! The mess you're making of our Abbey!'

He looked comically taken aback. '*Your* Abbey?'

'Yes,' said Laura, trembling with passion. 'Ours, ours, ours! You'll see!'

He was going to laugh – she knew it and couldn't endure it.

So she turned on her heel and left, finding some small satisfaction in having the last word.

Stamping back to the Lodge in a fury, all her new-found serenity vanished, she thought, '*Pa was right all along! Of course we should hate them!*'

Chapter Eleven

'I want to know about family trees,' said Janice. At her old library in Guildford, she'd only ever sought out popular fiction. Now, for the first time in her life, she found herself in a reference section and an atmosphere of study that was intimidating. She could see a boy of about Justin's age absorbed in making notes at the end of a long table. A few seats away from him, an elderly man with shopping parked by his feet was poring over an enormous volume while a bottle of gin lolled like a secret lover from one of his plastic bags.

She envied her younger son's easy, disrespectful relationship with books. His bedroom was strewn with toppling piles – comments pencilled in the margins, pages turned down – and his interests were eclectic. Besides his set science subjects, there were works on astrology and philosophy and anthropology, like a motley gang of gatecrashers who'd inveigled their way in. Otherwise, there were very few books in the Abbey. There were the twenty-four volumes of the *Encyclopaedia Britannica* she'd bought for the children when they were little, and a big *Reader's*

Digest do-it-yourself manual, which was never used because Mark knew everything about the subject and, anyway, they could afford to employ builders now. There was a collection of paperbacks – James Micheners and James Clavells, and quite a few of her Jean Plaidys and Danielle Steeles – strewn around the guest bedrooms. *The Joy of Sex* (also neglected) was hidden away on a top shelf of her wardrobe. By contrast, there were magazines everywhere, a great many of which specialized in interior decor and gardening, plus the odd *Cosmopolitan* to flick through in the bathrooms.

'That'll be in family history,' said the librarian, seeming to sum up Janice in a glance. She had drooping hair and tired clothes and powerful spectacles. She spoke in the same precise, confident way as Fred Delancey. She could have been one of her friends, also fallen on difficult times.

'Oh, it's not for mine!' said Janice, reacting just as defensively as she might have with Fred. What gave these people the idea they were superior just because they spoke differently? And where did their overbearing confidence come from, anyway? She'd be ashamed, she thought as she tapped her long painted nails on the counter, to come into work dressed like that. She prided herself on the efforts she made to look good: the hairdresser twice a week, the painstakingly applied make-up each morning, the expensive coordinated clothes. Though Mark seldom signalled appreciation, she knew he'd notice soon enough if she slacked off. She told herself that someone so hard on himself was bound to expect a lot from others, too. In fact, whenever she felt particularly upset about the situation he and his father had got them all into, she'd remind herself of the long years of striving, as man and wife, to create a better life for the family.

'What is the surname?'

She believed she managed to pronounce it without expression. However, it seemed to her that there was a knowing sneer in the librarian's voice when she responded.

'You won't find *them* in family history.'

'Pardon?'

'The Delanceys of Melcombe Abbey.'

It sounded like the title of one of the historical romances Janice loved. She was unable to stop herself snapping back, 'Not now, they're not.'

'More's the pity!' The librarian had turned her back by now, was already in the process of sorting out books, and Janice noticed a tatty Marks and Spencer label hanging lopsidedly out of the neck of her jumper. 'I hear the new owners are making a pig's ear of that exquisite house.'

For a moment, Janice considered walking out. Then she told herself that the librarian could have no idea of her identity. It made her feel miserable, though, to learn what the county thought of her efforts to turn the chilly, uncomfortable Abbey into a home.

She was given a couple of substantial tomes: *Burke's Peerage, Baronetage and Knightage* and *Debrett's Peerage and Baronetage.* 'You may be interested in these, too,' said the librarian, piling several more books on top.

Janice settled herself down in an empty space at the table. She was already out of sorts. '*Wouldn't you know?*' she thought bitterly. It seemed that, even where works on family trees were concerned, a snobbish hierarchy operated. She would have to accept that, in this unfriendly milieu, getting on socially had little to do with material success. It seemed to be largely about time – a family remaining in the same house for centuries – and how could you buy that? But even this wasn't strictly true. After all, though the Delanceys were now dispossessed of their precious Abbey, the same people still wanted to know them, didn't they?

They took up a lot of space. They even possessed a family crest – a gloomy looking owl perched on top of a shield. She could see that nearly all the families enjoyed this privilege, with simple images described in terms she'd never come across before – peculiar words like gules and chevrons and bezants and, most puzzling of all in this context, escallops. Under the heading 'Lineage', she discovered that the Delanceys had been granted Melcombe Abbey and its lands in 1539 for unspecified services to King Henry VIII, with the impression given that nothing had changed. *'But who earned it fair and square?'* she thought, strongly tempted to pencil in a correction. An idea had occurred to her. What was to prevent her own family from purchasing a title? She'd the feeling that nothing might annoy Sam and Fred more.

Delancey, Delancey, Delancey . . . The names went on and on though, for some reason, the long imperious line seemed to falter at one point, mysteriously becoming first one name and then another before recovering itself a couple of generations later. It caught her attention for a second – she'd seen the first name somewhere very recently – but it had little to do with her quest, so she put the thought aside.

A little crazily, she'd fantasized that *the* name – the one belonging to the woman who'd written the letters – would leap out at her with the emotional impact of a telegram. But there was nothing to indicate if she was Emerald Frances Delancey (1804–1880), for instance, or Antonia Emilia Delancey (1822–1921). And to make things even less interesting, there were no illustrations. *'I'd know her if I saw her,'* thought Janice quite irrationally, as if the mysterious woman was a long-lost friend. She'd already combed the Abbey's attics for more portraits, without success.

However, she was reluctant to lose face with the librarian by leaving so soon. So, mostly for show, she started leafing through the other material she'd been given: two or three books that seemed to be about the Abbey.

'*What do I want to bother with this for?*' Like her husband and father-in-law, she'd made a virtue out of ignorance. It was because, according to Lily, the Delanceys had never stopped droning on about the history of the house. Professing boredom was another way of putting them in their place.

The first book she opened started with a description that was more than two hundred years old: 'No other building in England can surpass Melcombe Abbey in beauty and interest . . .'

'*You don't know about the perishing cold,*' thought Janice a little tartly. '*Or the thousands it's costing us to repair the roof. Or the big patch of dry rot the builders have just found.*'

'Its outdoor scenery is a paradise of green fields and sparkling waters with, in the immediate vicinity of the house, glorious gardens filled with fruits and flowers . . .'

'*Tell me something I don't know!*'

'Built in 1147 and started by a small number of Cistercian monks, Melcombe Abbey eventually became one of the wealthiest and most cultured monasteries in the south-west . . .'

'*Yes, yes, yes . . .*' Everyone knew it had been a monastery – why else was it called an Abbey? – though she was ignorant of what a Cistercian might be. A Catholic of some kind? She had an idea that England had once been predominantly Catholic.

She remembered a film about the six wives of Henry VIII . . . something about the King breaking with the Catholic religion so as to be able to marry one of those wives, only for her to come to a very sticky end. She leafed through the book, hoping to happen on a gripping drama of betrayal and execution.

'At the beginning of the sixteenth century, monasteries owned well over a quarter of all the cultivated land in England . . .'

'*Really?*' thought Janice, interested despite herself. The word 'monk' had always conjured up an image of poverty besides, of course, chastity. But it seemed she'd been mistaken.

'Though individual monks took a vow of poverty, monasteries were usually very wealthy. Many of them set up profitable businesses . . . The Cistercians at Melcombe Abbey were especially successful sheep-farmers . . .'

Janice looked up from her book with a triumphant smile. There! Not even Justin knew that. Even so, she'd come to the library on a mission to find out about her mysterious letter-writer and it had proved unsuccessful and there were a million jobs waiting for her at home. She flipped through more pages, as impatiently as she'd often anticipate the end of a novel, and a single paragraph sprang out at her.

'The destruction of the English monasteries by Henry VIII must be regarded as one of the great events of the sixteenth century. In April 1536, the twenty-seventh year of his reign, there were over 800 monasteries, abbeys, nunneries and friaries that were home to over 10,000 monks, nuns, friars and canons. By April 1540 there were none.'

It was an astounding piece of information for someone so ignorant of her country's history. Janice glanced up once as if checking her surroundings, making sure she was still in the twentieth century. She'd forgotten about going home. Finally, history had hooked her.

Melcombe Abbey, she discovered, had once been like a mini kingdom, which was another reason for Henry VIII's determination to do away with it. Like other monasteries, it was independent, able to organize its own finances and decisions: its ultimate head being not the King but its own abbot, one Father Dominic.

However, according to the King's specially appointed vicar-general, Thomas Cromwell, the monasteries were often also sinks of vice. There was 'manifest sin', he reported in 1534 when charged with carrying out an audit – completed, with the help of only four men, in just six months. 'Vicious, carnal and abominable living is daily used and committed amongst the little and small abbeys . . .'

Whatever the truth of these reports, the King now saw fit to pass an act which allowed him to shut down all religious houses with an income of less than two hundred pounds a year. Then he seized their lands and property to finance his wars against France and Scotland. In less than two years – following Henry's excommunication by the Pope – the larger monasteries, like Melcombe Abbey, would suffer the same fate.

'*Didn't they do anything?*' thought Janice. And, even as she read on, she learnt of the fierce opposition to Henry's Act of Suppression: the demonstrations in the North of England and the army of rebels – the so-called Pilgrimage of Grace – who'd demanded the restoration of their monasteries.

At first, it seemed that their voices would be heard. In return for disbanding, they were offered a meeting of Parliament to discuss their complaints. But the King reneged. From every village and town that had taken part in the pilgrimage, a good number of people were publicly hanged, drawn and quartered. And, in the big religious houses that had supported the rebels, some of the abbots were executed.

By the end of 1537, even the most devoted monks and nuns were required to declare that their way of life had been a 'vain and superstitious round of dumb ceremonies'. It was a story of greed and destruction to chill the blood: of altar plates, goblets and vestments stolen to become part of the King's jewel house; of the annihilation of sacred shrines like Thomas Becket's (the final straw for Rome); of prayer bells turned into cannons, and lead roofing melted down in the furnace created by a monastery's own timbers and subsequently used as shot.

But Melcombe Abbey had survived. It was astonishing really because it seemed that its abbot, Father Dominic, was one of the very few who'd refused to switch his allegiance from the Pope to the King.

'*I know what happened!*' Janice told herself, all caught up in the excitement of the story. Father Dominic – a wonderful man, obviously – had made a passionate speech in defence of his beliefs and the King had been so moved that, in this unique instance, clemency had been granted.

Longing to read on, she caught sight of the time on her platinum wristwatch and was suddenly made aware that hours had sped past and the reading room had emptied without her even noticing, and it was all of five o'clock. Mark would be home soon and she hadn't even thought about the evening meal.

Very reluctantly, she'd have to wait for the next instalment of the story. She decided to say nothing to her family for now. It was partly because she was a little afraid of being teased, especially by Justin, who'd seized hold of his good education and made the very most of it, unlike Joe and Genevieve, who'd let it wash over them.

'Any use?' asked the librarian with a smile that seemed only friendly now, already reaching for her coat so she could let them both out before locking up for the night.

'Thank you!' said Janice most sincerely and, all the way back to the Abbey, she thought of what she'd learnt, like a lover remembering each precious touch, each word.

Chapter Twelve

Effie Trafford felt isolated, stuck in a tiny cottage with Stanley's parents and an insomniac baby. She missed Stanley dreadfully and now she was missing her fellow workers at the munitions factory, too.

Thank goodness for her friend, Hester Delancey. It was becoming a familiar routine to wheel her little son, Mark, up to the Abbey in his pram most afternoons. Often, the jolting motion and the peace would send him to sleep and then Effie would loiter, enjoying the fresh air and the sunlight while she scoured the hedgerows for something to make the evening meal more palatable. If Mark stayed awake, she'd talk to him: a running commentary on everything she was doing, a valiant though useless attempt to engage him in proper conversation. 'When's this war ever going to end, my handsome?' But Mark was as powerless to answer that as everyone else.

As usual, she ended up pressing some of her booty on Hester. Today it was dandelion leaves. 'It makes a grand salad,' she said, 'if you can spare a pinch of sugar.' And then, 'He were fretting all night, Hester. He were dreadful.'

There were dark shadows under her eyes, though this didn't stop her from having the usual effect on the men. 'Care to give me a bed bath, miss?' one of them called in a way he'd never have dared (or perhaps wanted) to use with Hester. A landmine explosion had blown away his hand, but it didn't stop him from playing cards with the others.

'Mrs. And no, thank you,' Effie muttered under her breath, impatient and embarrassed by the attention, as always.

It seemed something had happened at the Abbey early that morning to lift the monotony. A brigadier general had paid a visit and, as he toured the beds occupied by men too ill to stand up and salute, the officious colonel everyone was finding such a trial had ordered them to lie stiffly to attention. But though Effie smiled politely as Hester related the incident, she was plainly distracted. She knew it was her friend's break: she'd timed her arrival perfectly.

She wanted to talk privately, of course, so after Hester had made them two cups of tea in the Abbey's kitchen, they sought out the Morning Room in the east wing and a sofa that was usable once they'd removed a small mahogany chest of drawers containing a collection of blown eggs labelled in a childish hand (Edmund's) and a large stuffed pike in a glass case (also Edmund's work, some years later). As usual, Effie stared at these objects wonderingly, as if astonished to find them in a home. Before the war, Hester had told her, the room had been a retreat for Delancey men to read the newspapers after breakfast. But, since the army had commandeered most of the place, it had been used to store pieces of good furniture and precious knick-knacks from the grand reception rooms, now stuffed to the gills with beds and soldiers.

Like reclaiming a piece of knitting, Effie picked up exactly where their last such conversation had left off. Her voice was a little plaintive, as if the cheerful carefree girl were gradually being edged out by another. 'There's Mark now, ain't there?'

'Indeed.' Hester was holding the solid sticky baby on her lap but only because Effie had put him there. She was hoping he wouldn't mess up her nurse's uniform. She found it astonishing how much space and time this tiny newcomer now took as a right. He was a party to all conversation, too. Once, Hester had wondered if this was the reason he seldom slept, because his mother's talk was so riveting when she got into her stride.

But now Mark was working himself up to a frenzy. Effie smiled a little helplessly as she took him back. Despite the disruption, she implied, it was sweet to be so needed. Very naturally, she lifted her blouse and pulled out an enormous blue-veined breast. 'There!' she said when the crying had ceased. And then: 'He don't understand . . .'

However, this time she wasn't talking about the baby.

Labour had been traumatic – twenty-four hours of excruciating contractions, mostly on her own, before forceps and heavy stitching at the end. It was a mercy, really, that husbands weren't allowed. 'I'm not rightly sure I should tell you, Hester,' she'd said, a little troubled because it was wrong to scare those who'd yet to give birth. And, then, very quickly, touching Mark: 'I wouldn't be without him for the world.'

'I wants to be a good wife,' she went on now, sounding a little bewildered.

'Of course you do,' said Hester automatically. She was watching the baby clamped to Effie's nipple and almost purring with contentment, and reflected that *she* could never behave in so animal a fashion. She was also hoping her mother-in-law wouldn't come in. Lady Delancey, whose sense of the status quo was unaffected by wartime, believed that if there was a place for naked bosoms it was certainly not at the Abbey.

'Stanley loves him really, Hester, but I hates to hear him cry!' Effie's pretty face became fierce. 'He's only little, ain't he?' She adjusted her clothing and tenderly shifted the baby to her shoulder so she could rub his back, and Hester noticed a dark patch flower on the front of her print dress.

The baby burped and, comfortably changing mood, Effie giggled and said, 'Just like Dada.'

Hester ignored this. She made herself touch Effie on the arm in a show of female solidarity even though she knew that, if ever she had a child, her attitude would be quite different. For a start, Mark was far too old – at almost a year – to be still feeding at the breast. 'It's a comfort,' Effie maintained, but Hester wondered for whom. In her opinion, babies needed a firm hand – Truby King, the acknowledged expert, said so, too – and you should start as you meant to go on.

Effie's troubles were starting to dribble out like the milk on Mark's chin. When Stanley did come home, she told Hester, he'd complain he was ignored. But the worst thing he'd said to her was that the passion had gone. She'd cried and cried, but mostly because it was true. When Stanley made love to her, she explained earnestly, she felt the same deep commitment as always. But that explosive pleasure in the dark field of the old days? Because of Mark, they were now obliged to stay in the cottage, and even as Stanley caressed her so tenderly and hopefully, she'd find herself listening for the baby. When he cried, she'd tense up. Whenever there was 'blessed silence', as Stanley put it (in other words, only the deep snoring of his parents to contend with), she'd worry that he'd stopped breathing. Stanley had started to call her 'Mother', with a mixture of affection and exasperation.

'Know what, Hester?' said Effie, looking down resignedly at the damp patch on her dress. 'I ain't smelling of honey and clotted cream no more.'

When Edmund came home, his first impulse was to remind himself what he was fighting for. Besides, the Abbey was his destiny. 'Look at that sublime strapwork!' he'd marvel to Hester as the two of them wandered round, hand in hand, eyes firmly fixed on the exquisite plaster moulding above the chaos. Or he'd lead her to the cloisters where he'd gesture eloquently at the ceilings fashioned of fan-vaulted stone. She could appreciate the comfort it must afford, after the horrors he'd seen. Then, frowning a little, he'd play her his favourite Schubert on the wind-up gramophone. 'Listen to the passion in that phrasing, darling . . .' Sometimes there'd be tears in his eyes.

Whereas on *his* snatched periods of leave, it seemed Stanley had only one objective in mind. He'd insist on his pleasure even when she was bleeding, Effie had told Hester without rancour, and the day she brought Mark back from the hospital, he'd burst her stitches open.

'I can't hardly say no to him, can I?' Effie's soft brown eyes were round with apprehension – even though a second unplanned pregnancy was a far more real fear than Stanley turning for consolation elsewhere. How would they manage? That pessary the doctor had given her was the devil to put in, she said, and when Stanley was around she could never take the blessed thing out. What was she to do when the war ended and he was home all the time?

No girl had ever talked to Hester so frankly. Effie involved

Hester in her menstrual cycles every time – the panic each month if she was late, the overwhelming relief when she came on. But she was so guileless and anxious and apologetic that it was impossible to take offence. Besides, though Hester maintained her usual mask of inscrutability, she was intrigued by the story of that other marriage; sometimes a little alarmed, too, even though Effie would erupt in giggles, at the same time glancing a little anxiously at Mark, lest his innocence be corrupted.

Stanley's rampant libido stalked Effie at every turn. If she was doing the washing-up at the sink with her shreds of old soap pressed into her wire container, she said, chances were he'd attack from behind. If she was laying her sheets out on the grass to whiten, like as not she'd be tumbled on them and forced to boil up the copper all over again. Most of her dresses had grass stains on their backs; she'd given up on trying to conceal the love bites. 'You have a nasty rash down the side of your neck, my dear,' old Lady Delancey had observed the other day.

'Do you trust him?' Hester asked her once, when both of their men were out in France.

'Trust him?' Effie had sounded absolutely astonished. 'I'd trust him with my life, Hester!'

And Hester had let it drop because, in her own way, Effie was such an innocent. '*Is it possible that I am missing something?*' she had once found herself wondering. But then she'd frowned and shivered, like slamming shut the lid of a box.

Effie had another secret, as it happened. But she was determined to keep this one to herself, lest she break the spell.

The fact was that, though they'd not once discussed it – just as they never ever talked about Hester's marriage – she was aware of her friend's longing for a child. She understood, too, that in Hester's elevated situation, there was no question but that she must have a son, and furthermore, what with the uncertainty of wartime, it must happen as soon as possible. Effie sensed the disappointment building up around Hester like a barbed wire fence. 'Rather you than me!' she'd say with a laugh; or 'Messy things, babies.' Effie emanated silent understanding and reassurance but, alone, she'd done more. She'd prayed for Hester. And when Christianity failed her, she'd turned to black magic.

It was her grandmother who'd taught her how. It had been a test of nerve, stealing out into the fields one dark night when the moon was waxing and therefore the spell would be at its most potent. She'd taken with her a fox skull picked up in the woods to amuse Mark, though she'd been terrified of allowing him near it since. She'd arranged the skull in a circle of elder saplings with a secret spring – a place that was naturally magic – and let the water bubble up through the sockets in the bone. Then she'd waited, shivering with fear, before sensing the looming of a dark force, a vast listening presence. She'd known for certain that whatever was asked for that night would be granted. You needed to be extra careful how you phrased it, though: this was black magic, after all. You must never forget, her grandmother had explained to her most seriously, that you were harnessing something 'powerful evil', as she'd put it. You had to ensure your wish couldn't possibly be misinterpreted.

'Make Hester Delancey pregnant!' she'd cried into the night. 'Oh please, give her a baby son what'll be healthy and live a long life!'

There'd been a moment of complete stillness and silence, like someone absorbing the information, quietly checking it over. Then, suddenly, the wind had caught hold of the leaves of the big oak trees nearby and shaken them violently, as if reminding Effie that a sacrifice was necessary. So, trembling with terror, she'd jabbed at her arm with the potato knife she'd brought along for the purpose, and then worried that her few drops of blood might not be enough.

She thought she'd covered all eventualities. Even so, she continued to worry – especially in sleepless stretches of the night – whether her friend's baby would truly turn out all right.

When the months turned into years and Hester failed to become pregnant, Effie realized that her one error had lain in omitting a time limit. However, she remained quietly hopeful. Sooner or later, Hester would conceive a son and heir.

You could trust black magic, she thought very confidently.

Chapter Thirteen

On 19 August 1985, Mr Vickers, the postman, delivered identical brown envelopes to the Abbey and the Lodge. He remained fascinated by the fluctuating fortunes of the two families. 'There's a turn-up,' he'd marvel as he approached the imposing mass of the Abbey glowing in the morning sun, with its gloss of new money, its startling glimpses of change. And, after peering into the darkness of the Lodge, searching for fresh evidence of poverty and despair, he'd invariably leave muttering, 'What a come down!'

'You'll be waiting for this,' he stated confidently as he handed the letter to Fred. He'd another half dozen in his bag for distribution around the county. It felt good to have real power for once: to know he possessed information capable of changing lives. It made him want to linger, accept a cup of tea if it was offered, suggest it would be welcome if not.

'Oh Lord!' said Fred, putting a hand to her mouth as if, until that moment, she'd forgotten about this most significant of dates.

A little taken aback, Mr Vickers couldn't resist entering into the kind of game Lily played with the Delanceys, though without the same malice. 'Just come from up there,' he said, gesturing in the direction of the Abbey. 'Mr Trafford wants to open it his self, but he don't allow him.' He added, 'Justin, ain't it?' with an unconvincing display of doubt because of course the name had been clearly typed on the envelope.

'Oh Lord!' repeated Fred. Naturally they'd been waiting for the letter even though, typically, David was behaving as if it was of no consequence to him. As for her, she was convinced that her clever but indolent son had failed to achieve the right marks in his A levels. None of her children possessed the degree of savagery required for success – but how could they, without an example to follow? The glory days were over. David would never get to Cambridge like his father and grandfather and great-grandfather before him. It was dismaying to have become so negative, the sense of failure firing up the hatred even as it steamrollered all hope.

'Three A's,' said the postman laconically as if reading her thoughts and, though she managed a cold smile, she could have killed him.

'Who's got three A's?' asked Sam, who'd appeared beside her, already beaming like a lunatic. That was the great difference between them, she reflected soberly. He went on genuinely believing their luck could change at any minute.

When she didn't answer, the postman did.

'Well done,' Sam muttered through his teeth. He sounded as if he'd choke.

The postman was still holding on to the letter as if forbidden to give it up to anyone except the addressee. But there was no way David was going to make an appearance until he'd gone. He shared his mother's pessimism. After all, what hope had he, coming from a country comprehensive, of achieving a place at Cambridge? Okay, so his father's old college had interviewed him as a favour. They'd even told him that if he got two A's and a B he'd be in with a chance – though only if he read engineering. But his father had seemed like his old energetic self as he'd pushed and encouraged him. 'Piece of cake,' he'd insisted the day of the interview. He'd even lent him a lucky tie.

'Lovely morning,' said Mr Vickers, still hoping to be offered a cup of tea. But they were obviously waiting for him to go and he didn't blame them really. Shame, because he'd have liked to know what was in the envelope. He could hazard a guess, though. Nothing went right for the Delanceys these days.

Next stop the Harcourts, who needed to have it confirmed that their adored son Archie was two ha'p'orth short of a farthing.

'The world's your oyster,' Mark told Justin as the whole family stood around on the lawn in front of the Abbey, beaming in the warmth of the sun. He'd broken his rule of no alcohol during working hours because this was an historic moment. Justin would be the first Trafford to go to university. The whole family had toasted his triumph with Moët & Chandon and Mark's smile didn't falter even when his exultant son seized hold of a second bottle, shook it up and released a fan of spray over shrieking Genevieve. They'd made it! What was more, Justin could take his pick because there wasn't a university in the country that would turn him down now with his three A's. It was Mark who'd advised him to delay applying till he'd got his results, when he'd hold a far stronger hand. It was about confidence; knowing luck was riding quietly by your side.

'To think a grandson of mine'll be going to Cambridge University,' said Stanley, eyes shining with pride like twin black spiders crouching in intricate webs.

'Or Oxford,' Janice pointed out, thinking of *Brideshead Revisited*, which they'd recently watched on the television. It wasn't really the others' cup of tea, though Joe had admired the acting. A lovely period drama, was her own opinion.

'Didn't them lot go to Cambridge?' But Stanley knew the answer, of course, and had already made a firm decision about which university Justin would be attending.

'Two A's and a B is *good*!' insisted Sam once he and Fred were alone together, sitting over the debris of lunch. They'd all told David so. They'd even opened up a bottle of very old Veuve kept for a special occasion. It was sour and dark, like tea, and most of the sparkle had gone but all of them except Hester had behaved as if it was a rare treat.

'Sherry's off,' she'd commented before finishing her glass, as usual.

'Is it good enough, though?' Fred hated herself for behaving like such a wet blanket. But she felt obliged to bring Sam down to earth.

'That's what they told him.'

'Only if he does engineering . . . Can you see it, Sam? He says he wants to be a sociologist!'

'Of course he'll do engineering. He can become a sociologist later. Anyway, what's he bothering with a non science for?'

'Oh, he does what we tell him, does he?'

'Fred! What is this?'

'I'm sorry, darling, I just can't help it.'

'Now look here,' said Sam, taking her by the shoulders and looking into her unhappy face. 'What boy in his right mind is going to turn down going to the most fun college in the finest university in the world – even if he has to adapt a little?' He went on, 'Best years of my life.' Then repeated the words a little sadly.

'You're right.' But she sounded unconvinced.

'I am.'

'Even if you are . . . How are we going to pay for his board and so forth?'

'Fred,' he told her very firmly, 'one step at a time. We'll think of something. Now, there's a spot of that left. And then I think a little siesta might be in order. Fizz and a zizz.'

Justin said, 'Dad?'

'Mmm.'

'I've done OK, haven't I?'

'You've done us proud, son.' But Mark sounded a little impatient, as if enough praise had been meted out for the time being.

The sun streamed through the mullioned windows in narrow shafts like the fingers of a vast celestial hand administering a benediction. But, inexplicably, the mood had changed. They'd all been so joyful celebrating Justin's triumph out in the garden, but once inside the cool Refectory, a strange discontent had fallen.

'Can I take the Rolls out, then?'

'No,' said Mark immediately. The Rolls was his pride and joy and the most potent symbol of his success. Not even Janice was permitted to drive it.

'You promised me a car!'

'I did. And we're going down the garage next week to see what we can find.'

'I don't *want* to wait till next week.'

'I've said no, Justin.'

'I did pass my test first off.'

'Take your mother's car, if you have to.'

'Ta for that!' said Janice.

'I don't want Mum's car.' Justin added like a sulky child, 'I only wanted to take it up the drive . . .'

'I've said no, and that's the end of it.' His father sounded really angry now. It was amazing how completely his bonhomie had fallen away.

But it was Stanley, as usual, who had the last word. 'Where's the harm if he stays on the property? The lad's earned it! Let him!'

Sam and Fred heard the first car roar past the Lodge while they were still in bed. They saw Janice Trafford's Peugeot speed by even faster a couple of hours later as they were enjoying home-made scones. They felt relaxed and full of well-being as they listened to David expounding on a game he'd just heard about. They were revelling in the company of their two youngest children and not even worrying about Laura, who'd been alarmingly tense and moody of late. She was off somewhere on her own. Hester was safely absorbed in her embroidery in a corner. She smiled every so often as her needle darted in and out of her circle of canvas, building up another dense miniature view of the Abbey. Fred noticed she'd included an ancient yew long since destroyed by lightning.

'It's called "Dukes and Dustmen". You get someone to put

on a peaked cap and immediately it shows up what class they are. You see, either they look like a duke out shooting, or a dustman.' He explained kindly, 'The idea comes from *The Uses of Literacy*. Hang on a sec, I've got the book upstairs . . .'

'I'm not *entirely* illiterate,' Sam pointed out a little wearily, though he'd never heard of this seminal study of the working class.

In a few minutes, David was back, obviously keenly looking forward to lecturing everyone, telling them something they didn't know. He regarded his mother as uneducated, just like his sisters. 'Here we go,' he said, opening the book where he'd stuck in a marker. 'This is how Richard Hoggart describes the working-class man: "He tends to be small and dark, lined and sallow about the face by the time he has passed thirty. The bone-structure of the face and neck then shows clearly, with a suggestion of the whippet about it." Now, who does that remind you of?'

'Stanley Trafford!' everyone cried at once.

David smiled with satisfaction. '"In general,"' he read on, '"these physical marks are observable early, and remain throughout life . . ."' He looked up to make sure they were all paying attention. 'This is the bit . . . "If I or some of my professional acquaintance who were born into the working-classes put on the sort of flat cap and neckerchief which go with looking 'county', or if we leave our collars open, the sit of the cap and the neckerchief, or the structure of the bones round the neck make us look, not like the sporting middle classes, but like working men on a day off . . ."'

But Fred had stopped paying attention. She frowned a little as she sipped her tea. 'That car was going awfully fast . . . Where are they all off to?'

'Hell, with any luck.' Sam sounded very jovial and nobody took offence, of course.

'Interesting, you must agree,' said David.

'It's very snobbish,' protested Maria – though laughingly because they'd picked up from their parents that it was OK to be class conscious.

'But it works!'

'Let's have a go, then.'

'Oh, it only works for men.'

'Oh men!' Maria sounded disgusted. As Laura had rightly pointed out the other day, the whole focus in their family was on male supremacy. She might be the eldest, she'd said, but it was David who was treated as the heir even though there was nothing left to inherit; he whose further education was considered paramount; he whose opinions (on politics and other so-called 'male' subjects) were sought and respectfully listened to, even though most of the time he talked nonsense. It was astonishing, really, Laura had continued, that their parents – intelligent and fairly liberal in other respects – went along with it. As for herself and Maria, in 1985 they were still expected to hang around until someone suitable (i.e. of similar class) wanted to marry them.

'Where's my cap, then?' said Sam, who loved this sort of game. 'I want to try it out.'

'No idea,' said Fred.

'What do you mean? S'pose I need my cap to go shooting?'

'It is around. I just don't know where. Anyway, it's August, so you won't.'

He couldn't be cross with her after the lovely time they'd had in bed. 'Oh well, it'll keep.' Then his tender tolerant mood fell away as Spectre seized half a scone from his plate. 'No, sir, you do *not* behave like that! Pleeving theb!'

Reminded of his obsession with the other family, his smile returned. 'Anyone seen Mark Trafford in his cap?'

'Loads of times, the cheeky chappie,' said David. He yawned. 'Told you the game always works.'

Chapter Fourteen

It was Janice who drove them to the hospital in the Peugeot, the only working car left. Mark and Stanley were in the back, with Genevieve squeezed between them, while Joe sat in front.

'He were going too fast,' said Stanley for the umpteenth time, though no less miserably.

'We don't know that, Dad.'

'Police said so, didn't they?'

'I've told you: they don't know cos they weren't there.'

'If anything happens to that lad, I'll never forgive myself. Never!' Stanley let out a harsh sob and, in the rear-view mirror, Janice saw Mark put an arm round his father, squashing Genevieve even more.

'Not your fault,' Stanley was assured yet again. 'Justin's a law unto himself. We all know that. It's *my* fault for being too soft on him. Shouldn't have let him have driving lessons in the first place.'

'He enjoyed them lessons.'

'Of course he did. Don't know what I'm saying. I'm *glad* he enjoyed himself.'

In the mirror, Janice saw her husband stare out of the window with a stony face as if he had to summon all his strength not to be undone by the memory of Justin full of vigour and happiness.

'He will be all right, won't he?' Genevieve sounded very tearful and childlike.

'Course he will, love!' said Stanley, suddenly remembering his favourite.

'We're here,' said Janice, swerving into the entrance, nearly hitting a gatepost.

Even in August, the windows of the hospital were closed. The heat seemed to rush them from all sides but Janice shivered as they sat in a room waiting to talk to the surgeon who would be operating. He was called Mr Porter, a nurse had informed them, and Janice found herself worrying that he couldn't be any good. They'd been allowed to see Justin very briefly and were still in shock. Looking at his motionless figure swathed in bandages, they found it impossible to believe that, just a couple of hours earlier, he'd been prancing across the Abbey's sunny lawn, spraying champagne over his sister. His right leg was broken in three places, they'd learnt, and his collarbone was smashed, too. Then there were the head injuries.

The door opened and a surprisingly young man came in, looking serious, and Mark touched Janice on the arm as if to say, 'Leave the talking to me.'

'I won't pretend it's a simple procedure,' said Mr Porter. 'But with luck we can reduce the pressure on Justin's brain.'

'Worst case scenario?' Mark snapped out.

Janice could have hit him, even though she understood that

it was part of his character to want to know exactly what he was facing. He'd always been brave.

The surgeon seemed to hesitate. Perhaps the bluntness had shocked him, too. 'There could be brain damage,' he warned very gently, and Janice didn't hear anything beyond that – definitely not Mr Porter's assurances that this was by no means certain and that everything possible would be done.

Sam said, 'Something rather awful, darling . . .'

'What?' Fred was laying the table in her usual eccentric though formal style, with sprigs of flowering plumbago pinched from the Abbey gardens that afternoon. It took away some of the bitterness from being able to afford only the cheapest of food. As an hors d'oeuvres they were having Chanterelle mushrooms from Melcombe's woods, which the ignorant Traffords believed were poisonous, for sure. And to follow, she'd made coq au vin from chicken drumsticks bought cheap because they were past their sell-by date and yesterday's leftover red wine, which had tasted so metallic that even Hester had abandoned her glass.

'It's all over the village.'

'What is?' She frowned as she put out her mother-in-law's increasingly threadbare napkin, as usual blotched with magenta lipstick.

'One of the Trafford boys has been involved in rather a hideous accident.'

Fred immediately stopped what she was doing, staring at Sam with a shocked expression. Someone from a different background might have inferred that 'rather' minimized the force of 'hideous' but, as always, she understood him perfectly.

'Wrote off the Rolls, from what I can gather. Wrapped it round a tree down by Millers Cross.'

'And?' she asked, looking increasingly concerned.

'He's being operated on at the Whitmore as we speak.'

'Oh Lord! This is awful!'

'Complicated business.' He paused then said, as if making a conscious effort to keep his tone as neutral as possible, 'He could have brain damage.'

'Oh Lord!' Fred repeated with a slightly different inflection. She was remembering her words, just a short time before, after discovering what had happened to their portraits: '*I hate them. I wish evil to befall them.*' What an appalling thing to have come out with, she thought. Unlike Sam, she'd had a Catholic upbringing, after all. She said, 'Poor things.' But, typically, it emerged clipped and dry as if there was no real sincerity there at all.

'Poor things,' echoed Sam, sounding as if he didn't know how to say it either, since this was the Traffords they were talking about.

'I feel sick!'

'Hush!' said Stanley, enclosing Genevieve's hand in his own. 'That's cos you ate all them Mars Bars.'

'Shall I fetch you another?' asked Janice distractedly. It seemed to her that they'd been crouching for ever in that stuffy little waiting room, drinking warm tea, starting up with fear each time the door opened. Justin had been in theatre for two hours and the sky – so blue and bright earlier on – was darkening as if in sympathy. She found herself thinking of the clocks at the Abbey, wishing that the hands could move backwards and the day be rewound. It seemed such a simple thing to ask for.

'Gen shouldn't be here,' said Mark as if suddenly aware of what they might all have to face, any moment now.

'I want to stay!' protested Genevieve in a panic.

'Scampi!' said Janice suddenly. 'It's way past his dinner time. Can you run the Peugeot back and see to him, Joe love? Take Gen, why don't you?'

'No, I want to stay! I want to see Justin!'

'Well, all right, love.' She added, sounding utterly unconcerned, 'He's probably piddled on the carpet by now.'

'Do you think we ought to . . . ?'

'What?'

Fred shrugged a little helplessly as she started setting out hot dishes on the table. 'A note or something.'

'A note?' echoed Sam.

'I don't know, darling. I just thought . . .'

'How would a note look, coming from us?'

'Yes, but . . . We can't do nothing, can we? I mean, imagine if it was the other way round . . .' She was throwing the responsibility on him. After all, he was the real Delancey and therefore flag-bearer of the feud.

'I think it would look hypocritical if we wrote a note. Think of it, Fred! We *hate* them! My God, how many times have I heard you say it?'

'Yes, but . . .'

'What?'

'Doesn't this sort of wipe away everything?'

He smiled at the absurdity of that, though he also seemed to ponder her question for a moment. 'Does it?'

'We can always go back to hating them later,' she suggested helpfully.

Such courtesies were mandatory in their world. It was part of the language they'd learnt: forget to send a thank you note and you could reasonably expect never to be invited again. They must have known how failing to react to that terrible car accident would be perceived. Even so, Sam and Fred decided that to behave in any way that suggested sympathy for the Traffords would indeed be hypocrisy.

Joe was used to seeing the Abbey lit up like a Christmas tree as soon as dusk fell. Since the move, his parents seemed to have made it a deliberate policy not to economize on electricity. But tonight, so black was the Abbey that it seemed absorbed by the starless, moonless night. It could have been returned to another century.

As he unlocked the door with the ancient heavy key they were still using, he was thinking about passing Millers Cross, where the Rolls had veered off the road. It had been terrible to see its shiny bonnet concertinaed into a tree, its silver lady knocked awry, its doors flung open to show expensive leather seats strewn with shattered glass. It had taken the firemen from High Regis more than half an hour to cut Justin free. *'Poor bro,'* thought Joe miserably, even though Justin had been profoundly unconscious throughout.

He could hear Scampi barking hysterically inside. The heavy door swung open on the yawning Great Hall and the inky depths beyond.

Strangely, Scampi didn't come bounding out but continued to yap hysterically somewhere in the distance. Then, still standing with his hand on the front door, Joe could have sworn he saw a shape pass very swiftly, black on black, across the darkness where the Great Hall led to the Refectory.

'Scampi?' he called. He snapped on the lights. But even with the shadows banished, his heart pounded with fear. It seemed insane that, not long ago, he'd implored the spirits of the Abbey to appear to him. It had come of spending too much time daydreaming. Now, all he wanted was to find the dog and feed it, then return to the hospital as speedily as possible.

Then a soft voice from the darkness outside almost finished him.

After the scene with her parents, Laura had stormed out of the Lodge. 'You *can't* not say anything!' she'd protested, utterly shocked, deaf to their reasonable voices, their careful explanations. 'Imagine if it had happened to David!'

'It didn't,' David pointed out unnecessarily. Maria had supported the parents' decision, too.

'*I can't be with them any more*,' Laura had thought, trembling and miserable, terrified of a return to the despair of a few months back.

It was just then that a car had passed by and, in the dim light, she recognized Joe Trafford at the wheel. It had seemed so natural to follow him up to the Abbey. Of course, her predominant feelings were anger with her parents and great sympathy for Joe. But returning to that house of her childhood for the first time felt like stumbling from a lonely dull place into a party she'd never wanted to leave.

'I had to come,' she told him. 'I heard about your brother and I'm so so sorry.' Then she cast a backward glance in the direction of the Lodge, and added very quickly, without expression, 'They don't know I'm here.'

'Thanks,' said Joe gruffly. So, the mission wasn't on behalf of her family. Even so, he found it incredible – after their last confrontation – that she'd come at all.

'Thanks,' he muttered once more. Seeing her again made him realize how very much he liked her and memories of the evening they'd spent together started to return to him.

For the first time, she made eye contact and – confronted by her sweet, worried expression – he felt as shaken as if she'd touched him.

'Please try not to worry too much,' she said very earnestly. 'My sister had her appendix out at the Whitmore. Justin couldn't be in a better place.'

He nodded brusquely: moved for some reason that she'd used his brother's name and also terrified he might break down.

'I *know* he's going to be all right,' said Laura very positively. Then, to his great relief, she was distracted. 'What's the matter with your dog?'

Justin was finally out of surgery and, within his own careful framework, Mr Porter had offered a measure of optimism. The operation had gone as well as could be expected, though Justin would remain on the critical list for the time being. Family members only were allowed to see him for just five minutes.

'My boy,' Mark murmured as he looked down at his unconscious son, now hooked up to machines and swathed in even more bandages.

Janice squeezed Justin's limp fingers, willing him to return the pressure.

'Can he hear us?' asked Genevieve anxiously.

'Every blooming word!' Stanley's seamy old face was wet with tears. 'See that? Lid twitched!'

Mark nudged his father because however much they all wanted to believe Justin was out of the woods, it was best to be cautious. He'd been so lucky as an adult, but now he felt fate hovering in the wings, waiting to pounce on complacency.

'There!' said Stanley. 'He done it again!'

'Shall I bring in some of my tapes tomorrow?' Genevieve suggested.

'You do what you like, Gen. He hates your Pink Floyd. But he's a fighter. Might be just the ticket. Trafford, ain't he?'

They found Scampi in the Refectory. He was planted on Janice's pink carpet in the centre of a spreading stain. It was as if someone had ordered him to sit, locking him in the same stiff, shameful position for hours.

'Oh Scampi!' said Joe and, at the sound of his voice, the dog slunk over to them, ears limp with mortification, tail wagging cautiously.

Joe watched as, looking about her with wide eyes, Laura took in her surroundings. He was laid back about most things – affecting to know nothing about interior decoration – but privately had always found his mother's renovations over the top. He'd not forgotten Laura's harsh words the last time they'd met, and didn't think he could bear another altercation. As she stared at the newly restored portraits, each now set beneath an individual spotlight, he thought he saw a movement in her throat, as if she were trying to swallow.

'It's different,' she commented at last. Then she smiled a little helplessly.

Joe melted. Could this thoughtful tactful girl really belong to the family which, for as long as he could remember, he'd been encouraged to hate? That moment was the beginning of him falling in love and instinctively he moved as if to take her in his arms.

'Not here,' she whispered to his astonishment and joy.

'No,' he made himself agree very reasonably. Then his smile faded. He was starting to feel it now – that alarming concentration of emotion he'd so often experienced in the Refectory, the only room where his close-knit family ever fell out with each other. And the strange thing was, it seemed to have become worse since his mother's changes.

It was Laura who fetched a damp cloth from the old scullery, braving the terrifying shadows, seemingly unaffected.

As they moved to leave the Abbey, the dog following closely behind, Joe whispered as if fearful of being overheard, 'It's like it wants the place to itself.'

'What?' asked Laura, sounding genuinely puzzled.

'Can't you feel it?'

'No,' she said, beginning to look frightened, too.

Then Joe understood. The Abbey had been free of malign spirits as she'd known it. Something had been activated when his family moved in. He was more than ever certain that he hadn't imagined the tentative but invisible touch on his arm as he was climbing out of the Refectory window some weeks back or the swiftly moving black shadow of a moment ago.

It seemed it wasn't only the Delanceys who hated his family and wanted them out. And now, with Justin's accident, it was as if a curse had been laid on them, too.

Chapter Fifteen

The war would be over very soon – everyone was saying so. Moreover, a four-piece band just a few yards away was belting out 'Chatanooga Choo Choo' and Hester was still young even though she was getting alarmingly close to thirty and, for once, she could wear a pretty dress (dark blue crepe with big shoulder pads and a matching belt). But the real delight lay in escaping from the Abbey. Two hours earlier, still in her nurse's uniform and in defiance of her in-laws, she'd caught the train to London, so exhausted she'd dozed for most of the journey. She was expected back early the following morning for a full day's work and might not get to bed at all (though this seemed irrelevant). It was extraordinary to remember that, only a few years before, she'd been taken to the Cygnet at least once a month. Odder still, it didn't feel awkward to be sitting in that exclusive nightclub with Stanley. But, then, he'd undergone quite a transformation.

He raised his glass of gin. 'Bottoms up!'

Hester made the same sort of face as Edmund did in such

circumstances, deploring the army vulgarity yet forgiving it because these were different times, after all. 'And well done, by the way,' she told him.

Stanley grinned and touched the dark curl that always fell over his forehead, as if making a mocking salute to himself. 'He looks the picture,' Effie had said of his new persona, half laughing, half tearful. Stanley in his officer's uniform, his silver coin medal pinned to his chest. 'Dada's a hero,' she'd informed Mark. 'And we think the world of him.'

'You must tell me the whole story,' said Hester in her dry way as if it were the last thing she really wanted to encourage. But she'd already had the gist of it from Edmund, who'd beamed with pride in his friend.

It seemed that, under enemy fire, Stanley had saved the lives of two fellow soldiers. It had been an extraordinary demonstration of selfless courage, said those who'd witnessed it. As a direct result, he'd been awarded a Military Medal, pulled out of the ranks and put into the Officer Training Corps. Only six months later, he was on a par with Edmund, and now he'd outpaced him. It was the talk of the Abbey. Even Edmund appeared a little stunned by the speed of his rise. But when Hester marvelled, 'Amazing!' he'd corrected her a little sharply, saying, 'Stanley's always had courage, as I should know.'

Despite the renewed bombing, it seemed as if half the young people in London were crammed into the Cygnet that night – or at any rate, the ones in Hester's acquaintance. The roar of refined merriment made it difficult to talk and the dance floor was filling up with more and more couples. She did a double-take, recognizing a fellow debutante, Freda McCarthur, surfacing from a deep kiss, who looked quite alarmed until she

took in the interesting fact that Hester wasn't with her husband
either.

'Hester!'

'Freda.'

'D'you know Simon?' Freda shouted over the din.

Her companion clicked his heels together in drunken
parody. He was short and fair and quite unlike Freda's
husband, whose family owned a large estate in Scotland.
Hester had to admit that Stanley looked far better in the same
uniform. It amused her to see how Freda kept glancing at him.
But, then, he glistened with vitality, as if he'd been liberated.
But for that (as Effie would point out increasingly wistfully)
he'd still be helping out in the Abbey's gardens, under his
father.

Freda was looking at Hester expectantly because it was her
turn for introductions. But at that moment the drummer went
into a frenzy of activity so Hester shook her head with a smile
and a shrug as if to say, 'Too bad!' To her shame, she was rather
enjoying the ambiguity of the situation.

The other couple returned to the dance floor and more
circumspect dancing though not before Freda had conveyed a
silent message. 'Different times, different rules,' she told Hester
with a helpless sophisticated shrug, as her eyes lingered
admiringly on Stanley.

'Pity about Edmund, weren't it?' Stanley had moved very
close so she could absorb the full strength of his West Country
burr, feel his warm breath against her cheek.

'A great pity,' she agreed, very prim now, realizing that he
must have witnessed the silent exchange with Freda and might
even be enjoying playing along with it. He was naughty. Effie
was always saying so.

'He were devastated, Hester.' But he wore a deadpan expression, as if he just might be sending her up.

The band struck up with 'You Were Never Lovelier' and Stanley said, 'Dance?'

'Why not?' Hester responded coolly with a shrug, as if unable to come up with a decent excuse.

Edmund had understood Hester's need to escape from the Abbey and indulge in mindless frivolity and she really appreciated it, but then his long-anticipated leave was cancelled at the very last minute. He was based near Salisbury now, engaged in some sort of surveillance work, while Stanley had been moved to a training camp in Surrey, where he was teaching leadership skills.

'Thank heavens, darling!' he exclaimed, on managing to get through to the Cygnet, where she was already waiting. The telephone crackled. 'Afraid I won't be able to make it, after all.'

'Oh no!' Hester had been unable to hide the disappointment. She was thinking she'd have to go straight back to Melcombe on the next train.

'Can't be helped,' said Edmund, controlled and stoical, setting the tone. He'd gone on in a quiet, important voice – 'All very hush hush' – hinting at secrets, reminding her that, like every trusted soldier, he was prohibited from discussing work, even with his wife. And after that, with the air of one producing a nice surprise, said, 'Look here, darling, Stanley's coming to the Cygnet instead.'

'Stanley?' Hester had echoed blankly. For a moment, she believed she must have misheard.

'He has to be in London on business,' Edmund continued. 'As a matter of fact, he's on his way to the club now.'

'They won't let him in,' said Hester very confidently.

'Oh yes, they will. I've just had a word.' She could hear the cheerfulness in his voice, as if he loved the idea of his wife and his best friend together.

'Effie's expecting him . . .' she began.

'Oh, he won't have time to get down there!' said Edmund, as if Hester understood nothing of war, even though it had been going on for almost six years now.

And Hester had thought a little indignantly, '*He should*!' She'd found herself briefly wondering: '*Does Effie know about this?*'

'Enjoying yourself?' Stanley asked in her ear but lazily, as if there could be no doubt. She had the uncomfortable suspicion that he knew full well about Effie's marital confidences and might even be speculating, in an amused way, about their effect. There was something disturbing about being so close to him on the dance floor, imprisoned in his strong embrace. Stanley's hard, muscular body was strangely graceful. She thought of the way her husband danced, holding her very lightly and loosely, scarcely seeming to touch her at all.

However, all she said by way of reply, keeping herself very stiff and separate, sounding as haughty as her mother-in-law, was, 'Quite extraordinary, being here with you, of all people.'

It was like cuffing him, putting him in his place: making it clear that he, the gardener's son, was lucky to find himself in such exclusive surroundings. But it stemmed more from uneasiness than unkindness.

She saw a spark of anger flare in his eyes but never discovered how he might have reacted next. For, at that moment, a raid began.

As bombs started to land alarmingly nearby, the band ceased

playing abruptly, the seats in the club bucked up and down, bottles and glasses fell off the tables and smashed, and the red curtains enfolding the room swished with strange wild movements. The next thing she knew, Stanley had flung her to the ground, covering her body from head to foot with his own, so close that she could smell his sweat, feel the strength in his arms and the bones in his hips and even register the black beard that was beginning to push its way through his freshly shaven face. Then there was an enormous explosion and pieces of ceiling and dust rained down all round them.

It seemed it was Stanley Trafford's destiny to save the Delancey family.

Chapter Sixteen

My dearest Pooh, if I close my eyes I am back in time in that most special of evenings, waiting so impatiently for your arrival. Did you guess at my happiness? I think not, for I wear a mask for the world and, besides, I did not truly recognize it myself. That evening was your idea it seemed, and I must confess that originally I harboured some doubt. But one of the many qualities I have come to love in you is your ability to expand my narrow world. But, there, we both know the nature of your priceless gift . . .

One of the old bells on springs jangled outside the kitchen and Janice jumped like a guilty servant and stuffed the letter into a pocket of her apron. She checked the top oven of the newly installed Aga, but the fish pie she'd made for lunch seemed only half done though it had been in for a good twenty minutes. She couldn't get to grips with this cooking, which it seemed was mandatory in the country. The Aga reminded her of their new neighbours. It had its own strange code of behaviour, and could be malicious, too.

She could hear the noise and laughter in the distance as she toiled up the stairs for the fourth or fifth time that morning. Since his return from hospital a week ago, Justin's bedroom had become the epicentre of the house. It was Mark's first port of call before the business of his day began; and the family would usually spend the whole evening in there, watching a new television that had been installed. Justin was revelling in the attention. *'Bless him!'* thought Janice with a lump in her throat because it was like a miracle to have their son restored with all his old sharpness, no worse for his accident except for his badly broken leg.

Joe was sitting on Justin's bed picking at a pile of grapes and, encased in his battered blue overalls, Stanley was staring out of the window at the gardeners working in the distance. He made a sudden movement like a cat noticing a mouse. 'What the heck?' he muttered.

'Lunch is nearly done,' Janice assured Justin. 'Joe can fetch your tray up in a minute.'

But it seemed hunger was not the reason he'd summoned her. 'Seen Joe's hair?' he said with a mischievous look, inviting his mother, with her special intuition, to confirm a suspicion that had just come to him.

'So?' said Joe, touching his newly gelled dark hair very delicately as if each strand had its appointed place, and it occurred to Janice that he was spending a great deal of time in front of the mirror these days. His skin gleamed with health. His beauty was astounding.

'Spit were good enough for us,' said Stanley, springing into action like an old boxer, trying to muss the hairdo and, as she

watched the two of them dodge around the room – youth easily
batting away age – Janice strove to find any similarity.

'Dad was a knockout, too,' Mark had said. 'He had the ladies
fluttering round him like nobody's business. Not that he ever
noticed. The only one for him was Mam.'

She plumped up Justin's pillows, though she'd done it only
half an hour before, and readjusted his bedclothes, noting that
the heavy plaster on his leg had even more messages scribbled
on it. 'Get well, soldier,' Stanley had written in his painstaking
fashion. Justin would be out of action for eight weeks at least
and, of course, all decisions on his academic future were now
on hold.

On her way back to the kitchen, Janice passed the builders,
who'd paused mid-demolition of an old chimney breast to eat
their sandwiches. It was Stanley's idea to make a cinema out of
the big ground-floor room where the Delanceys had
apparently once stored guns. 'Mind you use those dust sheets,'
she warned, and one of them called after her hopefully,
'Wouldn't say no to a cuppa . . .' even though there was nothing
to stop them from making tea for themselves.

It was only now – a month after the accident – that she was
beginning to pick up the reins of her life once more. The
Abbey's past still fascinated her, though the mystery of the
lovelorn letter-writer had been overtaken, to an extent, by the
conundrum as to why the house had survived the seemingly
indiscriminate destruction of the sixteenth century. However,
because of Justin, she'd been obliged to postpone her return to
the library.

Back in the kitchen, she pulled out the letter from her apron
pocket. She'd not even revealed her find to Mark yet. She felt
responsible for the secret that had been hidden so carefully

away. '*It's all right*,' she caught herself whispering once, like soothing an anxious spirit.

... You were right, of course, and it was the most wonderful party ever to have been held in the Abbey. I shall hold for ever in my heart the memory of the candlelight and the music you were so rightly proud of – and a feeling like no other in this ancient, occasionally unfriendly place. It was you, my secret love: your aura and your essence. Why did we not dance together, you and I? I watched you, though. Oh yes, all through the night . . .

At this point, the writing was smeared into illegibility as if, all those years and years ago, a tear had fallen on the fragile paper. But at least this letter was signed, in a manner of speaking. 'Your Figlet', it looked like. Figlet and Pooh! Odder and odder! Why hadn't the author used their real names? So she, too, had not always felt at ease in the Abbey. It made Janice warm to her even more. Furthermore, she'd made a discovery. Once, there'd been a hugely successful party here – though exactly when was a mystery.

She was reminded of Stanley's suggestion to hold a costume ball. One plan to court local society had gone by the wayside. Justin had complained it would be unfair to hold the pheasant shoot without him, especially when he'd been looking forward to using his new Purdey. So Stanley had immediately cancelled it. He'd seemed oddly relieved, Janice had noted, as if some gentle and secret part of him agreed with Joe that rearing birds for shooting them was obscene.

The whole family was still seething about the Delanceys' failure to make any gesture of sympathy after Justin's accident.

The poaching of their pheasants and all the other deliberate provocations seemed trivial by comparison. A line had been crossed and there could be no going back. Janice understood, for the first time, that Sam and Fred were truly evil. To add to the bitterness, if that was possible, Lily had just let slip that David Delancey had been awarded a place at Cambridge.

Holding an expensive party without asking the other family would be like smacking them across the face. It would be a celebration of Justin's survival. Besides, the renovation of the Great Hall was now complete. It was time for a proper house-warming.

Justin's bell jangled again and Janice cheerfully stowed away the letter. Again, she wished there'd been a date. If only she knew more history. She was beginning to feel her lack of education most painfully but at least she was eager to learn and that was a real advance since coming to the Abbey.

Then she forgot all about the past because there was an unmistakable smell of burning coming from the Aga.

Chapter Seventeen

On 15 May 1945, at two minutes past eight in the evening, Edmund's father, Sir Michael, pitched forward into a bowl of onion and potato soup and died. Perhaps he was succumbing to the weak heart that had seen off so many Delancey males or maybe he no longer wished to continue living now that one of the most enjoyable periods he could remember was drawing to a close.

A week before, this ancient aristocrat, who'd been a guest at the coronation of King Edward VII and who deplored vulgarity of any kind, had encouraged gaudy bunting to be strung throughout his Abbey. Afterwards, a huge bonfire had been lit on one of his hills, where he'd joined in wholeheartedly with the rowdy songs and the speeches and applause. With Germany's surrender, the war was effectively over. Soon the bustle of patients and nursing staff would be gone and his family could leave the makeshift but surprisingly pleasant way of life they'd created in the east wing to reoccupy the freezing and cavernous main body of the house. The silence of centuries would descend once more: that patient, infinitely adaptable, occasionally savage flavour he'd long since suspected contributed to the famous Delancey depression. There was a sense of claustrophobia, too. But, then, one might expect that from a great house which had been in the same family for generations.

He was an old-fashioned unimaginative person of privilege nearing eighty. Even so, the democracy of the past six years had seeped into his joints, making him both more sociable and less intolerant. He wasn't alone. If his friends' houses hadn't been requisitioned by the military, too, they'd been obliged to take in evacuees. And it was impossible for any of them – with all these new influences – to maintain their usual lofty social stance. After all, hadn't even the Royal Family made a point of showing solidarity with those from the poorest and most vulnerable areas of London? He'd watched the exposure to different people with their unfamiliar ways astonish and sometimes infuriate his friends, too.

For the first time in his life, Sir Michael Delancey had come to perceive those who'd worked for him for years as individuals, with hopes and fears, just like him. His gardener, Reg Trafford, was a case in point, even though there'd long been an awkward-ness between the two families because of the friendship between their sons. But with the coming of war, any tension seemed to melt away. Everyone had sons in the forces. Stanley Trafford had served in the same regiment as Edmund Delancey; they'd even ended up in France together. It became entirely acceptable for them to see each other openly. When back on leave, Stanley Trafford would pop into the Abbey, just as his wife, Effie, did, to be greeted most graciously by the Delanceys. He was a splendid chap, everyone agreed, and a credit to his family.

'Worrying business,' Sir Michael would comment to his gardener, now engaged full time in the growing of vegetables. Then they'd both think about the dreadful unremitting anxiety, and the way the war had lasted against all expectations and the terror of losing a child, especially an only one. Usually Sir Michael would utter some gruff anodyne words of comfort like, 'We must keep faith,' even though, whilst a churchgoer, he was not a religious man. And after that, they'd engage in an enjoyable discussion about the curse of rationing or the horrors of fascism or what a fine job Churchill was doing.

For some time now, however, the relationship had come under strain. It had been expected, of course, that Edmund would be put on fast track to become an officer. After all, public school was generally considered by the forces to be a fine preparation for leadership because, by example, it taught command. What hadn't been expected was that, through nothing more than his own efforts, Stanley would quickly achieve the same rank as Edmund and then surpass him. He was a colonel now, whereas Edmund had stuck at major. Because the estate was very feudal, Reg Trafford probably expected his employer to feel the same pride as he did; and it might not have been boastfulness that impelled him to return again and again to the subject of Stanley's decoration for valour. 'He'm having a hero's welcome for sure . . .' Eventually Sir Michael took to turning on his heel and stumping off on his stick – and even then his gardener failed to get the message. For the fact was, Edmund had passed an undistinguished war. There'd been no mentions in dispatches. He'd done exactly what was required of him, but no more.

One part of Sir Michael was deeply relieved, of course. After six long years of anxiety, his son was coming home for good. But why couldn't he have acquitted himself with honour *and* returned in one piece? To rub salt in his personal wound, the gardener's hero son was coming home to his beautiful young wife. Sir Michael had never forgotten the scene he'd once interrupted in the Morning Room, early on in the war. He'd have feared for his reaction if his daughter-in-law, Hester, hadn't been present, too. But, instead of covering the naked bosom her child was still feeding from, the girl had just giggled. Hussy!

But now it was all over: the disappointment and the shameful lusting and the taken-for-granted privilege and the spoilt despair. The moment he slumped forward, lifeless, into his tepid, insufficiently seasoned soup, everything passed to Edmund: the Abbey and its estate, together with the responsibility for running them. Not to mention the crucial, increasingly worrying matter of continuing the line.

Edmund's first major decision, on assuming his father's mantle, was to arrange a grand Victory Ball. For all his gradual softening up, his father would never have allowed such a thing – at least, not the sort of party Edmund had in mind – and his mother had expressed her disapproval most forcefully. 'Hasn't the Abbey been through enough?' she'd demanded.

It was true that the Abbey had taken a severe battering, though its treasures – including the family portraits – had been carefully hidden away. After the years of occupation by the military, there were dents and scuffs everywhere. The flagstones still bore the marks of too much harsh scrubbing and the scraping of beds and heavy trolleys, and dozens of tiny panes in the huge windows were either cracked or smashed. Worst of all, the historic panelling was badly damaged. The marvellous ceilings had survived best – although, in a corner of the Great

Hall, a strip of moulding was shattered, as if someone had slung (or even fired) a heavy object at it.

But Edmund was adamant his ball should take place there, though even the vicar had suggested the village hall was more suitable. It would sum up the breeze of change that had characterized the wartime period and herald the arrival of a democratic new era, he explained excitedly to Hester. So what if it resulted in a few more cracks and breakages? The house was going to need redecoration and expert repair, anyway, just as the gardens would have to be remade, all over again. He got quite carried away as he enumerated the reasons why his idea was so excellent.

'The war was an education for me,' he continued earnestly. 'No one welcomes such terrible events. Never!' A shadow passed over his face as if – for a second and against his will – some of the terrible things he'd seen and heard on the long retreat to Dunkirk had come back to him like ghosts. Women and children cut down by machine-gun fire from enemy aircraft; comrades in arms blown to bits before his horrified eyes; the dreadful shrieks of pain. He'd never gone into the details. 'It was quite a thing,' was the most he'd admitted to Hester, and, typically, she'd not pressed him though Effie had confided that Stanley once wept in her arms.

'But if I hadn't been through it . . .' Edmund left the sentence unfinished and, after a minute, Hester saw that he was smiling, though his eyes looked quite shiny. 'When I think of some of the fun we had, in spite of it all . . . You ask old Stanley! The times we had!'

'We need a guest list,' she said, briskly bringing him back to the point, though gratified to see his cheerfulness return.

'Not necessary, darling.'

Hester raised her eyebrows, perplexed and a little amused. 'Why not?'

'Everyone's invited.'

'What, *everyone?*'

'That's the idea. The village, the estate . . .' He threw his arms wide in an extravagant gesture and beamed. 'Everyone!'

'And do our friends get a look in?' she enquired with a touch of her old asperity.

'Our friends?' he echoed, looking puzzled.

'The Fitzherberts . . . The Askews . . .' She sounded a little impatient because it was only the beginning of the list.

'Of course!'

'This needs a bit of thinking about.'

'Nothing to it,' he assured her. It was typical of Hes to fuss over detail, he thought. She was a perfectionist: another quality he appreciated in her. 'It'll be wonderful, you'll see. And Stanley says the village band will be terrific, so long as the drummer doesn't drink too much.' He laughed.

'You've talked to Stanley about the party, then?' she asked, taken aback.

'Of course!'

Effie wheeled Mark up to the Abbey in his battered pushchair, thankful, for once, to be apart from Stanley. He was not in a good mood. It was understandable, thought Effie sympathetically. One moment, he'd been a conquering hero with the world at his feet; the next, he was back in the overcrowded gardener's cottage. She'd assured him that, with his record, there was sure to be some wonderful job in the offing. The second time she said this, he snapped at her badly. It felt very natural to seek out Hester, as she'd done so many times before.

'Leave it,' Stanley had advised. 'They's things to do with the earth on the old one's grave yet to sink.' But Effie was anxious not to irritate her husband further.

'Baby wants his walk,' she said and, like a tiny ally, Mark started stamping and shouting 'Walk!' until Stanley put his head in his hands and bellowed.

'For God's sake, get him out of here, woman!'

Mark ceased yelling the moment they started up the long and bumpy lane leading from their home to the big house. He now loved these trips as much as she did. They'd sing in celebration of their escape from the stuffy dark cottage as they dawdled, searching for wood for the fire and, if the corn had just been harvested, stray ears for their few chickens. Every trip was an adventure; each return a long but enjoyable business of unloading the pushchair of all the bits and pieces they'd accumulated. They were lucky to live in the country, Effie often thought, and at least, during these straitened times, everyone could be sure of rations of butter and sugar and fat, however tiny.

On this occasion, she foraged for nettles, too, carefully stowing them under the seat where they couldn't sting Mark. She'd rather turn vegetarian, she told him indignantly, than eat whale meat or that disgusting snoek everyone was so fed up of. It was a shame it wasn't hazelnut season yet. When you shelled them and hammered out the kernels, they added real flavour and texture to cakes made with dried egg powder and lard. A month or so back, oranges had suddenly appeared in the greengrocer's like brightly coloured toys, but by the time she joined the queue they were all gone. She wished it were possible to prepare a feast for her husband – a proper joint of beef with Yorkshire pudding like in the old pre-rationing days – but nettle soup cost nothing and was nourishing. And after that, they'd have a special treat: the sheep's brains picked up from the butcher's for a few points. You needed to soak them in salty water for several hours and pull out the slimy strings but, stewed with tomatoes and onions from the garden, they were delicious.

'See?' she murmured to Mark as the Abbey came floating into view, like a golden ship on its choppy sea of dug-up lawn. She noticed that a Union Jack had been run up on the flagpole. 'That be Edmund,' she said fondly. Hester was very preoccupied these days. Of course, her husband was home for good with a whole new weight of responsibility. Sir Edmund Delancey! Whoever could have dreamt that her own dear Stanley would be best friends with a sir?

She went to the front door, as usual, only to find to her astonishment that it was locked. So she stowed the pushchair under a nearby yew tree and went to the servants' entrance, which was open. Once inside the seemingly deserted Abbey, she made for the inner side of the front door, pretending to have come in the way she always did while smiling at her own foolishness.

It was a fortnight since the last traces of the hospital had been removed, but the Abbey was still in a dreadful mess. It was worn out by war, as exhausted as the rest of the country, and nothing had been mended for years. The damp had come through the plaster where guttering had collapsed. The musty breath of mould was everywhere.

She peeped into the empty Refectory, remembering the dozens of beds filled with cheeky card-playing officers. 'Hello, darling!' they'd called, and 'Good morning, my lovely!' Though she'd affected not to notice, she found herself missing them now. They'd been so chirpy, even the ones with the worst injuries; often she'd found herself wishing she could work at the Abbey, like Hester. Making people better had to have the edge over helping in the manufacture of war weapons. But it was girls like Hester who did the nursing, ones like herself who worked in the factories and she'd long since accepted the division without rancour. The portraits were back on the brown walls, she noticed, as if to stress that the real owners had at long last reclaimed their inheritance even if it meant camping in squalor until the house could be set to rights.

She shivered a little as she walked through the Great Hall. It wasn't just the damp chill. Though it was deserted, she felt observed. Thank goodness, she told Mark, that she had him parked on her hip for comfort. The two of them would say boo to any silly old ghost!

'Ghost!' he echoed. He was four now but still clung to her. He was bemused by the surroundings, head swivelling like a top-heavy flower on a stem as he absorbed the novelty of a house with endless space. Then he put a sticky little hand over her mouth as if checking she was still present and breathing.

She snorted suddenly, like a pig, and he gave one of the fat chuckles she adored.

She could hear distant voices coming from the Library and smiled as she recognized Hester's precise yet languid tones. She knew what a contrast she presented with her soft West Country patois. Hester would mock her sometimes but it was only her style. '"Proper antsy"? Whatever can you mean, Effie?' Then, after Effie had explained with much shy giggling: 'Oh well, if the baby's restless, why not say so? "Antsy" indeed!' But Effie would never have considered trying to remodel herself. Sometimes, she'd mentally step back from the two of them as they talked and be put in mind of one of the gramophone records Edmund loved to play: herself a plaintive broad-hipped cello, Hester an elegant violin. They got along just fine, which was all that mattered. It was the same with Stanley and Edmund. Proper friendship paid no account to differences and all four of them were the proof.

Through the closed doors of the Library, Effie heard a fragment of conversation. '. . . as well as for the Abbey,' Hester was saying with peculiar emphasis.

Effie wasn't consciously eavesdropping but there was something about Hester's tone that made her pause before announcing herself. She was still hovering, hand on the doorknob, when she heard Edmund say, 'Ah!' There was something unusual in the way he uttered this, too – something desperate yet comprehending, almost like it was forced out of him, thought Effie, more and more puzzled.

Afterwards, she wished she'd crept away like a mouse. But Mark cried out and so she had no choice. 'Just me!' she said as she pushed open the door. It was the same humble greeting as always, though she'd come to feel so welcome at the Abbey. It was funny to remember that, before the war, she could never have imagined finding herself in such a grand house, unless it was to sweep and dust and polish. But for years now, she'd been running in and out like a member of the family.

As soon as she saw the two of them – Hester seated on the sofa, Edmund standing up – she picked up something disturbing, pungent as perfume and very serious. All she knew was, she didn't want to be there. But it was too late to back away. Besides, she lacked the confidence to manage such an exit.

Edmund was very pale, she noticed, almost as if he'd just received some shocking news. Then he appeared to recover himself, perhaps for her sake. 'Effie, my fair one!' he exclaimed in the courteous overly flattering way that always lifted her spirits. This was a joke in itself, of course – she being so dark. 'How *are* you? And this young fellow? I say, he's grown! What do you feed him on? Spinach?' But there was something mechanical about the way he said it, almost like he was reciting poetry.

Effie went on smiling in her shy anxious way, though her thoughts were darting everywhere.

'Effie,' murmured Hester in her cool fashion. But Effie was used to that because Hester wasn't a naturally effusive person.

Then a silence fell and the bewilderment started. Effie realized that she hadn't seen her friend properly for months now. Suddenly, Hester was always too busy to talk, and there were no more invitations to tea. Effie could see, too late, that she should have taken Stanley's advice. But there'd been nowhere else to go.

Hester was very elegant in a new dress – fine green wool that picked up the colour of her eyes – and Effie wondered where she'd got the coupons from. As usual, she was wearing her pearls. Once she'd explained that the more she wore them, the more beautiful they became because something in skin enhanced the lustre. 'When I'm old and wrinkled, Effie, they'll be at their very best.'

She'd be glad Edmund was home, thought Effie. Glad, too, that the Abbey was theirs now, even though the war had left it in such a mess. Effie appreciated that, in the nicest sort of way, Hester liked being in control as, for all her bossiness, old Lady Delancey would find out.

'Stanley were on about the party . . .' Effie began, remembering her husband's excitement before he'd shouted at her. Edmund had enlisted him to help with the planning of the Victory Ball, he'd told her. But now, even to herself, she sounded timid and rough. She felt very out of place in the cold and cavernous Library with its shelves of books, its clock ticking ponderously away from a high mantelpiece, even though, in honour of her visit, and as a form of thank you, she was wearing a dress Hester had most generously passed to her on the last real occasion they'd spent as friends.

She'd been invited up to the Abbey specially and then Hester had made a little presentation. 'I'd like you to have this, Effie. It will look so much nicer on you.' The cream linen clung to her body as it never had to Hester's spare and elegant frame. But now she saw Hester glance at it coldly and realized, with a sinking sensation in her stomach, that it had been an error, though she was baffled as to why.

Trust Mark to be sick just at that moment, as if he was forcing them all to take notice of him; but it was true his stomach had been bad for days. Like a little jug, he poured out a stream of smelly liquid, most of which landed on a beautiful patterned carpet. To her further chagrin, Effie saw Hester wince.

'Here,' said Edmund, handing over his handkerchief: an enormous white monogrammed thing, very clean and pressed. He didn't seem a bit bothered about the rug; he actually smiled indulgently as he watched her go down on her knees to deal with the vomit whilst grasping Mark awkwardly with her other arm in case he took it into his head to dash off and smash something. She was still concentrating on sopping up as much as possible when she heard him say, 'Might as well get used to it, I suppose.'

Puzzled, Effie glanced at Hester. Edmund couldn't have meant it how it had sounded. Then she saw his awkwardness and, for the first time, noticed the giveaway softness that had settled on Hester, the sleepy look of her eyes and last – though certainly not least – the smile of pure happiness she bestowed on Edmund.

It was ironic that she, of all people, hadn't guessed. Hadn't she called on the dark forces to help her friend? For years she'd been waiting for just this moment. The only wonder was it had taken so long. But she'd come to understand that had been her fault: a time limit being the one detail she'd forgotten to mention.

Why wouldn't Hester meet her eyes? Instead, she beamed encouragingly at Edmund, who said, 'We're having a baby, Effie! It's tremendous news, isn't it? I'm sure it'll be a son.'

'Tremendous!' Effie echoed a little uncertainly, like someone copying a foreigner. She knew, of course, that Edmund was right: there was no way they'd be having a daughter. 'When?'

'When?' Edmund asked Hester, though he must already know. It was as if, thought Effie, he'd picked up on the tension and was trying to force Hester into addressing her directly, to jiggle them back into their usual easy friendship.

'November,' said Hester, still looking at Edmund. 'Not long to go.' It was as if she were reassuring him.

Effie was more hurt than she could remember. It seemed Hester had been pregnant for all of four months but had not thought to share the marvellous news with her. However, all she said was, 'Happen the first . . .' She was going to point out that first babies sometimes came early, though she'd no idea if this was true. It stemmed from a wish to establish her credentials as a friend who knew about motherhood and could definitely be helpful.

But Edmund interrupted her, rubbing his hands together briskly. 'No peace for the wicked.' It was an unlikely phrase for him to choose but, then, she'd noticed he spoke differently since the war. 'Back to the grindstone.'

Was it another of his jokes – especially for her? You never could tell with Edmund. He was so charming, with those perfect manners, but occasionally she'd get the odd feeling there was a mysterious space behind it all or, at least, something quite different from what was being presented. She'd never have dared say this to Stanley, of course. Her husband loved Edmund like a brother, as he so often told her.

'*Now he's going, she'll get us some tea and then we can talk,*' thought Effie, humming with anticipation.

But instead Hester said, studying her nails, 'I'm afraid I must get on, too. Forgive me, Effie.'

Effie announced dully to her family, 'She'm expecting, ain't she?' As she said it, a hen squawked past her in a flap and she made a mental note to search the cottage for eggs. Yesterday evening, her father-in-law had crushed one, pushing his chair back, and it had felt like a small death.

Coming so recently from Hester and Edmund's, she was struck by contrasts. The Abbey still smelt of dried rose petals though there'd been no flowers cultivated in its gardens for years. With a different stamp of permanence, the dark little cottage breathed stale cooking and insufficient bathing. Whereas the Abbey seemed to bloom from the ground like an enormous flower, this crumbling wattle house sank into it, further oppressed by a leaking thatched roof infested by rats that scuttled about in the night. There was no privacy. One of the reasons Effie had fled was that each tiny room led into the next (as if even doors had been economized on) and all conversation could be overheard, especially disagreements, and Stanley's mother had given her a nasty look for annoying her hero son. The only place you could for sure be alone was the privy at the bottom of the garden, infested with maggots and blowflies. You had to push your way through a thicket of vegetables to reach the rotting door. Effie would tear off a furry aromatic tomato leaf to press to her nostrils like a pomander. What would it be like, she thought without envy, to live in a house with countless enormous rooms, where your bed chamber was as private and peaceful as a high branch on a tree? Once she'd seen Hester's – four times the size of the room where her family were presently drinking tea – and by now, of course, they'd have moved into the even larger White Room, dominated by an ancient four-poster, where the master and mistress always slept.

'Her young Ladyship expecting? That's right grand!'

Effie shivered a little. It was because she could hear herself so precisely echoed in her mother-in-law. The Delanceys talked like each other, too – though in a quite different way – but they often didn't mean what they said. For instance, when Hester had told her just now 'Forgive me, Effie', what she'd really meant was 'run along'. There'd been no real contrition. It had been painfully obvious that she couldn't wait for her to leave.

The Traffords possessed courtesy, too, but didn't hesitate to speak plainly. 'It's only natural, ain't it?' Stanley's father would say, glorying in the sight of the wonderfully juicy tomatoes and superbly bloated marrows that crowded his tiny garden. 'Only natural,' he'd repeat with a frown, as if puzzling over old Sir Michael's reaction when he'd explained why his vegetables were a lot more succulent than those grown up at the Abbey. The smell of raw human sewage hung around the cottage like a compelling but loathsome visitor.

'Not before time!' he commented cheerfully now, and then he and his wife started talking about what a shame it was the old master hadn't lived long enough to see this happy day.

Effie glanced at Stanley for his reaction, but he was staring into the fire. Another disadvantage at the cottage was that if they wanted to boil the kettle for tea – and when did they ever not? – they were compelled to keep a fire going, even in summer. But at least, thought Effie, looking on the bright side, there was always plenty of wood from the estate. It was a particularly warm June and Stanley was sweating a little and his sultry beauty moved Effie afresh.

'Does you know this, my love?' she asked softly.

He shook his head, still absorbed by the sight of the flickering flames, but she didn't believe him. He was Edmund's best friend so of course he'd been told about the baby. She was bewildered; mortified, too, that he hadn't let her in on it before she'd made a fool of herself.

Effie started mentally rewriting the afternoon from the beginning: herself selecting another dress, even if it was old and tatty, and then lingering on her way to the Abbey to pick a pretty posy of campions and cow parsley to give to her friend. Hester was the sort of girl more used to orchids and lilies, of course. Nevertheless, 'How nice!' she'd have said in her familiar lightly mocking way.

However, it was Effie's firm belief that actions from the heart never went unrecognized.

Chapter Eighteen

When he'd blown out the match, Joe told Laura as casually as he could manage, 'We're meant to be having a party.'

A moment before, the two of them had been lying in a long loose tangle like one of the skeins of wool her crazy old grandmother was always leaving around the Abbey. He'd felt languorous and happy after the lovemaking, all complications banished, registering only the faint breeze on his naked skin and his Barbour bunched up beneath his back, and the scent of apples from her soft hair. He'd been thinking – if he'd been contemplating anything at all – that this was the only way to make forbidden love: in a profoundly silent place, under a canopy of stars. But now he felt her body stiffen and draw away. He cursed himself and silently passed across the cigarette, watching the little red end of it glow in the darkness, thankful he couldn't see the expression in her eyes.

'Are you?' Laura asked after a moment, sounding utterly uninterested. She was thinking, '*Don't you realize we hear about everything from Lily? My parents and their friends have been talking about nothing but your fancy-dress ball for weeks!'* She wished that she *had* been kept in ignorance because even to know about these things felt like betraying him.

Joe made a miserable face because, despite the passion he felt for Laura, he was still a Trafford and couldn't bear to see his mother so worried and, besides, he was starting to get suspicious himself about what was going on.

Laura was thinking of the numerous phone calls her parents had been receiving lately, and the conversation between them at breakfast that very morning.

'Isn't it brilliant?' her mother had crowed, sounding like a spiteful child. 'If *we're* not going to be invited, none of them are accepting.'

'As if!' her father had exploded. All his children became a little afraid when he laughed in that particular way. 'As bloody if!'

'Oh I know!' her mother had admitted with an unpleasant-sounding laugh of her own. 'Them inviting us! Can you see it in a million years?'

'No!' her father had responded with that terrifying murderous amusement. 'Can you imagine us ever going?'

Joe was thinking of all the work his mother had put into the ball. First there'd been the ordering of the invitations. After trying and failing to get input from his father – always so wrapped up in his own affairs – she'd been forced to make decisions on her own. Then there were the caterers whose menus she was painstakingly pre-testing; the florist who'd been instructed to provide hundreds of pink roses with which to decorate the newly renovated Great Hall; the band that had been booked. Even Genevieve's costume had been bought. She would be the Snow Queen in a marvellous white dress, with a décolleté neckline to show off her best feature. *Haute couture*, his grandfather had bragged to Lily, though nobody French would have understood him either.

It was his grandfather who'd insisted there wasn't a person in the county who'd pass up an invitation to such a grand do. But, of course, the people on the guest list – those long-established families his parents seemed so anxious to get to know – were all good friends of the Delanceys. It had been typical of his granddad to blame his mum when not a single one of them accepted. According to him, it was she who'd brought this about, thus letting down the entire family.

'Dress to impress?' Joe had heard him rail, voice trembling with outrage and disbelief. 'You went and put "Dress to impress"?'

It had been amusing (in a painful kind of way) to listen to him banging on about etiquette in his funny old accent when he couldn't even pronounce the word right. And, true to form, he was as protective of Mark as ever. 'Don't you go bothering him,' he'd ordered Janice, as if she'd *want* to upset her husband.

'Yes,' Joe agreed. 'We're meant to be having a party.' He threw away the stub of cigarette and watched the tiny red dot plummet into a dark mass of undergrowth and vanish.

Until his brother's near-fatal accident, he'd had little interest in the feud. OK, many years ago, Laura's grandfather had sacked his, plunging the family into poverty. But on the other hand, without that harsh background, his father would never have made such a success of his life, as he'd readily admit. And though Joe would never have dared say so, part of him had appreciated why the Delanceys were so put out by the loss of their Abbey. Furthermore, hadn't his granddad made it crystal clear they'd come back for revenge? He'd watched the increasingly crazy antics, more amused than distressed and very thankful for his detachment.

Since Justin's accident, however, Joe had changed. He loved Laura but now heartily disliked the rest of her family. Their silence had been unforgiveable, and – as if that weren't enough – they were obviously intent on sabotaging his mother's party.

Laura was thinking: '*Of course, it was dreadful of them not to write and I know they're behaving badly now even though this party is almost certainly being held to pay them back. But it feels so weird not being able to talk to him about them. If only I could make him understand that they're just wounded and miserable . . .*'

The implacable hatred that divided their two families lay between them like a starting pistol. Once it was fired, there could be no going back. Whilst feeling ashamed of their parents' behaviour, they remained deeply protective of them. Their own relationship was too new and vulnerable to take risks with. If they wanted it to continue, they understood without conferring, they must behave like orphans.

It had occurred to Joe that perhaps this taboo added to the excitement, like the ever-present terror of being found out. There was no doubt that coming together had the force of lighting a flame, every time.

Fred said, while admiring two beautiful antique silver candelabra that cast a soft light over the company, 'Serve them right if nobody comes.'

She and Sam were dining with their great friends, the Harcourts, who lived in an exquisite Jacobean manor house called Haxton, set in the bowl of a valley. Rupert Harcourt came from a wealthy, long-established family, too, but – unlike Sam –

had been clever with money, using an inheritance to set up a classy wallpaper business, which had prospered. In front of his beautifully maintained home were parked three top-of-the-range cars: his own green Daimler; a neat little Toyota belonging to his wife, Sara; and a sporty MG, which had been a coming of age present for their son Archie.

'*Good for you!*' Sam had thought very positively as he set alongside his own ancient Volvo. Nice to see a mate doing so splendidly, he'd remarked to Fred. Even so, as she'd pulled her Indian shawl around her shoulders and adjusted the wilting peacock feather unearthed from a drawer, she'd found herself wishing for a moment that she could afford to buy beautiful fashionable clothes – even though Sara Harcourt, sleek in her Kenzo suit, had marvelled, 'You look sensational, Fred! How *do* you do it?' All very welcome, thought Fred, who was beginning to worry that her famous style was fraying at the seams.

Since moving to the Lodge, she and Sam felt increasingly under pressure to sing for their supper. Sometimes Fred wondered if the compulsion to be more and more amusing might even have exacerbated the feud with the Traffords. 'Do tell about the time you dumped a load of steaming manure in their drive,' their friends would urge, especially if strangers were present. And sometimes Sam would be inspired to invent some amusing new torment – only to feel duty bound to make it happen.

In pride of place on the Harcourts' mantelpiece was the invitation to the Traffords' costume ball.

'Even more cringe-making than that thing we got when they took possession of your Abbey,' said Sara, making a face because everyone knew that, whilst it was acceptable to send change of address notices, it certainly wasn't to deliver flamboyant moving-in cards, which – they'd all agreed – had been nothing more than a thinly veiled gloat.

Everything about the invitation had been mocked: its naff, glittery edging and the wording, of course, and the fact that it had been printed rather than embossed. 'Do you see this?' Sara had asked incredulously, indicating 'RSVP Janice', with the 'i' beneath a tiny circle instead of a dot.

Now they were on the subject of Genevieve.

'A lump by all accounts.'

'Total waste of money, if you ask me . . . Archie's seen her in the Lion and Unicorn . . . I can tell you she's not *interested* in meeting suitable men . . .'

'According to Lily, they've kitted her out in a hideously expensive "dress to impress".'

'A frock to shock?'

'Remember that bit from *Cold Comfort Farm*, when the gorgeous Starkadder girl makes her entrance at the ball?'

'Elfine.'

They'd all been brought up on this classic satire on the Mary Webb novels and Sam quoted to maximum effect: '"Lost is that man who sees a beautiful woman descending a noble staircase . . ."'

Rupert took over. '"Here was beauty! It silenced all comment except that of eager praise . . ."'

They laughed for a long time, thinking of beefy Genevieve Trafford, notorious for snogging bits of rough at the local pub, and Sam reflected that this was what friendship was about: picking up on the same references, enjoying the same sense of humour and, most crucial of all, trusting each other implicitly.

'I can't say we weren't tempted to go,' said Sara. 'The omnipresent pinkness . . . the spotlighting . . . It all sounds *so* over the top I'm quite longing to check it out for myself. Not to mention the "champagne and nibbles"!'

'Oh, it's every bit as bad as we've told you.' Sam made a gloomy face though he felt very content. He sipped his 1970 Chateau Monlot-Capet, which Rupert had served with ceremony. Thank goodness he and Fred weren't for ever cut off from drinking good wine. He'd savoured every mouthful of the crown of lamb, too, and the excellent smoked salmon that had preceded it. At times like this, he felt only lucky. He could see a box of expensive cigars laid out on the sideboard next to the port that would follow the raspberry pavlova, which looked delectable despite Sara's laughing confession that it wasn't her own work – 'I've just discovered this perfectly marvellous shop called Bejam's near the council estate' – and the truckle of fine stilton.

'Your turn to be thoroughly indulged, old boy,' Fred had told him earlier, promising to pilot them home. She'd pointed out that the last straw would be to get done for drinking and driving, which had happened to one of their friends a few weeks back.

'You didn't really consider accepting that invitation?' she said now, but she sounded strangely uncertain, even a trifle sharp.

'Sara's joking,' Rupert confirmed, touching Fred's arm for reassurance. 'We wouldn't dream of it. Besides . . . you know how I adored your Abbey as it was. Couldn't bear to see it ruined.' He shuddered. 'What dreadful vulgar people they are!'

Later, Fred was able to conjure up Sara's expression exactly: a strange mixture of irritation and caution. And she also remembered thinking for the first time, '*There are tensions between these good friends of ours that we really have no conception of . . .*'

'Didn't stop you from sending over some of your samples,' Sara observed tartly, as if quite unable to prevent herself.

'That was business,' Rupert corrected his wife, frowning, but he appeared suddenly uneasy.

Sam was looking at him now. It was clear that an explanation was expected.

'Lucinda asked me to.' Rupert smiled very charmingly. He had a wonderful even white smile. 'You know, the interior decorator they've hired? She's a mate.'

'And by the way,' said Sara with meaning, 'she is quite pretty, if you admire the Princess Di type.'

However Rupert continued very smoothly as if he'd not been interrupted. 'Of course, the Trafford woman hasn't taken a single one of her suggestions. Don't know why she bothered to hire Lucinda in the first place. It's all upset the poor girl dreadfully. Can you imagine having people thinking all that was *her* idea? Believe me, I was only trying to limit the damage . . .'

It was no good. Sam and Fred had already exchanged a glance that conveyed everything.

Nobody could have blamed Fred for exacting a small measure of revenge as she and Sara sat drinking coffee in the stylish drawing room decorated with Rupert's wallpaper, while they waited for their men to finish with port and cigars in the dining room.

'By the way, we're so sorry Archie didn't get into Oxford. Isn't it mean that we can't all be lucky?'

Once they were alone together, Janice said, 'I know we've spent thousands on the party so far, but it's not going to work out, Mark, and that's all there is to it.' Then she pulled her nightgown over her head as if trying to hide from his reaction.

She heard him say very sharply, 'Pardon?'

A moment before, he'd been sunk in his usual

preoccupations and operating on bedtime autopilot: emptying his pockets of change on to the big chest of drawers and arranging the coins in neat piles, setting out his Mont Blanc pen and his Dupont lighter, hanging up his expensive suit, checking the alarm was set for 6.30 a.m. and was in sync with his gold Rolex. But now he sat down on the four-poster bed in his black silk pyjamas, waiting for her explanation.

First she settled herself, trying to derive comfort and confidence from her crisp new Egyptian cotton sheets and pillowcases and the soft welcome of the excellent mattress that had replaced the Delanceys' ancient horsehair one. But it was no good. What was happening made her feel quite worthless, a non-person. 'I took such care with those cards, Mark, I assure you, but I might as well have flushed them down the toilet.' She winced as she thought of the letters of refusal: sent at the very last minute, when she'd assumed they were all coming. 'Mr and Mrs Rupert Harcourt regret they are unable to accept the kind invitation of Mr and Mrs Mark Trafford . . .' They had a cold and formal courtesy that seemed more like a slap in the face.

He was furious when he learnt the full story, though not with her. 'Shit!' he exploded, punching the mattress. He added contemptuously, as if he'd never shown the slightest interest in courting local society and had failed to see the business opportunities to be gained from living in this ancient, impressive place: 'Wouldn't have them in my house anyway!' And then, with passionate bitterness: 'I thought those bastards prided themselves on their manners!'

Janice said very tentatively, 'Mark, I've an idea. Listen to me, please, will you?'

'I'm listening,' he said, to her considerable surprise. But it was true that since Justin's accident the family had grown even closer.

'S'pose we ask our old friends instead?'

'Our old friends,' he echoed as if, until that moment, he'd forgotten all about them.

'I've missed them so,' she rushed on, and a tear came to her eye as she assembled more compelling reasons for persuasion. 'Most of it's paid for and they won't give refunds, Mark, believe me, I've tried. We've the band booked, and the caterers and the florist – and there's Genevieve's dress. This way, it won't all be wasted, like the shoot. It's not as if we haven't the space to put everyone up. They'd *like* a costume ball. And we could enjoy ourselves, for a change.'

If Stanley had been there, he might have vetoed her plea, come up with some new and cunning ploy to entice the Delanceys' friends to the party. As it was, Mark seemed to understand, for the first time, what sacrifices she'd made in moving to the Abbey.

'That's a grand idea, love,' he said. 'You do whatever makes you happy.' He kissed the top of her head tenderly. Then he pulled back and looked a little anxiously into her eyes as if, for the first time ever, he was unsure of her. 'You OK, Jan? You seem different, somehow.'

'Couldn't be better, darling.'

She decided then and there that one person they'd keep in ignorance about the *volte face* was Lily. She'd a good idea of the role the cleaner played. What a mixer! Let her think what she pleased; and if the festivities annoyed the Delanceys, all the better.

Chapter Nineteen

The evening of the ball was terrible. They'd been anticipating a show of solidarity from their friends, all of whom had sworn they'd refused the invitations, and seeing their beloved Abbey ostracized and their enemies publicly humiliated.

Instead, soon after eight o'clock, they heard a steady procession of cars speeding past the Lodge. They hung back, anxious to avoid the further mortification of being observed spying from their own windows, but couldn't help being aware of one masked and elaborately dressed-up set of guests after another. Once, Maria glimpsed a Bentley piloted by a Pierrot who could have been their friend Johnny Saunders (who owned just such a car). After that, the family tried to ignore what was happening, but it was impossible. When Fred rushed up to Laura's bedroom to get a good view of the Abbey, she saw it blasting light. It was shocking how vulgar that beautiful, ancient house now appeared. Every couple of minutes or so, the huge oak door was flung open to reveal a butler in tails and, through Sam's binoculars, she made out a man in a devil's suit being admitted, his tiny horns and forked tail black against a strangely fiery interior.

'They might just be having a few friends,' suggested Laura. The evening before, in their dark field, Joe had informed her very casually, before changing the subject, 'That party I told you about . . . it's only for people from where we lived before.' Had he guessed at the poisonous paranoia in the Lodge? And was he encouraging her to relay the truth to her parents? But how, she wondered miserably, did he think that would be possible without incriminating herself?

'Hired flunkeys?' her father barked. 'Caterers' vans? A band?' Just now, when he'd briefly flung open their front door, he'd been infuriated by the strains of light music drifting across the night. Laura wondered anxiously if hearing 'A Surrey With a Fringe on the Top', almost certainly performed in the venerable Great Hall, might lead to bloodshed.

'Well, they might not be anyone you know.'

But the Delanceys' experience the evening they'd dined with the Harcourts had planted fatal seeds of doubt. If they couldn't trust those good old friends to stay one hundred per cent loyal, who *could* they count on?

'And on what do you base that?' Sam sounded extraordinarily like his father.

'Well, I don't,' Laura agreed after a moment.

'Exactly. So shut up, please.'

'Now now!' said Fred, hair springing round her face in a frenzy of corkscrew curls. 'Supper will only be a minute.'

She'd taken even more trouble than usual with the meal – laying the table with old party lights and a pattern of faded blue azalea petals, creating something delicious and remarkable out of very little in an attempt to distract her family from what certainly appeared to be an act of mass betrayal.

'What's this?' Sam enquired, lighting a fresh cigarette from a stub and peering into the pan.

'Not pheasant,' she assured him. Since the Traffords had lost interest in their shoot, it was as if the birds were competing to get killed off by any other means. They rose squawking at the very last minute beneath booted feet and scuttled across lanes with fatal mistiming. It had taken the fun out of poaching and, besides, everyone was sick of the taste. She glanced at him anxiously as he went into a fit of coughing. 'I don't like the sound of that, darling. I wish you'd cut down.'

He was momentarily cheered as he realized what was for supper. 'Breet sweds, if I'm not mistaken! *What* a feast!'

'Done with tomato and garlic and butter. I've made roast parsnips, too, and – oh joy! – sorrel. Did I tell you I've discovered a bush of wild sorrel?'

'What have I done to deserve such a wife?'

'Sweetbreads again?' Maria queried a little nervously as they sat down to eat. 'What part is that, anyway?'

'Nothing wrong with the pancreas,' Sam informed her, his temper returning. 'Very important organ, as you'd soon realize if yours stopped functioning.'

'We ate sweetbreads in the war,' Hester observed in her chatty refined way. 'I believe Parker used to bake them in the oven – and very delicious they were, too. Oh, we kept her on all through that ghastly time. *What* a good cook she was!'

'Parker,' Sam intoned in a bored testy voice. 'Interesting how our memories differ. I remember Parker being an appalling cook. The food was always cold and overdone and she didn't know how to make proper gravy or custard. *And* she had a moustache.' He paused with a little frown, as if he'd missed a trick. 'I thought you enjoyed the war, Mama.'

But Hester wasn't listening. 'We held a big party at the Abbey once,' she said with a smile of fond reminiscence, oblivious to Fred's fierce glare. 'I wasn't sure at first, but it was all *such* fun! Different, certainly . . .' For a second, she seemed to bask in her old mocking intelligence. Then her expression changed, becoming first wary, then shut off. It was as if she'd been made aware of the tragedy of awakening a marvellous memory, only to watch it break up and become meaningless.

One of the remarkable qualities of the Abbey was its ability to change. Chilly and frightening one minute, it could become wonderfully seductive the next. That evening, flickering with candlelight (Janice's idea) and resonating with music, it gave an unforgettable welcome to a whole host of guests in splendid fancy dress, with their grown-up children in tow. It smelt delicious, too, of the roasted baron of beef that would be served up in the Refectory. Mickey Mouse had come along and Miss Piggy and Kermit the Frog and a Godfather and at least three mermaids and one red indian and a couple of cowboys. After a lot of thought, Stanley had dressed up as one of his heroes, Admiral Nelson. Justin, on crutches and thoroughly spoilt by everyone, was Long John Silver, while Mark and Janice had opted to be Anthony and Cleopatra.

It was only recently that they'd occupied the same rung of the ladder as these old friends of theirs: all of them successful, though none multi-millionaires. Had they striven harder or simply been luckier? However, even as Janice pondered this, she understood that Mark's experience had given him a savagery of purpose, a fiercely guarded autonomy possessed by none of their former circle. She saw his reaction when their friend Stuart Walters announced he'd become a name at Lloyds. The great advantage, said Stuart, very earnest in a scaly green dragon's outfit, was that you could make your money work for you twice over (whereas Janice knew it was engrained in Mark that nothing ever came for free). However, the news caused a ripple of interest among the rest of the company, especially when Stuart suggested that joining this ancient and distinguished institution was more of a status symbol than all the possessions money could buy. Now was the time to do it, he urged, flicking his tail casually over one arm, because they were relaxing the rules – 'But get in quick, before the rush!' At the interviews, he said, you were warned of unlimited liability with a quip about the possibility of losing the buttons off your shirt. He laughed heartily because it was only a formality.

Anxious to avoid local gossip about her party, Janice had selected caterers from a different county. They'd brought along dozens of young waiters and waitresses to weave in and out of the throng serving champagne and delicious canapés. A four-piece band played softly in the background – lovely old tunes like 'Start Spreading the News' and 'Chicago' – and when Genevieve made her entrance in her beautiful white dress, there was quiet approval for the girl everyone remembered as a proper tomboy.

'Don't she look the picture?' Stanley kept demanding.

The guests were bowled over by the Abbey. It was spectacular, they kept repeating. They made light of the drawbacks, such as the enormous size of the place, with jokes about laying trails of breadcrumbs for themselves like Hansel and Gretel. But, in the privacy of their rooms, which had been provided with wonderfully comfortable beds, they murmured about cleaning help and the astronomical heating bill. No en suites had yet been installed, so they were obliged to brave freezing corridors and share bathrooms shockingly lacking, as yet, in mod cons. Still, they had a good laugh at rusty hollow cylinders that served as plugs and strange slatted wooden trays for soap and sponges that fitted over the baths. They could see that the builders had a way to go, but imagined the Abbey would always retain a certain creepiness, what with its shadowy corners and sudden secret staircases. For all its impressive old-fashioned staginess, they decided their friends' new house was somewhere to enjoy visiting rather than covet.

For once, Janice could be knowledgeable. However, she was brought up short when asked, 'But if Henry VIII was into doing away with the monasteries, how come your Abbey survived?'

'I'll find out for next time,' she promised, already impatient.

She thought of Guildford and the life she'd believed she was in mourning for. But, while delighted to see all her old friends, she felt strangely disconnected, even critical in a quite new way. '*Was I like that?*' she caught herself wondering as Susie Walker enthused about spotting Joan Collins dining at the Post Office Tower.

She and Mark had come to live in a place utterly unlike any of their friends' comfortable, well-equipped houses – and only now was she beginning to appreciate who might have the advantage.

Laura had expressed alarm about Joe meeting other girls at the party, even though he'd assured her this was crazy. In the end, he'd come up with a plan to soothe her.

'You've a good view from your window, right?'

She nodded with a rueful smile. 'You know I have!'

He made a face. 'I'll find a room where I can see you and you can see me . . .'

'OK.'

'. . . and at nine on the dot . . .'

He'd been impatiently consulting his watch for an hour now. There'd been many admiring glances cast his way, but he was oblivious. He'd already ascertained which of the Abbey's many guest rooms was suitable and now he stole in there, picking his way through a clutter of visiting suitcases, inhaling the trace of a parting squirt of Je Reviens.

He leant on the wide stone sill, thankful to be alone. A slight breeze cooled his hot cheeks and the expanse of dark lawn stretched away beneath him. The Lodge looked very small and neglected in the distance, with only one light on, and a frail pipe of smoke issued from a chimney.

Music and talk and laughter floated up from below but he felt very separate, as if all those friends from the past meant nothing to him now. He was confident yet impatient, strangely anxious yet so filled with happiness that he almost wanted to be sick. It was two minutes to nine. He recrossed the room and flicked on the old ridged, brass light switch by the door. Then he stood a little self-consciously in the only costume he'd known would be right for this party, even though it had scared him a little to put it on. To his amazement, his mother had been able to advise on detail. He reflected, '*I must look a right prat,*' because Laura had only ever seen him in jeans.

As soon as she saw the Abbey window lit up – with a monk in a white habit and a black scapular standing very still in the centre, staring at her from under his cowl – Laura, who'd been waiting, switched on her light, too. The moment seemed very symbolic: a Trafford in the Abbey, dressed as Father Dominic, its most famous ghost, a Delancey in the Lodge – the two of them exchanging a secret love message across the divide.

She thought of her parents downstairs, picking at their anger and misery, exacerbating them. The truth was, she'd come to understand, with great sadness, her father *needed* to blame someone as a way of diverting attention from his own failures. And, anxious not to damage their relationship, her mother went along with it, not appreciating that it might be far kinder in the long run to be tough.

She wished it was possible to confide all this to Joe without feeling disloyal. They weren't going to be able to avoid discussion of the feud for much longer.

For Sam and Fred, seeing the Abbey lit up for the party was like watching a film of the life they'd previously taken for granted. Once, they'd entertained lavishly, too: with annual fixtures like a huge drinks bash at Christmas and an elaborate egg hunt for their friends' children in the gardens at Easter. For Sam, this over-the-top hospitality had been a reaction to an upbringing where, despite the presence of great wealth, the re-using of envelopes and string was encouraged as a virtue. He'd never learnt to live within his means.

He and Fred were so paranoid by now that they imagined they could hear in the distance faint roars of laughter at their expense. Thank God they had each other! No one else understood the depth of the humiliation and the terrifying, escalating rage. They felt so upset and angry, they could scarcely breathe. It was like madness. For the first time in their lives, they could understand real violence. And to make things worse, Lily was sure to drop in over the next few days to leak hurtful details, like measuring out poison.

Sam tossed back his drink, winced, and said, sounding very casual, 'You know, it has crossed my mind to take out a contract on them.'

It was just a few weeks back that, filled with remorse for her vicious thoughts and secretly terrified they'd had an effect, Fred had slipped into the local church to offer up a prayer for Justin Trafford's full recovery – '*Let him live and be exactly as before. And . . . I swear I'll be magnanimous even if he gets to Cambridge and David doesn't.*' Yet now she appeared only faintly taken aback. 'You mean, the whole family?'

'Well, perhaps just Mark. It doesn't cost that much, apparently. Happens all the time.'

'Really?' She sounded quite interested. Then she seemed to gather up the shreds of decorum. 'You can't be serious, darling!'

There was a pause before he agreed, a little reluctantly, 'Not really.' He lit another cigarette. 'Anyway, who's going to lend us the money?'

'I think,' said Fred after a long pause, 'that we're letting them win even to be discussing such a thing.'

They'd laid a fire mostly for comfort because the meagre fireplace gave out little heat. But having lived at the Abbey for so many years, they were used to a cold house. Of all the dreadful changes the Traffords had inflicted on their beloved former home, it was the installation of central heating that offended most. When they'd owned the Abbey, it had been like a badge of honour to endure the icy winters with only layers of moth-eaten clothes and log fires and old china hot water bottles. They saw it as nothing but cheating on the part of the Traffords to expect constant warmth.

Because they couldn't afford wine, they were drinking cider that had for decades been made by an apple farmer living nearby. It was very sour but cheap and potent and better than nothing. They listened to the wind moaning in the narrow chimney and thought of the revelry going on a few hundred yards away.

'I know I've always promised I'd get the Abbey back for you . . .' Sam began.

'Oh darling!' Fred sounded distressed.

'I'm beginning to doubt it now.' His voice broke a little. It was such a shaming admission.

'I'm not!' she told him very staunchly, willing him to recover himself. It was strange, she reflected, how none of their friends guessed what lay beneath his urbane exterior. To them, the feud was, at best, a source of amusement at dinner parties; at worst, a bit of a bore. Sam and Fred never told it like it was – mostly because socializing remained a great comfort.

'No man could ask for a better wife,' he went on. 'But I've let you down dreadfully. I plainly haven't got it – whatever *it* is. I mean, look at him!' He gestured angrily in the direction of the Abbey and its new owner. 'He came from nothing, as I should know – the very dregs of the pit. Him and his unspeakably ghastly father. Whereas I . . .' He shrugged helplessly. 'Look at all the advantages *I* was given.'

He was right, thought Fred. However, she replied very positively, 'Stop it! What about your thriller? The bits you've let me read are brilliant.'

'But you know I'll never finish it,' he complained a little bitterly, almost as if he blamed her for understanding him too well.

'Who says?'

'It's like all my ideas.'

Fred smiled at him but said nothing. '*You could get a job!*' she thought. Their tiny savings were almost spent now, and she was terrified for the future. Trying to lessen the sense of disloyalty, she wondered, '*Perhaps I should get a job, too — now the children are grown up.*' But, unfortunately, neither of them was in possession of marketable skills. Sam had been expected only to run his father's estate, which he'd done badly, when finally given the chance, and she'd been brought up to marry a rich man. A further problem was that, for all his rapidly declining sense of self-worth, Sam would never consider getting a menial job for fear it would compromise his only residual asset, which was his background. Despite her frustration, she felt similarly trapped. '*I suppose I could always start cooking for other people's dinner parties,*' she thought dismally, because that was just about acceptable for women like her. So was designing other people's houses and gardens. It was because the work was obtained through personal contacts so that, despite money changing hands, both sides could somehow pass it off as a favour. 'You *are* clever!' the employer might say. 'I can never make up my mind!' Or 'Can't *think* why I never learnt to cook properly!'

And what could Sam do if he refused to consider working for someone else? '*Well,*' thought Fred, '*he could always take up carpentry.*' It was acceptable for men like him to make beautiful furniture. However, an apprenticeship would certainly be required. And where would the money for that come from?

'I tell you, Fred, I'm no good. I can't provide for you properly. I'm pretty useless, all things considered . . .' Then he stopped abruptly. Something had happened — or, more accurately, failed to — in bed the previous night. It had been most upsetting. She'd not commented, of course. They'd not discussed it at all even though she'd heard him mutter, 'Fuck!' as if it were the absolute last straw.

'Now, listen to me, Sam,' she said fiercely. 'I don't care about having things. You know I don't.'

'You should,' he said bleakly. 'You deserve a better life. So do the children.'

'You know what sort of upbringing I had,' she went on.

'Plenty of money,' he pointed out, making a pained face.

'And a father who screwed everything that moved!'

Sam blinked because she was usually quite sanguine about her father's philandering.

'I saw the misery it inflicted on my mother.' Her eyes glistened with sudden emotion. 'You've given me absolute fidelity and loyalty, which is the greatest gift one person can bestow upon another. And if you think I'd rather be rich, Sam Delancey . . . Well, you're out of your mind!' She paused. 'At least *we've* given our children a happy childhood.'

He didn't even need to consider this. They were far closer, as a family, than he'd ever been with his own parents. There were jokes and discussions, certainly a lot more affection. They were still beaming fondly at each other when Hester burst in, back from one of her nocturnal rambles. Her face was ashen. She gasped for breath.

'Where am I?'

Sam frowned though he made an effort. 'You're with us, Mama, Fred and me.' He added with meaning, 'In the Lodge.'

'Go and check your message board,' Fred suggested in the same kindly, firm manner. That morning, after inscribing the correct date and the usual reminder about the Abbey, she'd appended, 'I had a boiled egg for breakfast. I am very proud of my grandson, David, who has just got into Cambridge.'

'I saw him at the window!' Her voice rose to a shriek and a dry leaf drifted gently off her tweed skirt to the floor. 'We were always seeing shadows, but that's all it was. Shadows . . .' A gnarled old hand fluttered over her heart; she shook her head, seemingly very afraid. 'That cruel old man, that hypocrite . . . He didn't love beauty!'

'Sorry, Mama, we're not with you.'

This time, the sound of his voice seemed to bring Hester up short. 'Where's Edmund?' she faltered, eyelids fluttering in panic.

'Papa died ten years ago now,' Sam told her, making his voice compassionate.

'Oh,' said Hester in much the same uninterested tone as she'd reacted a few weeks before when informed on her message board that Boris Becker was the new Wimbledon champion.

When she'd stumped up the stairs to her bedroom, Fred asked, 'Was she talking about the ghost?'

Sam shrugged as if it were immaterial.

'She's getting worse.'

'Yes,' he agreed helplessly. Hester was still breaking into the Abbey and inflicting damage on the Traffords' property, which didn't exactly displease him and Fred. But how would they manage if she became dangerously out of control? 'Remember my mama as she *used* to be?' He shook his head because the comparison between the two Hesters was so tragic.

'I've never understood why that marriage was quite so bad,' said Fred, returning to a favourite conversation like picking up a piece of knitting. It was one of the great comforts of marriage, she thought, being able to gossip like this without fear of boring each other. 'They had separate rooms for years, didn't they?'

'Well, he was depressed.' Sam added lightly, making a joke of it, 'The family curse.'

'I know that, darling,' she agreed. 'But why did she go on with it?'

Sam shrugged because people from his parents' generation and background hadn't believed in divorce and, besides, he'd always understood that *he* was the main reason why his mother had stayed married to his father.

'All the same . . .' said Fred, frowning. She was remembering Edmund's almost perverse refusal to find joy in anything – even the grandchildren who'd confirmed the survival of the dynasty, knotting it into place. It brought tears to her eyes to imagine how it must have been for Sam to grow up in that gloom and stifling atmosphere. Why had Hester shown such equanimity for the silent mealtimes, the terrifying bursts of rage? It was almost as if she were atoning to Edmund for some unmentionable transgression. She'd adored the Abbey, of course, and made it her life. But even so, thought Fred. Even so . . .

She concluded briskly, '*I* wouldn't have put up with it!'

'You're different,' Sam told her fondly. He added, 'We both are, thank God.'

Chapter Twenty

In her diary, in the space for 14 November 1945, Hester recorded in her beautiful handwriting: 'Appearance of Samuel Hadley.' And after that, as an elegant aside: 'Wd have appreciated a touch more gas.' It was her only nod to the ordeal of labour, which had lasted for more than forty-eight hours.

'Funny little prune,' was Edmund's reaction on first sight of the baby.

'Isn't he just?' Hester looked very wan, he noticed with a pang, though it seemed nothing could affect her composure. She touched the crib parked by the four-poster where she reclined. It was like an ornate wicker pram without wheels and thirty years before, Edmund had lain in there, too.

After intently studying the baby's minute wrinkled features for a few moments, Edmund pronounced very decisively, 'Looks like Horatio.'

'Do you think so?' She glanced at him, then frowned thoughtfully. Perhaps she was trying to summon up the features of this eighteenth century slave-trader ancestor whose portrait hung downstairs in the Refectory, and of whom Edmund never failed to point out: 'He cared a very great deal about his men.'

'I do indeed . . . Something about the chin . . .'

'You may be right,' Hester agreed in her detached fashion.

'Splendid!' He went on staring down at the baby. 'Does he always caterwaul like that?'

'Seems to,' said Hester – even though Samuel Hadley had only that second started to mew very faintly – and she signalled to Edmund's old nanny, waiting tactfully by the door, to remove him to his own little bedroom (Edmund's childhood one) where he would be bottle-fed with Cow & Gate every four hours on the dot. 'Thank you, Narnie,' she said graciously, using the nickname Edmund had conferred a quarter of a century before.

'Yes, thank you, Narnie,' Edmund echoed fervently, as if the old nanny had agreed to come out of retirement and look after Samuel for nothing.

When they'd gone, he asked very solicitously, 'Are you up to visits, darling?' He noticed that Hester was in the antique cream lace bed jacket all the Delancey women traditionally wore after their confinements, which looked very pressed and starched but was getting quite threadbare now.

She said, 'Depends.'

The fire crackled noisily in the grate, as Edmund informed her, 'There's a whole queue of eager chums waiting to see you. Miranda Askew's telephoned . . .'

'Love to see Miranda.'

'So has Clarissa . . .'

'How nice,' said Hester with a smile.

'Good, good!' Edmund rubbed his hands together at this sign of improvement. 'And dear little Effie's been popping in and out ever since you . . .' His voice trailed away because he'd never been any good at facing mess or pain and hated to think of Hes suffering. After a moment he went on, 'She seemed most anxious to . . .' He paused, as if searching for the right anodyne phrase. 'Hold your hand when you . . . but I didn't think . . .'

'No,' she agreed with a faint smile and Edmund reflected that, in force of character, she was much like his own mother, which was one of the reasons he'd married her.

'She's downstairs now,' he went on, picturing Effie in the freezing Great Hall in her familiar old blue wool coat, eyes shining with excitement, breath like white smoke, a strange bunch of dark leaves (a home-made winter bouquet?) by her side. She'd been there, on and off, for hours. It occurred to him only now that she was probably hungry as well as cold. He should have thought of it, he told himself guiltily – asked for a fire to be lit, got Parker to rustle up something from the kitchen. He wouldn't have shown such insensitivity a few months back, he acknowledged a little uncomfortably, but since taking over his inheritance, he'd been very preoccupied.

Not that Effie had seemed fazed. 'We're right thrilled for the both of you,' she'd told him with a catch in her husky voice. 'I says to Stanley, now Samuel Hadley and Mark can look out for each other just like you and Edmund always done.' He'd pressed her shoulder at that, as if overcome by strong emotion.

'Has she the boy with her?' Hester asked him.

'Of course!' For when did Effie not have her beloved son by her side? They were inseparable. Even so, he'd have thought someone could have cared for him at the cottage. Perhaps, during her brief absences, Effie had been trying to arrange that – though, of course, everyone was still so busy trying to put the Abbey to rights.

Mark had been misbehaving last time Edmund had been down. He'd heard Effie murmur, 'Hush, my love. This is important, see?' and Mark immediately ask why. His nose had been pink with cold, he'd noticed. He was making an odd whooping noise, too, which was amplified in that echoing place, and he kept pulling his hat and gloves off, though Effie would patiently fit them back on.

'Perhaps not, then,' said Hester after a moment.

'Not?' Edmund echoed, like picking up a thread. Possibly he was admonishing Hester for her lack of consideration for Effie who, alone among their friends, had stood such faithful guard; or simply saying he understood her wish to be alone. She was certainly exhausted, he reminded himself, and hardly up to the company of a rumbustious child. 'Perhaps later?' he suggested.

'Perhaps.' Then Hester closed her eyes and sighed and, after bestowing a tender kiss on her forehead, Edmund crept out, leaving her to her own reflections on new parenthood in the ancient, stately peace of the White Room.

Soothing her fractious son as she waited patiently in the Great Hall, Effie was oblivious to cold or hunger. She wore a dreamy little smile. She was reliving the most extraordinary night of her life, where it had happened, four months before.

The journey from the little cottage to the Abbey for the Victory Ball seemed very symbolic. Emerging from a pitch dark rutted track, hand in hand, she and Stanley saw the vast shape of the house loom up, defined by soft light. All around them, huddles of figures were converging from the shadows. They heard someone exclaim in a panic, 'Blackout!' before a gale of laughter erupted because, of course, the air raids had finished and there was no longer any need to seal doors and windows. Effie recognized the local butcher, Charlie Symes, and his wife, Florrie, weaving their way through the ranks of smart cars parked in the drive and reflected that rationing was not going to go away for some time yet and neither was queuing. It seemed Charlie had been unusually generous with his sausages – 'I hear some cats and dogs went missing,' Stanley had commented with sinister meaning. As Effie herself had merrily suggested, they could always pretend they were eating that caviar stuff instead of spam or sandwiches made out of guava jam, or whatever other strange food surpluses came their way. Only the spirit of the gathering mattered and it was wonderful, in a sense, to be reminded of the sacrifices that had been so unifying: of the six long years of terror and loss and hardship that had broken down the class system that had previously divided the county as rigidly as the hedges criss-crossing the fields.

She felt about to burst with happiness as she and Stanley walked through the big oak door of the Abbey alongside Edmund and Hester's grand friends, like a prince with his princess. They could hear music – the soar of a trumpet, the scream of a fiddle and the whispering clatter of drums.

'That's the Rhythm Rousers!' Stanley announced excitedly. He looked round as if checking he was being properly listened to before demanding, 'Weren't I on at Edmund to grab that band?'

She heard her new shoes clack on the flagstones like applause – the hinged wooden clogs Stanley had brought back from London, assuring her they were *à la mode* (a phrase he'd picked up in France), though it seemed that tonight, with so many elegant women present, she was alone in her choice of footwear.

The party was entirely lit by dozens of white candles burning
in saucers, and it baffled Effie. Why use them when, with the
flick of a switch, you could magically illuminate each room? She
and her family were dependent on candles, and she never
stopped scraping up the wax that spilt and hardened, clogging
the ragged old rugs. She dreamt about electricity, sometimes.
Fancy being freed from the nightly terror of burning to death
in your bed if you forgot to extinguish a wick properly!

However, she was forced to acknowledge that the soft
flickering light did a grand job of masking the damage that had
been inflicted. Since there were no flowers, a garland of cabbage
leaves adorned the huge white marble mantelpiece in the Great
Hall and, for once, she didn't mourn the shocking scratches and
chips, the burn marks from carelessly abandoned cigarettes.
Someone had put a lot of thought into dressing up the Abbey.
Hester, for sure, thought Effie affectionately. People always
remarked on her style.

Guests stood in knots and Effie couldn't help noticing that
Edmund and Hester's friends seemed to be sticking with each
other, the men in dinner jackets and black ties. But, then, the
estate workers and shopfolk were also keeping to tight clusters
of their own.

'Wait till they gets stuck into the cider,' Stanley murmured in
her ear laughing, and she thought how much she'd loved
watching him help plan the party. It had taken his mind off the
worry about finding suitable work.

And then Edmund strode across in a dress suit, which was
obviously old though nicely cut like all his clothes. He was
rubbing his hands together and beaming. 'Effie! Stanley! How
wonderful! Isn't this all splendid?'

'Edmund,' Stanley responded in his deep voice. He kept his

hands in the pockets of the same suit he'd worn that time at the White Lion Hotel, when he'd taken Effie to meet his very best friend – and Hester, of course. His dark brooding looks only seemed to improve with time and the war had left him very lean and fit. '*And I'm all washed out*,' thought Effie, thinking a little sadly of what feeding Mark for all those months had done to her breasts. But at least *he'd* filled out like a stuffed toy. The lipstick she'd treated herself to hadn't worked either, though the shade was meant to adapt to a girl's natural colouring.

'You look a right tart, my love,' Stanley had told her fondly as they left the cottage. She was glad, really, when he'd kissed the orange stuff off, seizing the chance of being alone together even if she was wearing her best dress and it meant arriving late.

'Have you seen my darling wife?' Edmund asked them and Effie glanced at Stanley before nodding shyly, as if Hester had just greeted them in the same friendly and welcoming way.

She'd spotted her the moment they entered. She was facing them in a pale flowing dress, talking to the Forsters, who owned a neighbouring estate. Effie had smiled and raised a tentative hand, but Hester appeared oblivious. Another moment and she'd turned away.

'*Never mind*,' Effie told herself. '*I can see her any time*.'

'Effie?' She emerged from her reverie to find Edmund standing before her, smiling a little awkwardly. 'So sorry, fair one,' he said. 'Hes isn't really up to seeing people yet.'

Immediately Effie was alarmed. Was this more than the exhaustion of childbirth?

'Whacked,' Edmund explained with a helpless shrug.

Effie felt momentarily relieved. She beamed sympathy, hoping to convey the message that she knew all about long labours and, even if she couldn't see her, was Hester's sister in spirit. 'Don't you fret,' she assured him. 'She'll be right as rain come the morning.'

'Of course,' Edmund agreed very positively. 'Look, you mustn't sit around here any longer. I'm sure you have things to do. Besides, that little chap of yours must be peckish.' He frowned. 'Time to take him home,' he added, quite briskly, as Mark coughed, the sound resonating round the room.

But Effie hesitated. She wanted to make quite sure that, after the apparent success of her spell, Hester's baby was in perfect order; you could never be one hundred per cent sure where witchcraft was concerned. 'Is he – just as he should be?' she asked tentatively.

'Samuel?' Edmund appeared to ponder the question seriously for a moment.

'Edmund!' Effie chided gently, for she knew how he loved to tease. 'Has he – all his bits?' She bit her lip, prompted shyly, 'Fingers and toes . . . ?'

Edmund smiled. 'Ten of each at the last count. Is that the correct amount? As a matter of fact,' he went on, sounding very pleased with himself, 'he's perfect!'

No cloven hooves or harelips, then. 'That's grand,' Effie pronounced contentedly. She picked up her drooping bouquet of leaves then laid it down again. She'd been longing to see the baby but now she knew he was truly all right, a great burden had been taken off her. She assured Edmund so he wouldn't feel guilty for her long and pointless wait, 'Don't you fret, I've a picture of him in my head.'

'If it's a cross between Winston and a baked potato,' said Edmund with a poker face, 'you're getting warm.'

'Edmund!' She whacked him gently with the leaves because

they were all limp and useless now, and Mark looked delighted. He tried to grab the bunch so he could hit Edmund, too, and, laughing, she had to restrain him.

'Actually,' said Edmund, turning serious, looking at a point above her head as if conjuring up the memory, 'we're both agreed he looks awfully like my great-great-grandfather, which is nice.' He went on, 'I'll get a message to you if Hester feels up to it tomorrow, I promise.'

When he'd gone, Effie's mother-in-law, Annie, scuttled in clutching a big bunch of silver cutlery and a polishing cloth, complaining about her painful legs, as usual. She'd been a guest at the Victory Ball, too, but had now been enlisted in clearing up the Abbey. Soon the repainting would start, the estate staff had been told, when layers of whitewash would obliterate the chocolate-brown gloss of the wartime convalescent home.

'About time, too.' Annie sounded very indignant as she watched Effie gather up Mark in her arms. 'That poor mite's had more than enough. He'll be starved as well as cold.' Then, as Mark let out another ringing whoop, she declared, 'That's the croup, if I'm not mistook. Needs his little head setting under a towel over some Friar's Balsam and hot water.'

'Poor Hester,' said Effie.

Stanley's mother sniffed noisily, as if making a point. 'Nothing wrong with Her Ladyship,' she informed her daughter-in-law. 'She'm preparing for visitors. She've only this minute asked Mrs Parker to send up a tray of tea to her room.'

Effie stared at her, dumbfounded. The very next moment, they heard the wheels of a car crunching the gravel outside, then confident voices. And after that, Edmund and Hester's friends Simon and Miranda Askew strode through the front door with big smiles on their faces, bearing a bottle wrapped in newspaper. Edmund had introduced them to her and Stanley at the party. But they couldn't have remembered. They swept past Effie and her mother-in-law as if wearing blinkers. They must have thought they were servants.

'*She knew I were set on seeing her baby,*' thought Effie sadly on the lonely walk home, trundling Mark's pushchair across the frosty ground. Hester was not an effusive person, or even a particularly thoughtful one, but it was now obvious to Effie that she and Stanley had done something very serious to offend her. What was more, she thought, this mysterious something could only have happened at the Victory Ball.

Hester surely couldn't be angry because Stanley, all tanked up on cider, had taken it on himself to make a speech? It had been a lovely thing to do, thought Effie, smiling at the memory.

After supper, Stanley leapt on a chair and hushed everyone, becoming quite stroppy when the laughter and talking didn't stop immediately.

'My friend Edmund don't entertain over much,' he began, gently mocking Edmund's parsimony. But he said lovely things, too: that Edmund was the kindest and best of men and, now the war was over, he was going to be the finest master the Abbey had ever seen. Stanley added that the whole Delancey family had made them both 'wonderful welcome', as he put it. 'My queen', he called her in front of all those grand folk – and Effie almost burst with pride. She caught sight of Edmund, head down as he listened, and knew he was moved from the familiar way he twitched at his cuffs and tie. Hester was studying the floor, too, but – because her bump got in the way – gave the impression that that was the real focus of her attention. Stanley ended with a rousing 'Hip hip hooray!' and then he called on everyone to sing 'For He's a Jolly Good Fellow' and – like conspirators – the Rhythm Rousers struck up the tune and, after an initial shyness, people joined in.

It couldn't have been that, thought Effie, as she tried to work out what they'd done to upset Hester. The party Stanley had helped organize had been a huge success, all the servants had told them afterwards. It was odd how, in retrospect, it seemed to her that she and Stanley and the estate workers and shop people had been outnumbered by the Delanceys' other friends, though this hadn't in reality been so. Then she remembered that, at one point in the evening, Hester herself had acted most strange. And that had certainly had nothing to do with them.

The Rhythm Rousers were a triumph, playing numbers like 'Goodbye Sally' and 'Run Rabbit Run' which they'd all listened to on the wireless in the darkest of times. And then they struck up with 'You Were Never Lovelier' and Effie whispered to Stanley, 'Let's!' even though nobody else had taken to the floor. It was because she'd danced to the tune with the recovering soldiers, music crackling from the old gramophone at the Abbey that needed rewinding every time. It had been a surefire way of getting them exercised because none ever refused her. 'You were never lovelier,' they'd croon meaningfully into her ear, trying to pull her closer – even Rupert, the dark and handsome one blinded by shrapnel, who'd never again be able to judge if a girl was beautiful or plain.

However, the minute she and Stanley moved into each other's arms, Hester marched over to the bandleader. 'I'm not having that tune!' they all heard her say with extraordinary passion. Even so, the band took a bit of time coming to a halt because the music had such a lovely swing to it and the bandleader – Eddie Saunders, who was the village baker by day – didn't understand because it was normally such a favourite.

'Hes?' Edmund asked, seemingly as puzzled as everyone else.

It was awkward for a moment or two, but then Hester seemed to pull herself together and laughed in her familiar cool way – as if laughing at herself, really – and everyone joined in because they were celebrating the end of the war and weren't pregnant women entitled to be difficult?

'What were that about, my love?' Effie whispered in Stanley's ear.

But he shrugged as if he'd no idea either, his black eyes quite blank.

Hester had been fearful, Effie concluded, trying to pretend that the unaccountable coldness hadn't been building for months. It was only natural, she told herself, for an expectant mother.

But that failed to explain why Hester didn't want to see her now Samuel Hadley was safely arrived. She'd been looking forward to seeing Hester with her baby: watching that most determinedly unmaternal person soften and surrender to love, like everyone else. She could never confront Hester about her coldness, of course. She'd slide away in the same way Edmund did. She'd likely become still icier if something specific was said, make Effie feel even more of a fool. For once, Effie blessed her own family's noisy uncomplicated intimacy.

Then Mark woke up and started wailing like a baby and she stopped worrying about Hester. Giving her son her full attention for the first time, she saw that he was very pale and his nose was bunged up. His head felt hot, too. What did anything matter, compared with his well-being? She'd take her mother-in-law's advice and get him fixed up with some Friar's Balsam and then she'd sing him to sleep.

She decided not to tell Stanley about Hester's snub. His mood was bad enough as it was. He hated the dullness of civilian life, he said often. For the time being, since no wonderful job had materialized, he was reluctantly helping his father in the gardens once more. It was better than moping, thought Effie, and he seemed to have inherited the talent, though she was careful not to point this out. And at least his friendship with Edmund was as strong as ever. Only yesterday, the two of them had spent the afternoon out shooting rabbits. For once, he'd come home relaxed and happy, slung with the makings of a fine supper.

Then she forgot about all these preoccupations because there was Stanley, yelling from the gate of the cottage as if he'd been waiting for her.

'Go back! Go back! Father's been in an accident!' He could hardly get the words out, he was in such a state. It seemed the tractor had tipped over in the woods when the Abbey's supply of logs was being replenished. His father's right leg had been crushed. It was a mercy the gamekeeper had heard his cries.

Stanley seemed not to notice the yelling, miserable little boy. 'Tell Edmund to phone for the doctor. Run, Effie! Run!'

Chapter Twenty-one

Janice was in the Refectory setting the table for her family's evening meal while, outside, a scarlet sun sinking into purple hills caused the window panes to sparkle and glow as intensely as if the Abbey was going up in flames, which so easily could have been its fate more than four centuries before. As usual, the air was very still, clotted with disquieting emotion.

A guest at their recent party, an unimaginative insurance salesman who'd kitted himself out as King Arthur with a paper crown and a plastic Excalibur sword, had claimed to have suddenly awoken in the early hours to find a tall gaunt figure staring down at him, its pallid face partly obscured, its eyes glittering. At first, he'd thought it might be Joe, still in costume and playing a joke. Then, terrified by the malevolence he sensed, he roused his wife (whose Queen Guinevere costume lay folded over a chair). Though the apparition vanished before she could act as witness, neither of them got any more sleep. 'I know what I saw,' he kept repeating at breakfast the next morning, looking very pale.

'I believe him,' his wife echoed stoutly.

It didn't help when Joe announced excitedly that the evil was spreading. And though the majority of the guests insisted they didn't believe in ghosts, by noon nearly all of them were on their way home.

The following day, Janice made a long overdue return visit to the library.

It had been terrifying to discover what had once happened in the Abbey and, more specifically, the Refectory. It mortified her to remember how pleased she'd been with her renovations. She'd understood nothing, then, of the house's long story, nor appreciated that to impose radical changes might be interpreted, in some quarters, as trying to obliterate the past.

At last she was beginning to understand this was not possible, that the past was made up of layer upon layer upon layer, like the papier mâché models her children had once constructed at school. People had lived at the Abbey long long before the Delanceys. She'd discovered for herself that there'd been monks there since the twelfth century. What was more, one of them had apparently been deeply proprietorial.

Still seething with violent images from the past, her mind was starting to play tricks on her. For one extraordinary second, as she set out her pink and gold plates and her fine crystal glasses, she believed she saw rough wooden bowls and pewter beakers instead. She thought she could hear a very faint high-pitched humming, too. It was as if the house was preparing to break its silence so it could tell the dreadful story for itself.

In 1539, the Abbey would have been even more peaceful. And, of course, it had been self-sufficient then. The smooth green lawn she was looking out at through the same long windows had probably been rough ground planted with lines of vegetables. The sheep the Cistercians were so adept at keeping would have been grazing in flocks in the surrounding meadows, their plaintive intermittent chuckling underscored by the soft drone of bees toiling away at honey-making.

Janice thought of the charge of Henry VIII's vicar general, Thomas Cromwell, that places like this had mostly been dens of vice. She'd learnt that the monks of Melcombe had cared for the sick and the poor in their remote, self-governing community. Did they have any idea, she wondered, what was coming? Chaos and violence were, after all, sweeping the country. If so, when the moment arrived, were they still taken by surprise?

The first indication of visitors would have been the sound of many horses' hooves clopping briskly down the long drive – a whole procession of armed soldiers, with orders to subjugate or, failing that, destroy. Had a monk on lookout duty tried to alert the community? Had the big iron bell been tolled as caution – perhaps the only time in its history when it had not been used to summon the faithful to prayer? But of what use was a warning, anyway? The sole hope of survival for those monks was to take the fixed pension on offer while accepting a way of life no longer ordered by the Catholic faith. The problem was that, most unfortunately for them, their future had already been decided.

Janice was remembering what she'd read about the abbot, Father Dominic, who, by all accounts, had been as forceful and charismatic as he was ambitious: 'The beauty of Melcombe Abbey today can be almost entirely attributed to one man. In the first half of the sixteenth century, Father Dominic masterminded its restoration, rebuilding the Great Hall and the cloisters, amongst so much else . . .'

So he'd loved the Abbey with a passion. Why had he not

submitted to the King's will? He couldn't have known, of course, that exquisite Melcombe was to be spared, even though the priceless illuminated manuscripts in its library would routinely be destroyed. Why had he not listened to his peace-loving colleague? 'Father Benedict pleaded with the abbot most reasonably and eloquently . . . "Let us go peacefully, Father Dominic, for our Lord shall give us solace in our secret thoughts . . ."'

Janice shivered as she stood in the Refectory, staring down at the long scarred table she'd intended to restore but never would now.

Once, she'd discovered, there'd been a chapel attached to the Abbey. It had been an exquisite thing, by all accounts, like everything conceived by Father Dominic. How had he sounded when he'd requested his monks to join him there for a last prayer? In her overexcited state, Janice fancied she caught a faint snatch of a wheedling, authoritative voice. Of course, his flock had allowed themselves to be driven into the church. They'd trusted him. And then . . .

And then, the abbot of Melcombe Abbey had thrown a burning firebrand inside that holy place and locked the doors. And, while still listening to the shrieks of his monks as they burnt alive, he was confronted by the King's soldiers. There would be no compromise and certainly no surrender: 'The abbot screamed defiance at Cromwell's men. He cursed all those who put the storing up of gold before the true faith . . .'

No wonder the Refectory still seethed with rage and terror. For it was in this very room, 446 years before, that the abbot had been chopped to bits, his blood fountaining onto the flagstones. According to the history books, it had taken a dozen soldiers to extinguish his life.

It was the hated Delanceys who'd directly profited from the killings, Janice had discovered. For, unlike so many other religious houses, the Abbey was not razed to a desert of ash. Henry VIII had already promised it to Thomas Delancey, a favourite, together with its rich land. It would become the cornerstone of the family's prosperity – until, that is, decline set in soon after the end of the Second World War.

Sam and Fred had known about the violence of the past, of course. And they'd bequeathed it to their enemies without so much as a word. Then Janice remembered Joe's strange remark once their party guests had left. 'D'you think maybe something about us has, like, activated him?'

'Us?' she'd demanded with unusual crossness. 'What's wrong with *us*?'

He'd shrugged. 'I expect I could find out somehow if *they* ever saw anything.'

'What? Them?' she'd responded sharply. 'And how are you going to do that when none of us is ever going to speak to that dreadful family again?'

Something was happening to Joe. He hummed with nervous energy, full of strangely childish questions for someone of twenty-one.

'Would you love me, whatever I did?'

'Why do you ask?' she'd responded, more teasing than anxious. 'Have you committed a murder?'

He'd been shocked. 'Mum!'

What could she say? 'Whatever you do, Joe, I'll always love you – even if I find it hard to forgive you. You know that!'

Chapter Twenty-two

It was Laura's foolhardy idea to sneak into Joe's bedroom at the Abbey. It was early November and getting colder by the day.

'It's been nearly two weeks,' she reminded him unnecessarily.

'Don't!' he groaned, remembering how he'd borrowed his mother's car to park in a lay-by off a lonely lane. It had been freezing even with the heater on and very cramped. But Janice didn't like lending the Peugeot, since she was not allowed to drive any of Mark's cars – especially the latest model Jaguar that had replaced the written-off Rolls.

Now they were out walking with Spectre and Caesar and Scampi (who'd seldom been better exercised) and had just exchanged a long kiss. The feel of Laura's warm body under her ancient raincoat was delicious torture for Joe. If it weren't for the rain, he said, and the cold and the mud and the gorse and the cow pats . . . It was as if the whole world was conspiring against them, he went on dramatically, water streaming down his face. 'I want a bed. We've never been in a bed.'

'Well, then,' she said, as if the matter was settled. She looked delighted.

But he seemed deeply worried. 'I don't know, Laura . . .'

'You're forgetting – I used to live in that house.'

'Of course you did,' he agreed with caution because they were still skirting around any mention of the feud. It felt bizarre because the quarrelling between their two families was the one thing they truly had in common. But it had become so explosive, and their relationship was too new and, besides, they had a more pressing preoccupation.

'If I turn up really late . . .'

He thought about this for a few moments. 'How are you going to get back into yours?'

'They never lock the door at night.' After a moment, Laura added, 'They never used to at the Abbey either.'

Joe was silent. He was thinking of the burglar alarm his parents had just installed and the piercing shrilling it had emitted when tested, and the new bolts on the enormous front door, and the internal security locks on the windows throughout the ground floor. It meant Laura's crazy old grandmother couldn't break into the Abbey again. But he could always let *her* out.

Laura was thinking that, for a long time now, her parents had not owned anything worth stealing. But, in any case, her father affected disdain for those who prized their possessions. It was a sign of vulgarity, he'd remarked after Lily had told them about the Abbey's new burglar alarm. He wouldn't be caught dead insuring his house either, he'd gone on to assert with a savage laugh, though Fred had pointed out that this was just as well since they were unable to afford the premiums. It was as plebeian as washing one's car, he said, and for a moment everyone visualized Mark Trafford's gleaming new Jaguar.

'But you clean your shoes, darling,' Fred had pointed out, speaking gently like she always did when he got worked up.

'What have clean shoes got to do with anything?' he'd retorted, genuinely taken aback.

Fuelled by its illicit nature, the affair was gathering steam by the minute. When they weren't tramping the soggy woods and fields, Laura and Joe longed for each other in the coffee bar in Magna Saunter. It was frustration, compounded by shockingly bad weather, which finally broke the taboo.

'This crazy situation . . .' Joe began, shaking his head, not meeting her eyes.

There was a long silence. Then, even as he was castigating himself, Laura muttered, 'Sometimes I want to bang their heads together.'

'Me too!' he agreed eagerly.

'If they only knew . . .'

Joe looked appalled. 'Don't!'

'Just as well *they* can't talk,' said Laura, gesturing at the three dripping dogs shivering nearby. They burst out laughing and Joe seized hold of Laura and kissed her passionately while the rain pounded down. The countryside had become like a greedy mud bath. It sucked at their gumboots as they explored each other's warm lips.

'This is driving me nuts,' he said, staring at the drops of water on her eyelashes, the hair plastered to her head.

'Me, too. It's *insane* we can't be together.'

'Insane!' Joe echoed with his sweet smile, as if the word had nothing to do with what had been going on between their parents for the past few weeks.

Laura seemed to make a decision. 'The thing is,' she said eagerly, 'you'd like my family.'

'Oh sure!' he agreed.

'They're a laugh,' she went on. 'Really!'

'Oh sure!' he repeated, unable to hide the bitterness this time.

There was a long silence then Laura enquired with a dangerous edge, 'And just what do you mean by that?'

'Forget it!'

'No,' Laura insisted grimly, rain trickling down her cheeks. 'I want you to explain what you meant just now.'

Joe's resentment spilt out. 'It wasn't very funny the way they acted when my brother had his accident.'

There was another nasty silence before Laura responded, giving a poisonous sting to each word, 'Oh, and your family know how to behave, do they?'

A short while before, Joe had been thinking how much he loved her. Now, for all his gentle nature, he wasn't far off striking her. She must have understood that this place so riven with class divisions had made his whole family extremely sensitive – and now she'd joined in the mockery, too. As though accepting the part, he tugged at the peak of his cap, stuffed his hands deep in his pockets and stared truculently ahead, refusing to react when, like an anxious peacemaker, Caesar deposited one stick after another in front of him.

It was their first quarrel since the affair had become serious. In silence, they crossed the same field where so many passionate encounters had taken place and, still without a word, parted: he to return to the Abbey with Scampi, she to accompany Spectre and Caesar to the Lodge. For all Joe knew in his anguished state, Laura continued to maintain her cold mask.

But he didn't hear her sobbing as she strode through the mist and rain. 'Fool!' she told the two baffled Labradors. 'Idiot!'

Sam said, sounding bewildered and a little hurt, 'I didn't *say* anything!'

One minute Laura had been having tea with them; the next she'd shot out of her chair, rushed up the stairs and slammed her bedroom door.

'No,' Fred agreed, almost as surprised. After all, the children were used to their father's rages about the Traffords. Starting with a rant about the noise made by their builders, this one had escalated into a full-scale explosion. It was true that the banging and music were getting worse. Scaffolding was presently being erected around the Abbey, like a cage to stop it fleeing from any more renovation.

'You were there, Fred,' Sam went on, still mystified by Laura's extreme reaction and thinking that he'd been really rather generous in saying he didn't object to his old home's window sills and so forth being mended. Perhaps he'd forgotten his subsequent threat to strangle Mark Trafford and his unspeakably vulgar old father, as he'd put it, if they dared lay a hand on the beautiful stonework. It was like the portraits all over again, he'd gone on, warming to his theme – a collision between limitless new money and old and tested taste. But try telling that to the Traffords! 'THEY ARE INCAPABLE OF REASON!' he'd bellowed at the top of his voice. All in all, it had been pretty standard behaviour – for him.

'I'm worried about her,' said Fred, twisting her hair. 'Something's making her miserable.'

*

'It's not fair you won't let me go to drama school,' Joe complained to his father after supper in the Refectory, as heatedly as if they'd been engaged in a lengthy argument.

'Pardon?'

'I *am* the oldest.'

'He is,' agreed Janice, who'd noted that Joe's strange contentment had vanished as abruptly as it had appeared.

'You have to earn your place in this world,' Mark told Joe with a stony expression, choosing to ignore the fact that he'd indulged his children from the moment they were born.

'Hear hear!' said Stanley, putting in his usual penny's worth. 'Look at Justin and his books.'

'It's high time you buckled to and got yourself a proper job.'

'Summat fit for a man.'

'Acting's all I want to do and you won't even let me *try*!'

When Joe had stormed out, Janice said worriedly to her husband and father-in-law, 'You're too hard on him.'

The deliciousness of making up was worth the horror of falling out, Joe and Laura agreed, feeling as if they were the first lovers ever to come up with such a novel idea. Their reunion was all the more wonderful for being in Joe's comfortable bed with its crisp duvet stuffed with down and its electric blanket.

'It's the first time I've ever been warm here,' Laura marvelled. The cold in the Abbey had once been relentless, but now she could fling a bare arm out of the covers as she talked.

She'd refrained from commenting on any of the less pleasing changes to her old home: the pink and red paint everywhere; the lamps fashioned like toga-clad Greek goddesses brandishing torches that beckoned the way at exact intervals along corridors formerly wreathed in darkness; the wall to wall carpeting that made exploring the house like treading on lush grass. She was trying not to think about the torn-off magazine picture she'd spotted pinned to an easel in the cloisters. It had depicted a southern scene: a pretty señorita serenaded by a handsome, laughing señor with a mandolin. It had looked horribly as if someone was playing with the fancy of a mural in that historic place.

As for this newly redecorated bedroom where they now lay, she'd known it as 'The Mulberry Room'. It had been a shrine to her great-grandfather's passion for big game hunting, with a balding leopard skin draped over one of the chairs and a zebra skin covering the narrow single bed and a stuffed, moth-eaten buffalo's head with glass eyes looming from one wall. It should, by rights, have been called 'The Shooting Room'. But there was already such a place behind 'The Coat Room' on the ground floor, where shotguns had for centuries been stored in unlocked glass-fronted cupboards. Laura wondered, trying to remain sanguine, if it still existed.

It had been past midnight before she'd dared leave the Lodge. Usually her parents went to bed no later than eleven, but – 'We haven't played Monopoly for ages,' her mother had mourned, for some reason, as they all shivered by the tiny fire. Laura had been appalled.

'Can't we play Scrabble?' She'd hurried through the game with her lowest score ever, for once not caring about losing to her brother and immediately agreeing with her sister that 'ent' was an acceptable word though everyone else insisted it be looked up in the dictionary. Meanwhile, Hester sat in a corner, chuckling softly every now and then as she pulled strands of wool into place.

When Laura finally stole out into the night, Spectre and

Caesar tried to tag along, too. 'Back to basket!' she hissed and, looking mournful, they returned to their lumpy beanbags in the kitchen as if remembering that, at the Abbey, they'd had a reeking cavern of a room hung with ancient saddles and riding rosettes all to themselves.

Joe was leaning against the wall of the cloisters and as he came forward to embrace her, Laura fancied – for an unnerving second – that she saw a shadow slide out alongside him. She could hear Scampi barking faintly in the distance, as if he'd got wind of a visitor. 'He'll calm down,' Joe reassured her.

The Abbey still glowed with soft light and, despite his promises that everyone had gone to bed hours ago, she felt very anxious as she followed him up the winding stone staircase that led from a hidden entrance in the Great Hall to the bedrooms in the east wing. Surprisingly, the house had not lost its distinctive scent of dried rose petals. Something was different, though. She found a new edginess in the air that provoked at least two backward glances on the way to his room.

It wasn't until four o'clock in the morning, safe in a warm embrace, that they finally got around to a proper discussion of the quarrel between their two families. Even so, mindful of what had happened before, they took great care to begin with.

'I accept that my parents should have sent yours a note after Justin's accident,' was Laura's considerable ice-breaker.

'It's cool,' said Joe, kissing her head and trying not to think about what his father and grandfather would have made of this comment. He added magnanimously, 'It must have been tough for them losing the house.'

'It was desperate,' said Laura, giving him an appreciative kiss back. 'Well, awful for all of us, actually. But my pa's family had

had it since the sixteenth century.' She paused as if weighing up whether or not to trust Joe with the confidence: 'He felt such a failure, you see – being the one to break the link.'

Joe was thinking of his own father who, he was pretty certain, had never seen himself as anything but successful. He could feel the silence of the vast house all around them: dozens of dark and empty rooms. It felt as if they were the only living, breathing people in that ancient place. At the same time, there were inexplicable sounds everywhere in the blackness. Once, he could have sworn he heard a suppressed sigh.

'Even if we hadn't bought it, someone else might have,' he said, because it seemed obvious.

Laura moved her body slightly away from his. After a moment, she asked, 'So, why our Abbey when your father could have had any house in England?'

'I think it would have been hard for your parents, whoever moved in,' said Joe diplomatically.

'I disagree,' said Laura, quite unable to stop herself.

Joe bit his lip, determined not to let this escalate, plumping for generosity, whatever the cost. 'Look, I know what my mother's done to the house isn't, like, exactly your style.'

'I didn't say that,' protested Laura. She'd rolled away from him by now and was staring angrily into the darkness, thinking of everything her family had had to put up with from his. 'Your lot have deliberately done everything they can to upset mine! And – don't let's forget – your grandfather laid a horrible, upsetting curse on us, too!'

'I wonder why!'

'He didn't have to take it like that!' Laura added, like a hurt child, 'It wasn't very nice.'

'Didn't have to take it like that?' Joe echoed disbelievingly.

'Your granddad turned mine out of his house! His parents couldn't even walk! My dad was six! They had nothing! You talk about your family being desperate. Think about mine!'

'Oh yes, of course,' said Laura. 'Let's be honest about why they really bought the Abbey.'

'All my dad wanted,' Joe began, once he'd taken a deep breath, 'was to, like, make it up to my granddad.' He added: 'And my nan. Only she died.'

'So it wasn't revenge?' said Laura with a nasty smile.

'Don't make it sound like that!'

'What else was it?'

'OK,' Joe conceded. 'But right from the beginning did your parents have to be quite so . . . ?' He'd been going to say 'unpleasant' but at the last moment changed it to 'unfriendly'.

'Did you expect them to be happy?'

'Maybe not. But they didn't have to stick around.'

'Didn't have to stick around?' repeated Laura, sounding as shocked as he had, a moment before. He'd really blown it now. And perhaps he'd also forgotten that, if her family hadn't stayed in the vicinity of the Abbey, the two of them would never have met.

'Sorry!' said Joe immediately, but it was too late.

'Why shouldn't they stay? Where were they supposed to move to, anyway? They couldn't afford anywhere else. But why should I expect *you*, of all people, to understand that?' She got out of bed. 'This is useless. I'm going.'

He switched on the light. 'No, you're not.'

She was busy gathering up her clothes, but it took some time. Her bra had landed on a white and gold reproduction Louis XVI chest of drawers, her pants were buried somewhere deep in the double bed, her jumper was draped over an ornate mauve box with a slit in it which she'd only just worked out was a paper handkerchief holder.

'Laura,' he said. 'If *we* can't talk . . .'

'We can't,' she replied, very tight-lipped.

He got out of bed, too, and came right up to her, feeling her warm, naked body against his. 'We are not them,' he told her with great intensity, holding her by the shoulders and looking down into her eyes.

There was a long silence and then she said, with a shiver, 'What are we doing?' It was as if she'd suddenly come to her senses.

'Going back to bed, aren't we?'

'I'll have to leave soon. Just half an hour, that's all.'

It was Genevieve – sent to find out why Joe hadn't made an appearance at breakfast – who discovered the lovers, still fast asleep in each other's arms. And by that time, Fred had discovered that her elder daughter's bed hadn't been slept in.

When Laura crept back to the Lodge, terrified, the game was up.

Chapter Twenty-three

By the late summer of 1947, two years after the surrender of Japan, the Abbey and its gardens had recovered their fabled grandeur – but very slowly, like a shaky old person dressing elaborately for a ball. In the deep silence that descended, it became harder and harder to conjure up the noise and mess of the recovering officers. Clipped, even grass rolled over the old vegetable patches like a green picnic blanket and roses dominated the gardens once more, their sweet summer perfume recorded in the dried petals heaped in the enormous blue and white bowl on the oak chest in the Great Hall. There were regular dinner parties, too, like in the old days: celebrations of survival with similarly placed friends, now the evacuees had been sent home and the debris of the hospitals and army centres had been tidied away. The experience of war had been interesting in its own peculiar fashion, everyone agreed, but thank God it was finally over! 'If it weren't for this wretched rationing ...' Edmund would say, more wondering than plaintive, as if all that chaos and upset might never have taken place. Life had readjusted to its old pattern. It was indeed, in every other way, as if the war had never happened.

'What an excellent gardener he's proved to be,' Hester remarked as they sat over breakfast in the Refectory. Through the enormous windows, she was staring at a patch of flowering clerodendrons in the distance – a white brushstroke against the green – as if memorizing its beauty for one of her tapestries.

'Indeed.' Edmund was studying his *Times* and not listening. He read at the table occasionally now, though Hester refrained from commenting on the discourtesy. He was frowning, perhaps because he'd just learnt that Cambridge University had voted to allow women to receive full Bachelor of Arts degrees.

'Not *quite* as good as his father yet, but we'll see.' Hester spoke in her usual offhand but amused way. A stranger over-hearing the conversation would never have guessed that it concerned her husband's greatest friend.

'Indeed,' Edmund repeated, as if he'd made a resolution not to take any notice of this nonsense. Now he was engrossed in a story about the growing success of the British film industry. He and Hester enjoyed their trips to the cinema in Magna Saunter. They'd loved *Great Expectations*, had a polite little spat about *Brief Encounter*.

'Silly,' Edmund had commented afterwards.

'Clever, though,' Hester had said with a bemused little frown.

'It doesn't happen like that!'

'What doesn't?'

He'd shrugged. 'Love.' He sounded as if the very word was an embarrassment. 'One minute Celia Johnson was perfectly content with her life even though it was excruciatingly dull and suburban. The next, she was desperately in love with Trevor

Howard and preparing to throw herself under a train!'

'You may be right,' Hester had responded after a moment. It was exactly the same phrase Edmund used when he disagreed with her. They never argued.

Now she returned to the conversation about their gardener. 'Well, clearly these things run in families.'

Edmund failed to react. He folded his newspaper up very thoroughly, apparently intent on making it into as small and neat a package as possible.

Then both of them were distracted as Samuel toddled in, dressed in a sailor suit, looking very clean and brushed and holding his nanny's hand.

'Ah, Narnie!' said Hester, smiling fondly at the child. 'Is he all ready for me to take him out?'

'He is, Your Ladyship.'

Samuel was impossible to ignore, as Edmund discovered all over again. First he made a rush at him, hands everywhere, and then he tried to climb on his knee. He always seemed to be either laughing or wailing. 'And Sir Edmund was such a wee mouse,' Narnie would tell them, shaking her head. Sometimes Edmund found it strange to remember that this old servant who now deferred to him, addressing him by his title, had once terrorized him into sitting before a plate of uneaten tapioca pudding for hours. Nevertheless, he'd not hesitated to entrust her with his heir.

He liked Samuel but there was only so much boisterous behaviour he could take. 'When I can hold a proper discussion with him . . .' he'd promise Hester. It was a relief when they left for a day of treats. First there'd be lunch with Miranda Askew at her exquisite Jacobean manor house, where Samuel had broken a valuable china ornament, a piece of Meissen, the last time, and then a visit with Miranda and her daughter to the travelling circus that had arrived in the town. There were live elephants, Edmund told Samuel in the quizzical, slightly threatening voice he used for talking to young children, and tigers, too. 'Mind you're on your best behaviour or they might gobble you up.'

Half-hidden by a swathe of white blossom, Stanley Trafford watched Hester Delancey and her diminutive son climb into the back of the Daimler, while Rogers, the chauffeur, held the door open for them.

His black eyes were quite expressionless as they followed the car's slow progress down the long drive. From the rise where he was positioned, he was perhaps admiring the wonderful topiary he'd achieved – the clipped yew bushes scattered across the lawn like a series of huge ornate chess pieces – or even the hedges dividing the fields that surrounded the Abbey, once full of gaps but now restored to their former impenetrability.

Then his gaze returned to the house. Such was its brooding intensity that it seemed to pierce the thick old walls. One might even have fancied he could see his friend Edmund, left on his own now, and revelling in a last patch of peace before addressing the business of running an estate.

It was Effie's mother-in-law who whispered that she'd heard Her Ladyship was taking Master Samuel to the circus.

'The circus?' Effie echoed before realizing her error.

'I want to go to the circus,' Mark said immediately.

'You can't, my love.'

'Why?' He sounded honestly puzzled.

'We've our jobs, my handsome.'

'Why?' It was as if he were trying without rancour to work out why one boy should be thoroughly spoilt in a palace run by a fleet of servants while the other was kept in a stifling cottage with nothing more thrilling on offer than helping his mother with the washing.

Stanley had come to adore the son he'd initially resented. He would talk to Mark as if he were a grown-up and, though the two of them were not so similar in looks, they had identical mannerisms. Mark would cross his arms when feeling obdurate and mask his anger with an inky unwavering gaze. He was nearly seven now. He'd started attending the little village school, whereas Samuel Hadley's destiny was to be sent to Eton, where his father had been so miserable.

'Effie!' came a querulous voice from upstairs. She sighed and said, 'Here we go!' and Mark rolled his eyes and lifted his hands, mimicking his mother's mixture of resignation and good spirits, making her laugh like always. But alongside the joy went terror now. She'd so nearly lost Mark to pneumonia. Worse, it had been her fault: her own child whooping away unnoticed when all she could think of was getting to see Hester's.

Effie was only twenty-five but no longer felt safe. Everything had come at once: Mark's terrifying brush with death and Stanley's father getting crippled in the tractor accident. It had been a dreadful time, when she'd seemed to live in the cottage hospital, seldom eating or sleeping. Edmund had come to visit once, all charm and sympathy, with a bunch of flowers from the Abbey gardens. But her former friend Hester had kept away, not even sending a message.

In the course of one shocking afternoon, the family lost not only its entitlement to be at the Abbey but also its main source of income. However, Edmund was wonderful. He immediately offered Stanley his father's job, even though there were other employees with a greater claim. But money was very tight on one wage – especially as no compensation for the accident was ever offered. Despite the excitement generated by the proposed welfare state, not a whisper of it reached the Abbey, which, for all Edmund's brief flirtation with democracy, continued to be run on the same feudal lines as always.

Effie's life was all drudgery now. Annie's bad legs had ballooned into enormous sausages and she was no help with the nursing and fetching and carrying. The two old people huddled together, grumbling at the loss of their health and independence, unreasonably suspicious of the young and fit.

Sometimes Effie would remember her conversation with Edmund the day Samuel Hadley had been born, her hope that their boys would be close and supportive friends, too. The wartime period seemed ever more distant and dream-like. Had she and Stanley and Edmund and Hester really spent whole periods of leave together? Had she run through the front door of the Abbey nearly every day, in search of her then great friend? Or worn her best yellow dress to the Victory Ball like a queen (and worried all evening about grass stains from an impetuous bout of lovemaking)? Their sons never saw each other except in the distance, by chance. Hester made sure of it. Well, thought Effie resignedly, she was Lady Delancey now.

But at least Stanley and Edmund's friendship had survived. For all Hester's efforts it was unbreakable. Somehow the two of them had even got over the difficult matter of Edmund becoming Stanley's employer. But then, Effie reflected, Edmund had such perfect manners he could make anything right. If she bumped into him now, he'd behave as if nothing had changed. 'Effie, my fair one,' he'd say with a smile as he

courteously raised his hat, just exactly as if she were one of his
grand friends. 'Why do we *never* see you?' And while she smiled
helplessly back, drawn into the charade, he'd go on, 'My word,
this sprog of yours has grown. We really must get him and
young Samuel together.'

In truth, she acknowledged a little sadly, Edmund had always
been weak despite a definite streak of stubbornness. It was
easier for him to give some ground to Hester, a far stronger
character, than rock the boat – provided, of course, that he was
allowed to continue seeing his great friend.

Sometimes Effie wondered about her husband's real feelings,
and if he ever relived his night of triumph at the Victory Ball.
She never asked him; just like she'd not asked his opinion on
why Hester had distanced herself. He was the same passionate,
proud man she'd always known, though burdened with anxieties
now. As for the ambitions that had come to nothing after his
heroic war . . . 'Beggars can't be choosers,' he'd sometimes say,
though without apparent bitterness. It was as if he put his
friendship with Edmund into a box that had little to do with the
rest of his life.

It wasn't in Effie's nature to brood on things either. Besides,
when was there ever the opportunity these grinding, careworn
days?

'Time for Granfer's sheets,' she told Mark with a smile,
gathering up a heap of painstakingly dried cotton to replace the
wet stuff and handing him a fresh towel to carry so as to involve
him.

Stanley stole into the Abbey as softly as a cat – through the front
door, which he found unlocked. It was like cocking a snook at
Hester, besides buffing up his self-esteem. He needed to talk to

Edmund man to man and why should he wait for the next time he decided on one of their expeditions, which might be tomorrow but could equally well be next week?

He'd not been inside the house for two years now and he glanced curiously around him at the grand, enormous rooms, redecorated and fully restored. The furnishings both amused and puzzled him. Why would anyone in their right mind want a big old chest of drawers in a sitting room or a small box-like table with a strange bag dangling beneath it like a cow's udder?

As he passed softly through, he encountered one of the maids attending to ashes in a fireplace, who glanced at him a little uneasily. She was a new girl from the village. He shook his head with a half-smile as if to say, 'Think of me as a visitation.' He even did a little dance for her like a merry ghost and she laughed out loud, immediately afterwards clapping a hand to her mouth.

Edmund was in the Refectory, as Stanley had guessed, loitering over the breakfast table, doing one of his crosswords though it was long gone nine. His newspaper seemed very crumpled, as if it had been folded a dozen times. He looked pale and slender in his funny old tweed plus fours. Stanley noted a series of silver domes enclosing dishes on a sideboard. From the looks of things, Edmund had been consuming a kipper followed by toast and marmalade. It seemed there was choice here – for all he knew, no rationing at all – and Stanley speculated whether a heap of still-warm scrambled egg and a sheaf of crisp bacon might rest under one of those polished covers. He'd been up since six and suddenly he felt ravenous.

At first sight of him, Edmund appeared very startled. Then he seemed to remember that Hester was gone for the day and smiled – that familiar, controlled beam showing pale gums –

and Stanley reminded himself, '*He's never more pleased to see anyone else.*'

'What ho, Edmund!' It was Stanley's habitual greeting in a voice as much like his friend's as he could make it.

'Oi oi!' responded Edmund in kind.

Stanley waited to be offered a seat – and perhaps even breakfast. He'd have liked to sit down at the long table and forget about his worries: pretend, for a brief moment, that he was a carefree aristocrat, too.

This room was so unwelcoming, he thought: spare and uncomfortable, like there was some strange virtue in denying wealth. Edmund had once told him it was where the monks used to eat. Stanley pictured Edmund and Hester's grand friends sitting down in fancy clothes at this long, badly scarred old table and wondered what on earth they made of it. He'd never envied Edmund's life, having seen the damage it had inflicted. He could taste the aloofness in this place; whereas, for all its poverty, the gardener's cottage breathed warmth and togetherness.

Then there were Edmund's ancestors, faces like pale spoons, everywhere he looked. It was like seeing Edmund in a series of distorting mirrors because the fair and handsome youth still only in his early thirties, just like himself, was inexorably becoming a Delancey. It was akin to watching free-flowing cream being very slowly formed into an oblong of butter, thought Stanley, amused by his flight of fancy. The women who'd been brought into the family throughout the centuries had, seemingly, made little contribution. The Delancey genes were too strong. You could see their hooded, narrow-set eyes and aquiline noses and insubstantial chins in every image. What must it have been like for Edmund to grow up knowing precisely how he'd age? Even as Stanley wondered, he heard the grandfather clock in the corner rev up to chime the half hour, followed by others pinging and booming all over the house: a sedate, scattered chorus to remind poor Edmund that his youth was dripping away in this morgue. The strange thing was, Stanley couldn't recall any clocks striking during the war, when he'd passed through the Abbey so frequently. Had they stopped being wound then, because of a dearth of servants and far more important matters to attend to? Or, looking back, had time somehow been suspended during that increasingly magical-seeming era?

'I was this minute coming to look for you,' said Edmund in his usual courteous fashion, and Stanley took it as a gentle reprimand. Edmund could never say anything straight up, he thought affectionately. He'd noticed that his friend was beginning to stoop a little, though he remained slender and athletic, and he thought of old Sir Michael at eighty, bent as a shepherd's crook, peering at the ground like a beetle. Edmund went on, 'I'm most anxious for your opinion on a buddleia.'

'*Oh, bugger your old buddleia!*' Stanley almost said it out loud. He was remembering watching Hester and Samuel climb into the gleaming Daimler a little while earlier, all dressed up for a day of pleasure.

Abruptly, he sat down next to Edmund at the table. He saw his friend blink with surprise before he gave a tiny frown and stared down at his newspaper: silently registering his disapproval. However, Stanley was all keyed-up and couldn't be bothered with pandering to Edmund's complicated ways. He needed to talk to him as a friend – he had a big favour to ask – and yet at the same time, resented finding himself in this situation. Why couldn't Edmund perceive his difficulties, with nothing needing to be said? It was pride that had held Stanley back until now. He was painfully conscious of his old check shirt rolled up to the elbows, his hands engrained with soil despite a hasty scrub. In his awkward, anxious state, he caught up a piece of toast from a silver rack and crunched a corner off. But it wasn't the way to behave in these surroundings – as he saw immediately from Edmund's alarmed expression.

He decided to lead up to his problem gradually. 'Remember me fishing you out of that trouble all them years ago?'

But, instead of acknowledging the debt, Edmund responded with a helpless shrug, like performing an elaborate, ironic bow. 'How could I not?' he drawled.

Stanley put the toast down. He wasn't enjoying its cardboard taste anyway. For some reason, he was reminded of watching Edmund with his friends on the tennis court, now returned to its pre-war splendour. For all his apparent fragility, he was an excellent player. He said a little sternly, 'Saved your life, or so you told me.'

'Did I?' Edmund murmured, sounding as though he could hardly be bothered to deny it.

Stanley reminded himself that Edmund often behaved like this: it was down to the peculiar way he'd been brought up. But he believed he knew him very thoroughly by now, appreciating the true person beneath the play-acting. He'd been a wonderful and supportive friend in his own oddly undemonstrative way. But, then, Stanley told himself, his own dependability couldn't be faulted either. He was entitled to make this request. There'd been only one moment in their long friendship when the thread of loyalty had very briefly wavered, but he wouldn't think of that because it was over and done with, forgotten.

'You knows so.' Stanley waited, but it seemed there was no way Edmund was going to help him out. He fixed him with a relentless treacle gaze. 'I only has to ask, you said . . .' he prompted.

But there was no response. Was Edmund remembering him saying he'd have risked his life for the dogs, just the same? Stanley thought of the other favours he'd done for his friend: for instance, the way he'd protected him from ridicule when they'd first joined the ranks together, once even using his fists. That was the loyalty that mattered, he told himself.

'*Whatever* I want,' he went on, repeating ten-year-old Edmund's fluting promise. 'You said you'd give it me. Anything. That means anything, you said. For ever, for what I done.'

Had Edmund forgotten everything they'd been to each other in more than twenty years? The fun and dramas, the shared experiences of childhood and marriage and war.

Stanley made a decision. He held out his calloused hand as if to shake Edmund's soft one and, when he responded, pulled him up from his chair. Edmund felt very passive – almost, it occurred to Stanley, like he'd done all that time ago when he'd hauled him unconscious up the river bank. Still holding his friend's hand, Stanley pulled him over to one of the huge windows and opened its stiff catch. He knew he was behaving as if he owned the place: impudently, like seizing hold of that toast. But he wanted to let freedom into this prison, make Edmund look at the woods and fields stretching away in the far distance so he could be reminded of all the wonderful adventures they'd enjoyed together.

The heavy window creaked open and fresh air floated in, carrying the faint scent of dying lavender from the flowerbeds beneath. Until that moment, the day had been chilly and dull. But all of a sudden the clouds shifted in the sky and the hundreds of tiny, newly restored window panes glittered like diamonds. Stanley saw the rush of sunlight seize on Edmund's hair, turning it to gold, and, glancing casually down, noticed it do exactly the same for the sheen on his own muscular forearms. He could feel the bright warmth on his face, like being probed by a searchlight.

Edmund appeared suddenly anxious, he noticed, as if he guessed what was coming. But he told himself, '*So what? Drop in the ocean.*' Look at everything Edmund had! He could be curiously mean about money. Stanley had noticed it before. '*I am owed*,' he reminded himself sternly. All of them must look to the future in these trying times. He steeled himself to keep his nerve for the sake of his family and saw Edmund give him an odd sideways glance, as if trying to work something out.

They were standing so close to each other that Stanley could smell Edmund's funny old man's scent of cigar smoke and mothballs. They both stared out at the landscape: the dull colours lit up, the whole aspect marvellously transformed.

'We can't manage,' Stanley told Edmund, coming finally to the point. 'There's five mouths to feed on the one wage now and Mark's a growing lad.' He turned to look at his friend, giving his radiant flashing smile as if to remind him that he also had a young son with a healthy appetite. 'It's only the once I'll ask,' he promised, honestly determined not to let this be the first of many begged loans.

It was a moment before Edmund reacted and, after that, everything changed.

It was the beginning of the long nightmare for the Trafford family.

Chapter Twenty-four

'Now you need to be told good and proper,' Stanley informed his grandchildren very grimly, nearly forty years on.

He'd gathered the whole family in the old Morning Room after the evening meal, and Janice had brought in a tray of tea. The grandchildren listened to the gloating crackle of the fire, rain charging the windows of that warm and comfortable place as if losing patience with being outside, and exchanged weary glances. The story of their family's journey from rags to riches was so familiar it had become like a creed. '*We* never had nothing like this,' their grandfather would invariably remind them as they tucked into a fine roast or opened an expensive gift. 'Mind you say thank you, now.' They were doubly blessed, he'd point out: growing up in privilege, yet aware that even the wildest of dreams could be realized. What was more (though he didn't add this), they'd been protected because Mark and Janice didn't like to talk about the poverty and squalor of former days. It was because they were all in a new life now.

The children were correct in one sense. Their grandfather

was indeed about to remind them of the family's painful beginnings. However, this time – with the blessing of Mark – he would make the story unbearable.

The rage was getting in the way, though. 'Trouble with them people!' he spluttered. Then: 'What he knew about plants!' He could feel his heart racing, his cheeks burning and didn't seem to notice the soothing hand Mark laid on his arm. If he closed his eyes, he could see and feel it all – the garden trashed by war that had been coaxed back to loveliness, and the searing shame and terror. He'd lead up to it gradually for maximum effect. He'd tell the story of a terrible injustice but, as always, keep the long history with Edmund to himself.

Why was it that the flavour of a day bore no relation to the events it held? That dreadful morning in October 1947 – four weeks after he'd finally gone to Edmund for money – should by rights have been black and stormy. Instead it was blue and crisp and beautiful as if nature was trying to fool everyone autumn wasn't coming, after all.

It had occurred to Stanley that gardening had something in common with cookery. Not that it was *his* problem – thank God! – to struggle to set adequate nourishment on the table. Day after day, he watched Effie and his mother create something out of nothing: the dry oats dropped into water at night for porridge next morning; hard turnips tossed into a thin broth that would eventually become a thick and tasty soup; scraps of offal seasoned with parsley and stretched with potatoes. The process was similar, in its way, to pricking out fragile seedlings that would swell into fat crisply layered lettuces, or cajoling a limp scrap of cutting to become a vigorous blossoming shrub. It was like inscribing a circle. It chimed with the dying in winter and the magical resurrection each spring.

That morning, he was operating to a timetable, of course. Working in a garden, you always did. There was a whole education he'd picked up from his father, without even being aware of it. It had started with following him around as a child and listening to him talk about his work at the end of the day. So he knew it was time for the vine.

Edmund had views on the subject, as it happened. He'd often talked about the wine produced at Melcombe by the monks in the Middle Ages. White it had been, apparently, 'with an excellent flinty quality'. Stanley had asked how a wine tasting of stone could be anything to brag about, but Edmund had pointed out in that annoyingly superior way he'd sometimes affect, 'It means the wine was clean and sharp.' Then he'd added, like a child offering a sweet to make up, 'It's the way one talks about wine, actually, and – you're right – it is rather silly.'

It had been Edmund's dream to restart the vineyard. He'd said it again the last real day they'd spent as friends, while out searching for wood pigeons, with Stanley expected to do all the shooting, as usual, because, once he'd seen action, Edmund never again killed for pleasure. He announced he wanted to make liqueur, too, something calling itself 'shartrooze', with herbs they'd grow especially.

'I'd enjoy the sense of continuity,' he said. 'Did you know it was first made at a Carthusian monastery near Grenoble, Stanley? A place called La Grande Chartreuse, hence the name?'

Of course Stanley hadn't known! First he'd swung up his gun without appearing to take aim and felled a pigeon and then he'd retorted there was a heap of things he didn't know and therefore, by implication, a whole lot more that he did. It was a typical exchange, really, demonstrating their affectionate, seesaw balance of power, which had easily survived Edmund becoming the employer. By way of an apology – obviously – he was given all four shot pigeons: 'I insist! And send the fair one my compliments, won't you?'

But that had been before the scene in the Refectory; before Edmund's appalling reaction after he'd asked for money and his own furious response. He'd known then that it was only a matter of time before he lost his job. However, he said nothing to his family even though, with each hour and day and week, the fear grew. But Edmund kept his distance. For a whole month, there'd been no sign of him, even though it was his practice each morning, come rain or shine, to walk through his gardens, taking the air.

That last beautiful, dreadful day he spent at the Abbey, Stanley had known exactly what to do about the vine. He'd even checked with his bedridden father to be sure. The thing was, vines were a special case. The time for pruning most trees, as any fool knew, was the very end of winter, February or thereabouts. But, save for summer pinching, you should never touch vines after New Year's Day. It was because, like birch and walnut and liquidambar, they'd bleed when the sap was rising, and with vines the wound could be fatal. So you'd cut away the dead wood and tidy up when the plants were relaxing after their summer labours but not yet ready to think about striving all over again.

He'd badly needed to be alone: away from Effie, too, who'd sensed his anxiety and not let up. 'What troubles you, my love?' she'd ask very anxiously. But there was no way he could go into it. Besides, he couldn't bear to frighten her.

He had another secret, as it happened, though a far more pleasing one. He'd come to love working in that garden. It had crept up on him slowly, like a spurned girl who'd won him round with sweetness, and for a long while, out of cussedness, he wouldn't admit it even to himself. But he'd been actually looking forward to putting the garden to bed for winter: seeing that the earth was dark and mulched and the plants pinned back to their bones. He found he relished the outdoor life despite its harshness but, best of all, enjoyed the power. He was the master there, for all he was a servant.

The main thing, he told himself resolutely as he attended to the vine, was to get on with the job in hand. He knew he was an excellent gardener.

He'd been sawing away for about half an hour – very carefully, stopping every few minutes to check his angles – when he suddenly became aware of Edmund behind him. How long had he been there? It made Stanley's skin crawl to think of it and he was painfully conscious that Edmund must have noted the way he hunched his shoulders instinctively, as if shielding himself. He couldn't look him in the face, either, though he took in the silly old suit with the waistcoat and the brown precisely dented Homberg hat. He waited a little sullenly.

'May I ask what you're doing?' Edmund's voice was very quiet and controlled, but the way he pronounced 'what' was ominous – the 'w' disappearing into the strung-out 'h'. In much the same way, he'd confronted deer poachers in Baines's Copse a couple of months ago, though it was Stanley who'd ordered them off the property and fired his shotgun into the air just in case they had any ideas about coming back.

'Pardon?' He was frightened, of course, but also confused by Edmund's question. After all, he had his saw in one hand and his bit of old string for measuring in the other. Furthermore, there was a blunt pencil parked over one ear, not to mention cut-off branches strewn all around his feet.

'You're pruning my vine!'

Stanley frowned. 'Pardon?'

'I beg your pardon,' Edmund corrected him icily, as if he was some oaf that needed teaching manners. Another silence fell. Stanley willed himself to keep his nerve. He held his knowledge of Edmund to him like the saw, and waited.

'In *October*?'

Stanley thought he comprehended what this was about now. He told Edmund, trying not to sound superior because it was obviously crucial not to upset him in any way, 'Vines is different.'

'I beg your pardon?'

'Vines is different,' he repeated, stammering a little, to his mortification. He was very nervous. It was because a vivid picture had suddenly come into his mind of Effie and Mark and his parents waiting for him at home.

'In which sense?' asked Edmund, using the trick with his h's once more. He was poking at the bits of cut-off wood with a silver-topped cane, acting like a fifty- or sixty-year-old. Before, Stanley would have mocked him and made him smile – and been loved for it.

'You don't never prune a vine come New Year.' He was looking at a point beyond Edmund's shoulder as he said it. He'd not once met his eyes.

There was a pause, while Edmund considered this. Then he drawled with a look of triumph, 'Exactly!'

'Pardon?'

'You've just admitted it. You were engaged in a deliberate attempt to destroy my vine.'

Then Stanley understood. This was the pretext for dismissal that Edmund had been waiting for, and the moment he'd been so dreading. It was of no use informing Edmund that his bedridden father – a gardener, after all, with a legendary reputation – could vouch for him. He simply wasn't interested.

'Edmund . . .' It was a last desperate shot. Fatal, it turned out.

He was a brave man, Stanley reminded his family – the old macho cockiness briefly surfacing – and didn't he have a row of medals somewhere to prove it? But none of the horrors he'd faced in wartime could compare with having to go home and repeat Edmund Delancey's words to his family: 'I want the lot of you out by the morning.' No ifs or buts. No consideration of the fact that it meant two ill old people being uprooted, not to mention a mother and a small child who'd been sickly ever since his bout of pneumonia. Tears came to Stanley's eyes as he relived the anguished journey back to the cottage, still clutching at his saw and his bit of string.

'He sacked you – for that?'

'Been biding his time, hadn't he?'

'Because of you asking for money when you couldn't manage on the pittance he paid you?'

Stanley nodded grimly. Telling the story to the grandchildren, he found he could almost believe it himself.

'But didn't you beg?'

Thirty-eight years before, Effie had asked him the same question. It was strange to hear it repeated just as urgently, though without the terror – *'But didn't you beg?'* As if, even in 1985, the years of desperate poverty the family had endured could somehow be averted: like stopping an old news film of a real-life massacre halfway through and substituting a happy ending.

'Course I damn well begged!' he responded a lot less gently

than he had back then. 'Did you think I were going to let that bastard . . .' Words failed him for a moment and he bunched his fists before burying them in his pockets and muttering, 'Without a fight?' He added bleakly, 'And neither were she.'

Effie tore off her apron in preparation for the visit to the Abbey, but for once left Mark behind. She sobbed as she ran up the green lane where she'd loitered so many times before, picking nettles and dandelions and berries. Hester would listen to her, she told herself, even though they'd had no contact for more than two years. It was inconceivable she'd allow this dreadful injustice, with their history.

She thought of Stanley's old parents waiting, powerless and terrified, in the cottage, and her little son, weakened by illness, too. She hadn't prepared a speech. All she knew for certain was that, once they were finally face to face, Hester would be unable to resist her. She'd intercede with Edmund . . . She'd save them all . . . She must! But the front door of the Abbey was locked, and so was the servants' entrance, which she'd never known happen before.

Effie circled the enormous house, looking in vain for a door or window left open, but the house that had welcomed her in wartime had turned into an impregnable fortress. She beat on the solid front door with her fists, at first softly but then with increasing violence, calling to Hester.

'Let me in!' she shrieked, just as desperately as – more than four hundred years before – the monks locked in the burning chapel had screamed to be let out.

Plainly, the servants had been given strict instructions, because nobody came. Then, for the first time, Effie noticed Edmund's Daimler parked by the side of the Abbey and, after that, caught a movement in the window of the White Room and, looking up, saw Hester observing her from above, face very set and pale before it vanished behind folds of curtain.

Effie gave up then, the only record of her visit the smears of blood drying on the oak door. She was never quite the same. It was the day she lost her faith in goodness and justice for ever.

Stanley wiped his eyes. However, the way he'd told it to his family – omitting the truth about Edmund and their great friendship – Effie could have been the desperate wife of any one of the servants. Therefore, a good deal of the true horror of that tragic scene was lost.

Mark could only dimly recall his mother returning to the cottage in tears. But he remembered the panic of packing up because that had involved him, too. He and his father began to describe it for the children, almost as if vying with each other.

'There weren't a wink of sleep for none of us that night.'

'I was seven!'

'Three months short, son. We all had to set to – even the old ones. Granfer on his backside, Grammer with her legs . . .'

'They couldn't stop crying . . . I can hear it now!'

'All them years of living in that hell-hole, for all it were home.'

'Specified he wanted it like a new pin, didn't he? The bastard!'

It was Edmund's final cruelty. Stunned and fearful but still reacting like servants, the family scrubbed and swept and cleared all night long. For as long as he could remember, Stanley had welcomed the dawn's pink fingers unwrapping each day – but all it meant, that awful morning, was that in three hours, two hours, one hour, they must be out. What to take and what to burn on the bonfire that smouldered all night long, which, in nightmares, turned into the flames of hell? There wasn't much to show, in the end, from their life in that little house. The saddest part for him personally was leaving the garden because, whereas you needed money to make a house nice, you could glorify a garden for nothing. It might have been a rich man's, he'd tell himself, revelling in his richly scented old roses, his plumbago and deutzia and choisya. But, in truth, that's exactly what it was – a rich man's garden assembled, bit by bit, with seeds and cuttings pilfered over the years. A seed could grow anywhere with no one the wiser. That much he'd learnt.

'Are we to be gypsies?' Effie whispered as they all stumbled into the terrifying future. It was then that he called up his last scrap of energy and all of his venom and laid his curse on the Delanceys. Then he ordered his parents and his wife to forget that he and Edmund had once been friends. If they ever mentioned it – to Mark or anyone else – he'd leave the lot of them. He said it with such passion that they almost believed him. They were allowed to hate the Delanceys, though. There was every reason for it now.

'How did you manage?' asked Justin, touching one of his metal crutches for reassurance, his usually confident voice a little shaky.

Stanley gave a savage laugh. 'How did we manage?' he repeated, as if baffled himself. It would come to seem to them all as if they'd been really spoilt in their crumbling cottage on the Abbey estate, and insane ever to have complained when there was a regular salary coming in, however insufficient it had felt at the time.

It took hours to reach the village, what with stops for the old ones, Stanley carrying his father all the way. Once there, they knocked on the door of a friend's house and begged for a room.

Jim Pitfield, the village blacksmith, who'd been a guest at the Delanceys' Victory Ball and witnessed Stanley's zenith, had taken them all in. There was no crowing, just sadness that Stanley had had to suffer such a brutal awakening, because you were what you'd been born and there could never be any changing it. The Traffords shared the rabbit hot pot prepared by Jim's wife and padded out with hastily made dumplings, and no meal ever tasted more delicious. It recharged the family, made them believe that true kindness existed outside the Abbey, after all.

For a week, they stayed put. But there were too many of them for an already crowded house so they moved into a dilapidated barn while Stanley tried to find work: not as a gardener – he couldn't hope for that – but labouring or whatever else was available. There was so little, though. This was post-war, after all.

'Lived off potatoes, didn't we?' Mark recalled.

'Mostly charity,' Stanley corrected him. He added, for the benefit of the children, 'February 1948, we ate a dead pigeon off the road. Thought it were still breathing, till we saw the maggots.'

'Mam would dry out our tea leaves over and over. I remember that.'

'Dried-out tea leaves was a luxury.' Stanley touched the fine china cup he'd been using, an oddly scornful look on his face. It was because he was remembering the jam jars his family had once used for hot drinks, which sometimes cracked, scalding them. In this lush new life, those old jars had all of a sudden acquired a strange glamour, like mugs used in wartime trenches.

Then he shook off the unbidden nostalgia and pulled himself together. The true smell of poverty, he informed his grandchildren, wasn't the stench of an outside latrine without running water. 'Forget soft toilet paper!' he said, with a stern glance at Justin, who was notoriously wasteful of the stuff, adding with seeming irrelevance, '*Daily Mirror* were a rare treat.' No, he continued, real poverty smelt of mould from the damp that crept up the walls and the omnipresent heaps of wet washing that never properly dried. There was no more free wood from the estate, of course, and they were all too exhausted to go searching for more than the bare requirements to make up a fire. That first winter was bitter and the two old people died within weeks of each other. Soon afterwards, Stanley and Effie decided that their only hope, for Mark's sake, was to move to London. They were country people, born and bred. It was terrible to give up the life. But they'd lost almost everything else. They were used to loss by then.

'Now do you see?' Stanley demanded angrily of his elder grandson. It was Joe, of course, who'd caused the full horror of that wretched time to be exhumed. For he had to be made to understand that there was no way he could carry on with his shocking romance with the Delancey girl. Stanley shivered at the very idea. He had to impress on Joe that to continue with this deceitful relationship for one second longer was to shame his whole family. It was no use Joe telling them Laura was this, Laura was that, Laura was different . . . It was out of the question. End of story.

However, instead of meekly accepting this, it seemed Joe only wanted to ask one thing. 'But why did you want to come back, Granddad?'

'Yes, why?' demanded Genevieve and Justin simultaneously, as if they, too, found it quite impossible to understand why their grandfather should ever again have wished to have anything to do with the Delanceys or the Abbey after the treatment that had been meted out.

'To teach them,' said Stanley after a moment. Wasn't this what he'd always maintained? It was the reason he collected sayings on retribution like 'Revenge is a dish best eaten cold' or 'The mills of God grind slowly, but they grind exceeding small'.

Joe said bravely, 'It has to stop somewhere.'

'Why?' his grandfather immediately snapped.

'Yes, why?' his father echoed.

For such a gentle person, Joe could be surprisingly obstinate. To see his family set against Laura only fuelled his determination. 'Couldn't I just ask her over?' he pleaded. 'Then you can judge for yourselves.'

But it was no good. Even his mother, who usually loved a good romance, shook her head sadly. And his grandfather was the most implacable of all.

Chapter Twenty-five

'Today is Tuesday, 17 December, 1985. My daughter-in-law Fred is taking me to Magna Saunter at ten o'clock. There is plenty of wool in my work box. The Abbey now has a burglar alarm.'

Hester frowned at her message board. 'Is there something about a horsewhipping?' But since she'd been searching for her glasses for the last ten minutes, plainly the writing appeared as a blur.

'What on earth are you talking about?' demanded Sam crossly. It wasn't only because he and Fred had spent a mostly sleepless night, worrying about Laura. He'd just had to watch a twenty-foot fir tree being manoeuvred through the front door of the Abbey. Fred had kept all the old Christmas decorations, of course, but of what use was an enormous antique angel when all they could accommodate in the Lodge was a three-foot tree? It was a bad time of year, underlining all the fun and richness that had gone. And his mood was further darkened by some of the cards the postman had just delivered, round robin letters tucked into them like lengthy boasts. How come everyone else was doing so splendidly? It seemed as if the whole world was buying a second home in Majorca. *'Dear All,'* he thought, with savage humour, *'not much to report since last Christmas. Still staving off the bailiffs . . . Remember our former gardener whose son stole our Abbey? We've just discovered that our daughter Laura is sleeping with his grandson.'*

In his irritation, he decided it was high time his mother had a short-term memory test. 'What have you just had for breakfast?' He watched as Hester frowned and bit her lip. 'You can't remember?'

'Yes I can!' said Hester triumphantly, as if she'd been puzzling over something quite different. 'Toast and marmalade and coffee!'

'That's what we always have for breakfast. And, by the way, Mama, if you're wondering where your specs are, they're on your head, as usual.'

'Why did you ask me, then?' She went on, brow still furrowed, 'I'm sure I heard something about a horsewhipping . . .'

When Sam failed to respond, she studied her messages for the day, now perfectly readable. She said, as if her old sharp self was popping in for a visit, 'I'm certain burglar alarm has a hyphen.' Then casually: 'Has Laura found herself a young man?'

Sam and Fred exchanged glances. Hester was going a bit deaf but, owing to the flimsy construction of the Lodge, it was certainly possible that she might have overheard part of their discussion the evening before. However, even if so, it was most unlikely she'd remembered it.

'My mama is a crashing snob,' Sam had begun, even as Hester was stumping up the stairs to bed – as if this was the real reason for excluding her from a family conference about the treacherous affair between his daughter and the son of his sworn enemy.

He must be trying to make out that class divisions were unimportant to him, Laura had reflected with a mixture of sadness and amusement. Had he forgotten all the jibes of the past? Poor foolish Mark Trafford, he'd sneer, who failed to appreciate that, even in the flashy eighties, it wasn't done to parade money. But, then, how could he? Her father would imply that only a thousand years of lineage could bestow his own brand of innate self-confidence. It was rather like having an army marching behind one, trumpeting one's identity. It meant, in effect, that if Trafford ate peas off a knife, he would only ever appear vulgar, whereas he himself could pass it off as eccentricity. Obviously, thought Laura wearily, her father was going to try and be cunning.

She was right. Her parents had had twenty-four hours to think about the situation and compare notes in whispers; a day and a restless night in which to progress from outrage and dismay to a cautiously agreed, 'The very worst thing we could do, from our point of view, is stress what *arrivistes* that ghastly family are.' Laura was going through a standard rebellious phase, they'd decided. After all, according to Hester before she'd lost her mind, even Sam's famously conservative father had once toyed with socialism. Take it gently, appeal to Laura's better nature, play it by ear . . .

Even so, once they were all gathered with the door closed they seemed uncertain how to begin. Sam lit another cigarette. Fred fiddled with her hair. Fortunately, Maria leapt in with: 'It wasn't her fault!' before explaining that both Laura and Joe had dissembled, to begin with. If only, reflected Laura, Maria had displayed a little more deviousness herself. She could so easily have concocted a story for their parents to explain that un-slept-in bed. '*I should never have told her,*' she thought. It was almost as if Maria had *wanted* the affair to come out in the open.

'So, he's a liar, too . . .' Sam began. But, catching a warning look from Fred, he deflected the anger in Maria's direction. 'As for you, miss . . .'

Fred said warmly, 'Darling, you do know, don't you, that all we really want is for you to be happy?'

'Yes,' Laura agreed warily.

'You're such a wonderful girl.'

'Indeed you are!' Sam chimed in.

'You deserve the very best.'

Silence fell.

'Far be it from us to . . .' Fred began, but Sam shook his head at her. It was his moment to take the floor.

'I've nothing against this young man personally . . .' His voice was very mellifluous and reasonable. Someone who didn't know him might have been fooled.

Laura kept her expression quite blank but she was thinking, '*So if you only want me to be happy and you've got nothing against Joe – oh yes, and you're not a snob – why have you called a family conference?*'

Sam answered the question himself in a heavy despairing tone, as if forced to face up to an unpalatable fact. 'There is such a thing as bad blood.'

'Oh Pa!' Laura felt quite helpless. When she was a child, Sam had talked to her about the Trafford family in the same over-dramatic terms – but it had been a joke, a mockery of his own humourless, grudge-bearing father. It dismayed her to see how serious he seemed now: as if age was turning him into exactly the same sort of person. 'I know they bought our house . . .' she began.

Sam stared at her, face flushing, expression hardening, as if all the rage was now directed at her.

'But if they hadn't, someone else might have.'

'I'm not talking about the house,' he told her brusquely.

'You're not?'

'I could, of course.' He gave a thin smile, implying that the list of atrocities committed against his beloved Abbey was endless. 'No. I'm talking about *them*. The fact of it is, no matter how charming one of them might have made himself appear to you, that family is a bad lot.'

'Now you sound just like Grandpa,' said Laura rather daringly.

'And with reason,' said Sam, who was about to be extremely unreasonable. 'After they left Melcombe, my papa went into a decline from which he never recovered.' He looked as sad as if he and his father had enjoyed a perfect relationship. 'They did something abominable to him – I've never known what. I blame them for his early death.' He started wobbling up into a rage again, pausing between words for emphasis. 'I am – telling you – that you will – kill me, too – if you go on with this, this . . .' He paused. 'Are you *trying* to torture us?'

'They're in love!' Maria announced triumphantly, as if this excused everything.

'Pass the sick bucket,' muttered her brother, newly returned from his first term at Cambridge and doubly annoying.

It made Laura cringe, too, to hear her sister talk about something so private, though she could only lower her head mutely, seeming to agree. She *was* in love with Joe, wasn't she? Why else was she letting this happen?

'In love?' It was too late. Her mother was frowning and twirling her hair frantically. 'What do you *mean*, in love?' It was so strange to hear her ask the question, as if her own passionate attachment to Sam hadn't forgiven all the anxiety and penury.

'It's serious!' Maria crowed, plunging her sister into even deeper trouble.

'Is this true, Laura?' Fred sounded panic-stricken.

It was then that all reasonableness vanished and Sam bellowed at the top of his voice, just as his fierce old father might have done, 'I'VE A GOOD MIND TO TAKE A HORSEWHIP TO THE PAIR OF YOU!'

'I'll take Mama Christmas shopping,' Sam told Fred. He smiled at her very cheerfully, as if – quite suddenly – he'd made a decision to put the worry about Laura to one side.

'Really?' She was surprised by the offer to help because Sam had inherited from his father a very precise picture of his place in the household. It was wives who organized the care of elderly relatives as well as everything else, even if husbands refused to find themselves decent jobs with which to support the family.

'I need to go into town and sort out a few things anyway.'

'Oh?'

But, instead of explaining, he glanced meaningfully in Hester's direction as if to say, 'Not now.'

'All right then,' Fred agreed amiably. 'Would you mind picking up some oranges and a bag of flour? Get the own-brand sort. And your mama is due for a haircut.'

Sam frowned because this might be asking a little too much of him, especially as the barber's shop, cheaper than the hairdresser's, was complicated to reach.

'Leave her there, while you do whatever it is you need to,'

Fred suggested. She smiled very sweetly. 'And don't forget my flour and oranges or there'll be no pudding for you tonight.'

'And I need more wool,' said Hester, as if the thought had just swum vigorously into her mind.

Once Sam had deposited Hester at the barber's shop, he got on with the real purpose of his trip to Magna Saunter, which was to use its reference library.

When he'd lived in the Abbey, there'd never been any need for such a visit because his father's collection of books was so comprehensive. It was another tragedy of moving to be compelled to give them away (or lend them to friends, as he and Fred euphemistically put it). But it was either that or selling them because there was no money for storage and, of course, no space in the Lodge. They could have been left in the Abbey, where they belonged, but as he himself had scornfully pointed out: '*They* don't read! Those sort of people buy books by the yard, for decoration!'

Once he'd revealed his identity to the librarian, she was extremely helpful. At the same time, she assumed a cautious though pitying attitude, as if dealing with someone recently bereaved. She kept glancing at his clothes – favourite much-darned jacket, same dog-spotted corduroy trousers as always – as if trying to gauge how far he'd fallen. It irritated him mightily, though he didn't let up on the charm. He wondered what a woman like that was doing there because, as he later explained to Fred, 'She was one of us.'

The librarian was clearly curious, too, about why he should wish to look up his own ancestry but he continued to smile, while giving nothing away – even when she tried to make out that he wasn't the only person interested in such information. Very recently, she told him, someone else had come on precisely the same quest. In other circumstances, he would have followed this up. As it was, he was short of time, anxious only to pursue the business in hand.

Leafing through the pages of Debrett's was rather like opening an address book full of friends. And here he was: 'Samuel Hadley Delancey b. 14 November, 1945', the scion of a great family, striding on stage to claim his prize. Only, it hadn't been altogether straightforward, he'd come to understand from his mother. It wasn't until six years into the marriage that he'd been born. 'I thought you would never come,' she'd once confided. But for him, she'd gone on to explain, the Abbey would have passed, on the death of his father, into the eager hands of a detested second cousin once removed. 'It was the thing about your father's family, do you see? Because he was the only one.' Almost from the moment she married, she revealed, her in-laws had watched her and waited – as if winning the war was of minor importance, by comparison. It was unusual for his mother to be quite so forthcoming. She'd added that she'd felt the spirits of Edmund's dead ancestors bearing down on her: an unbroken line, all of whom had passed the Abbey directly from father to son.

Only it had just dawned on Sam that this might not be strictly true. It had come to him, like a bell tolling in the distance, even as he was taking out his frustration on Hester. It was because of something she'd said. He'd been transported back to childhood, reminded of a conversation with his father when he was about twelve. He was putting it all together now: padding out the remembered fragments with fact.

His mother had gone out and he was waiting to have lunch in the Refectory. His father put great store on punctuality, as did the family cook, so Sam had got there early and was casting around for a subject of conversation. Mealtimes were almost invariably miserable. His father was well into the grip of the family depression by then, but there was something about the Refectory that made it even worse, some residual emotion that fell on him like a veil. It was, of course, where the King's soldiers had chopped Father Dominic, legendary abbot of Melcombe, into pieces. Sam shivered enjoyably, imagining the whirling swords, the fountaining gore.

He had an inspiration while he waited and, when his father came in, precisely at one o'clock, pointed to one of the portraits and asked, 'Why's his name got a dash in it?'

'Does Parker know we're in?' was Edmund's testy response, as if the very sight of his son was an irritation.

Sam tried not to let this get to him, because he was a naturally cheerful child. 'I've just told her.'

'Ah!' said his father. Then, slightly appeased because, as Sam well knew, his ancestry was a favourite topic, 'I assume you're referring to the tobacco merchant?' Each subject in the portrait gallery, from the MP to the admiral, had his title and role in the family. He went on, 'It's a hyphen, not a dash.'

'Seymour Hadley-Delancey,' Sam confirmed. And then they both sat down at the long table and waited for Mrs Parker to bring in the soup.

His well-read father could be interesting, and the two of them were never so close as during discussions about long-dead Delanceys, whose lives had sometimes been extraordinarily dramatic. Sam liked to hear about Thomas Delancey, the King's favourite – one moment a relatively humble courtier and the next, saviour and squire of Melcombe. Very occasionally he was allowed to see Thomas's diary, in which the King's historic visit was recorded, and even to touch it. 'Charming fellow,' Edmund would comment, as if he'd known him personally. Sometimes Sam would get the feeling that his father was truly enjoying his company, as if the pleasure had taken him by surprise; but then he'd invariably become sarcastic and gloomy as if he only wanted him out of his sight. It was as if, Sam once thought bitterly, his father had made up his mind not to love him.

He wasn't really that interested in why a hyphen was apparent on one of the portraits. It was amazing he'd seen it at all beneath the patina of ancient grunge. As they ate, they listened to rain beating against the myriad window panes. The room had darkened but there was no question of switching on the lights because Edmund refused to allow electricity in the daytime. The portraits crouched in the gloom, keeping their secrets.

'Dreadful business, the Civil War.' Sam's father would ruminate on the distant past in much the same fashion as, after reading his *Times*, he'd pronounce on current events. 'Good fellow!' he'd commented earlier, after reading that Harold Macmillan had kept the Tory party in power with a thumping majority. 'Awful thing, losing Jasper,' he went on.

Sam could hear the minutes ticking past on the grandfather clock in the corner. He knew about Jasper Delancey, a Cavalier and family hero. Jasper had been commiserating with friends at a dinner party in Bristol after the city had fallen to the enemy when he received a message that a group of marauding Roundheads wished to speak to him outside. He'd made his excuses – 'Please don't wait on my account' – only to be torn to bits. ('Anything to avoid pudding,' Sam would joke to his own children, years on.) Jasper had surely eaten lunch at this same table with his own father and Sam wondered if they'd liked each other.

'Good boy. Pity. Twenty-five, that's all.' There was a long pause. 'There was only Jane left then, do you see?'

Sam was no wiser but sensibly kept quiet.

'Not as if they hadn't tried.' Edmund chewed on his roast mutton as if it were more of a chore than a pleasure. 'Six stillborns before Jasper. All boys.' He took a piece of gristle out of his mouth and deposited it on the side of his plate. 'Too late for a spare after that.'

Gradually, in elliptical fashion, with many stops and starts, the rest of the story emerged. The death of Jasper Delancey had plunged the family into crisis, Sam's father told him, because, without an extant male heir, it looked as if the Abbey would have to pass to distant relatives. The one daughter remaining – Jane, aged twenty-eight – was not particularly well-favoured, according to Edmund, and firmly on the shelf.

'And then Seymour Hadley came along, do you see?'

Sam was thinking about spending the afternoon catching newts in the canal while his father spoke of Seymour Hadley, the man whose portrait he'd noticed, who'd made a fortune from tobacco in the New World. He had vivid dark looks, a vitality that seemed to spring through the dingy oil paint.

'Big estate in the north, but no name to speak of.' Edmund considered this as they were both served with bowls of anaemic-looking stewed cherries in syrup. It quickly became apparent that Mrs Parker hadn't removed the stones so Sam waited to see what his father would do. It seemed that the correct way to eat this pudding was (after a lot of thoughtful masticating) to spit out the stones into one's spoon before depositing them, one by one, around the rim of one's bowl. Edmund then slurped up the syrup in the same noisy way that he supped his soup.

Although Seymour Hadley had possessed great wealth, there was no impressive family background and so he had taken the sensible decision that Jane's name was worth more than his. Such things happened occasionally then, Edmund pointed out. Upon their marriage, Seymour had changed 'Hadley' by deed poll to 'Hadley-Delancey'. The couple went on to have four sons, all healthy; and, within a generation, the hyphen had disappeared, with 'Hadley' becoming the family's middle name for all males thereafter.

Edmund never failed to refer to Seymour as 'the tobacco merchant'. It was as if he couldn't forgive the fact that, for all his success (and generosity, too), he had not been what he considered a gentleman. But he would always point out that the bargain between the Hadleys and the Delanceys had been justified. When the future of a great house was at stake, he told Sam with formidable gravity, no holds were barred.

Seated in the reference library at Magna Saunter, Sam experienced a kind of dreadful excitement. For a change, he told himself, he'd conceived a plan to win back the Abbey that really was brilliant – with a far greater chance of success than trying to write a bestseller. But was he prepared to sacrifice his beloved daughter? '*It's not a question of that,*' Sam assured himself and really believed he meant it. '*Laura is crazy about the Abbey, too – after all, it nearly did for her having to leave it. And if she loves this boy, why can't some good come of it at the same time?*'

He decided to keep his plan secret, for the moment – especially from Fred, whose reaction he could guess. But, then, she was only a Delancey by marriage, thought Sam for the first time ever. He felt a strange affinity with the father who'd dispensed his affection so sparingly, infusing his childhood with gloom. The Abbey had been all-important to him, too. But how far would *he* have gone to save it? He was lucky, thought Sam, that he'd never been put to the test.

He presented Fred with a bunch of roses when he came home at lunchtime.

'What's this for?'

'Does it have to be *for* anything?'

'Were they horribly expensive, darling?' was her predictable response.

'Don't you like them?'

'I love them.'

'Well, then.' Occasionally, Sam implied, bouquets stolen from the Abbey's flowerbeds weren't quite special enough for her.

She studied him. 'You look pleased with yourself.' It was odd in the circumstances, she thought. She herself was still miserably preoccupied by the business with Laura and the Trafford boy.

'Where is everyone?' he asked because the house was very quiet.

'Out.' She added quickly, in case he was worried, 'Laura's with Maria. They went Christmas shopping. And David's off somewhere. It's just us. Cheese on toast. We can give Mama hers on a tray. She likes that, and *Brief Encounter*'s on. It's already started, but she won't notice.'

Hester's outing seemed to have done her good. There had been men at the barber's, she told them as she watched Fred prepare her tray, and even reminded her not to forget the Branston Pickle. She disliked having her hair washed in front of men, she complained. Because she went so rarely, she'd been given a cut that made her look like a wizened boy.

When she was settled in front of her film in the sitting room,

Fred remarked to Sam, 'You were gone for an awfully long time.'

The television was on at full volume and they both heard a precisely enunciated male voice enquire in a tone that simultaneously managed to be intimate and urgent and slightly threatening: 'You know what's happened, don't you?'

'Actually,' Sam told her, 'I've come to a decision. And I hope you're going to back me up.'

'Oh?'

'If Laura's really serious about this boy . . .'

'Oh dear!' said Fred and immediately began fiddling with her hair.

'I think we should give her our support. I'm only thinking of her happiness. Besides, she's nineteen now. Quite old enough to know her own mind.' And, before she could protest, he pointed out, 'You were eighteen when I married you.' It was true. But she'd also been pregnant with Laura. He went on: 'I'll talk to her when this farce is over' – as if Christmas nowadays was no more than an endurance test.

Chapter Twenty-six

'I don't like it,' said Laura.

Walking across the Abbey's frosty lawns under a cloudless blue sky, leaving a trail of jumbled-up footprints in their wake, she wondered if they were being observed. She shivered and pulled away from Joe's embrace and saw his expression become even more disconsolate. She'd been so sure of her feelings when the relationship was secret but now felt only confused.

'I mean,' she went on, trying to repair matters, 'you should have heard him before!' But, on reflection, this was hardly tactful even though she understood that Joe's family were incandescent about the romance.

'Perhaps he really does want us to be happy,' Joe suggested in his gentle amiable way and for the first time ever Laura experienced impatience with him. Why was he quite so trusting? Why wouldn't he take her word for it when she assured him there was something deeply suspicious about her father's behaviour?

*

'Tell me about Joe,' Sam had asked with his most charming smile, appearing genuinely interested. But when she started talking about Joe's ambition to become an actor, his reaction was very plainly boredom verging on contempt. As soon as he decently could, he changed the subject. 'Do you really love him?' came next, with a sentimental yet strangely eager look in his eye. It had embarrassed Laura horribly. She had no wish to discuss her feelings for Joe with either of her parents.

Most extraordinarily, her father appeared to have softened towards the family he'd hated so obsessively. But, then, she now knew from Joe – via his grandfather, Stanley – the full horror of their banishment from Melcombe all those years ago. It was she who'd told her father about how Edmund had refused to give Stanley financial help when he'd begged for it; the feeble excuse for dismissal that had been fabricated; and the family's descent into terrible poverty. The death of Effie at only fifty-four, weakened by years of struggle, just when her life had become really comfortable, was the final unforgiveable piece of the picture.

She'd expected him to dismiss it all as the Traffords' version of events. But, to her amazement, he'd expressed what seemed like sympathy. He'd only been two years old when it happened, he'd pointed out, but conceded that his father had probably been far too harsh in turning out the gardener and his family. 'Even if he really did ruin our vine,' he added with a poker face. After all, it had been a time of nationwide unemployment and there were ill old people involved, not to mention a young child. It was small wonder, he'd actually said, that they should have harboured some resentment. As for the man that child had grown into – 'He's done well for himself, I'll give him that.' He went even further. He accepted, he said, that his own provocative behaviour towards the Traffords had been over the top at times. 'But it was only a bit of fun!'

By this time the others had come in. They listened in astonished silence.

'Shall we give him a message board, too?' David suggested. He picked up an imaginary pen and wrote in the air. 'They have poisoned my life and ruined my house and stolen my friends and only three weeks ago I was talking about hiring a contract killer.'

Something even more unlikely and dismaying had happened since.

That very day, at Sam's instigation, both sets of parents were to meet and discuss 'the situation', as Fred had begun to call it. Sam had telephoned the Abbey (because Fred refused to) and once more, listening to his unctuous voice, his family scarcely recognized him.

'I'll get back to you,' Mark Trafford had responded curtly and, half an hour later – only marginally less brusque – had invited Sam and Fred to lunch.

Afterwards, Sam said, with a return of his old form, 'Well, we are, after all, the sort of people they've been trying so desperately to associate with.' But Laura knew the truth from Joe. His parents must have agreed to meet hers in order to hammer out a plan to separate them.

Joe said, sounding anxious and placatory, 'They'll be arriving soon.'

'Yes,' Laura agreed. Her father had yet to see the changes to the inside of the Abbey. She knew his explosive nature. There'd be no way he could hide his real feelings. For once, she found herself looking forward to one of his rages. At least, then, everyone would know where they stood.

None of the children had been invited to the lunch, though it had been decided that Joe and Laura should join the company afterwards for coffee: presumably so as to be ordered to terminate their relationship.

Fred said as they approached the big oak door – each dent and scratch achingly familiar – 'You're going to get a shock, darling.' She was fiddling with her hair while glancing at him anxiously, though he didn't seem to have noticed the new wooden sign with 'Melcombe Abbey' burnt into it in Gothic writing. However, despite her warning to expect changes, she'd not adjusted her own memories of the Abbey in winter and was wearing a multi-coloured woollen shawl over a thick sweater and vest, and heavy tights under her long felt skirt. She'd also put on a pair of dangling earrings, after announcing that she had no intention of dressing up. She'd support him in this meeting, of course, because she never let him down; but that didn't mean she was happy about it.

'Don't you worry about me,' said Sam, sounding in excellent humour. And why not? The night before, giggling like children, he and Fred had acted out a sexual fantasy. He'd tied her wrists to the brass headboard of their bed with his old dressing-gown cord and made love to her twice. He'd felt like a young man again. Thank God, he'd remarked afterwards, that this one great pleasure was free, adding, 'Bet *he* never has such a good time with Crimplene.' It was unfair of him to have coined this nickname for Janice, since she was always expensively dressed, but he knew it would amuse Fred.

He dropped his cigarette, stamping it into newly laid gravel that had very recently been raked. However, after a moment's reflection, he picked up the stub and secreted it in a pocket of his old tweed jacket. He was glancing at the flowerbeds either side of the door as if he approved of the splashes of yellow winter pansies that had been arranged there. 'Of course,' he said, as if reminding himself what Stanley Trafford had once been.

They'd left Hester behind without explanation, just as they'd decided to keep her in the dark about Laura's love affair with Joe. But she'd picked up something in the air and, surprisingly, kept returning to it. 'What's the name of Laura's young man?' she'd asked that morning, though they'd fobbed her off.

'What's the point in distressing her?' said Fred afterwards, adding a little despairingly, 'Not that she'll know who we're talking about, anyway.'

She saw Sam's determinedly jovial expression waver as the chiming doorbell sounded. But as the last note of 'D'ye Ken John Peel' faded away, he seemed to recover himself. After all, he knew about the bell. Fred was remembering the night he'd stormed up to the Abbey in a vain attempt to confront the Traffords after learning about their outrageous treatment of his portraits. She'd feared for his health then. Now, there was the added worry that he was up to something. She'd felt it for days.

'Pink everywhere, remember!' she hissed.

However, to her astonishment, Sam responded very cheerfully and positively, 'Nothing that can't be undone.'

And then Mark Trafford opened the door. He was wearing a formal dark suit, as usual, and Fred was struck, once again, by the great difference in the two men. Mark was so restless and humourless: he gave the impression that every moment spent away from his work was a waste of time.

She forced a smile, even as she took in the newly renovated Great Hall in the background. It was now painted a deep glistening red, like the inside of a healthy throat, although, to her very great relief, the famous plaster moulded ceiling had been left untouched. '*They'd call it a feature*,' she thought grimly. She heard Sam, beside her, let out a sort of a groan, though he immediately coughed, while scrabbling on auto-pilot for his cigarettes. They maintained sphinx-like expressions as they absorbed the toning crimson carpet, the brilliant white gloss paint that now masked the old wood panelling they'd treasured.

'We're in the upstairs lounge,' Mark informed them. He suggested, looking a little awkward, 'I'll lead the way, shall I?'

Fred exchanged an appalled glance with Sam – '*More than one lounge?*' – because humour was their only lifeline. She was being assaulted by warmth. The whole Abbey luxuriated in it and very reluctantly (even sulkily) she had to concede that it was quite pleasant, on this wintry day, not to be suffering the usual discomfort. She noticed new radiators everywhere and even believed she could identify a skin of double glazing over the ancient windows, whilst profoundly hoping Sam would not.

Janice Trafford and the old man were waiting in the former Morning Room, now painted sunny yellow and fitted with a chocolate shagpile carpet and cream blinds. Even more warmth came from a newly installed arrangement of glowing – but most certainly fake – logs. There was an enormous television set in one corner and a light melody tinkled softly from a very sophisticated music-centre. This was obviously where the Traffords relaxed. Had that icy, uncomfortable room, with its moth-eaten shooting and fishing trophies, where generations of Delancey men used to read the newspaper after breakfast like an endurance test, ever really existed? And could any of them, in their worst nightmares, thought Fred, have imagined *this* scenario?

'Do come in,' said Janice unnecessarily and immediately proffered overly sweet sherry – perhaps to avoid shaking Fred's hand. She seemed very uneasy and Fred wondered yet again why the Traffords had agreed to Sam's strange suggestion.

Stanley Trafford didn't get up and failed even to greet them. He was staring at Sam very fixedly. Clearly, thought Fred, he was baffled as to why anyone had let this loose cannon into the Abbey. However, she imagined that, a little like Hester, Stanley no longer had any real say in family decisions. She only hoped that he wouldn't be overtly hostile. But whatever happened, she was determined, for Sam's sake, to behave well.

Janice thought, '*What are they* doing *here?*' It made her miserable to think of Joe being involved with a Delancey, though he'd told her over and over the girl was special, not like them at all.

'I love her, Mum,' he'd added unnecessarily. But, for once, she'd been unmoved.

The thought of discussing Joe's private feelings with these dreadful, heartless people made Janice feel quite ill. Mark hadn't wanted to invite them, either. As if! It was Stanley who'd seized on the Delanceys' suggestion, insisting – despite all their objections – that there should be a lunch invitation. 'Need to nip this in the bud good and proper,' he'd explained, using a typical metaphor.

In spite of Fred's manners, which couldn't be faulted, Janice was dismally aware of critical glances and pointed silences and even caught the other woman giving a half bitter, half triumphant little smile at one point. 'An abomination,' she'd called the newly decorated Refectory not long ago.

But the truth was that, despite having banished the cold and most of the gloom, even Janice was beginning to doubt the wisdom of her renovations. It was since learning about the Abbey's past. History demanded respect. A little too late, she was starting to appreciate it.

There were niceties to be observed, even in a social situation as tricky as this. The Delanceys were, after all, the Traffords' guests. Just as, at a business lunch, it wasn't done to get straight down to the matter in hand, so the Traffords postponed discussion of the troubling romance until the first course – chicken supreme – had been cleared away.

But there was not much that could be safely talked about and, to begin with, the two families ate mostly in silence. The Refectory was brightly illuminated now, by ranks of spotlights embedded in its high ceiling. But it had lost none of its old oppressive aura, Sam was glad to note. If anything, this had intensified. 'Joe says it's got a ghost,' Laura had informed him during one of their talks and he'd thought gleefully, '*Good old Father Dominic!*' He used to joke about the Abbey's legendary ghost, when his children were little, treating it as a real presence. At mealtimes, he'd say courteously, 'Do sit down, Father.' And, after he'd pulled out a chair, he'd pour an extra glass. 'Are you a claret man? I forget . . .' He liked to think of the spirit of the old monk hovering ominously in the background while the Trafford woman chattered inanely away. Father Dominic had loved the Abbey with a passion, too, despite a fatal inability to compromise that had resulted in the destruction of his chapel. It was hardly surprising if he'd returned from the dead to terrorize its new owners because of their dreadful taste.

But none of the ghastly changes really mattered, Sam told himself, touching the ancient scars of his table for reassurance under the hideous gold tablecloth that had been laid. He could even be sanguine about the abysmally restored portraits – while exchanging a meaningful glance with Seymour Hadley-Delancey (whose hyphen was now in sharp relief). No, if his brilliant plan succeeded, all of this could be reversed. The secret knowledge gave him an edge over the whole company, including – to his shame – his beloved wife. But he knew her character too well. She'd be horrified by the notion of exploiting one of their children, even if it turned out that Laura was perfectly content to go along with his scheme. It was probably unwise to drink when he needed to keep his head, especially as he noted Mark Trafford was on fizzy water, but the wine was too good to resist. Anyway, he thought defiantly, why shouldn't he celebrate?

'What d'ye do with y'self all day?'

At first, he didn't realize the question was being directed at him. Stanley Trafford hadn't spoken till now. His voice was very gruff, with a strong rural accent. It was unnerving the way he stared with his black eyes. '*What a liability!*' thought Sam. It was farcical to imagine this old man being permitted to sit at the head of the Refectory table in the old days.

But before he could decide how best to respond, Stanley said sombrely, almost accusingly, 'My Mark's done well for himself.'

'Indeed!' Sam managed to agree. He could sense Fred's indignation. He told himself it was only to be expected that the other family couldn't resist flaunting their good fortune. He was quite determined not to be provoked.

'With all them disadvantages . . . Only goes to show, don't it?' He bared blackened, uneven teeth.

Even as Sam boiled with fury, a quite separate part of him noted that Stanley's smile had a strange appeal, in its rough way.

It hinted at an appetite for life and a merriment that had somehow survived the ruin of everything else.

To his credit, Mark interceded at this point. 'We're met here to discuss the young ones, Dad,' he pointed out, and immediately Janice got to her feet, like someone anticipating trouble, and started clearing away. 'That can wait,' said Mark shortly.

'I'll just fetch in the dessert.'

Sam watched with barely concealed enjoyment as Mark drummed his fingers on the table while Janice set down a pile of slightly smaller but equally hideous pink and gold plates and started slicing up a big meringue topped with whipped cream and tinned peaches. It seemed there was some tension in the marriage. But, then, Sam couldn't imagine what it must be like to live with Mark Trafford. All that exhausting energy: eyes darting everywhere as if, even now, he might be missing some opportunity to make himself even richer. When did the man ever take time off to enjoy it all? '*At least I know how to have fun*,' thought Sam smugly. Furthermore, he congratulated himself, he had his Fred with her cool and perfect eye. All the money in the world couldn't buy taste, as had been most comprehensively demonstrated.

There was a sudden crash as a fist was slammed on the table.

'We'll not *allow* this thing to happen!' said Stanley very forcefully and, simultaneously, both Delanceys realized they'd been guilty of a serious error of judgement.

Joe said, as he and Laura toyed with hamburgers and chips in the coffee bar in Magna Saunter, 'I wasn't going to tell you . . .'

'What?'

He sounded miserable but, nevertheless, there was an edge of excitement to his voice. 'Dad's said he'll pay for me to go to drama school in London.'

'I see.'

'It's pathetic! I've been asking for months and months. He told me it wasn't a proper job for a man.'

'Great.' Laura didn't tell him that her father clearly shared this opinion, though he'd resisted the temptation to say so.

'Even Granddad's said "yes".'

Now that she had such evidence of his family's opposition to their romance, Laura felt her passion for him start to unfold again.

He laughed unhappily and repeated, 'Pathetic!' If only they sincerely believed in his acting talent . . .

'Will you go?' she faltered.

Joe fiddled with the ketchup. Then he chopped his gherkin into tiny slices and pushed them into a line. 'If I do . . .' he began.

So he'd decided. She felt despair settle on her.

'. . . will you come with me?'

After the shock of discovering who really held the reins of power in the Trafford household, Sam pulled himself together. He believed he managed to sound relaxed, even amused, as he drawled, 'That's a little extreme, surely?'

Stanley stared at him, breathing hard.

'We've had our differences, certainly,' Sam continued with a genial smile, as if all the poisonous hating had been a game. 'But don't let's take it out on the young.' He smiled. 'It's hardly *their* fault! Fred and I haven't yet had the pleasure of meeting . . .' He fumbled embarrassingly for the correct name.

'Joe! But Laura does appear genuinely in love.' His expression softened. 'All right, she's only nineteen. But it seems to me . . .'

Another vicious thump on the table which made the crystal glasses shiver and the fine china clatter.

'And who might you be?' enquired Stanley in his funny old accent. He smiled, showing his blackened teeth once more.

Sam found the question more puzzling than offensive. He was still frowning, wondering how best to respond, when Stanley barked out, 'For pity's sake, man! Look at the shape of you!' For some extraordinary reason – in the space of a second – he'd become a parody of a hectoring drill sergeant.

'I beg your pardon?' Sam could sense Fred bristling and willed her to control herself. After all, he was managing to keep *his* temper, in spite of all this provocation . . . And, if she only knew it, there was far, far too much at stake.

Then he had to suffer more offensive staring and tut-tutting. Finally, sounding utterly disgusted, Stanley spat out, 'Flipping grasshopper!'

It was now obvious to Sam why he and Fred had been invited to this lunch at the Abbey. Stanley relished the piquancy of insulting them in the comfort of their old home. But it was his own fault, of course, Sam told himself ruefully. It was he who'd made the first move. He'd set them up as sitting ducks.

'Fascinating . . .' he began, grasping at sarcasm, though still determined to keep his temper. It would be a kind of victory, after all this goading from Stanley. Besides, he'd not lost sight of his objective. But before he could feel his way further, Fred's voice drowned him out – all the ruder for its perfect crystalline delivery.

'How dare you speak to my husband like that, you fucking little upstart!'

Laura and Joe heard a distant hubbub as they entered the Abbey, hand in hand, and glanced at each other triumphantly. So, everyone was having a good time! Brilliant! They paused to kiss in the Great Hall and Laura closed her eyes against the new red paint. By the time they reached the Refectory, the noise had stopped and the two families were on their feet, as if a decision had just been made to decamp to a more comfortable room for coffee.

'Darling!' said Fred, sounding as if she'd forgotten all about the two of them. Her hair, so carefully done for the occasion, had become a real frizz, Laura noticed, and her cheeks were bright red.

'Ah, Laura!' said Sam, puffing away at a cigarette.

'Laura?' exclaimed Joe's grandfather in an eager, friendly way. To her surprise, he came right up close and clasped her hand in his rough, grimy one. He, too, seemed a little flushed.

'*They must have had a good lunch,*' thought Laura. '*Does he always look at people like this?*' she wondered, while reclaiming her hand as soon as decently possible. So thorough and searching was his black gaze that she felt violated. It was extremely disagreeable to be subjected to such lechery but, for Joe's sake, she made herself smile back, even though she could sense her father scowling in the background.

'You're a nice-looking lass and no mistake.' He sounded as if he were licking each word.

'Told you, Granddad!' said Joe with innocent happiness. He should have waited, of course, like they'd agreed, but the unexpected approval derailed him. To Laura's horror, he announced, still smiling like a lunatic: 'We've wonderful news for you all. We're getting married.'

The effect on Joe's grandfather was terrifying. One moment, he was winking and smiling, the next it was as if someone had punched him. He staggered and crashed into a chair before sliding clumsily onto the floor and letting out a dreadful groan.

'Where's his tablets?' cried Mark and Janice set off in search.

Joe instantly removed his hand from Laura's, looking stricken.

Mark knelt beside his father and took him in his arms. 'Tell me where it hurts, Dad,' he enquired very anxiously and tenderly.

'Here!' said Stanley, putting his hand on his chest.

'Hold on!' When Mark had measured out pills and administered them with a glass of water, he urged, 'Breathe deep now.' Then he asked Janice, 'You've phoned for the doctor?'

'Over my dead body,' Stanley muttered savagely.

'You don't want him?'

Stanley shook his head, said with an attempt at a smile, 'I'll be OK, son.'

'It's not your heart, then?'

'Oh, it's my heart all right!' Stanley went on very piteously, 'How could he do this to me? How?'

'See what you've done!' Mark snapped at Joe, and Laura was mortified to find herself on the point of tears.

'That's unfair,' Sam protested.

'I think you've said enough,' Mark responded, looking pointedly at his watch. Then he told Fred grimly, 'As for you, lady . . . I *don't* think!'

'Don't worry, we're going,' said Fred, sounding very assured.

Of course, Laura went with them. She didn't want to linger outside the tight fence of this family, with Joe too distracted and upset to protect her. But she heard what Stanley said all right, even as the three of them made their way to the front door.

'I'm telling you, son . . . If we let that lass into our family it'll finish me off – same as Hester tried to. Over my dead body! Have to kill me first!'

They found her at her embroidery, as usual, seated before a meagre fire, muttering under her breath as she threaded her needle in and out, absorbed in another portrait of the Abbey. She was shrinking with age, thought Sam: dwindling away, the only excess flesh around her ankles. She was using the unpicked wool from a previous work – something she'd been doing more and more, lately. She was like a photographer shooting from every conceivable angle, as if reminding herself over and over again never to forget this one most beautiful thing.

'Where are the children?'

'The children,' she echoed with a bemused frown. Her voice quavered a little, underlining the helplessness.

Sam ground his teeth with exasperation. But he made an effort to speak reasonably and gently. 'David and Maria, Mama – your grandchildren.'

Laura had shaken off her mother's tender concern and straightaway run up to her room where she'd be in tears for sure. And, instead of making them all tea, Fred had marched out to the cold garden. He could see her through the window, hair blown everywhere, tugging viciously at the ivy that crept over the flowerbeds.

'Out?' Hester sounded unsure, though the house was patently quite empty.

Sam thought of Stanley Trafford, who was more or less exactly the same age yet still sharp as a knife. He shivered with fury as he remembered the disgusting way he'd looked at Laura. He was a dead giveaway for any family set on social advancement and yet none of the Traffords had seemed the slightest bit ashamed of him – quite the reverse, actually. Sam could see that anyone who wanted to get close to the son would first have to become accepted by the father, however appalling the prospect. 'Flipping grasshopper,' Stanley had dared to call him and, now that his fury had abated slightly, he could see there was something very odd about it. The meaning had surely been unambiguous, but how could that semi-illiterate possibly be familiar with Aesop's fable of the industrious ant (Mark, in other words) and the idle pleasure-loving grasshopper? As a child, Sam had been read the story by his own father: not, it was made clear, for pleasure, but as a homily.

Far more importantly, what could Stanley have meant when he'd warned Mark with such passion about Hester, of all people? Hester, whose mind was unravelling at wretched speed! It was ironic, thought Sam with some bitterness, that it was his own mother – sent demented, after all, by the trauma of losing the Abbey – who might yet wreck his brilliant plan to win it back.

'*I'm going to get to the bottom of this somehow.*' But he dreaded the prospect. Attempting to get any sort of sense out of Hester was like approaching a warren of rabbit holes and trying to figure out which one didn't end in a cul-de-sac. He'd have to be cunning, too, because, for all her senility, she could be obstinate.

Moving to the Lodge was a fine metaphor for what had

happened to her. The huge accumulation of the past had disappeared virtually overnight – packed up and sent off to an unknown address. Nobody who'd known elegant, witty Hester in the old days would even recognize her now. It was interesting, though, that she'd lost none of her skill for needlework or, indeed, her old class consciousness, which was another reason why he dreaded explaining about Joe Trafford. He decided to go slowly.

'Mama . . .'

'Mmm?' He noticed that she was engaged in stitching brown wool around her tiny Abbey, as if some cataclysm had occurred and its emerald lawn had been ripped up. It was not a good omen.

'You know the gardener's family?'   ·

'Who?'

He sighed in exasperation, though he should have expected this. 'The Traffords, Mama.'

'Oh, them! Is that what they're called?' She sounded amused.

'You know they are! Remember, they took our house?'

'Oh? Which house?' Hester seemed very serene as she batted back his questions. She bit off a piece of wool and it left a small wisp of fluff on her upper lip which, as usual, was smeared with sticky pink lipstick.

Sam thought, '*Why can't I lean forward and pick that off with a loving smile? Why don't I give her a hug and make her feel all right, in so far as I am able, about being lost and garish and foolish?*'

As if she could read his mind, Hester removed the piece of fluff herself and smiled at him, looking very composed. Then she searched in her sewing box and produced a tiny pair of scissors.

'You know perfectly well which house!' he told her, starting to lose his temper, to his shame. 'Don't pretend you can't remember the Abbey!'

'Which Abbey?' she asked, preparing to snip off another dangling thread.

He seized hold of her tapestry frame and shook it at her like a tambourine. 'What's this, Mama?'

'Oh, that!' she said calmly, taking it back.

'Yes, that! The house you lived in for almost half a century!'

'What about it?' she snapped like a bad-tempered dog. It gave him a shock momentarily. But it was only the ghost of her old autocratic self, he realized – an engrained reaction, like wincing when someone used the word 'toilet' or mispronounced 'exquisite'.

He decided to come straight to the point. 'I know Papa sacked them . . .'

She glanced at him and, for a second, he fancied he caught a gleam of the once acute intelligence. It was like dropping a stone into a pond thick with slime and seeing the vegetation part for a glimpse of inky depths. The doctor had told them it was a feature of her form of dementia – a last cruel trick – that, very occasionally, a streak of lucidity appeared. He'd observed for himself that his mother had good days. With luck, this might be one of them.

'And it seems he *was* unreasonably harsh, in the circumstances. You see, I've heard their side of the story now.' He added, hoping to engage her, perhaps even prepare her, 'From Laura.'

Was any of this getting through? She ran a finger over the bumpy surface of her embroidery, sighed as if disappointed with herself. '*At least something still moves her,*' thought Sam a little bitterly. It had for long been obvious to him why she'd married his father. Her first sight of the Abbey must have tempered all her perceptions of that distant, difficult man, even if it later became her prison. Sam had seen for himself the treatment she'd suffered. The whole of his upbringing had taken place against a background of festering rage and deep, self-centred misery.

'I'd very much like to hear it from you, too, Mama.'

He waited, even though he told himself he didn't know why he was bothering. And, as he did so, he remembered Stanley and Mark Trafford at lunch – the way the son had constantly looked to the father for a reaction and the pride the father had shown in the son, the unmistakable tenderness and understanding humming between the two of them like messages passing along a wire. He couldn't imagine Stanley holding anything back from Mark or vice versa.

'Did you know that was what he was going to do?'

But she wasn't even listening to him. All her attention was still on her work. Sam grabbed the tapestry frame again, keeping it out of reach.

'Did you, Mama?'

'Did I what?'

He made a great effort. 'Did you know Papa was going to sack them?'

'Who?'

This was pointless, thought Sam. He might as well stop trying to find out what lay at the heart of Stanley's extraordinary dislike of his mother. Even so, he found himself saying, 'Stanley Trafford seems to have got it into his head, Mama, that you mean trouble for them. And it's all got to stop – now.'

In the old days, he would never have dared talk to her like this. Hester had been too strong a mother, suffocating him with her attention even as she repelled any attempts at true closeness. For all that, he could recall shafts of tenderness: a look of pride shut off before it could be properly enjoyed, embraces all the more precious from someone known to dislike intimacy. She'd been against his early marriage, of course, even though Fred was perfect for him in every way. But, then, his mother could always upset him. He would never forget his hurt at her reaction when the estate was sold to the Traffords, even though he'd managed to hang on to the Lodge. 'You and your idiotic ideas!' she'd shrieked. 'Only you could bring us to this!'

But now Hester couldn't even remember the names of her own grandchildren.

Nevertheless, he found himself informing her, 'You see, Laura wants to marry Joe Trafford. They've just broken it to us.'

He heard her needle tinkle to the floor, but thought nothing of it. Hester dropped things as often as she mislaid her handbag. Besides, he was all bound up with his own feelings: still engaged in talking himself round and thinking guiltily of Fred and the confusion he could identify in every one of her clumsy savage movements, outside in the cold garden. He could tell that she was secretly entertaining the idea of the marriage – and hating herself for it. He felt similar self-loathing for the way he'd manipulated her. 'You know what this means, don't you?' he'd whispered on the way back from lunch. 'Laura can get married in the Abbey, after all.' Did she think he didn't know how long she'd cherished that dream? Or planned it down to the last detail?

'Joe Trafford?' Hester repeated.

'We don't like it either,' he said, the tone of his voice telling a different story. 'The very idea of her becoming part of that appalling family! But Laura is nineteen now. And if it's what she really wants . . .'

'She can't!'

'What?'

His mother had gone very pale. Her hands were shaking and her eyes were terrified. It seemed that all she was capable of saying, with a kind of awful desperation, was: 'Can't, can't, can't!' But once she'd said it a dozen times, the sense went, just as it did with everything else.

Chapter Twenty-seven

'Drink?' asked Sam.

'Yes, please.' Joe was hoping without much confidence that it would be the same fine malt whisky that awaited his own father after a hard day's work – and a double, too. It was a few days since the disastrous lunch at the Abbey. He was feeling rattled in spite of the fulsome speech he'd just been given about being most welcome and Sam wanting to get to know him better. Very deliberately, it seemed, they'd been left alone together in the lounge, apart from the old lady muttering away in the corner over her needlework.

Remembering his grandfather's dreadful description of his grandmother beating on the locked door of the Abbey, coming home with bleeding hands, he'd given Hester Delancey a cold look – quite obviously wasted. He could see for himself that this confused old woman was to be pitied now. And in fact, since his grandfather had sat them all down to tell them about the inherent wickedness of Laura's family, he'd actually started feeling more kindly to Sam and Fred, not less. After all,

Edmund Delancey was the real villain of the piece and he'd been dead for ages.

He was trying to forget the scene he'd left at home: his grandfather clutching at his heart and bellowing that he would disown him if he insisted on going through with the marriage; his father telling him, very angry and distressed, 'This is unacceptable, Joe!' and his mother shooting him an anguished glance as if she could only agree. Even Justin and Genevieve had had an angry go at him. It took real nerve to resist all that, but some madness, some perversity, was urging him on.

'I love her,' he'd told them all and paused for effect, just for a second, before striding out of the Abbey into the dark and windy night.

But since arriving at the Lodge, he'd felt deflated: trapped and vulnerable, too, as if his private feelings were being hijacked for some as yet mysterious purpose. There was a cold look in Sam's eye that belied all the friendliness. *'But why's he invited me here?'* thought Joe.

He could hear the rumble of family just out of sight: Laura chattering away to her mother in the kitchen, and her brother and sister upstairs. The walls were so thin in this house. Presumably, this conversation was also being monitored. It only added to his unease.

'Hope you like gut rot,' Sam went on, baring his teeth as he handed over a glass of amber-coloured liquid. Then he made an elaborately courteous gesture in the direction of one of the sagging, cluttered armchairs arranged around a very small and ineffective fire. He was playing the amiable munificent host, apparently oblivious to the absence of props, the bareness of the stage – not to mention the extreme sourness of the cider.

Sam took no notice of his mother whatsoever. Joe couldn't imagine his own father treating his grandfather like that and it added to his discomfort. He could feel Hester's gaze settling on him like mist and glanced at her very quickly, without expression. There was anguish in that gaze: a fierce bewilderment, almost as if she were seeing someone else.

Joe and his siblings hadn't been consulted about the move to the Abbey. It was their grandfather and father who'd made the decision, almost from one day to the next, overruling their mother, as usual. They'd seen their new house for the first time only when the removal vans had departed and all the familiar furniture from Guildford was set in place. Apart from the strange assortment of junk left behind, they'd little idea how the Abbey had looked before. It was only now, glancing about him, that Joe started to build up a picture not just of its past but of the real character of the family he'd become entangled with. It was like diving beneath the surface of a fairytale.

Those grand but threadbare damask curtains bunched in bulky horizontal folds either side of the lounge window like a mother's dress tried on by a small child must once have framed a window of a grand reception room. These worn rugs overlapping one another like the leaves of a cardboard box would have softened the sound of footsteps on the old flagstones before his mother's fitted carpets had obliterated them. There were strange little stools everywhere, seeming to grow out of the rugs like mushrooms, each encrusted with embroidery, and countless embroidered cushions, too. He could recognize the Abbey on every one – depicted in sunlight and in rain and, once, lit up like an ancient lantern against the darkness. The fraying, holy old sofa and mismatched armchairs had bolts of patterned cloth flung across them as part of a bold but casual style very different from his mother's uneasy attempts at brightening up a house. Behind a damaged Chinese-looking screen, he spied an old and very small television set. Clearly, unlike the enormous one in the upstairs lounge at the Abbey, it was not watched much.

By contrast, the shelves here were stuffed with books and several lay open and face down on the arms of chairs as if, in this house, reading was as constant and time-consuming as talking. There were no gadgets like the line of hanging silver balls on his father's desk at the Abbey which, when set in motion, set up a self-perpetuating pendulum effect. Here, there were only strange objects on display, like a badly stuffed heron, balding in several places, with an obvious bullet mark on its breast, imprisoned in a glass case with a handwritten label curling off it: 'August 1944'.

The place was freezing, though nobody remarked on it. The wind whistled through gaps in the sash windows and under the doors. Even Spectre and Caesar, parked in front of the dismal fire, looked offended. The only comfort was a delicious smell of roasting meat that filled the whole house. It made the dogs sigh and lick their chops. They started up every so often, too, as if hearing the strains of a familiar tune associated with happier times.

'Venison,' said Sam, sipping at his drink and nodding sagely, although Laura's mother had already mentioned what they'd be having for supper. Joe's father's nickname for her was 'the fridge', but she'd turned out to be surprisingly warm and friendly in her own home. She was also, it seemed, an excellent cook – which surprised him because, unlike his own mother (who he had to concede was not talented in this respect), she'd apparently been brought up with servants.

'Three cheers for Sam!' she'd announced proudly, before disappearing into the kitchen with Laura. According to her husband, he'd come across a dead deer in the road immediately after it had been hit by another car, which had apparently sped on regardless.

'Criminal!' he'd told Joe with a very serious face. And then, as if the thought had just struck him, 'I say, I do hope it wasn't one of your father's!'

Unfortunately, he'd explained, there was nothing that could be done for the animal and it seemed a shame to let it lie in the road and rot, especially as he'd seen for himself that it was perfectly fresh. It was just lucky he'd had his own car there to load it into. Very lucky, he'd repeated. Joe couldn't help remembering his grandfather's story about the maggot-ridden pigeon his family had once been forced to eat. However, it seemed that, among the Delanceys, scraping dead animals off the road was a matter for celebration.

In fact, in this shabby yet oddly stylish little house, he felt as if everything he'd been brought up to believe in had been turned upside down, with Laura's dad the greatest conundrum of all. Used to a self-made workaholic of a father who abhorred wasting time, he couldn't get a handle on this man who had no profession or regular salary and yet acted so superior. 'What does he do all day?' he'd asked Laura. Hadn't the question been asked often enough in his own family?

'He's writing a thriller,' she'd replied very defensively and Joe could see that there were indeed three very new-looking notebooks on a desk in an alcove with several pens neatly lined up beside them – the only touch of precision in this otherwise chaotic room. He couldn't help noticing that there were also about half a dozen carefully painted miniature model aeroplanes suspended by threads from the ceiling. They could only have been made by Laura's brother, surely? But this didn't seem to fit with the sophisticated, articulate boy he'd been introduced to.

In their speech and jokes, Laura's brother and sister were surprisingly similar to his own. And though Maria Delancey was a lot more girly than Genevieve, David Delancey was a bit of an intellectual show-off, exactly like Justin. Joe could even imagine meeting him in different circumstances and making friends.

Even as he was thinking about all this, Sam returned him to reality. 'Any thoughts yet on the wedding?' he asked, and Joe caught a sudden sharp movement from Hester on the periphery of his vision.

Taken aback, he shook his head. He was reminded of Laura's warning. 'Don't let him push you into anything. If we really want to get married eventually, we can always elope: get on a train and go to a registry office.'

Sam nodded. 'Early days,' he said. 'Early days.' Then, as if contradicting himself, he went on, 'I have to tell you, her mother is set on it taking place at the Abbey.'

'Oh,' said Joe, thinking with some trepidation of his own family's reaction to this.

'Pity the chapel's gone.' Sam made it sound as if it had been done away with very recently, instead of more than four centuries before. He continued smoothly, 'Very exciting! Excellent thing to get married young – I did it myself.' He was behaving as if the matter was settled, and Joe felt very young, helpless and tongue-tied, and profoundly wished Laura would join them.

'The summer might be nice,' Sam added casually.

Silence descended and Joe felt the terrifying prospect of imminent matrimony press down on him. Laura's father was behaving as if a vast unstoppable operation had been set in motion and, furthermore, had somehow managed to suggest that *his* family would be footing the bill.

'Water off a duck's back,' Sam said with a smile. '*Lots* of chums to invite on our side,' he went on, as if even the guest list had already been decided.

'*But I'm only twenty-one!*' Joe had proposed to Laura on the spur of the moment – as a romantic gesture, really – in reaction to his father's clumsy attempt to split them up. It might have been nice to be engaged to her, more or less permanently. But now he could see that if he wasn't very careful he was going to end up like his sister.

Ever since the costume ball, where she'd re-met a friend from Guildford days called Edward Morton, Genevieve had been a reformed character. The days of drunken, promiscuous pick-ups down at the local pub were well over. Now it was 'Edward thinks . . .' and 'As I said to Edward . . .' She'd thrown away her raffish individuality and become part of a couple, with every opinion filtered through another person – who wasn't that interesting anyway. She'd gone on a diet. She'd taken to wearing skirts and make-up. She'd even abandoned her old interest in horses. Worst of all, she'd become censorious of all those who didn't subscribe to the same conventional way of life. It was even unimportant to her that her grandfather had reservations about her boyfriend.

'You can do better than that, Gen,' he'd advised, but it was useless. It seemed Genevieve had found what she wanted, which was to make a life with someone who came from more or less exactly the same social background as herself.

'You'll live at the Abbey, of course,' said Sam. 'Very nice life indeed. Beats me why anyone should want to do anything else.'

It threw Joe into a state of such nervousness that he found himself accepting another glass of the disgusting cider.

Chapter Twenty-eight

'We need to talk, son.'

'Now?' As usual, Mark was exploring possibilities, calculating risks, mentally setting up deals – all the ceaseless activity of the successful property tycoon – because if you took your eye off the ball for one second, as he liked to say before setting the pendulum gadget on his desk in motion . . .

'Chop chop!' said Stanley, just like when Mark was little and pleading for delay, as any other child might, before getting the wood in or clearing the step of snow, or any of the innumerable chores expected of him then. If age taught anything, thought Stanley grimly, it was that procrastination was a gamble.

Now, entirely through his own fault, he'd found himself in the nightmare he'd for so long dreaded. No, he corrected himself, that wasn't quite right – yearned for and dreaded was more the ticket, because some devil was pushing him closer and closer to the truth. It was like his insistence that Sam and Fred Delancey be invited for lunch at the Abbey. What had possessed him, in retrospect?

'Give us a minute,' said Mark, looking worried, and it turned out to be ten at least before he was ready to offer most of his attention to his father. He was still patting his pockets, glancing at his watch, seizing a notebook to scribble reminders to himself.

'Not here,' said Stanley. He needed to set his explanation in the right context, for himself as well as for his son. 'Let's take a walk,' he suggested.

'I've a meeting in London this afternoon,' said Mark, checking the time yet again. 'I need to leave the house by twelve – latest.' Besides, walking was for weekends, not a busy Tuesday when the phones would be ringing.

'It's not even 9.30,' said Stanley firmly. 'And it's important.'

So they left the bustle of the Abbey, where Lily was hoovering rolls of fluff from the new red carpet in the Great Hall. Stanley led the way, since his son had no idea where he was taking him.

'Half an hour max,' Mark reminded him, dressed more suitably for a board meeting than for a country walk.

The day was cool but sunny, with a skein of white clouds drifting across an azure sky, and Stanley felt his spirits lift, as always, in the fresh air. As they approached the open land behind the Abbey, he attempted to paint a picture of the countryside he'd known as a child.

In 1925, he said, these exhausted over-fertilized fields they were skirting had been a paradise of long grass woven with brightly coloured wild flowers.

'I remember the buttercups,' Mark admitted a little sulkily.

'Oh, gil' cups!' said Stanley a little contemptuously, using the old rural term. And then he reeled off a whole list of unfamiliar names like weasel's snout and lamb's succory and mousetails and corncockles (with a deep pink flower, which the farmers had abhorred, he said, because, cut up with the harvest, it made the bread bitter). Drifts of butterflies had settled on the scented meadows during that lost era and Stanley told Mark that the year he was ten was the last time the Black-veined White had ever been seen in England.

'I need a botany lesson?'

'No, son,' said Stanley a little humbly. 'Summer of twenty-five were when I come across Edmund Delancey, in a manner of speaking.'

They'd reached their destination now and he needed his son to understand that this dried-up trickle blobbed with rainbow detergent foam had once been a wide river of clear, rushing water.

'Cruel,' Stanley went on, shaking his head as if remonstrating with his own foolishness. 'Even then.'

For, before he was made to see the error of his ways, Edmund Delancey had enjoyed collecting insects to impale on pins. That day in July, sixty years before, Stanley told Mark, Edmund had been after a dragonfly with his net – an Orange Spotted Emerald making its darting, hovering way over its favoured patch of bank.

'Tail like a stick of speckled liquorice, bright green body like a gobstopper.' In fact, Stanley pointed out indignantly, if Edmund hadn't slipped and fallen in and nearly drowned, that beautiful endangered insect might have met with the same fate as countless butterflies and moths. 'Stuck away in a silly old box some place in the Abbey.' He shook his head in dismay.

'So you *did* save his life!'

'Who said?' asked Stanley, instantly suspicious.

'Mam, right at the end.'

'So what?' He was annoyed with himself. The whole point of coming down to the river had been to set the scene, lead up to the thing gradually. But his feelings had got the better of him. He made an effort. In order for Mark to understand the whole painful, complicated story, he must put aside the unfairness and bitterness of what happened later. He must try and conjure up for his son the exact nature of his friendship with Edmund Delancey and why it had been so special: what it had felt like for him, the gardener's boy, to be taken up by a young aristocrat. Because it was Edmund Delancey, the son of the great house, who'd done all the running – at any rate, to begin with.

'He were always turning up at the cottage, asking for me. Took it into his head I were the only one he liked.' Stanley actually smiled fondly as he remembered it.

'You were flattered,' Mark pronounced a little sourly.

'Course I were flattered!' That was how it had started, anyway, Stanley conceded, but he'd come to love Edmund like a brother. They were both only children, he explained, and before making friends with Edmund, life had been very solitary. Perhaps that was why he'd felt so close to animals and birds, he said, as if this had only just occurred to him. But having the company of another boy of the same age had been wonderful, and it was obvious Edmund felt the same. Once a firm foundation for friendship had been established – 'After I fished him out,' he told Mark, 'he were laying right where your feet are' – there was no stopping them.

Edmund wasn't particularly popular with the servants, and that included the Trafford family. 'Your grammer said he were a right Lord Fauntleroy.' However, Stanley maintained that they all had it wrong because, once you got to know him, Edmund was 'champion'. It wasn't *his* fault he gave the wrong impression: it was his background.

Warming to his theme, Stanley explained that folk reared in great houses by nannies then sent away to boarding school weren't encouraged to show feelings. Quite the reverse. Edmund once told him, in a rare moment of vulnerability, about being cruelly taunted the first night he arrived at school, when he was caught weeping for his Narnie. It was no wonder, really, that he'd come to fear owning up to sadness or anger, or even joy. Getting Edmund to admit he was having a good time was a triumph, Stanley pointed out, because he seemed to believe that a kind of amused cynicism, like looking at life through a layer of thick glass, was the only safe approach. Edmund had a droll wit waiting to be discovered. 'He were a right funny one.' Stanley sounded extraordinarily affectionate and proprietorial, in the circumstances.

For years, he said, they met in the woods and fields surrounding the Abbey, enjoying the freedom from their different worlds and the novelty of each other's company. Despite being sent away to school and, after that, university, something always pulled Edmund back to the friendship. Neither set of parents was any happier and it caused talk locally, as it was bound to. Once, said Stanley with a rueful smile, he became involved in a nasty punch-up at the pub. 'Then the war come along,' he announced with a beaming smile, as if the world had changed miraculously for him at that point. 'And I had your Mam and Edmund were with Hester. She weren't a beauty, like your Mam,' he said. But there was something very elegant about her all the same. 'She knew who she were, see?' But, then, Hester came from the same confident, grand world as Edmund. Stanley added quickly, 'She were a joker, too.' If he hadn't got to know Edmund quite so well, he explained, he might have dismissed Hester as stuck-up; but she had the same dry, amused way about her – dropping the witticisms so casually and quietly you almost missed them.

Even so, he was surprised when the engagement was announced, because somehow it hadn't looked to him like things were going that way. He couldn't have said why, he told Mark, an odd blankness in his eyes. Once, he went on, he'd wondered if Edmund's surprise wedding had anything to do with him marrying Effie so suddenly. But far more likely, he pronounced, it was the imminence of war. Everyone was jumping into marriage. The terror and uncertainty of that time was impossible to convey – especially in the early days, when Germany was still allied with Russia. 'It were like we was up against the devil himself.'

After a bit of initial awkwardness, said Stanley, Hester and Effie hit it off like a house on fire. The friendship was a godsend for Effie, he explained – 'specially after you come along' – because she was only young and very lonely for company her sort of age and missing him dreadfully. She'd loved helping out at the Abbey's hospital. It had to be said, Stanley conceded, that all the Delanceys made her feel very welcome and for that, he went on, sounding a little pious, he blessed them. He seemed to forget that, only a few years later, he'd laid a chilling curse on them. It was as if going back to the good times momentarily expunged the bitterness. He was remembering being young.

It was towards the end of the war, late summer of 1944, Stanley told his son, that Edmund had joked about his seeming inability to produce an heir. At this point, Stanley took out the pipe he occasionally smoked and, using a dead matchstick, rootled around its bowl very concentratedly for several minutes. Then, with a faint sigh, as if longing to get this over with, he resumed his story.

They were out searching for a heron at the time, he said, enjoying a shared leave and the pretence that the world was sane: trying to forget that it was always possible this might be the last such expedition through the woods and fields and marshland they loved so much. 'I never seen it more beautiful,' he recalled with a misty look. He wanted to tell Mark word for word what had been said because that private conversation between friends acquired increasing significance for him.

'We've been married for five years, you know,' Edmund remarked, whacking at a reed with his stick. 'It's not that I care for babies overmuch. Noisy little beggars, if you ask me. But the pressure's on now.' He paused because they both knew very well what he meant. Then he shrugged with a little smile as if even the possibility of imminent death could be mocked. 'Who knows when this wretched war will end? If we don't get cracking, Hes and I might be the last Delanceys to enjoy the Abbey.' He made another amused face. 'Ghastly thought – handing it over to my philistine second cousin once removed!'

'You're lucky,' said Stanley with his cheeky smile because he was always worrying about getting Effie pregnant again. One child was plenty in such scarce and frightening times. That pessary of hers was dodgy. Coitus interruptus was his usual method of birth control, but it was risky, too, and took away a lot of the pleasure. Even so, there was no way he'd ever use a sheath. Passion-killers, he called them.

'There's a story about the Abbey . . .' Edmund began in his languid drawl. He was always telling stories about the house. He could afford to relax because it was understood Stanley would do any shooting. Besides, he was a far better shot.

Stanley had spotted the heron standing motionless in reeds, one twig-like leg bent at a perfect right angle behind it. This particular bird had been attacking nests, the women at the Abbey had complained, picking off baby ducklings with its sword of a beak. Even so, before the war he'd have abhorred the destruction of such a beautiful creature. Now, with part of his mind, he found he could blank off all thoughts of pain or waste. He took aim, only half listening to Edmund's ramblings, which seemed to concern the inability of a couple of his ancestors to produce an heir.

'The story is, they went through the whole performance of a pregnancy and, when the nine months were up, a baby was smuggled in. It was the son of the steward's daughter, legend has it, who was paid handsomely for the favour.'

Bang! A clean shot straight through the breast, so death was at least instantaneous.

'I say, well done! Never even saw him!'

Edmund fired blanks, so Stanley was given to understand. However much he tried, he was incapable of creating a child with his wife. Why else did he say, with a rueful smile, 'It's hard on Hes cos there's nothing wrong with *her*'? Stanley felt a rush of warm sympathy. He knew what it had cost for Edmund to confide such a humiliating secret: it was another proof of the strength of their friendship.

Edmund was touching the dead heron cautiously, stroking its warm feathers as if considering whether or not it merited stuffing, another bizarre upper-class pursuit of his. He had a familiar look on his face now, as if he wanted to back away from the intimacy they'd just shared because he'd learnt that any display of vulnerability was dangerous. Accordingly, Stanley changed the subject.

'It were natural,' Stanley muttered as miserably as a condemned man. He meant that what happened on a chilly evening in 1945, about six months after he and Edmund went looking for that heron, had struck him, at the time, as entirely impulsive – for both parties involved.

'It were about fear,' he told his son, who regarded him as a hero but had never served in a war and so knew nothing of the dreadful terror of bombardment, or the strange things that could happen when you found yourself alive and unharmed, after all.

He risked a quick glance and saw that Mark had stopped his clock-watching and was beginning to look distinctly agitated.

'*My number's up*,' he thought, somewhere between the air raid sirens going off and the bombs landing so close, making the ground judder. He'd faced danger before, but there was something dream-like about this, especially now the war was almost over. It would be just his luck, he told himself, to cop it in a club full of nobs after surviving the horrors of Dunkirk and so much else.

All the lights went out. Then there was that familiar though peculiar silence after the ground had finished shaking and the glass shattering and before the screaming began. His ears were still ringing from the blast and something quite heavy had landed on his back. Hester was lying very still and limp beneath him. He cautiously flexed first one leg, then the other; and, after that, he tested his arms and his back. Everything was still in working order, though his officer's uniform was covered in dust. The relief was indescribable.

He rolled off Hester, in the process dislodging the piece of ceiling that had fallen on him, and – after someone had found a candle and lit it – inspected her anxiously. Her eyes were closed and she appeared to have fainted. Her lovely blue dress was all dirty and ripped in places, though her string of pearls still gleamed against her throat. She seemed very childlike and vulnerable suddenly.

'Hester?'

She opened her eyes then shut them again, as if she couldn't believe she'd survived.

'We're still here!' Stanley assured her. He bent down and brushed some of the dust off. 'Give us your hand, love.'

As he pulled her up she slumped against him – Hester, who never admitted to any sort of weakness – and Stanley found himself hugging her very close and hard. '*We're alive!*' the embrace said. It was immaterial that, just before the air raid sirens went off, she'd been putting him in his place, stressing the yawning social gap between them.

She was crying. He could feel her tears against his neck.

An unbroken bottle had rolled on to the floor and it still had liquid in it. '*Whisky?*' thought Stanley. It seemed too much to hope for, especially when whisky was like gold dust. But, on taking a sniff, he discovered that miracles very occasionally did happen.

'Let's get out of here,' he said, and Hester looked at him tremulously, eyes still very shiny, and nodded fervently.

'It were nothing,' Stanley insisted, after relaying the bare, shameful facts. But Mark was looking very grim and accusatory because, of course, his father's whole behaviour and attitude indicated otherwise. Why else was he telling him the squalid story?

Nothing and something. A hasty, passionate fusing of bodies in a dark doorway littered with rubbish, which Hester had seemed to need as much as he did. It was a celebration of being alive: surviving one of those devilish V2s that exploded with no warning. 'Took out a six-storey hotel hundred yard away,' he remembered. 'Smouldering bungalow when Jerry were done.' Couples married to other people had probably fucked all over London in the aftermath of that bombing. It was what you did, Stanley attempted to convey to Mark, man to man. He wasn't going to tell him that the same thing had happened in France a couple of times, for exactly the same reason: sheer relief, like pinching himself, and, in the case of those French women, almost as impersonal as blowing his nose. But he did tell his son most passionately that he'd never felt he was betraying Effie with Hester. He'd loved his wife deeply, as Mark well knew.

The episode with Hester had been nothing in the sense that – once beyond a rush of guilt, which was on account of Edmund, too – he'd put it away, deciding it had been inevitable and not really his fault. This wasn't difficult because it was obvious Hester was of exactly the same mind. There was a definite awkwardness between them after that, and clearly she felt guilt about Effie because she made a point of avoiding her, too. He felt sorry about that, for Effie's sake. But at least his friendship with Edmund seemed unaffected – until their confrontation in the Refectory.

When Hester had become pregnant, he'd thought nothing of it, he told Mark. He wasn't surprised Edmund had got it wrong about being infertile. It was only much later, long after his family had been forced to leave Melcombe, that he started to ask painful questions, forcing himself to remember things he'd

vowed never to think of again, rearranging the pieces of the
past until the evidence seemed overwhelming.

Silence fell. Mark had got it now, of course. He was very pale
and licking his lips. He kept glancing at his father, as if he simply
couldn't believe he'd kept this secret from him. He'd forgotten
all about his business appointment. He sat down on the grass
in his beautiful, expensive suit and put his head in his hands.

Was he recalling the never-ending drumming up of hatred
against the Delanceys during the years of exile? And, more to
the point, the contempt rained down on Sam, once his family
had taken over the Abbey? The motive for coming back was
revenge, they'd always been given to understand. Stanley had
encouraged the bad feeling! And look how he'd behaved when
the Delanceys had come for lunch!

'But you hate him!' he said eventually.

Stanley's first reaction was to nod agreement. Then he shook
his head, appearing miserably confused.

It wasn't as simple as that.

The revelation came with a dream: a recurring one with a
shocking new twist at the end. They said dreams were the
expression of the subconscious, didn't they? So perhaps he'd
been mulling over the question marks for years.

In his recurring dream he'd find himself back in October
1947 on that terrible morning when his family were forced to
leave their cottage. They'd endured the scrubbing and the
washing and the clearing and the burning and now, exhausted
and frightened but with no time to rest, they were compelled to
begin a journey. They were halfway up the grassy path that led
to the Abbey when he suddenly ordered them to stop. 'I forgot

summat,' he said. He made them all wait while he went back. He opened the flimsy door he believed he'd closed for the very last time, and began to search the empty cottage. The thing was, he knew he'd left something very important behind, but for the life of him couldn't remember what. He'd search with increasing desperation, but never ever find it.

However, this time, the familiar dream cut to a different scene: the river where he'd once saved Edmund from drowning. He was back in 1925, aged ten, and saving him all over again, struggling desperately to pull him from the water before both of them were swept away, rolling him on his back so as to administer the kiss of life. Edmund coughed and spluttered, just as he'd done then, before the vomiting took over. But when he opened his eyes, instead of the familiar blue they were the colour of black treacle.

He'd woken himself up with the shock, he told Mark. He'd listened for Effie's breathing, as usual, and it was very laboured and stop-start and the room felt stifling because she couldn't get warm, however much they turned up the heating. A part of him longed to share his complicated reactions with her.

The thing was, he *knew*. He'd lain there shaking, assembling all the bits and pieces of evidence. 'It were staring me in the face.'

Samuel Hadley Delancey (a healthy, full-term baby) had been born on 14 November 1945 – he remembered the date, he said, because it was exactly three months after Japan surrendered – which meant he must have been conceived in February, which was when he and Hester had met up at the Cygnet. And for the whole of that month, he now recalled, Edmund had been away in Salisbury: in the end, he hadn't managed to get home once.

'It must have occurred to you before,' said Mark, grim-faced.

'No.' Stanley sounded very innocent. But, then he wasn't the sort of person who totted up months on his fingers and anyway, as he'd already explained, the thing with Hester was so fleeting it might not have happened. Especially when both of them pretended afterwards that it hadn't.

'It must have seemed to others there was something not right.'

'The servants?' If there'd been mutterings, said Stanley, he was unaware of them.

'That's not what I meant,' said Mark sternly.

'Course Edmund knew!' exploded Stanley.

'Hester could've had other ...' Mark searched for an appropriate word. 'Liaisons.'

'No,' Stanley said very definitely. He gave the impression that he had more powerful arguments in his possession but was reluctant to reveal them out of delicacy. 'Samuel were mine.' He was pretty sure now, he went on to explain, that Edmund had known the baby was his from the start. 'He were only what they wanted. They could keep the Abbey, then.' He'd come to believe he'd been manipulated, but very subtly, with nothing ever spelt out, like the Delanceys did everything. Hester was poison. Look at her treatment of Effie!

Once he'd got it, he said, he found himself thinking about Sam Delancey continuously.

'You're everything to me, son, and always will be.' But, after that, he sighed disconsolately. 'Effie and me, we'd set our hearts on making us a big family when the hard years was over, but by the time we was fit, it were too late for my poor dear.' His voice became a little plaintive, as if even he was losing patience with his own complicated feelings. 'It got so's every hour of the day he'd crowd my head. I'd puzzle over what he were at, the type of person he'd be. When Effie passed, God rest her, I were *compelled* to see him. And when the Abbey come up for sale – it were like a sign.'

The day they went to view the house and met Sam Delancey, he knew for sure he was his son. 'You mind his hands,' he advised Mark. 'Soft as they are, they're my own.' He added, 'Hair grows the exact same way, too.' It was astonishing, really, that nobody else had spotted it.

There'd been an unexpected bonus to the visit. 'When I saw the state of Hester . . .' he began. He was remembering thinking that, now Hester's mind had gone, he was the sole person in possession of the truth.

'So we uprooted all of our lives for that?' Mark paused. 'Why couldn't you have caught a train from Guildford, on the quiet? You could've fed him some excuse.' He paused before adding bitterly, 'Not so difficult to tell a lie, is it?'

Stanley flushed because it was terrible to be spoken to so harshly by Mark. He admitted humbly, 'You've every right.'

'You could've seen him the once and come away,' Mark went on. 'But no! You had to involve every one of us!' He paused again. 'All that trouble and expense. Not to mention the rest.'

'I needed to know him,' said Stanley very softly. Then he started to become angry, too. 'We *had* to buy the Abbey! How else would folk like us have got to know the likes of them, for all our wealth?'

'And did we?'

'No,' Stanley conceded very bitterly. But he'd tried, he insisted. When they'd looked round the place that very first time, he'd made an effort with Sam Delancey. Maybe Mark hadn't noticed him trying to make conversation in the background? But all he'd got back from Sam and his wife, right from the start, was insults and ice.

He was delighted when the Delanceys announced they intended to stay on at the Lodge. Looking back, said Stanley, they most likely hoped it would be a deterrent – but, for him, it had been the clincher, the moment when he knew they *must* buy the Abbey. As for the Delanceys' hostility . . . Never mind, he'd thought, once he and his family were part of the place, they'd all make friends. With Edmund dead and gone, it could be a new beginning. After all, weren't they helping the Delanceys out, in a manner of speaking? Nobody else seemed interested in buying the property.

However, he went on, once in the Abbey, every one of his friendly moves was deliberately misinterpreted. Take the offer to keep those portraits. It had been motivated by kindness, he said, because it was obvious the Delanceys had nowhere else to put them. He didn't add that he'd enjoyed contemplating that notional dynasty, and the secret knowledge that he'd interrupted the bloodline. 'But they acted like it was *them* doing us the favour!' It had been his idea to get the pictures properly cleaned up, as a surprise. 'Won't go into that now!' he said, shaking his head.

When he delivered Hester back from one of her crazed break-ins, he complained, the Delanceys were more churlish than grateful. None of them were allowed to socialize with their friends. Look how they'd sabotaged the costume ball! Then there were the so-called jokes: the knocking off of his carefully reared pheasants – and tying them to the door knocker, in case he'd failed to notice – and the dumping of manure in the driveway so none of their cars could get past. Not to mention the constant pilfering from the Abbey gardens and letting their dogs gallop round wild, depositing shit all over the lawn. But the very worst thing, the final straw, he spluttered, had been the failure to make any sort of sympathetic gesture after Justin's accident. He'd realized then that, for all he was his biological father, Sam was in every other way a Delancey.

'Look at you!' he told Mark with the usual pride. 'Trafford through and through. From what I hear, he spends his days constructing model Spitfires.' He added contemptuously, 'Closest *he'll* ever get to combat!'

'Don't know why you had to tell me this in the first place.' Mark sounded as if the words were wrung out of him.

'Well, I wouldn't've,' Stanley admitted. 'It were cos of Joe, weren't it? Could've knocked me down with a feather!'

The realization that Joe had been having a secret affair with one of the Delancey girls – and, though he couldn't know it, his first cousin – had come as a dreadful shock. However, he'd believed he could stamp on it – especially with the cooperation of the Delanceys, whom he'd assumed were equally appalled (though for a different reason). When Sam had phoned to suggest a meeting, he'd been all for it, as Mark was aware. The thing was, Stanley confessed, a little shame-faced, even now, a part of him still hoped for some kind of reconciliation.

'So you'd have gone on keeping it yourself, would you? Even if he'd been friendly to us all?'

Stanley nodded miserably.

'And you banged it into me from when I was knee high that family was everything!'

'So it is, son,' said Stanley, seeming almost as bewildered.

Mark was more furious than he ever remembered being. Out of sheer foolishness and misplaced lust, his father had risked a good marriage, thereby ruining the health and peace of mind of the mother he'd adored. Not content with that, years later, he'd made them all move from a happy and comfortable way of life to one they'd detested. He'd provoked a state of such poisonous relations between the two families that, at least once, Mark had feared he himself would have a heart attack. And finally, he'd caused his innocent grandson to become drawn into an incestuous relationship.

And then he looked at his father and saw that he was just a little, frightened old man, who needed protecting now.

It was going to be all right. They'd shared too much tenderness and history. He was already adjusting, beginning to forgive his father for deceiving them all. There'd been more words exchanged between them this past week than in forty-five years: his father peeling away the layers of the past until, finally, the real story of his family's banishment from the Abbey was revealed. Edmund had guessed the truth or, more likely, Stanley had lost his temper when denied money and spilt it out. It was strange how, in later life, he seemed to have convinced himself that Edmund had orchestrated that one-off conception so badly needed to continue the Delancey line. Mark thought of the heroic, tough father he'd idolized. But in some strange way, this distressing confession of weakness might end up bringing them even closer. He frowned as the thought came into his mind: *'For as long as I can remember, I wanted a brother.'*

'Laura's a fine lass,' said Stanley, but he shook his head, nevertheless. He'd been comforted to find this illicit granddaughter so thoroughly nice and normal. But as for a marriage and the possibility of children . . . 'Joe'll come to his senses.'

'Has to,' Mark agreed.

'Don't matter if it's legal. Ain't natural.'

They were united on that.

'There's no way we can keep this under wraps,' said Mark. But he didn't sound alarmed. He even gave the impression that he was quite looking forward to Sam Delancey learning the truth about himself.

There was just one more question. 'Is that it, Dad?'

'What do you mean, son?'

'What I said,' Mark cautioned him with extreme seriousness. 'No more surprises?'

'That's the last,' Stanley promised, clenching a fist so tightly that his nails bit into his palm.

Chapter Twenty-nine

'My dearest Pooh,

I never meant for it to happen – this you must believe. It was like falling under a spell orchestrated by mysterious, invisible forces. That terrifying yet wonderful moment was as great a shock for me as it was for you. After all the years of pretence, everything suddenly seemed to me so simple. I am glad I was foolish – oh yes, oh yes – despite all the grief and trouble it caused. Part of me is so very thankful I dared, at last, to be truthful even though that brief moment of ecstasy – of recognition – was also when I started to lose you for ever.

My only solace now is remembering the happy times. Nothing comforts, not even beauty though I try, I try. Nor even the child, though in my heart I am glad of him. I move through this exquisite place as if in a prison, appreciating none of it. And if I wander in the gardens my only thought is that, by some miracle, I might happen on you.

Today, I believe there was a sign. I found myself leaving

the familiar paths and following that old one, all overgrown with brambles now. Oh, it was terrible to see the thatched roof fallen in, rats whisking among the ruins. But when, scarcely able to breathe, I pushed open the broken-down door and entered that place of desolation, I was confounded to feel more comforted than afraid – almost as if, by some strange alchemy, your soul still inhabits that place. How fanciful I am growing, in my old age! But I shall not go again. I dare not. I shall hold in my heart the memory of that brief respite from this anguish: as if, once again, you'd taken my hand in yours.

I curse the streak of evil that caused you to hate me so. But the loathing you feel for me is as nothing compared to the revulsion I have for myself. And still you remain the one I love, the source of my only joy. You kissed me – remember? – though you mocked me cruelly at the end. I would forfeit the rest of my life for a single glimpse of your lovely eyes, your beautiful smile. Pity me, my dearest. Pity and, I beg, forgive . . .'

There, the last letter of all ended with 'Figlet' scrawled beneath, as if the usual perfectionism had been swept away by the passion of the author's feelings. When Janice held the thin paper to bright sunlight, it seemed as if the precisely executed handwriting was visibly fading away. Darkness had preserved the old ink for all these years – as thoroughly, she now understood, as a collective shame had shrouded the truth.

The story of the real identity of Sam Delancey's father had been revealed to the children the evening before, in the Refectory. Mark had returned from his walk with Stanley angry and confused but, for once, had shared his emotions. It was the first time Janice had ever heard him criticize his father. 'How could he do this to me, Jan?' The two of them had never been closer.

'Granddad has something to tell you all,' said Mark, just as the children were shifting impatiently, about to slide from their seats once supper had been eaten.

She saw her father-in-law shoot an imploring look at her husband, and, after a moment's hesitation, Mark nodded brusquely, as if he'd just taken up position as leader of the pack. So it was he who relayed the bare facts of the case without expression.

Stanley sat with his head bowed in shame. 'It were wartime,' he muttered wretchedly.

Normally, very little fazed the children, but this shocked them into silence. Then Justin and Genevieve began shooting each other incredulous glances, Genevieve chewing her lips as if fighting hysteria, unable to look at the grandfather she'd revered.

'So if he's really your brother,' said Justin, spelling things out as usual, 'then that makes . . .'

But poor Joe had already worked it out for himself. White as a sheet, he shoved back his chair and left the room.

'I won't have Granddad shouted at,' Mark warned, to the further unhappiness of Stanley, who, until then, had known nothing but respect from his family. 'We've told you now and that's the end of it, do you hear?'

However, for Janice, the extraordinary revelation had solved a mystery.

'Wicked and scheming,' was how Stanley had described Hester and there seemed little doubt she'd applauded Edmund's decision to banish him from the estate. However, it was now apparent to Janice that Stanley had missed a trick. The letters she'd found in the cupboard revealed Hester's secret anguish. The disdainful shell had masked a desperate heart.

The realization that she loved the man who'd fathered her son would have come gradually, Janice decided. The memory of their single sexual encounter must have acquired increasing poignancy because Stanley only ever loved his wife and was, anyway, gone for good. Hester must have betrayed herself in a hundred ways to her husband. No wonder Edmund had come to hate her and the marriage had turned so poisonous. How dreadfully ironic, thought Janice, that when, finally – in circumstances she could never have imagined – Hester got to see Stanley again, she probably didn't even know who he was.

For all her great dislike of Fred – who, it now appeared, was her sister-in-law – Janice was actually finding herself starting to pity the Delanceys. Poor Joe (who'd recovered a little) had told her Laura had broken the truth to Fred, who'd been put in the unenviable position of having to tell Sam. And now everything Sam believed himself to be was exploded, the deep-seated arrogance and pretensions ripped away like a set of shabby old clothes. What effect would it have on him? She couldn't even imagine.

She could see Stanley out of the window, talking to a gardener by one of the flowerbeds and, for a second, toyed with the romantic idea of playing postman and delivering the letters at last. Then she heard him bellow, the anger penetrating the newly installed double glazing, 'You daft or what? Dahlias has to be lifted and stored, come the frost!'

It was odd to feel protective towards a demented old woman who'd never shown her the slightest bit of friendliness.

*

Laura mumbled, 'All this stuff . . .'

'Doing my head in,' Joe agreed.

They sat in the coffee bar in town, so recently the scene of longing glances and whispered desires, and found they could scarcely bear to look at each other. But none of this excruciating mess was their fault. It seemed they'd been innocent pawns, caught up in a forty-year-old story of manipulation and revenge.

'It was so unbelievably irresponsible!' she raged.

He nodded, just as confused and upset, not knowing how to play the scene at all.

'I blame Gran more than your grandfather. Gran *always* knew! And the worst thing is – she's got away with it!'

Joe mumbled, looking at the floor, 'I wanted to let you know I'm catching the train to London this afternoon.' He added, 'Think I'll probably stay for a bit.'

'Good idea,' said Laura briskly. 'I'm worried about my pa,' she went on, as if talking to herself. 'I've never seen him like this.' Then, in a matter-of-fact though kindly tone, as if she wanted to get this enforced meeting over and done with in the most civilized way possible: 'I understand, Joe. Honestly.'

She hadn't looked into his beautiful black eyes once, let alone confronted the memory of his luscious mouth. '*I'm not even* going *there*,' she told herself angrily, unaware that her grandmother had gone into a similar kind of denial forty years before.

When the time came to say goodbye, she shook hands, refusing to be disturbed by his warm touch. But he didn't appear surprised by the formality. So far as she could tell, he welcomed it.

A little later on, still giving the impression of being more cross than bewildered, she asked her father, 'Are you just going to sit there like that?'

The truth was, he terrified her. Although it was past noon, he was unshaven and unwashed, still in his old tartan dressing gown. He was engaged in painting the cockpit of a tiny model Hurricane, using a magnifying glass because he refused to go to the optician and be fitted for spectacles. To Laura's very great relief, her grandmother was nowhere to be seen. She was in the doghouse. It was impossible to imagine her and Stanley young. As for them having sex . . .

She could hear her mother desperately whisking away in the kitchen as if, in sympathy with the collapse of Sam's world, egg whites were refusing to stiffen. 'I don't know what to do,' she'd just whispered. 'He won't eat. He won't talk to me!' Then she'd looked stricken by her own disloyalty.

Typically, David and Maria had distanced themselves, for once volunteering to walk the dogs so they could carry on discussing the extraordinary developments in private.

Laura longed to be able to escape into selfish immaturity, too. But then she remembered how her father had come to her rescue the year before, packing her off to India when the Abbey was sold. Besides, she was the eldest and, in so far as favourites were allowed in their family, had always enjoyed a special connection with him.

At the sound of her voice, he hadn't stirred. His previous glooms now appeared to her theatrical, even insincere – as if, secretly, he might have enjoyed playing the part of dispossessed heir to a great house. But how, thought Laura, could he possibly come to terms with this? He was the son of his family's former gardener. The worst enemy he'd ever had had turned out to be his own brother. No wonder he'd taken refuge in a scaled-down universe where all that mattered was applying the right colour paint to the correct minuscule area of plastic.

The noise from the kitchen had ceased and she pictured her mother twisting her hair and blinking as she listened through the door.

She said carefully, though not over-sympathetically, 'I know this has been dreadful for you, Pa.'

He didn't look up. He sighed as if she couldn't begin to comprehend his despair. Then he dipped his brush into a tiny pot of grey paint, picked up his magnifying glass and approached a minute propeller. But his hand started to tremble. He shut his eyes, seemed to be trying to control himself, but it was no good. He laid the brush down, stared into space as if waiting for her to go away.

'But you're not the only one,' Laura pursued earnestly. 'Everyone's upset that Gran could have . . .' She left the sentence unfinished. She was thinking that her father didn't look anything like Edmund in the old photos. However, from her limited observation of Stanley, it was hard to find a resemblance there either. In speech and manner and outlook, her father appeared exactly what he'd for so long believed himself to be: an aristocrat, fallen on hard times. It wasn't his fault he'd no sense of a work ethic, she thought fiercely, when Edmund had apparently considered giving the odd direction to staff and attempting *The Times* crossword a day well spent. There'd been no encouragement or guidance when he'd tried his hand at running the estate: only blame when it went wrong. No wonder he'd never had any real confidence. But he should have, she thought – and wished she could tell him so. Despite being deprived of good parenting, he'd gone on to be a loving and funny father himself and, unlike Edmund and Hester, had enjoyed an extremely close and happy marriage.

She sounded very abrupt as she informed him, 'That thing with Joe Trafford . . . It's over now.'

He didn't respond, though he was sitting very still and seemed to be paying attention.

'I think I know how you felt, Pa,' she went on, making her voice gentle because the last thing she wanted was for him to feel guilty. 'You might not have been crazy about him, but perhaps you liked the idea of me living in the Abbey?'

She saw him shut his eyes briefly, as if in pain.

'I liked him before I knew who he was.' It was a fact, though the way she put it suggested more of a friendship than an instantaneous attraction. She was remembering the night she'd followed Joe to the Abbey after his brother's accident, the way the anger and disappointment with her parents had fallen away as the beauty and magic of the house reclaimed her once more. 'I think maybe a lot of what I came to feel for Joe was because he lived there.' She added with the same painful honesty, 'That, and knowing it was forbidden.'

Her father reacted at last. To her horror, he let out a sob. Then she heard him mutter as if each word hurt, 'I don't deserve you.'

She let it go even though she'd suspected, all along, that he'd had his own Machiavellian reasons for encouraging the marriage. Besides, it was crucial – now that they had finally engaged – to encourage him to look outside himself. 'I think we should try and understand Gran and Grandpa,' she suggested. 'They loved the Abbey, just like we do. And they did manage to keep it – for you.'

'No,' Sam corrected her sadly. 'They had me so they could hang on to the Abbey. But not to tell me . . .' He sounded as if he would never forgive them.

'How could they have?' She paused. 'I think they were right

not to. If it hadn't been for the Traffords coming back here, you'd never have known.'

'No,' he agreed with a grimace.

She said very positively and encouragingly, as if he should be pleased, 'Joe told me Stanley said the real reason for buying our house wasn't revenge.'

'No?' He made a despairing face. 'You could have fooled me!'

'It was because he was desperate to get to know you.'

'Is that so?' But he appeared more appalled than flattered. The last thing he needed, he implied, was another hostile parent.

'He's your father, Pa!'

He shuddered. 'Don't remind me!'

Laura decided to change tack (while Fred, listening through the door, marvelled at her diplomacy). 'Was Grandpa that wonderful to you?'

'You know he wasn't!' Sam was thinking that he'd enjoyed such intimacy with his own children, by comparison. For years, they'd behaved like his mini army – parroting his likes and dislikes, hating or loving the same people he did. He'd relished that absolute allegiance. If only, he reflected a little wistfully, they hadn't had to grow up. And now here was Laura behaving as if *he* was the child!

'Joe said his father and grandfather have a great relationship.'

'I'm ecstatic for them!'

'It's not nothing!'

'Oh, so now I'm being ticked off for my failure to get on with the man who passed himself off as my father?'

'No, Pa!' She was getting really exasperated with him now. What had happened to his famous humour? The ability to laugh at himself along with everyone else? 'I'm saying it might be a *good* thing Grandpa wasn't your real father.'

'How so?' He picked up his magnifying glass again, which was a bad sign.

'Think about it!' she ordered. 'Look at what Stanley's done with his life! Being a war hero and surviving all the rest. Then look at Edmund. I know which father *I'd* rather have! You're not a Delancey, Pa!' She made it sound the best thing that had ever happened to him, and was about to explain why. 'It means that however gloomy you're feeling, you're not suffering from the Delancey depression. And you haven't gone bald. You'd have hated that! And you're not likely to keel over with a bad heart, either. *I* think that's all *good!*' There was another plus about not being a Delancey. 'It means you're not under some stupid curse.' Then, with a flourish, she produced her trump card. 'Also, we haven't really lost the Abbey now we've found out we're all related.'

He let out a snort. He was looking at her as if she were quite mad.

'Oh, I know we don't live there any more,' Laura went on. 'But isn't that sort of an advantage? Don't you remember how it was at the end, Pa? The dreadful cold because we couldn't afford any more oil or coal, and the rain coming through the ceilings. There were mushrooms growing out of the walls . . .'

'Fungi,' he corrected her pedantically, but it was like music to hear him behaving like his old self.

'Whatever. And remember that chunk of stone that fell off the house and missed David by an inch?' ('A fuss about nothing,' Sam had insisted at the time, though he'd been as shocked as the rest of them by the deep dent in the lawn.) 'There was no way you could afford to mend any of it, was there?' He'd no money to maintain the Lodge either, of course, which was also pretty dilapidated in its scaled-down fashion.

However, she continued undeterred. 'It's *their* problem now. Joe told me it cost a fortune to fix the roof.'

'Really?' He sounded interested despite himself.

'Fifteen thousand for the lead alone, apparently.'

He let out a whistle.

'And all the walls have had to be re-pointed, because the guttering had collapsed. Who else would have been prepared to take on all that? They only bought it because of us. We'd have had to move out sooner or later. At least you got some cash!'

'Pretty well all went in debts,' Sam reminded her sourly.

'But you got it. What would have happened to us if you hadn't? We'd have gone bankrupt. And the house would have been taken away anyway.'

'It nearly broke your heart,' he reminded her sharply, as if trying to recover his authority.

She was silenced momentarily. This was over-dramatic talk, of course, for whose heart had ever been truly broken? And what were you supposed to feel, anyway? A sudden splitting sensation in your chest, after which you were unable to care about anything? She'd loved every stone of the house, certainly. But what exactly had provoked those panic attacks and fits of violent weeping that had so troubled her parents? Had they really been caused by the removal from a beautiful environment and the ever-present sense of tracing a long line of footprints?

'*I'm not even a Delancey,*' she reminded herself. Once past the shocking realization that she and Joe shared the same blood, it wasn't such a huge disappointment. She was beginning to understand that there could be greater freedom in a small space than there ever had been in the Abbey, so redolent with expectation. And as Stanley's granddaughter, she found she was developing a different perspective on the house. Generations of Delanceys had reigned there, basking in the splendour. But it was also where Edmund had turned down a most reasonable request for money from a close friend and, a little later, Hester had shut her ears to Effie's desperate pleas. A family had been put through terrible poverty for almost twenty years and the Abbey had colluded in the injustice and cruelty. Its beauty was still breathtaking but, to Laura's astonishment, she was no longer in love.

She looked at the tiny model her father had constructed and experienced an overwhelming desire to be on a real aeroplane again.

'Maybe I've grown up finally,' she told him. She added very daringly, 'Perhaps it's time you did, too.'

He stared at her expressionlessly and for a moment she actually found herself scared. Was he about to strike her for her insolence, even though the only violence she'd ever seen in him had been directed towards another family?

Sam was actually thinking that he'd never have dared talk to his own parents like this. He was reflecting, too, that he'd never become close enough to either of them to learn how to manipulate their hidden fears and weaknesses. It was a little alarming to be so well read, but he was quite unable to be cross with Laura. She looked so wonderfully young and fresh and indignant. All he could feel, he found, was intense affection and pride.

She was astonished – and quite extraordinarily pleased with herself – when he made a gesture of surrender and said simply, 'I agree.' Then he looked down at himself with a sort of disgust and smiled sheepishly. 'Let me get washed and dressed and then we can all have lunch. Poor Ma must be waiting for us.'

Chapter Thirty

Fred approached the Abbey with Spectre and Caesar loping after her, spun off course every so often by the tease of a departed fox or mysterious rustling in faraway undergrowth. It was still cold, but a froth of white blossom had alighted on the blackthorn trees and a wave of yellow daffodils lapped at the distant shores of the lawn. The whole garden was extraordinarily neat and tidy, as if it had been lined up for a military inspection: each shrub stringently groomed yet gleaming with health; the soil raked and dark and free of weeds. The long canal in the distance sparkled – ready, when the time was right, to reflect the glorious colours in the herbaceous border set alongside. In Fred's day, it had heaved with newts crawling through weed. Now, there was only the discreet flash of rare goldfish.

As usual, she could hear hammering in the distance – metal on stone – though the bulk of the outside repair work was finished. Without its cage of scaffolding, its tatty embroidery of creeper, the house looked scrubbed and very naked. Yet now it was equipped to shrug off the heaviest rainstorms, the wildest of winds. It seemed ready to weather another eight centuries at least.

It took Fred a moment to identify exactly what felt so different. And then she understood that, though she would never stop reacting to the beauty of this place, the feelings of savage bitterness she had lived with for so long had vanished. She found she could observe all the evidence of new ownership quite sanguinely and feel simple happiness that it was spring and, for once, there was a little money to spare and, best of all, Sam was content. It seemed to her now as if the two of them had been through a long illness. What had been the point of all that poison and paranoia? And had they really gone for good now or, like some hideous virus, were they hovering somewhere in the ether, waiting for the right climate to fasten on someone else?

Janice Trafford had telephoned that morning to ask her to tea. She'd sounded hesitant, speaking with care, fearful, as always, of making a faux pas. But there was an eagerness, too, as if this were important to her. 'Just us,' she'd said a little apologetically, in case Fred was expecting a whole entertainment to be laid on.

The front door was open, like in the old days, which meant that, to Fred's relief, she didn't have to use the chiming bell. Through the gap, she could smell fresh paint. '*Oh Lord!*' she thought, more cheerful than alarmed. '*What now?*' The evening before, Sam had composed a limerick about Janice's passion for redecorating. 'The stink of pink,' had come into it but his poem was more affectionate than mocking.

'Stay!' she ordered the Labradors, and they sulked briefly before the Traffords' dog trotted out to put them through the usual lengthy programme of circling and sniffing, just in case these animals it had enjoyed itself with countless times had suddenly become enemies. Then they all ambled off happily in the direction of the cloisters.

She was still marvelling at the newly decorated Great Hall – plain white once more, just as it had been for centuries, only fresh and cobweb-free – when Janice came clacking down the stairs in high heels. She was wearing a suit and her hair and make-up were immaculate, as usual.

'This looks terrific!'

Janice looked simultaneously gratified and embarrassed. 'Well, it wasn't right for the Abbey before, was it?' she said, as if she'd finally accepted that her role was to play servant to the house rather than the other way round. It was a let-out, too. It meant she could appear uninfluenced by the Delanceys even though it was Fred who'd mentioned very casually that when Henry VIII had visited in 1549, the Great Hall had been white. There was a reference to it in Thomas Delancey's diary, she'd claimed, adding warmly, 'What a pity we had to sell it and I can't show you.' Now she couldn't resist asking, 'Are you planning to strip the panelling back, too?' though she straightaway regretted it.

However, to her relief, Janice responded a little uncertainly, 'Do you think we should?'

'Well, as a matter of fact, there are only about two houses in the country that possess panelling this ancient. It *is* mentioned in a couple of books. I could try and track them down, if you like.'

'I'll talk to Mark.' But Janice sounded as if it was already settled. It would cost even more money to strip the expensive gloss paint off the old wood, restore it to how it had been. But there was no arguing with history.

'*Next time I'll broach the carpet,*' thought Fred. Like a reward, she produced her bouquet from behind her back.

'For me?' asked Janice, very pleased. 'Primroses, aren't they?'

'I picked them from our garden,' Fred told her. 'But they're everywhere now.'

'My mother-in-law loved primroses,' said Janice as she led the way upstairs to the old Morning Room. 'She was incapable of coming home empty-handed, was Effie. Even after the move to Guildford, she'd turn up with her bits of wood for the fire – couldn't help herself though, of course, we had central heating then. Once she brought in an old cabbage she'd picked up off the street. Even insisted on cooking it, if you please!' She was talking too much. Worse, she'd made the gift of primroses sound cheap. It was down to nervousness. She went on hurriedly, 'And dock leaves. She never could resist her dock leaves! I said, "We've plenty of Savlon in the first aid box, Nan."' Didn't make a bit of difference.'

However, Fred was amused: not offended at all. It was another thread to weave into the portrait that was building up – a history of all that had happened during the long and toxic silence between the two families who had turned out to be one. Effie Trafford still puzzled her, though – that much-loved woman who'd never suspected her husband or her best friend. '*There's no way I wouldn't have known,*' thought Fred confidently. She'd been shown photographs, but what could you deduce from a pale round face with apprehensive eyes for the camera and a luscious, tender mouth? Effie had been lovely all right, but had she been unable to see the bad in people, as Stanley maintained, or was she just plain simple? What a shame, Fred thought, that she couldn't get Hester's take on it.

The room now known as 'the upstairs lounge' was still a

shock. However, she could tell from Janice's pleased expression that there'd be no recanting here. It had to be admitted that it was warm and cosy and bright, with sunlight pouring through the sparkling windows and bouncing off the walls. The moths and silverfish had vanished. The Abbey was astonishingly clean these days.

'I've given Lily her marching orders,' said Janice, as if following Fred's thoughts.

'Oh?'

'A real stirrer. Sloppy, too.' She ran a finger along the surface of a gleaming table and smiled with pride.

Tea had been laid out on a tray, including a cream sponge cake with a cut wedge backing out of it. Fred noticed there was champagne, too, cooling in an ice bucket on the floor.

'For later,' said Janice with a slightly embarrassed laugh. She poured milk into the cups before asking worriedly, 'Oh, you don't like lemon, do you?'

'This is lovely,' said Fred, though the tea Janice was now dispensing from a pot looked very strong and she did prefer lemon to milk. The other woman had turned out to be very friendly once past the armour of social uncertainty, as – to a slightly lesser degree – had Mark. But it was the children who'd shamed everyone into a proper reconciliation. They liked having a surprise lot of cousins, they'd told both sets of parents; and nobody could go on with the fighting unless, of course, they enjoyed it.

'Hey ho, all part of the family!' Stanley had taken to announcing. He'd got over the embarrassment and was only proud now, though he acknowledged that his relationship with Sam would take a bit of working on.

'How's Joe?' Fred went on.

'Loving London!'

'Oh good!'

'He phoned us yesterday evening to say he's still set on acting,' said Janice, trying to forget that three drama schools had turned him down so far.

After a moment, Fred said, 'Well, I do believe that if you want something enough, you get it.'

'Really?'

'Oh yes. Most definitely.'

There was another pause while they both considered this, then Janice enquired a little uncertainly, 'And Laura?'

'Laura's just fine. Thinking about doing A-levels at a crammer.' For her elder daughter had announced that she intended to go to university, which was a breakthrough for a Delancey woman, not to mention a Trafford one.

'Genevieve said.'

After that bit of awkwardness was over, Janice went on, sounding far more relaxed, 'I hear Sam's enjoying himself.'

It was Stanley who'd suggested Mark was in a position to do his half-brother a favour and, after a bit of token opposition, Mark had come round. Actually, he'd gone further. He'd created a job for Sam and, in so doing, displayed surprising tact. He was planning to go upmarket, he'd explained in his brisk fashion. A number of his friends were getting badly burnt by Lloyds and, consequently, he had an inkling that a whole swathe of grand properties would soon be coming up for sale.

'I need someone who can approach those people,' he'd continued, as if thinking out loud. 'Talk to them . . .' Before Sam could utter a word, he'd held up a hand to stop him. 'Take your time,' he'd urged. 'There'll be a proper salary in it, of course.'

When Sam told Fred, he was pitifully confused (one half of him secretly gratified, the other still toying with a play of outrage) – and utterly dependent on her reaction. 'You won't believe this but he's offered me a job!'

Sam was a different man now. It was a job made in heaven. It amused him to play an upper-class salesman and, moreover, to be so good at it. The work gave him structure and purpose, and more dignity rather than less; and, though he occasionally grumbled about Mark, it was more of an assertion of self than an expression of discontent. He was beginning to like him, he admitted. More to the point, he'd come to feel respect. It was amazing to watch Mark in action, he'd marvel. The cunning and daring of the man! No wonder he was so rich! To hell with the comments of friends, he told Fred. Let them speculate away to their hearts' content about why he'd lowered himself by working for that upstart. Murmurings had already reached him and Fred that they weren't considered half such fun, these days.

'We could have a party,' Stanley had suggested hopefully. 'Introductions all round?' He was testing the water a bit. But the fuss had died down now and – as he'd point out whenever given the chance – it had all turned out for the best, hadn't it?

However, both couples agreed that announcing the truth would be going too far. The secret must be kept within the family. Only one question mark remained: since there would never again be real Delanceys at the Abbey, was there any point in continuing to display the portraits? But over malt whisky one night in the Refectory, Mark and Sam decided they should stay as a reminder of the dreadful strife that had once divided them, and a caution against it ever happening again. Blood was edging them closer all the time, forgiving their differences. To have discovered a brother was a marvellous thing.

'For God's sake, don't let's get sentimental!' said Sam in his laconic way.

'I'll drink to that,' Mark responded, refilling their glasses because they could always blame it on alcohol.

The benefits of reconciliation weren't entirely one-sided. Once the Delanceys – still seen as a very distinguished family – appeared to accept the Traffords, the rest of the county cautiously started to follow suit, especially after Mark Trafford made a generous donation to the village school. An invitation to an important local drinks party was in the pipeline. When all was said and done, the Traffords were the owners of an historic house and, after all, they'd been there for nearly two years now.

Fred decided the champagne must be to celebrate Justin's acceptance by Leeds University. He didn't want to go to Cambridge any more, he'd insisted to David over a beer in the pub. 'Too snobby,' he'd said dismissively. 'But I might come for the weekend to see how you're getting on.' Or maybe it was to break the news of Genevieve's engagement. It was on the cards, Maria had said.

There'd been enough observance of the social niceties, Janice decided. It was time to get to the real point of this meeting. As she peeled foil from the champagne, while glancing a little guiltily at the ornate carriage clock on the mantelpiece because it hadn't even chimed five yet, she asked, 'Do you find yourself thinking of those two, in the old days?'

'Funny you should ask!' exclaimed Fred with a smile. 'All the time! I think of Edmund – not as he became, so miserable and impossible – but sweet and eager. It's been a revelation to me, learning about the past. I see those two little boys exploring the estate all those years ago and I think how lovely it must have felt for Edmund of all people to taste such freedom. So much was expected of him, you see. I'm glad that once upon a time he had a friend, because he wasn't much good at friendship, my father-in-law.' She stopped with a laugh. 'I should stop referring to him like that, shouldn't I? He didn't trust people, you see.' She paused. 'If only Sam had had a Stanley!'

'He had you,' Janice offered with a shy smile.

'Well, later on he did,' said Fred, basking in the unexpected compliment. But the truth was, she realized, Sam had possessed a secret weapon for enduring his own bleak childhood. Edmund and Hester had messed him up, certainly, but couldn't rob him of his humour. It was a strange and rather heartening idea that the reason lay with Stanley and his valiant old genes.

Janice poured champagne into two ornate crystal flutes. 'Here's to new beginnings,' she said very seriously.

They clinked glasses with care. It was excellent champagne – Roederer, Fred could see from the label.

Janice came to the point. 'As a matter of fact, I wasn't referring to Stanley and Edmund.'

'Oh?'

'No. I meant, Stanley and your mother-in-law.'

Fred was off again, talking too much. It was as if she were striving to make up to Janice for the months of haughty distance. Or perhaps it was just the effect of alcohol. 'I know Stanley's convinced himself he was set up. A plot so Edmund could keep the Abbey? I find that *very* hard to believe! The four of them seem to have been such good friends before it all went wrong. And it was wartime. These things happen. Hester got carried away that night – just as Stanley did – and, when she found herself pregnant, wasn't going to get rid of the baby. I don't blame her. She was nearly thirty, after all, and she and Edmund had been trying for ages. The situation suited her, of course, because they did desperately need an heir. Edmund went along with it for that reason. That and the fact that he always had beautiful manners.'

'She didn't love Edmund,' Janice interrupted with a strangely knowing smile.

'Who says?' Fred didn't mean it to sound quite so rude. After all, hadn't she seen for herself the chilly distance between Hester and Edmund? But Janice's comment had annoyed her. After all, she'd never met Edmund and had only known Hester as a travesty of herself. It was not a good omen. The relationships between the two families would work well, but only providing certain boundaries were respected.

To her surprise, Janice rose from her chair, which had strange buttons embedded in its tan suede upholstery, and went to a Louis XVI reproduction desk. She came back with an old and quite dirty packet of what looked like letters.

'I think we need a refill.'

'What's this?'

Janice topped up both flutes, took a large sip of champagne for courage. 'I found a secret cupboard.'

Fred waited.

'It was an accident. I touched a section of wood in my study—'

'Your study?' Fred interrupted very politely.

'The room at the top of the stairs.'

'Oh,' said Fred. 'You mean, the Yellow Room!'

Janice frowned because the room they sat in was the only yellow one now. And besides, before its sadly overdue makeover, her study had been a sort of dingy beige.

'The panelling by the window?' There was an odd note in Fred's voice, as if she regretted living alongside another secret for years without ever suspecting it.

Janice nodded. 'They're love letters.'

Fred stared at her.

Janice paused before delivering her bombshell. 'They're from your mother-in-law. From Hester to Stanley. But she never sent them.' Janice concluded triumphantly, 'She *did* love him!' She tapped the packet with a long polished nail. 'It's all here. She adored him. She never got over it. It broke her heart.' She became grave, confidential. 'I haven't even told Stanley, Fred. I wanted to let you know first.'

Fred put her champagne down on one of the coasters that scattered every polished surface. Hester had loved Stanley? She couldn't take it in. Loved him throughout her miserable, silent marriage and, even sadder, loved without hope because Effie had always possessed his heart. Poor, poor Hester, she thought. No wonder the loss of the Abbey had tipped her over the edge. She thought of how you could never tell, looking at the outside of a person, what went on inside; of how tenderness and passion turned in on themselves could so easily become their opposites.

'They're heartbreaking,' Janice confirmed, passing over the packet.

Fred untied the old white satin ribbon. Then she looked at the dozen or so dirty envelopes, all unaddressed. 'I wonder if we should really be reading these,' she said, making Janice flush. However, she was already opening the first one.

'She calls him "Pooh",' Janice supplied eagerly. 'And she was "Figlet"!' Then she giggled because the names were too ridiculous for words.

'So, they're unsigned,' observed Fred. She went on with a frown, 'Piglet, surely?' – as if the names were familiar, not finding them funny at all. Then she pointed out, 'There's no date either.'

'No.' Janice agreed. She couldn't understand why Fred was being so downbeat about this. Surely the proof that love had been tangled up in that brief, mismatched coupling would crown the extraordinary discovery that they were all part of the same family?

Fred read in silence, frowning slightly every so often. When she'd finished the first letter, she laid it aside. Then she read the rest, one after the other, without expression. Finally she commented: 'Interesting.'

Janice looked even more crestfallen. Was that all Fred was going to say about her thrilling find?

Fred started to replace the last letter in its envelope. The paper stuck and, as she shook the envelope to open it, a small blue-green feather floated out, spiralling slowly downwards to settle delicately on the chocolate brown carpet. Fred picked up the feather and smoothed it, keeping it in her hand as if it belonged to her family now, just like the letters.

They weren't in Hester's handwriting. However, Fred had recognized that distinctive, elaborately formed script immediately. But there was no way she was going to discuss this extraordinary revelation with anyone except Sam.

Chapter Thirty-one

Wandering in some foggy wasteland of the mind, Hester was made aware of the front door banging shut. Then she heard Sam and Fred come in, talking all the while. They'd gone to the supermarket, she remembered now. 'A *super* market,' Sam called it very enthusiastically and emphatically. They were going a lot suddenly, for some reason.

'Well, I don't know,' she heard her son say with a touch of exasperation, as if they'd been discussing a problem for some time without coming to any conclusion. 'Miranda Askew? Clarissa Fitzherbert? Pooh could have been any one of a number of women. They were pretty sociable until the depression . . .' Then his voice died away suddenly, like someone turning down the volume on a television set.

Hester had already forgotten the mention of those oddly familiar names. 'You could have been any one of a number of women,' her brain absorbed. 'Pretty sociable until The Depression . . .'

Then she heard her daughter-in-law exclaim brightly, 'Look what we have here!'

'Shrotted pimps!' Sam sounded astonishingly relaxed and happy. '*What* a treat!'

'At least he could love,' said Fred. 'That was what it was about – all the misery and raging.'

'Raving, too, some of it. Perhaps there never was anyone.'

'Your poor papa.' Her voice was very soft and sad.

'Pity Mama more, darling . . . You saw it, too . . .'

Hester could hardly hear her son now, but some part of her flinched away from the sympathy in his voice because she didn't deserve it: that much she knew. The guilt lay very deep. If only she could remember why.

'It's a mercy really that . . .'

And then all that came through the closed door was mumble, mumble, mumble until Sam said very positively, as if terminating the conversation, 'Well, there's no one left to ask now, is there?'

'I'll show you beauty as you've never seen it, my love,' Edmund had promised her. But with war looming, the churches and art galleries of Italy would have to wait.

Privately, though, Hester was quite content to be spending the first few days of married life in a hotel just twenty miles from the Abbey, relishing her new status and the freedom it had brought. In 1939, there was a very great difference between a spinster of twenty-four and a bride the same age. As they sped away from Melcombe in her newly acquired father-in-law's Daimler, hat like a fat pink pancake pinned to her freshly waved hair, she felt she could relax at last. Getting married in a hurry had involved a storm of guest lists and dress fittings, and still more complicated arrangements because, of course, a union between two such grand families had to be properly effected. There'd been no opportunity for reflection: she felt as if she knew Edmund even less than when he'd proposed. But now, at last, there was time to explore the charming but elusive man she'd married. They were right for each other and he knew it, too, thought Hester happily – even if he might occasionally hanker after something else. That time at the White Lion Hotel, she'd noted his unease around Effie, because nobody could deny the girl was pretty. '*But he doesn't need a little popsy!*' thought Hester indulgently. He required a wife who could help him run the Abbey, which was his destiny.

She saw him smile as he recklessly swept the big car towards a blind corner, its whole width taking up the narrow, sunken lane, cow parsley and campion crushed against its gleaming doors.

Hester smiled, too. 'You're thinking about Guy's speech!' Edmund's best man, Guy Gore-Brown, had a bad stammer. It had been excruciating waiting, with polite expressions, for him to bring off his punchlines.

But Edmund couldn't have heard her above the noise of the engine. 'Hope they're having a good time, too,' he said.

'Who?' But Hester already knew because he was always talking about Stanley and Effie even though it had been tacitly understood they could not be invited to the wedding.

'Poor things can't afford to get away.' He shuddered. 'The stench of that place! When we were boys, I used to pick him up and it almost took my head off!'

'And that's enough about them,' said Hester, a little daringly, laying a hand on his, enjoying the sight of her new ring, which wasn't really new, since it had once belonged to his great-grandmother.

But she thought about the gardener's son and his girl late that night, and the emotion that had pulsed between them like heat haze. They'd behaved very decorously at that tea they'd been invited to, never touching once – and yet, for some reason, she would remember hands everywhere, even the stolen brush of lips.

Edmund undressed in the bathroom and, while he was there, Hester undressed as well, selecting one of the beautiful new nightdresses from her trousseau, watery blue silk cut on the bias with thick bands of ecru lace. She cleaned her face with Pond's Cold Cream at the dressing table, dabbed a spot of pink on her pale mouth with her new Elizabeth Arden lipstick then rubbed most of it off and, by the time he returned in voluminous blue and white pyjamas, was in bed.

'Tired?' he asked, politely covering a yawn.

Hester was taken aback, though nobody would have guessed. 'Moderately,' she replied with a smile and a shrug. After all, they'd got married in the morning and it had been a very long day. However, what she really meant was that she was his wife now and anxious to be neither too eager nor off-putting.

'I'm exhausted,' said Edmund. He got into bed as well and then he leant over and seemed to think about kissing her on the mouth like he'd done throughout their courtship – brief kisses like thank you notes – but pressed his lips to her forehead instead. He smiled encouragingly just before he turned out the light. 'Better get a good night's sleep, darling.'

'Good idea,' said Hester.

When she awoke to the second day of her honeymoon, Edmund was already up and dressed: hair sleeked down, in tweed plus fours for walking. He looked very fresh and enthusiastic.

'See you in the dining room,' he told her with a smile.

After breakfast, they went down to the seashore.

'*Love* being with you, Hes,' he said, as they picked up shells and held them to their ears, like listening for the whisper of secret lives.

'Do you?'

'Love our talks,' he went on, though they'd not discussed the night before. He'd spoken of the Abbey and the sacrifices they would all have to make and how they should relish this special time together. It was impossible to escape the threat of war, even on honeymoon.

'Do you?'

Edmund was not a demonstrative man. Even so, he had a way of speaking, very occasionally, that hinted at deep springs of emotion. 'I never thought marriage would be so wonderful.'

'Neither did I,' she said, much moved, too. They were perfectly matched socially and intellectually. And she was so innocent. Her only piece of advice from her mother had been, 'Never say no to him.' So far as she knew, all husbands behaved as if naked bodies were to be hidden and treated their wives with tender respectful patience – especially Edmund, with the courtly sensitive nature she loved. It was, after all, only the second day of her honeymoon.

On the fourth night, they had two Gibson martinis each before dinner and a bottle of Burgundy with the meal, followed by brandies.

After Edmund got into bed with her and switched off the light, as usual, Hester lay there for a moment, feeling her head spin, and then, with an abrupt movement, turned and embraced him. She could feel him through the silk of her beautiful nightdress and the thick cotton of his pyjamas: a long and slender male body that must hold the same mysterious promise as her own. 'Oh, my darling husband,' she said as she began to kiss him, lengthy passionate kisses of a sort never before exchanged. She was very drunk. In her wild intoxication, she put her hand between his legs because, of course, she knew something about the act of love. It would have been difficult not to, as a country girl.

He removed the hand, but not before she'd felt his absolute flaccid passivity. He didn't rebuff her exactly. Very politely and with tenderness, he made her see for herself that she was being a little ridiculous and even improper – but that, most importantly, he forgave her. And then he gently disentangled himself and rolled over to his side of the bed.

Two days later, he was called up and, for the next six years, became a visitor to her life.

And then there entered – like a guileless, apologetic Scheherazade – Hester's unlikely wartime friend, Effie Trafford. Her tales of a passionate marriage, where sex was embraced, cherished, joked about were shocking, certainly, but addictive. Each time Stanley returned to Effie from the theatre of battle, Hester found herself looking forward to a fresh story.

'*Supposing I say something,*' she'd pondered once as Effie chattered on, staring down at an unfinished tapestry in her lap. But she was hardly the sort of woman to seek advice on her marriage, especially not from someone younger and, more to the point, from such an inferior background. Besides, she'd been taught to consider discretion and stoicism as virtues. Better to stitch up life tightly, guard the picture presented to the world. It would be different when the war ended, she told herself, holding on to the hope with decreasing conviction.

And then one evening at the Cygnet club early in 1945, there was quite literally an explosion in her life.

*

Stanley Trafford, the gardener's son, hurled former debutante Hester Delancey to the floor and leapt on her. But it was still wartime and a raid had started.

'*This is the end,*' Hester thought, with an odd feeling of resignation. Stanley plainly believed it, too, because she could feel the tension in his protective embrace, as if he were bracing himself for that final explosion which would blow them to smithereens. The lights had gone out and she could hear the sirens outside and pieces of plaster still raining down around them.

She'd heard that when you believed you were about to die, your life passed before you in a flash. It was true, Hester discovered, because the resignation didn't last. She found herself thinking with deep, deep sadness of the past six years and the tragedy of dying without having properly lived. She felt closer to Stanley at that moment than she ever had to Edmund because there was such honesty in their embrace. '*Why pretend?*' thought Hester, for whom make-believe had become a way of life. She and Stanley were so close physically that she could feel the bones of his hips grinding into her own; and, for all his courage, knew he was as terrified as she.

Eventually, she felt him roll off her and someone lit a match. But she kept her eyes closed because, to her consternation, she could feel tears welling up behind the lids.

'Hester?' she heard Stanley enquire very anxiously, so she opened her eyes briefly and was rewarded with a flash of his white teeth in the dim light.

'We're still here,' he assured her, and then he bent down to brush some of the debris away, before offering his warm hand and pulling her up. But her legs were giving way beneath her and she slumped against him.

Once more, Stanley hugged her close but, in this very different embrace, she felt his absolute joy in being alive. He did a little dance with her in his arms. He hummed and laughed into her ear.

Then an air raid warden appeared and said the building was on fire and everyone must leave immediately.

'Let's get out of here,' said Stanley, clutching a bottle he'd picked up from the floor.

And she nodded, feeling as joyous and eager as he. She'd no inkling, then, what was about to happen – but until reason faltered, would continue to question her own integrity. '*Did I make it happen? Was it all my fault?*'

'You need a son,' she'd dared to tell Edmund in the one really truthful conversation of their marriage; then wondered why she'd put it like that. All the pressure for years and years from her in-laws, only to find, to her astonishment, that she yearned for a child herself.

There was a short silence. Then he agreed with an understanding smile, as if she were equally to blame for the failure to produce an heir. 'That is certainly true.'

Stung, she responded, 'Edmund, I'm almost thirty. I'm not *going* to have a child at this rate!'

He raised his eyebrows, seemingly only amused. 'No?'

'Not unless someone else gives me one!' It was a sudden hot fury, an uncharacteristic longing to cut through the play-acting that had pushed her thus far. But she was ashamed of the unkindness later.

'*There's* an idea!' said Edmund, with the same equanimity, as if reducing everything to a joke was his own subtle form of reprimand.

Hester flung out of the room. Outside, she leant against a wall, feeling her heart plummet with fathomless despair.

'All right?' asked Fred, sticking her head round the door. Her hair looked tidy, for once, Hester noticed, as if – at last – she'd gone to a proper hairdresser.

She nodded. They always asked if she was all right, as if that was the most she could hope for, at her age.

'Sam wants to go up to the Abbey and talk about work,' said Fred, mystifying Hester. Sam? Work? What on earth was she talking about? Then Fred laughed for no apparent reason. She was very merry suddenly. 'But I'm going to fix you something to eat and then I thought you might like to watch television.' She gestured at the message board. 'Today is Saturday, 5 April 1986,' she'd written neatly at the top. But underneath that, Hester now noticed, someone had scrawled as if completely exasperated: 'If I have to read one more word about Prince Andrew's wedding . . .' Who was Prince Andrew?

They were still laughing as they made their way along the street, the pavement hot beneath her ruined best shoes as if hell had suddenly moved closer. They could hear the roar of burning buildings and the crackle of lesser fires and the shrieks of the wounded and trapped; and a whole cacophony of more positive sounds like the wail of the all-clear sirens, an ambulance skidding round a corner, the shouts of rescuers. There was the crunch of broken glass, too, and Hester knew it had cut into her ankles, ruining her one remaining pair of stockings. She could feel blood congealing on her legs, snagging the silk, but only smiled. Her heart was thumping in her chest with excitement and all her senses felt vivid and greedy, as if she'd just arrived in the world. The acrid, smouldering smell in the air was surely of death, but it seemed far more like life. She could still taste the unaccustomed whisky in her mouth and clutched at Stanley's hand in the soupy darkness.

'Don't you dare lose me!'

'No chance, Hester.'

A moment later, she was pulled abruptly into a black doorway. Then he was tugging at her neckline with such urgency that her buttons popped off, running his warm hands over her body, hoiking up the blue dress ruined by the bombing, tearing at her knickers, fumbling with the zip of his officer's trousers.

Hester surrendered to it all without hesitation and it was like being taken on a journey she'd heard described a hundred times before.

'There we are!' said Fred, as she arranged a tray of food in front of her. There was a grilled pork chop with apple sauce, new potatoes and salad, even a glass of wine. Hester greedily eyed a slice of white bread. She loved the processed food that had started creeping into the house. It was wonderful not to be fed gritty home-made soda bread or tricked-up offal any more. There was a delicious bought trifle for pudding, too, with brightly coloured hundreds and thousands scattered over it, and Fred had laid a new packet of bright green wool on the tray, like a rose. 'Present!' she said.

'I feel like a child,' said Hester, looking down at her old liver-spotted hands.

'What?' exclaimed Fred, and she peered a little anxiously into her mother-in-law's face.

Hester patted her arm. 'It's all right,' she said soothingly. 'It's quite all right.'

Fred seemed to come to a decision. 'I don't know if I should be asking you this, Mama . . .' she began, curling her smoothed down hair around her fingers. But when Hester looked up with a polite smile, she simply said with a sigh, as if she'd changed her mind, 'You enjoy your lunch.' And switched on the old television.

Hester relaxed in her chair, enjoying the freedom to be: a respite from Sam and Fred's eternal nagging on the plastic message board. Things came back to her sometimes like figures looming out of a mist – frighteningly sharp feelings of pain or hurt or sorrow. But what had caused them? And why the eternal stain of shame? All she knew was that, once, she'd done something dreadfully wrong. If only she could remember what . . .

She gasped and stiffened at the moment of penetration and felt Stanley falter just for a second. Like reassuring him, she pulled him so tight that, when his moment of climax came, he was unable to pull away in time. She felt his energy pump into her, the gradual slowing down until the last drop was spent.

A little later, cleaning herself up in the washroom of Waterloo Station for the return to the Abbey, she discovered blood on the hem of her dress. For a second she felt dismay, knowing Stanley would have been blooded, too. Then she remembered that he often made love to his wife when she had the curse. Effie had told her so. She imagined he'd feel only relief. They'd both been astonishingly careless.

Sitting primly in her nurse's uniform, watching the green landscape speed past the windows of the train, quite oblivious to the other passengers, Hester sighed every so often and chewed her lips and shook her head and, once even, shut her eyes. But the spell had lifted as suddenly as it had fallen. There'd been no lingering goodbyes, no plan to set up a further rendezvous: certainly no need to agree that Effie and Edmund must never be told.

She was horrified by what had happened, disbelieving and mortified. She was feeling the guilt, too, though more on Effie's account than Edmund's. She decided that, by way of expiation, she'd invite Effie up to the Abbey tomorrow or the day afterwards, when she was feeling less exhausted (and besmirched) and give her one of her frocks. It would be as if the episode with Stanley had never happened. It was the only way to manage it.

When she failed to menstruate the following month, Hester's complicated mixture of feelings quickly gave place to joy. It was astonishing how easy it had been to become pregnant. '*How many other children have waited to be born?*' she wondered a little sadly. All the same, an enormous problem had arisen.

'I've something to tell you,' she began. She and Edmund were in the Library and, to bolster her confidence, she'd put on a pretty new frock made of fine green wool, which felt more than a little tight. It was very soon after Edmund had come home for good, a month or so after his father had been buried. It was the last moment to break the news before it announced itself because she could feel her body changing: her breasts swelling and her waist thickening. Her face was different, too: softer, sleepy.

He looked suddenly apprehensive and it never occurred to her that he might be thinking she was about to leave him; or that anything she said instead would come as relief.

'We're having a baby.'

He glanced at her sharply, and then she saw him swallow, as

if he were trying to absorb the information physically as well as mentally.

'A child,' she confirmed. 'Quite soon.'

'Well!' he exclaimed, as if confounded how to proceed.

Hester went on, very nervous but with each word carefully rehearsed, 'The men have all gone now. It will be a new life for us, as well as for the Abbey.'

'Ah!' he said and glanced at her again.

And then, just at that most precarious of moments – as they faced the greatest hurdle of their marriage – Effie and Mark interrupted them. But though initially mortified to see the other girl, whom she'd been avoiding ever since discovering she was pregnant, Hester very quickly realized the visit was fortuitous. Edmund joked with Effie in his usual fashion – it seemed nothing could affect his manners. And then, to Hester's astonishment, he told her about the baby. When he rubbed his hands together, which always meant he was looking forwards, rather than back, she knew it was going to be all right.

In June 1945, she led Edmund to believe that an anonymous officer in the Abbey's makeshift hospital, one of the men she'd nursed – and a gentleman – had fathered the child who would inherit Melcombe.

To Edmund, as she well knew, all new babies looked the same: tiny, wrinkled, cross red things. They made far too much noise, too: there was no way of holding a conversation. He would ignore most children until they were about ten.

But Effie wasn't like that at all. Effie loved babies. She couldn't have enough of them.

All newborn babies looked exactly like their fathers, she'd told Hester very confidently. 'It's nature's way, ain't it?' Nature's trick to persuade a man to stay and take care of the family. The thought of Effie bending over Sam's cradle with her sweet, open face and guileless eyes, frowning with puzzlement before the dreadful realization came ... It was not to be contemplated: easier by far to initiate a coldness that, by the time the birth arrived, had set like concrete. Besides, all Hester wanted now was to keep as far away as possible from Stanley and Effie.

The day she took Sam to the circus, on 20 September 1947, the Delancey depression swooped on Edmund, gripping him in its talons, shading him with its black wings. When she and her son returned from their expedition, he was a different man. It was hard, at first, to identify how. Then Hester realized that, for as long as she'd known him, he'd given the impression of being a spectator of life, someone amused by the susceptibilities or enthusiasms of others, but fundamentally disengaged. Now, all of a sudden, he seemed simultaneously terrified and vulnerable. The urbanity had fallen away. He was like a man under siege.

'Nice day?' asked Hester.

'Average.' But she heard his voice falter, almost as if tears were threatening. His face was ashen.

Hester knew Edmund to be a deeply private man who hated any kind of fuss, so there was no way she could question him gently, soothe him into a confidence. She was alarmed by the way he kept glancing at her. Something had upset him greatly while she'd been gone. What could it be? Even as she speculated, a dreadful suspicion started taking shape. However, she smiled as she handed Sam back to Narnie, and said, 'We had a wonderful day.'

'Wonderful . . .' Edmund repeated, sounding as if he'd never heard the word before.

'Did you see anyone?'

She felt, rather than saw him glance at her carefully, anxiously. Then he said, 'Nobody,' in a tone that forbade further discussion.

Afterwards, one of the new maids informed her that the head gardener had come into the Abbey whilst she'd been away. He'd gone to the Refectory where the master was still sitting over breakfast, she said, and she'd heard shouting in the distance. She told the tale against another servant very brazenly.

That night, Hester awoke suddenly, seemingly for no reason. She heard the clocks chime three throughout the Abbey, on and on as if they were calling to each other and answering, and then she saw in the dim light from the moon filtering through a gap in the curtains that the other side of the four-poster was empty.

Edmund did not return. It was the last time he ever slept in the White Room.

What was she to think in the days that followed, when Edmund seemed to abhor the very sight of her: shutting himself away, failing to appear for meals? He didn't go out either, though the high point of his day had always been walking slowly around the gardens after breakfast, relishing the fresh air and inspecting progress and – of course – talking to his great friend, Stanley.

Guilty Hester asked no questions, said nothing, carrying on with the same cool assurance as always. And then, one day, when she was finishing breakfast, she heard the great oak door bang shut and, after a moment, saw Edmund set off into the frosty gardens with his silver-topped cane, walking like an old man.

He was away for perhaps half an hour. When he returned, he was trembling. He frightened her now. He took off his hat and smoothed his hair and then he said, 'I've told the Traffords to pack up and leave. They'll be gone by the morning and after that I don't wish them ever to be mentioned again.'

Later, she heard from the servants that, as a last unnecessary piece of cruelty, Edmund had ordered the Traffords to clear their cottage completely. He was punishing Stanley, of course, and all those close to him and – filled with dread and acceptance – she understood that the retribution was about to begin against her, too.

'Hester?'

She heard the desperate calling very faintly, through the just ajar window of the White Room, long before Effie came into sight.

It was Edmund who'd ordered the servants not to open the doors. He must have guessed Effie would come to the Abbey, thought Hester, cowering behind her curtain. She *knew* what had happened now. For some insane reason, Stanley had told his best friend Edmund the truth about Sam's conception – which was why Edmund had sacked him – and now Stanley had confessed to Effie.

'Hester!' She could see Effie now, her cheeks wet with tears, looking utterly bedraggled. She wanted to run downstairs and fling the doors open because it was a terrible, unjust thing Edmund had done. She wanted to tell Effie the truth about that night when the bombs had fallen and she'd had sex with her husband, but she was too ashamed.

She could hear Effie knocking. 'Let me in!' she shrieked. 'Hester, you have to let me in!'

On and on it went, like torture, Effie roaming round the Abbey crying, bashing against the doors and windows like an exhausted moth, until she looked up at Hester's window and saw her and – quite suddenly – it was over.

Hester put aside her tray with its empty plate and glass and picked up her tapestry – heart pounding with strange, inexplicably violent emotion. It happened like that, sometimes: feelings lying in wait, staging a sudden ambush like playing grandmother's footsteps. But creating pictures of the Abbey soothed her, as always. Perhaps an appreciation of beauty was one of the last things to go.

The Abbey was the other reason besides atonement why she stayed on in a marriage that became progressively worse. Edmund would remain sunk in deep depression, no sort of companion at all, hating her, obviously. But Hester had the exquisite house to look after and the child she would train to inherit it: both of which she over-indulged. Increasingly, she forgot about Sam's real father. Very occasionally, with a look or a gesture, her son would bring Stanley Trafford sharply to mind. But otherwise, he appeared exactly what the world assumed him to be: the scion of a dynasty.

Edmund never forgot about Stanley, though – despite his edict that the very name of the family was taboo. 'Those damn bloody Traffords!' he'd shout, as if all Stanley had ever been to him was a servant. He'd put a curse on them, he'd tell Hester, who didn't need reminding. She'd tremble as he ranted on, knowing the rage was directed against her, too, though he never once referred to the lie she'd told him. Bad blood, he'd say over and over again. Then he'd look haunted and uneasy, almost as if it were himself he condemned.

Against all advice, trifling with its destiny – and probably too depressed to care – he'd procrastinated about making over the Abbey to Sam, the cuckoo in his nest. 'I'm thinking about it!' he'd growl. When he died unexpectedly, thus incurring a huge bill for death duties, Hester started to believe in Stanley's curse. Less than ten years later, after Sam had lost even more money for the family, the Abbey was put up for sale. To add to the pain, only one purchaser came forward.

Hester was holding a blue glass vase, a pretty thing she'd filled with pink roses just cut from the garden. She went on doing the flowers for the Abbey long after Fred moved in and often there'd be two sets of displays, vying with each other for attention. She loved these old, densely petalled, gorgeously scented Bourbons that climbed up the south wall. They were made for the place.

'Some people want to have a look round this afternoon,' Sam informed her, seeming strangely worried.

'Oh?' The day was overcast, reflecting the mood of the family, with Laura most distressed of all. Such a sensitive child. She'd been crying all afternoon, Fred had said. Something would have to be done.

'I've been putting them off,' Sam told her, rather mystifyingly.

'Is that a good idea?' For all her apparent coldness, Hester ached for her family. She'd always been strong – far more so than her profligate son, she told herself – and now took the decision, on behalf of them all, that they must sell the Abbey. If they did not, she pointed out, the bank would take it anyway.

'They keep phoning to ask if anyone else has made an offer.'

Stranger and stranger . . . 'They sound keen,' she commented with a bleak shrug, thinking that they could do worse than let the house go to people who really wanted it. But why had Sam not told her about this before?

'Seems so.' Then, as if he'd come to the same sad conclusion, 'Perfect day for viewing so long as the rain holds off.'

They were silent for a minute, thinking of the buckets and saucepans arranged under the holes in the roof and a telltale orchestra of pinging; or, equally undesirable, a rush of bright sunlight that would reveal every crack and stain.

'Who are they, darling? Do we know anything about them?'

Sam paused almost as if he sensed that one second later the vase would come crashing down on the flagstones, together with any future peace of mind. 'It's those Traffords who used to work here, Mama. The ones Papa never stopped banging on about. Remember?'

Never, for one second, had she been tempted to tell her son the truth. Why? When it could only be destructive?

When Stanley Trafford appeared back on the scene, clearly intent on revenge, and Sam refused to reconsider the move to the Lodge, the stress proved too much for her. Or perhaps the dementia was, even then, fingering her mind. Her own mother had, after all, fallen prey to it.

The day she knew something was very wrong was when she found herself in Maria's bedroom with no memory of getting there.

She was sitting before her granddaughter's dressing table in one of the poky little bedrooms in the horrible new house, staring at her unadorned patrician features in the mirror. There were pots of foundation and powder, pencils and lipsticks, bits of cottonwool littered everywhere. Automatically, she started to tidy up. As she did so, she thought of Maria on her way out the evening before, sweet pudgy face all of a sudden full of contrasts and shadows, whole persona mysteriously altered. Suddenly, she was painting glossy lips onto her own thin mouth, smearing blue on her wrinkled lids – and staring at the floozy who confronted her. Some seed must have been planted, a strategy for escape. The next day, she went into the local Boots to buy more make-up for Maria, but never handed it over.

She felt her descent keenly, though not as her mother had done: because, in her own situation, surrender brought some measure of relief. Those break-ins to the Abbey had been ill thought-out, hysterical. Perhaps, at the beginning, some rational part of her had believed that if she could keep up the siege, ruin the Traffords' furniture and sense of well-being, they might be driven away. But the fog thickened at the sight of Stanley: old and out of breath and almost unrecognizable, yet patently unforgiving.

Dementia played strange tricks. She could experience dismay and even relive terror, without understanding why. The sight of Joe Trafford sent a shiver through her, and the news that he was to marry Laura had propelled her into an anguished spin. Wrong, was all she knew in her old bones. Wrong, wrong, wrong.

And now, for reasons she couldn't understand either, the anger and disappointment that had for so long pulsed through the house had evaporated. Furthermore, she no longer felt fear in the presence of Stanley Trafford. Perhaps, in some distant recess of her mind, she appreciated that, without him, this houseful of people would not exist. There'd be no chatter and banging of doors, no soft murmuring from the kitchen. No mess, no fun, no rows, no life.

'Thank you, treasure,' Hester told Maria when she came to collect the empty lunch tray; and then she touched her own rouged cheek, shook her head with a little smile, indicating that her young granddaughter was wearing too much make-up.

'Treasure?' repeated Maria, ignoring this latest example of double standards, watching the flickering images on the television set and thinking that she'd never grow old. 'That's a funny name, Gran!'

'Treasure,' Hester repeated slowly, like tasting the word before judging it was exactly right.

Chapter Thirty-two

In the end, Janice Trafford's changes turned out to be minimal, shrugged off by the Abbey with the same patient equanimity as the wars and the bloodshed. History had triumphed, but should anyone be surprised? In that place teeming with secrets, the past nudged the present, coloured it, and at times even seemed to be trying to overtake it.

The worst violence ever to befall the Abbey was its dissolution and those of a fanciful disposition would sometimes imagine they caught the sounds of it. The faint hollow clopping of the horses' hooves of the King's soldiers coming ever closer up the drive to disband a peaceful and austere community; the frantic tolling of the bell before it was cut down; the shrieks of the burning monks and the defiant curses of the abbot even as his blood spattered on to the flagstones.

But alongside the terror and drama had gone the quietness of ordinary life. After the monks had disappeared, generation upon generation of the same family lived and loved and died in that place. If you believed that anger and terror could leave a stain in the air long after a wickedness had been done, could it not also be true of love? Love had twined through the Abbey in all its forms – family love, married love, secret love, and spurned love.

It was in the Refectory that the last abbot of Melcombe had suffered his terrible death. But almost four hundred years later, it was the scene of another tragedy. This time, there was no bloodshed involved and, far from becoming a legend, what happened remained, for a variety of reasons, a closely guarded secret between the two people involved. Did some remnant of it hang in that still air? If you shut your eyes and struggled to tune into the past, might it not be possible to conjure it up?

It is almost 9.30 on a dull late summer morning in 1947 and a mundane though comfortable day lies ahead for a man still sitting over the remains of his breakfast. He is certainly not expecting anyone, except, perhaps, a servant to clear away the debris. Suddenly, a friend enters. Correction. This is no ordinary friend. This is the person who once saved his life and, over the years, has become the one he trusts and loves above all others.

Does our man sense, even then, that there's something perilous about this meeting? On the face of it, he behaves no differently. He fails to express the pleasure he feels, as always, at the sight of his friend because hiding his real feelings has become part of his nature. He doesn't even invite him to make himself comfortable. It's as if he's testing the strength of his friend's affection. And then, continuing to behave like a mere employer, he pretends not to understand why he's come, though he is perfectly well aware that a request is about to be made that

will involve no sacrifice on his part at all. It is deeply unfair –
and he knows it – but it's as if something in him is striving to
be perverse.

Then comes revelation. And this time, it's the Abbey that's
responsible. A rush of bright sunlight through mullioned
windows has the same effect as a switch being clicked. The day
is transformed and a beauty lit up and perceived as such for the
very first time. Alongside it comes a dreadful but wonderful
realization, and everything falls into place. It seems so
straightforward to our man, and also strangely innocent. This is
not friendship, he understands, but infinitely more. No wonder,
he thinks, that his marriage has been an unconsummated
charade. Tracing the friendship back to its very beginning,
everything now writes itself differently. It's like watching a
tapestry being unpicked and reworked. It is his own fault, he
chastises himself, for being so guarded, for approaching life like
a spectator. This is the person who, right from the beginning,
mitigated his deep loneliness and, over and over again, cheered
his spirits. And now he believes that each act of escalating
friendship actually spoke of love.

What is he to do? This man who's been brought up to think
there's only one form of love? That any other is 'unnatural'?

There's no choice whatsoever, as it turns out. No time even
to think. For the first time in his life, he is governed by impulse
rather than reason. Before he can stop himself, he has laid his
hand on the bare arm of his friend (which feels to him like
touching an electric current) and is stammering words of love.
It's the first sincerely heartfelt declaration he's ever made – the
only time his words come straight from the soul without passing
through a filter of irony and repression and expectation. And
the relief is indescribable. It's like feeling himself whole for the

first time in his life. He's so caught up in his own excitement – racing to tell everything he now understands – that he fails to notice the effect until it's too late.

Oh, the humiliation! His words are greeted initially with incredulity and then disgust and, after that – most terrible of all – with hilarity. He shrivels back into himself at the dreadful, unforgettable things that are said. There's a rush of shame before it becomes anger that will harden into implacable hatred. The man who scorned his outpouring of emotion must be punished. But he cannot guess at the sentence he'll inflict on himself. It will feel as if he's cut out his own heart. There's no other way of describing it. His life's a desert. He says so over and over again, to anyone who'll listen.

His one comfort and form of atonement is to write letters into the emptiness, posting them in a secret place. In this way, Piglet will dare to say things to Pooh that Edmund never could to Stanley. Love remains love – the deep and passionate attachment of one human being for another – however it may once have been received.

Small wonder that when Stanley finally returns to the Abbey with his grandson, Joe, who is the image of his younger self, the unhappiness that has lived on after Edmund's death acquires fresh impetus, stalking the Refectory, unsettling the house, adding to its layers of suffering and history. It's like someone pleading for forgiveness from a dark and distant place, telling his story in the only way he is able. The irresistible but fatal impulse to lay a hand on a bare young forearm, followed by a clumsy attempt at a kiss. The infection of hatred, cloaking a dreadful loss . . . The searing humiliation that seeps back out of the thick old walls it once slunk into.

It's magic, like the ability of the sun suddenly and fleetingly to turn a dull day into paradise; or a piece of witchcraft, carried out for the best of motives, that maliciously seizes the chance to go awry.

Epilogue

It is mid-June 1986 as Hester emerges from the trees and starts off – slowly but very purposefully – across the Abbey's expanse of bright green sunlit lawn, like an old bent toy guided by radar. She is wearing a new frock, as she'd call it, which is decorous but pretty, and her make-up is, for once, subtle. It looks suspiciously as if she's been taken in hand.

In fact, this is the latest in a series of stage-managed meetings: Hester hustled into the company of Stanley, who reacts in a bemused but gallant fashion. The feeling among the grandchildren is that it would be appropriate for Hester to apologize for the sufferings of the Traffords on behalf of Edmund, grandfather to none. OK, she's not all there. But everyone's noticed that now and again (though less and less often) Hester seems *compos mentis*. If only they can time it right, so that a shaft of clarity pierces just as she's in the company of the former servant she and her husband caused such grief to . . . Well, it'll be a most welcome full stop.

The grandchildren have a secondary motive, perhaps. These

are two bereaved old people – not lonely, yet alone. And how nice it would be – says Maria often – to have her grandparents properly united. But it invariably makes her laugh. Somehow, they can't picture it at all.

Stanley is waiting in knife-edge creased trousers and a new jacket (a military-looking thing with brass buttons) at a table that's been set up under a big canvas umbrella. There's a comfortable chair bed for each of them, and lemonade has been laid out, together with two tall glasses. There's a home-made chocolate cake bursting with cream, too. The drink is cloudy and not over sweet, with lumps of ice floating in it – real old-fashioned lemonade. You can hear the bees in the lavender, catch the scent of the pink velvet roses massing the flowerbeds. Gone are the mournful, formal patches of the garden like the dark yew bushes Edmund so prized. Since Stanley's return, it overflows with strong colours and sweet smells: the garden he always yearned for.

'You set yourself down on one of them loungers,' he suggests.

Hester eases herself onto one of the chair beds, dropping her stick on the grass and wincing slightly – perhaps more because of the use of the word 'lounger' than from genuine discomfort.

'Could murder a beer,' he grumbles gently as he fills their glasses. Hester would have preferred a martini. Perhaps real drinks will come later. They feel indulged yet controlled, like children at a tea party. Very likely, thinks Stanley, they're being spied on from one of the windows.

'Nice,' she says. But her gaze seems a little filmy. Can she really take in the beauty of the gardens, Stanley wonders? Does she even know where she is?

However, he enjoys their afternoons because these amiable comfortable days, reliving the past is more to be welcomed than dreaded. It's extraordinary to think of Hester as she once was, acerbic and smooth-skinned – and, just for a second, he finds he can remember the exact feel of her small breasts under his hands, hear her gasp as he entered her. *'How does it happen?'* he wonders: the imperceptible decay until suddenly one looks in the mirror and, there's no arguing with it – one is old. He feels exactly the same as when he was twenty, he reflects a little indignantly. It's another of life's jokes.

Hester says something, but Stanley's getting a little deaf now, though he refuses to let Mark buy him a hearing aid.

'Pardon?' he says, looking at Hester, and suddenly her green eyes no longer seem to him vague and wandering.

'He always loved you,' she says, raising the volume slightly.

Stanley scents danger. He crosses his arms and his black stare gives nothing away. He's heard about the letters, of course, and was deeply uneasy when the real identity of the writer was revealed. To add to his embarrassment, Janice repeated whole chunks with a daft look on her face. However, thankfully, everyone's still under the impression that a woman was involved – identity unknown. He doubts Hester was let in on the scandal at all.

In the light of this, he pulls himself together and assumes a dignified, indulgent sort of attitude. 'That's very true, Hester,' he agrees. 'I were Edmund's best friend for more than twenty year, all told.'

Hester takes his rough old hand in her gnarled one, as if she wants to make sure he's paying attention: as if her real message to him will explain everything, so there'll never again be any need for an apology.

'He always loved *you*,' she repeats, and this time her meaning is stark, unambiguous. 'Always,' she adds. It's as if she can finally recognize it. Her expression is sad, though full of understanding and kindliness. It's far far too late, she conveys, to mourn the unfairness or the waste. The dementia has given her a childlike quality. Such candour would have been unthinkable, before.

Stanley immediately cases the area, but they are the only people on the huge, sunny lawn. Nobody can hear this. For the second time in their lives, there's no pretence between them: none. Besides, he reminds himself, the intimacy is as fragile as that ball of thistledown drifting across the grass. Another second and it will be broken up and gone for ever. The secret is safe, however he chooses to respond.

He squeezes her hand back. 'I know it, Hester,' he says very softly and tenderly, as if overwhelmed by pity for them both. 'I do.'